THE DEVIL'S KNEE

Other Books by Irving Shulman

NOVELS
The Amboy Dukes ⎫
Cry Tough!   ⎬ A Trilogy
The Big Brokers   ⎭
The Square Trap
Children of the Dark
Good Deeds Must Be Punished
Calibre
The Velvet Knife
West Side Story (A Novelization)

SHORT STORIES
The Short End of the Stick

BIOGRAPHIES
The Roots of Fury
Harlow
Valentino

AMERICAN CULTURE
"Jackie"!

THE DEVIL'S KNEE

by Irving Shulman

 TRIDENT PRESS : NEW YORK

Copyright © 1973 by Irving Shulman
All rights reserved
including the right of reproduction
in whole or in part in any form
Published by Trident Press
A Division of Simon & Schuster, Inc.
Rockefeller Center, 630 Fifth Avenue
New York, New York 10020

FIRST PRINTING

SBN 671-27092-3
Library of Congress Catalog Card Number: 72-76773
Designed by Irving Perkins
Manufactured in the United States of America

FOR

*Gail Louise Eddy,
Brian David Alexander
and
Craig Andrew Alexander*

AUTHOR'S NOTE

Although some of the principal and secondary characters in The Devil's Knee *have appeared in other novels of mine, they were neither then nor now based on people in real life; the same holds true for every other character in this book. My one and only reason for using real locales and for occasionally mentioning people in the news has always been to give my readers a sense of time and place.*

If someone affirms that people and events in real life are far more idealistic, reverent, elevated and moral than those in this book, and my story should only be read as fiction, I fully agree. However, if someone presumes to identify any character in this book with a person of his acquaintance, or if he claims to have knowledge of the verity of any event I have described, his claims are without any basis in fact.

THE DEVIL'S KNEE

CHAPTER ONE

LARRY: I'd been doing it for many years now, working the curls of Simon's *payess* into his bushy beard.

"Very nice," I said after one of the curls got an extra touch of my pocket comb. Then I winked to keep Simon patient. "Now I'll do your moustache."

Simon clasped both hands behind his back and sighed. "You already did my moustache."

"Sure," I agreed. "But I don't like the way it looks. Besides, it'll take all day if you keep talking."

We stood in the two-story center hall of Joyce's English house, a mansion inside and out. With walls of faded red brick and white wooden trim. A house good enough for a picture postcard. While I combed Simon's moustache, he looked at himself in a beautiful antique mirror in a very old frame that must've cost a bundle when it was new, so it cost more now. So I moved him to one side, but that wasn't any good either because he wanted to get close to an antique display case against the opposite wall. Maybe he wanted to see his reflection in the glass-paned doors, but when I told him to stop trying to see himself, Simon said he was just looking at the china flower-sellers, the candlesticks made out of porcelain figures and the dollhouse furniture and musical instruments of gold, silver and—I guess you could call it enamel?—that filled the shelves. All of these too were antique. And there were other antiques in the center hall. Some of them were a grandfather's clock, very tall, in a case of turtle—I mean tortoiseshell—and ivory, and a chest under a mirror that Joyce's combination chauffeur-butler, Tom, told me was almost three hundred years old. He said it was from the time of William and Mary, which meant nothing to me at the time. But the clock interested Simon and me most, seeing as it told us the morning had almost two and a half hours left.

Simon raised a hand to hide his eyes from the strong light that came through the church-sized stained-glass window halfway up the staircase, just above the landing. The window was in three parts, just like in a church, and the frame was all carved and looked as if it'd been made by someone who knew everything about churches.

"It looks like nice weather outside," he said, which was his polite way of telling me to let him go.

"Stop talking. Please?" I also took a squint at the window. "I don't like it."

"And I do," Simon said. "Besides being elegant, there's nothing Christian about it. So it won't bother me."

Religious or not, the window just didn't fit the rest of the house, its architecture and furnishings. Later on, Tom and Milly—Tom's wife—told me some interesting things about the house. It was built almost fifty years ago by a silent-movie star who was all screwed up about history and really believed it'd been made much better by De Mille and guys like him. Honest, from what Milly said, she was one stupid broad, very conceited, who was convinced that anything over a hundred years old was as ancient as the pyramids or Christopher Columbus.

So, once, when she was in Europe someplace, making a super-epic with thousands of slaves and chariots, she was having this house put up in Beverly Hills. At last the house was finished, she came back to the States, and when her chauffeur opened the limousine door and she got out and saw what the architect had built, she sort of screamed and fainted on the sidewalk in a blue fit. Once she came to, she cursed for almost an hour that she would cut the bastard's balls off because she'd expected to return to a stone castle with towers and those notches on top of the walls where archers could shoot arrows from. Instead, she had a balanced Georgian mansion that anybody with money could've owned. Straight out her studio president warned how people would say she was nuts if the house got torn down, like she planned on doing, because architectural professors and students from as far away as Chicago had come to see this house, which they said was a masterpiece. All right, she finally agreed, she'd keep the house, but one part of the upper back wall had to be torn out for the stained-glass window made for her by an English studio artist who could trace his ancestry way back to King Arthur of the Round Table. That the window kind of ruined the appearance of the house inside and from the garden didn't bother her. She owned the house and let no one ever forget it. Other owners of the house besides Joyce always planned to take out the window until they realized how it clued in the real dumb personality of the first owner. It also proved how whacky Hollywood once was, when stars tied big velvet bows across their pianos and one cowboy star, I think it was Tom Mix, had a limousine that looked like a stagecoach. Buster Keaton had a yacht on wheels and Harold Lloyd, to this day they tell me, has a Christmas tree all year in his house.

Simon just couldn't stand still. First his eyes traced one of the patterns on the lobby-sized Oriental rug under us. Then he squinted again at the window where the big shot was a knight with long blond hair and a hunting bird on his left wrist. To one side was his horse. On the ground, the knight's helmet and shield were guarded by a greyhound.

"Like I've said for how many times since yesterday," Simon just had to keep talking, "this place cost a bundle of bundles. And Prince Valiant looks pretty good, don't you think?"

"For someone with long hair, at least he's neat," I said. "And that's how you'll look if you give me half a chance."

Simon touched one of his *payess*—those are religious sidelocks—then gave me one of his hard but funny looks. "I hope you didn't make them Shirley Temple," he warned me, his best and only friend.

"Because we're going to live here doesn't mean I want you to go Hollywood," I said to my best and only friend.

Now Simon smiled because he saw I was in a pretty good humor. "That's the last thing to expect from me. But it's past nine, Larry. So I'd like to get going."

I grabbed his chin, turned his head slightly before I touched a *payess* with my comb and smoothed some hairs in his beard. Sure I wanted Simon to look neat, but more important than that, combing Simon's hair every morning and sometimes during the day helped me get a long, close look into his eyes, which were like windows that let me see what Simon was going to be like for a couple of hours, maybe more. This morning, thank God, his eyes were clear and friendly. Without trouble. Actually innocent and trusting, which relieved me because this past month I'd worried long and hard about what might happen to Simon as we got ready to leave Mexico for the States. Because, you see, it was almost seventeen years since we'd left Vegas for Mexico, and at that time Simon—who was then called Bull by everyone—was really sick in the head.

Yes, it was almost seventeen years since all hell broke loose in New York after our good friend Mitch Wolf, who'd been one of us since we were kids together in the old Amboy Dukes, had spilled his guts to the cops. We had to blow Vegas in a hurry and Simon-then-Bull, who was a raving maniac, actually dangerous, cried and screamed when he wasn't cursing me from under a couple of blankets on the floorboards of the back seat as I drove just about nonstop through Arizona toward the Mexican border. Once across we attended to the first order of business, which was to find doctors, hospitals and sanatoriums for Simon. These had really cost. Of course there was almost two hundred thousand dollars in cash under the front seat, but in a foreign country whose language we didn't know, a country with a history of bandits who'd kill a man for a pair of socks with holes in the toes and heels, staying alive depended upon my being sharp all the time. This meant I had to give up boozing, so I did. It wasn't too hard, which surprised me pluswise, and from then to now I haven't averaged two shots a week, and only if the people I'm with make too much out of my not lifting an arm with them.

Anyway, when we got our tourist cards at the Nogales border crossing I wasn't thinking of Mexican bandits, but of the *gonovim* we'd left behind in the States, who'd be after us with every hood they could spare after they realized how much I'd taken the Riviera and its bank account for. Or, they might wait a while because of certain—make it all—the roles of microfilm I'd taken with the cash. These, you see, were our insurance policies. Meanwhile, as we drove through Guaymas and along roads that appeared and disappeared between Mazatlán and Guadalajara—the first civilized city we dared rest in for more than one night—we kept Simon under with sleeping pills, enough of them to make him into a zombie and maybe just one or two short of killing him, which I thought of more than once. That's the way I especially felt in Guadalajara, a city I really liked, and where we let Simon come awake long enough for him to attract attention, which any maniac can do, especially when someone is screaming like crazy that you're the devil dressed up like a man. That was his subconscious screaming—but for him to call me, who was taking care of him, a devil, that bothered me. Still, after I decided to make it to Mexico City, we got more sleeping pills in a *farmacia* because you don't need prescriptions for anything in Mexico, shoved them into Simon and got him into the back seat again. Then I told Joyce to sit with him while I drove and to do anything and everything she had to—except kill Simon—to keep him quiet, and I really meant anything and everything. A blow job not excepted. Joyce understood. She put Simon's head in her lap and sang little baby songs to him when she wasn't crooning like a mother to her kid that God had honest-to-God decided to forgive Simon for everything bad he'd ever done, and he hadn't done so many bad things at that, and proof of His forgiveness was our getaway from Vegas. For sure, she said, without Simon we'd never've made it.

Joyce was wonderful to him, so I was able to drive straight through to Mexico City and to a motel where Joyce really charmed the owner, a *machismo* stud, into getting us a doctor who spoke English and could tell us what he was doing for Simon, who twitched, moaned and wept in his heavy sleep. Things were below bottom when the doctor arrived. You see, we were just about out of sleeping pills, even aspirin. And we had to stop running sometime, finally stop in some place I felt might be safe. But how could I think of that when Simon and the way he was filled my mind?

Because it was still early afternoon of our second day in Mexico City, and Simon was sleeping, Joyce spent just enough time with the *macho* motel owner to make him into a chauffeur, guide and translator. Right after she put him back into his *pantalones* he drove her to the American Embassy, where she got bedrock information about things and how to make the best of them. Before she started there, we figured there was nothing to worry about from the government because my taking the cash and microfilm, which had been put in my care, was a private arrangement between some certain people from the East and me. So I thought over Joyce's suggestion of going to the embassy, decided it was all right, and watched her nervously as she drove away with the stud in *his* car because that left me alone with Simon.

Trust Joyce—she got things done at the embassy, where a junior officer decided her problems were red-alert emergency, so he telephoned a specialist—he also spoke English—and he was at the motel even before Joyce got back. Dr. Raul Marroqui De Vetiz pumped Simon's stomach and kept him calm after he came to. The next thing he did was telephone Vera Cruz and arrange for Simon's admission to a small, very private, very confidential but very good hospital. Then he advised me to get Mexican driving coverage before I next turned the ignition key. Naturally he had a relative who sold honest insurance. Joyce showed her appreciation to De Vetiz and his cousin, the insurance broker, who got us a driver, also some kind of relative but not too close, to drive us to Vera Cruz whenever the doctor gave us the go-ahead.

Meantime, while we waited for Simon's health to improve, because one of his complications was a bad flu that kept us in Mexico City about three weeks, I had plenty of time to think about myself. Where did someone stash almost two hundred thousand in cash, an item that was making me jumpy, and some rolls of microfilm, maybe worth as much as the cash or more? Again, and because she deserves every bit of credit due, Joyce took care of these through her embassy contact, a nice enough college type who was delivering more than one hundred percent for what he got in trade. Not that we ever talked about it, but I knew what she was doing with her survival kit to keep Simon, her and me alive.

After the embassy cluck arranged for me to get a bank vault and even helped us get some American-trained nurses for Simon, who was still running a fever but not so high, Joyce asked me for enough cash to set herself up for the right now. She bought the outer and underclothes that were the work uniform for the fifty-and-up trick, and in one of her basic black dresses, good hose, shoes, gloves, purse and pearls, in a black foundation garment with snappy garterstraps, she hustled the lobbies and bars of the best hotels. Some days she worked the lounge at the Hipódromo de las Americas, where they hold races about four days a week. Joyce did all right and because the nurses took good care of Simon, I went out and jackrolled some American drunks and faggots, who shook down with lots of tears because, I guess, they couldn't get anywhere with cops who didn't care about the problems of non-*macho* types. At best their complaints would've been handled as jokes.

To avoid the jokes turning sour, and to get Simon the intensive treatment the doctor said he hadda have, we started south the day right after the doctor okayed travel. With our good, reliable driver at the wheel, we were on our way to Vera Cruz and the hospital which was as good as Dr. De Vetiz said. At the hospital the psychiatrist—he was Swiss—said Simon was a schizoid paranoid with religious delusions that could make him violent enough to murder, and after he explained what hadda be done, I agreed. They managed to get Simon reasonably well in about four months and after he was discharged from the hospital we stuck around Vera Cruz because every so often Simon slipped and had to be hustled back by the white coats for more treatment. This cost, but the way I figured—which did and didn't surprise me—half the money in the vault was Simon's. So if it ever came down to it, Simon was paying his own way. Thinking that way bothered me, so I decided right then and there that Simon wasn't Mitch, the dirty bastard, and until the money or time ran out, I'd stick with Simon. And Joyce, too, if she wanted to stay on.

Thanks to his *Adonoy Eloheynu,* Simon's been on the outside since 1958, years after Joyce left Mexico. Six months of south of the border was about all she could take and after she sent some international telegrams to Winnie Dobby, her first and only pimp, she left for New York to report to the right people how I'd burned the microfilms—she saw me do it— because that wasn't my way of holding them off. I wasn't Mitch.

No one came after us. Time proved that. And Simon finally got well enough in every department except religion to live with me all the time. If I would've cared to discuss it, some stupids might've said that the way Simon was still hung up on religion proved he was still sick. But I don't go along. Whatever kept his brains from scrambling was good, and if the whatever was religion, then it was very good for Simon.

There was something else, a funny sort of thing, but it even helped me. You see, Simon's faith finally convinced him of something very important—that God had forgiven him *everything*. Including murder. Because God was generous, capable of really noble forgiveness, Simon insisted—funny how he remembered calling me a devil while he was out of his head—I was forgiven, too. Which was all right with me. Not that I was as convinced as Simon was, but if believing this made Simon feel better in the head and heart, who was I to make him feel bad? Then, who really knew? Couldn't Simon—I used to hope and I guess still do—be right?

"They really sleep around here," Simon said after the grandfather's clock chimed for the quarter hour.

"From what Tom and Milly told me—she never begins to move toward the edge of her bed much before noon," I said. "So I won't see her for at least three hours. The *schvartzers* let me know that even the gardener doesn't come here until way in the middle of the afternoon. That's so he won't disturb her with the electric mower."

"But even Tom and Milly aren't up yet," Simon went on. "Suppose someone wants breakfast or something? Suppose we were hungry?'"

"We've cooked before so we'd cook again," I said before I ordered Simon to hold still because his looking around kept me from finishing his hair.

Simon motioned for me to let up a minute. "There's plenty to see around here. Still, it isn't right for people to sleep so late," he insisted. "Not every day in the week."

"You know an awful lot for someone who hasn't been here a full day," I said.

"I spoke to Milly and Tom," he said. "They told me." Again he raised his hand for me to let him alone. "And the way she looks. My heart actually bled when I saw her."

"She certainly doesn't look like the Joyce we remembered," I agreed. "Still, there's a resemblance left."

"She was really so beautiful," he went on. "You know," he lowered his voice, "I don't think she's really glad to see us. But looking that way—" his voice trailed off.

"It's been a long time," I said as if it didn't matter what she felt about us, or me. "And I guess she hasn't been feeling so hot for who knows how long."

Again I told Simon to stand still because I wanted to finish up, and by that I meant not only with his hair but thinking about the past which for us included murder-one. But we'd been forgiven, so Simon said, which meant, if I understood things correctly, because Simon's explanations could be short in words but very far out in ideas, that the past was nothing he or I should ever again worry about. Not that Simon ever discussed our memories specifically, because lots of the past was as closed a book to him as the New Testament, but his faith in the *shul*'s God made him able to clean his conscience of fear because of what we'd known and done together when we were hard kids in Brownsville, before we did some reformatory time, and later, after we got out, as ambitious *shtarkers*. The way we operated got us promoted to Vegas. Then not long later, we made a very particular trip to Los Angeles. Bull-now-Simon was alongside me when I pumped more than enough slugs into Freddy Davis's chest to kill him. God in heaven—I've thought since then—what was I trying to prove? That I was a big heat who did his own big hits? Later on I admitted, but only to myself, that it'd been pretty stupid business, especially when satisfaction-guaranteed local mechanics were handy for anywhere between two and three bills.

It was best to agree, say, believe the past was as dead as Simon insisted it was. He had buried the forties, the early years of the fifties when we worked direct for the big brokers, and the later years of the fifties, which were, for Simon, mostly blanks of time. We could remember the sixties because they hadn't been bad, Simon'd got well and we were able to get along real nice on the income from our investment in a nice portfolio of blue-chip American stocks which'd split more'n once and from the interest we received on certain privately contracted certificates of deposit that're only identified by numbers and letters. These last averaged about nine percent after taxes. Two hundred thousand *pesos* a year was more than enough for us to live on, and after devaluation, which didn't hurt us for long, we got a third more *pesos*. So it felt good to know we had an intact nut that'd gone up nicely in value, especially after we made selective ventures in the market through a broker who was an uncle of De Vetiz and the insurance broker too. This uncle often mentioned Joyce, told us how sorry he was not to've had the chance to meet her, so I guess he was especially careful of us because he hoped someday how she might visit. So I made good money for us by following his advice about taking a position and letting go before the absolute high.

For me, the nut, and how it worked for us, was really the only link to the past I cared to remember. But for Simon Bronstein, since hell couldn't handle him, so he'd been forgiven by God, there was no past. Only the present was real because it helped him prepare for some time in the future when he would die without fear of the *malchemuvess* and be buried in an orthodox cemetery, or at least in a plot reserved for a *frummer Yid*.

I laughed when Simon pretended to tip me. That always pleased him. "Now brush me off and I'll be on my way," he said.

"No hurry," I told him. "It'll take at least five minutes or so for a cab to get here after we call."

"Please, Larry, no cab," he said to me. "I'm walking."

"You can't," I argued. "You don't know where you're going. I mean how to get there," I corrected myself.

"Walking'll teach me," he said. "And it's a nice morning."

"Nobody walks in Beverly Hills. Not unless you're attached to a dog."

"How far is it anyway to Fairfax?" he asked.

I tapped the comb against one of my palms, but that didn't help. "For someone who has to ask, it's too far," I said. "And I don't understand your rush. We only got here yesterday."

Simon played with his beard. "Well, while you were getting acquainted yesterday——"

"Some getting acquainted," I interrupted him. I put the comb and case in my shirt pocket and moved to sit on a polished hardwood step of the wide staircase that curved from the landing to the second story. A gallery ran from the top of the stairs toward the bedrooms and sitting rooms and bathrooms in both wings of the house. "Some getting acquainted. As soon as you were taken up to your room she started to blast me in the library. I mean it," I replied to Simon's astonished expression. "I'd forgotten what a mouth she had for curses. And how much she really hated me. Enough so she wouldn't slap my back even if I was choking to death."

Simon looked toward the ceiling, as if he could see right into Joyce's room. "It isn't a good situation," he admitted. "But like I said, she doesn't look well. She could be sick."

"Let's hope it isn't a small thing," I said and turned away because Simon was shocked. "Personally, I'd rather be a widower than a married man. All right, Simon," my voice became edgy, "I shouldn't've said that. But take it from someone who's been there. All she has to do is climb outa the bottle and she's just gotta look better."

Simon sat next to me and patted my arm. "You're becoming nervous. But believe me, everything'll be all right."

"Thanks for telling me."

"You'll see. Just as soon as she gets used to being married to you," he continued. "And it's good that you're married. I like it," he said with force. "And I want to buy both of you a very nice wedding present. But with a house—a place like this." He shook his head. "What do I know about buying anything for a museum or art gallery?"

"Get flowers," I suggested. "Or just forget it. Some marriage."

Say it again, a hundred, times—some marriage. With Simon, that nut, who insisted on dressing up for the occasion in his Pesach-Rosh Hashanah suit, my *abogado* and his secretary, we went to a recorder's office in Mexico City, where the secretary, with a little veil and a bunch of orange blossoms, stood in for Joyce, my bride, who was going through a similar ceremony, just as strange but just as legal, in Downey, with an old bum she'd got at a mission for five dollars and a gallon of red. That's the way she saw me, she'd told me last night—if not in appearance, certainly on the inside. Unluckily for her, my proxy'd been sober enough to sign his name to the legal documents that became a record. Strange as it was, and impossible even then and even now for me to believe, it was all legal. Mexico was a real country. It had—let me get the right words —reciprocal treaties with the United States. And if people wanted to get married with proxies acting for the principals, the marriage certificate handed me in Mexico City was legal and binding in both countries, others too. So was the pretty marriage certificate Joyce got in Downey. We were married. Mr. and Mrs. Lebel Tunig. That's my real name. Not Tunafish. And Lebel is my real name too but it hasn't been used since I went to junior high on the records as Lawrence, then Larry.

"That could be it," Simon interrupted my blue thoughts. "The ceremony bothered her just like it bothered me."

"It's who she's married to that bothers her," I said.

"It's the ceremony," Simon insisted. "You know I didn't like it. I said so before and after."

"You did. But you weren't involved."

"I was the best man," he said. "So maybe you could have another one?" he suggested. "A nice one? Right here? The garden would be a great place for a reception. And I'd like the ceremony to be Jewish."

"Who'll we invite? Gorillas and the FBI?" I gave Simon the elbow. "So maybe you should get married."

"Me?" he grinned. "Who'd want an old *meshuggener* like me?"

"Don't say that," I said sharply. "Never. You're a lot smarter and all right than most people. Lots more for sure than the people who got me involved in this. Or for that matter—me for going through with it."

"You did it for me," Simon went on as if I'd said nothing and only shrugged or nodded. "So if that's crazy—God, forgive me, please—I don't want it any other way."

"Get up and turn around," I said after I stood with my back toward him for a couple of seconds. "I want to comb around your *yarmulkah*."

Simon was sweating nervous like a horse when, for the last time, we left our rented house on Avenida President Masaryk in Polanco, which is the pretty-well-off and substantial Hooish—funny how they can't pronounce a "j" in Spanish like it should be—section and not too far from El Centro Deportivo Israelita. That means the Jewish Sports Center. We moved there in 1966 because it was convenient for him to bike to the Center, where he worked in the kosher kitchen and helped the boxing coach and weight-lifting instructor. Right off, some of Simon's pupils called him *el brazo fuerte*—strong arm—but he didn't like it, so they quit. Once on the plane Simon asked me if he could sit by the window. Then he fastened his safety belt, looked out to wave good-bye to the city below us and closed his eyes until we were level in flight. He refused, but like always—politely, a straight or mixed drink and smiled okay because I ordered a Coke. In pretty good Spanish he told the stewardess, no—he wouldn't have lunch—but would appreciate a glass of wine for the cheese sandwiches on *bolillos* that were in his metal lunchbox. He'd made the sandwiches with Mexican hard rolls and cheese from the Center, whose *kashrut* had been certified by the orthodox rabbi from the Ashkenazi synagogue.

I knew Simon's *frumkeit*—or religiousness—was going to make for real problems in this mansion, all of whose rooms and grounds we hadn't seen yet. If Joyce and me—and I certainly did—wanted Simon at the table, we would have to throw out all the pots and pans, dishes, tablecloths and silver —and get two new services of each, plus two more for Passover. Naturally we would have to get new freezers and refrigerators, maybe even a new range and oven. And a cook who could keep a kosher kitchen? Could Milly be taught that? Was there a kosher butcher in Beverly Hills? It was going to be murder, especially during the time of inspection, when Simon would take a rabbi through the kitchen, butler's pantry, storage rooms—one of which Milly said was called a buttery— breakfast room and dining room to prove how everything matched up with the Law. Suppose the rabbi said we—I mean Joyce—had to get rid of the very big dining room table where she had late supper even if she was the only person served? Knowing Simon, he'd be willing to eat in the breakfast room, even the kitchen, but the problem of the kitchen and what to do about it, so that Simon would eat with us, was bound to set off real explosions. That being the case, to keep the explosions small, to keep them from setting off others, would take some doing. Exactly what, I didn't know.

At LAX the immigration inspector figured he had a real one in Simon when he appeared before the waist-high desk in his full beard, *payess, yarmulkah* and *tzitzit*. Those are religious fringes and they hung below Simon's vest and outside his pants. Talk about surprises, the inspector couldn't believe that Simon was a Brooklyn boy who still had his accent although he and his friend, Mr. Tunig, had been out of the country since 1951 and'd lived in Mexico for more than ten years as *Inmigrantes Rentistas,* which explained why Simon was allowed to hold a job. After the inspector eagle-eyed copies of our birth certificates, which Joyce'd got for us long ago, after she returned to the States from Vera Cruz, he searched his ledgers to see if there were any instructions or charges to hold us. Both of us were nervous until the inspector shook his head that we were A-okay, which compelled him to welcome us back to the land of smog and Chicken Delight. Becoming real friendly because he wanted to make up, I guess, for the way he'd first stared at Simon, he advised us to stay off the freeways until we could handle the traffic and the insane nuts driving cars. Then he told Simon how he oughta carry a guitar case. That way people would believe he was a rock 'n' roll musician. But then he might get stopped by lots of cops who'd shake him down for pot.

So we went from immigration to customs, where we declared a little used clothing, Simon's religious books, *tefillin*, prayer shawl or *tallis*, lunchbox now empty, and a copy of *Los Angeles on Five Dollars a Day*, which Simon insisted would be useful until he went to work because he'd never accepted that more than a hundred—then a hundred and twenty-five, then a hundred and fifty and now something more than three hundred thousand dollars of the money on deposit in Mexico City Swiss-type accounts, the income they earned, or that even half of the stock portfolio—was his. Not that he refused to believe in the cash or stocks being real, but like with his wages, he made me handle everything and give him an allowance because, he said, his head was so filled with God there was little room left for anything else. And certainly not for money. He got along fine with my managing things, didn't he? Weren't the stocks, bank and certificate accounts in both our number-names, with either-or withdrawal and survival setups? Let things be, leave them alone, he would say whenever I argued that he ought to take some interest in our financial condition, which—since my agreeing to return to the States after my proxy marriage to Joyce, and to live in the same house with her—had just about doubled because of my public deposit of the letter of credit made out to me by Fred Rory, Esq., which was to prove how good, generous and sincere were the intentions of the people who had arranged everything—including our being kicked out of Mexico if I refused to marry Joyce and come home. So what if we had about fourteen-plus million *pesos,* all told, in Mexico, which is more than a million dollars? So what if we were going to get generous five-figure allowances as pensioners? Simon still intended to get a job. And until he did, a book on how to live inexpensively was a good buy.

Not a cop stopped us, not one official held us up at the airport. Simon got plenty of looks but so did anyone with long hair and far-out clothes, and Simon's *tzitzit* had even stopped people at the Center because Mexican Jews are a lot different from American and other kinds of Jews, I guess. A porter carried our light bags as we walked from the satellite through the airport lobby. My camera with no film in it, as always, was around my neck, but nothing made me raise and focus it. We tipped the porter after he got us a cab and about twenty-thirty minutes later, because I warned the cabby to take his time, he stopped outside Joyce's house on Lexington Road and whistled. We joined him after Simon checked the house number stenciled on the curb, for whatever we'd expected, no matter how good, had been lots lots less than this. And the cab-driver, really fascinated by the way Simon looked and was dressed, now was convinced that at least one of his passengers was someone famous, maybe an international star, because he couldn't figure how anyone less than absolutely important would be admitted to this house, which stood on at least a full acre of grass with nice bunches of plants here and there. Later I learned their names: sun azaleas and camellias. A big oak stood in a fieldstone well not quite centered on the east lawn, just about halfway between the sidewalk and the house. And the brick path to the very big—huge—doorway, set way back like in a castle or church, was bordered by low hedges—boxwood—with spaced topiary clusters. That's really a word, but we'd seen lots of topiary in Mexico City in the gardens of houses in Chapultepec, Lomas and Jardin Pedregal, but these were just as good. The house stood apart from the Spanish monster on its left and the house on the right, which actually had a couple of little minarets coming up outa the roof. But neither of these was as wild as two very special houses in Beverly Hills. One was like the house of the evil witch who was so mean to Hansel and Gretel. The other place, Joyce told me, imitated Stonehenge, some sort of big pile of rocks in England that was supposed to be a caveman temple or something like it.

"I'm finished, Simon," I said at last because I couldn't go on combing or brushing single hairs. "Now let me take a good look at you." I stepped back, took off my not-so-dark glasses which I used for indoors, and looked him over again, knowing all the while how I was stalling because I didn't want Simon to leave me alone in Joyce's house. "I never minded the *yarmulkah*," I let him know as I pointed to his *tzitzit*. "It's those that really bother me."

"They shouldn't," he said.

"Believe me, right after we're settled down I'm gonna see an orthodox rabbi and find out if you've gotta wear them. So why not take them off until we find out?" I suggested.

"First find out. Then I'll think about it," Simon said. "And finally, I've got your permission to go?"

There were times, say like right now, when Simon wasn't as easy to get along with as say an ordinary person. And some of those times, and right now, I felt like telling him that how come, since he'd gone so far with the way he dressed and behaved, he didn't go all the way and have some plastic surgeon put a hook in his nose or at least make him big nostrils so he'd really look really Jewish? But I never did because I'd start worrying how Simon might react if I actually said it, even if I did my best to make it sound like a rib.

Simon often said I worried too much about him. Still, I had reason. First, there was what'd happened to him. Second, there were too many *goyim* in the world, too many anti-Semites. Even in Mexico, for a pretty long time, troubles happened almost every day for Simon until people all around accepted him and spread the word how he was strong, could break a man's face as easy as his arm, and just as easy weep for pardon and forgiveness because he wanted to live in peace with everyone, to turn the other cheek, even back off from *mendigos,* slobs and creeps because no one, not even Simon himself, knew when he might grab someone who was giving him a hard time. Then the slob would be left busted up and bleeding in the street. Still, after he was able to control himself again and wipe away his tears, Simon would be the *Número Uno* Samaritan to help the man or men he'd hurt, before he ran to the *shul*—and I mean it, he'd run all the way—where he'd start crying again, rocking up and back as he punched his forehead and chest with both fists, sobbing as he pulled on his hair and beard, all the while pleading with God to forgive him because he promised that never again, no matter whatever was said or done to him, even spitting in his face or worse, would he ever again lift a hand to anyone. The very next time creeps started to give him a bad time, he would just run away. Never, never again, would he hit anyone.

"Just how long'll you be gone?" I answered Simon's question with one of my own. "And because you won't answer directly, I take it you're gonna go around here with your *yarmulkah* and *tzitzit?*"

"Of course," he said. "What people think, if they think bad, doesn't bother me. What God does, does. So stop worrying, Larry," he told me again. "Stop worrying so much."

I saw him look again at the clock before he shook his head because like earlier I was sitting on the step again and massaging my knuckles. This told him how nervous I was. The heavy wedding ring on my left hand looked strange, funny to me, I guess to Simon too, but the proxy bride'd given me the ring as a gift and it wasn't the time or place to say no-thanks. Of course I could've thrown the ring away after we left the recorder's office, or given it to an Indian beggar woman, but Simon would've said something. And the ring told me I'd made a contract, so like it or not I'd have to perform. Another thing, as I worked my knuckles and played with the ring, I hoped the sight of me as a married man, with a ring, certificate, wife and house, might—this morning—make Simon think of me first.

At last, finally, he got the message. "Maybe you want me to stick around?" he asked. "Come to think of it, what's my hurry? I can get to Fairfax tomorrow, next week. Isn't that right?"

"You don't have to stay with me," I said.

"I never said I had to," he replied. "But I want to."

Just to show how screwed up I was, I shook my head. "No. But I still don't want you to walk," I added, and my eyes got smaller to show I was impatient because he was giving me another argument. "All right," I gave in, "walk. Just one thing. You'll call me when you're ready to come home?"

"I will," he said.

"And you'll take a cab? No buses?" I knocked out any ideas Simon had of trying to live on five-a-day. "A cab?"

Giving in, Simon raised his right hand. "A cab."

"And you've got cash?"

"A hundred for sure," Simon said as he patted the hip pocket where his wallet was. "So I'll call you before I leave Fairfax. Do you mind if I bring home some kosher delicatessen? And paper plates for myself?" he added after a second.

"Mind?" I laughed. "You'd better. And anything else that'll make you feel better."

"I'm glad you said that, Larry."

I licked my lips for him to see. "Look, I'm tasting. So you're ready to take my order?"

"I'm ready." Simon sucked in his stomach, squared up his shoulders and made like he flipped a napkin across his arm before he took a pad and pencil from an inside jacket pocket. "What'll it be, Mr. Tunig?"

"You'll bring home a sandwich rye," I began. "And while we're sitting up tonight to watch color TV, you'll cut the bread in half, then slice each half right through and make us real thick club sandwiches." Simon grinned so happily that I patted my stomach. "Buy everything. Corned-beef and pastrami. Rolled-beef too. Sour pickles and sour tomatoes and lots of potato salad. Not so much cole slaw. Get French fries and we'll reheat them. Get sponge cake. You got all that?"

"Everything," Simon said. "It'll be a feast. You think they'll have Dr. Brown's?"

"You could ask." For a second I thought of going along and walking around Fairfax to see what it was like until Simon met me. Then we could've shopped together. But I decided against it. "Now for sure you'll have to take a cab home," I said. "So I'll see you to the door."

Simon made some stroking lines across the pad. "Everything's underlined," he said before he put away the pad and pencil. "Just leave the order to me. And I'll be back as soon as I can."

"My friend the caterer." My mouth formed again in what was for me a smile. "You might look into that," I suggested. "Your own business."

Simon stared at me. "You're kidding."

"I'm serious," I said. "Why not? With so many *unserer* out here you could do damned good. I'm just suggesting," I added real quick because Simon's eyes filled up with fear of responsibility. "Nothing else, Simon, believe me. It was just talk."

He was relieved, grateful that I'd said this. So he thanked me by saying he wouldn't take any job without first talking to me. So when he pointed again to the front door, I stood, took his arm, and we left the house together. Without speaking, we walked down the brick path and were almost at the sidewalk when the sight-seeing bus came around the far corner, toward us, as the driver spoke into the microphone and his tourists stared at the houses. The driver looked us over as the bus came abreast of Joyce's house, then he shook his head before he spoke into the microphone to tell his passengers, I guess, that the house behind us once belonged to a famous star but its present occupant wasn't in the entertainment industry. Suddenly the driver really slowed the bus and looked at us again, especially at Simon, and said something else into the microphone. The man with the beard might be Al Hirt or Sebastian Cabot or Burl Ives is what I'm sure he said.

"So"—Simon said after he waved at the bus and was pleased because some of the people waved back—"say it to me."

"Be careful," I said. *"Und geh mit Gott."*

"Thanks, Larry." He patted my shoulder. *"Bleib mit Gott."*

I kept waving at Simon as he walked along the sidewalk. Broad as a bull, which he was no longer called, he held his head high as if to make the most of his *yarmulkah*. Not fat, although he did have a pot, shoulders back, legs and arms pumping, Simon looked like a wrestler or a defensive lineman. And in his neat blue suit, white shirt and blue tie with little figures on it, black shoes and blue socks held up by garters, he might've been a professor. Then I saw his *tzitzit*. A rabbi. Win, place and show, he could pass for a rabbi.

"Simon," I called after him with my hands cupped to my mouth. "Simon."

He stopped and turned. "Yes?"

"Just a second." He waited patiently for me to reach him. "There's something else you're to get. You don't have to write it down," I told him as I flicked some lint from one of his sleeves before I pointed toward the house. "First, you're going to live here? You won't move out?" I had to know for sure.

My question surprised him. "Why should I?"

"Good." I was relieved. "So you might's well buy a *mezuzah* for the front door. But one thing"—I turned him toward the house—"you can see it's really a mansion. And furnished like one."

"No museum could look better," he agreed. "And you'll never know how happy you've made me by saying I should buy a *mezuzah*."

"So make me happy by getting one that's simple. In good taste," I said. "Nothing flashy."

Simon was very solemn because of the real responsibility

I'd given him. "Depend on me," he said after he relaxed his jaws and mouth. "I'll call you when I'm ready to come home. That'll be after I buy the *mezuzah* and delicatessen. And I'll come home by cab."

"Good," I said. "So I'll see you later."

"You'll take things easy?" he wanted to know.

"I will," I said. And hoped I could.

I didn't move until Simon reached the end of the block, where he waved before he turned right into Beverly Drive to walk toward Sunset Boulevard and from there, I wasn't exactly sure. But if Simon said he had directions to get to Fairfax Avenue, then he had them. And he had our phone number and enough cash to get back without trouble. And our address was written on a tape and stitched inside one of the breast pockets of his jacket. All of this I'd attended to before we left Mexico City.

This was a good street, I told myself, but it wasn't Mexico where most little houses had their walls to the street and bigger houses, worth something, stood behind brick or adobe walls or high, wrought-iron fences, and every window, cabinet, drawer and closet had its own lock and key. People were more trusting here, or had reason to be, I figured, which meant they worried less about break-ins. Still, these houses along our street and all around it screamed at thieves and burglars that their insides were loaded with five- and six-figure loot, that their women had furs and rocks really worth the risk, and the amount of cash a mechanic with a gun might pick up could be hefty. I'd have to find out from Joyce if the house had an alarm system, although on second thought it would be the last house anyone in the know would pick for a break-in. But there were always beginners around, mavericks who'd burgle their own mothers or the orphanages that raised them with loving care and kindness, Gypsy types who came into a city for a quick hit-and-run. So I'd have to ask Joyce about burglar alarms and—the humor of this didn't go over my head—other things about the house and accounts, but not immediately because talking to her wouldn't be easy. She'd proved this last night.

Still, turn it any way you wanted, examine it from top, bottom or sideways, she'd furnished the house, she said so, which proved that what she'd done at the Riviera hadn't been an accident. At that time too, because we had to find something for her or have her crack up with doing nothing, we'd asked her what she'd like to be in charge of, and after thinking about it for a little while she told us maybe she could work with the decorators. Everyone but them thought it was a good idea, but their opinions didn't count. For that matter, Simon-then-Bull made his contribution to the Riviera, and I can still remember, and always laugh to myself when I do, how Cherry, the featured crime above the mirror of the Clubhouse Bar, for which S-then-B was responsible, made the interior look like the parlor of a not-so-expensive joint. Joyce also screamed that Cherry—who she hated as if she was a human being—worked harder in her dirty movements when I inspected the bar to see that everyone was nose to the grindstone.

Lifesize and nude, stacked where she had to be, Cherry lay with a little patch of black velvet on her crotch. And every hour on the hour, while the rosy nipples of Cherry's real-skin rubber bombs glowed like little coals, the doll's stomach would bump and grind for about a minute. For this steamy toy B-now-S had screamed like a maniac, pounded his fists into walls, threatened to call Itzik in New York, and almost choked the life outa one of the interior decorators when it was stupid enough to say that the only place he'd put Cherry was in a garbage can. But Simon had his way because I said so. And Cherry was installed on an imitation leopardskin rug above the bar, where her ready-for-it position balled the customers, especially when her belly revolved, her hips ground figure-eights and her nipples lit up to illuminate, I guess, the hots that most women, maybe all, could never know. It was possible, I used to think.

Maybe Cherry did work harder when she saw me enter the bar. . . .

Then after her sponsor, poor Simon-then-Bull, became so sick that he almost lost the use of an arm and even sicker in the head so that he almost lost his mind, he begged me to get rid of Cherry, to take her down from the bar, because she was a graven image and against God's second commandment. Maybe it—or she—was, I thought at the time, but I'd never done anything about Cherry because I was too busy with more important things concerning the Riviera—just to keep the plant running smooth every day—than to think for more than two, three seconds about something as silly as a doll that the customers were crazy about even if Joyce and Bull-now-Simon weren't.

I'll say it again. The Riviera took everything I had to keep it going. When, not too long before, when I'd been a tough j.d. who hoped to make it big, and president of the Amboy Dukes, I ran the gang without argument by busting most of the guys, warning others and cursing the rest, that's if I had time to waste. But most often I got action by kicking or belting anyone who crossed me. Assigned, then ordered by Itzik Yanowitz to get the Riviera moving again, to give a new image to a hotel that'd been operated as a crummy hot-pillow joint with a lousy kitchen, tonky floor show and a casino no sane gambler would use for his action, I just did there what I'd done with the Dukes. And it'd worked and helped me keep everyone in line, from top management to half-drunk porters. One of the worst things anyone could do, even worse than stalling, was to steal, and two of the bigger thieves'd been Johnny Lachetti and Freddy Davis. Lachetti was smart enough to put oceans between him and Nevada, but Davis, the jerk, had only gone as far as California, where I saw him in the flesh —for the very first and only time—through a window and I put two—or was it three?—holes in his chest.

"Sure they're afraid of me," I'd once said to Itzik—may he

rest in peace in a place where he was made welcome by Fat Dovel Apfelshpein and his *haimische* wife, who had forgiven Itzik so that they were once again the best of friends until all things ended. Simon included this prayer, which he'd made up all by himself, with those of the *Kaddish* which he said for Itzik, whose death was very recent news to us. "And they've gotta be scared of me. I've gotta keep them so scared that they're always nervous even when I'm not around because they could never be certain I wasn't somehow watching them. What'm I working with, Itzik?" I asked him. "Hustlers and creeps who'd even steal poison ivy? Guys who'd rather sell phony watches even if good ones were cheaper and more profit? Pitchmen?" I went on because Itzik was nodding that I was right and he understood. "Scum of the earth in good dresses and haberdashery?"

How had I kept them in line? By making my mouth, a really evil piece of machinery when I put it to work, more to be afraid of than my fists or shoes. By ordering them to stay on their feet when I had them in my office and never letting them sit down, while all the while I fooled around with a long steel ruler that I might suddenly swing at them. By throwing a paperweight, a couple of dry inkwells just kept on my desk for that purpose, a box of cigars, even a roll of coins or a bottle—empty or full—at anyone from a busboy to a pit boss if I read them right and figured that would make them most afraid of me. So people at the Riviera had learned right off not to argue with me, not to contradict me with even a word like "but," the smallest look or gesture, so that I wouldn't think they weren't with me one hundred percent when I cursed them for what slobs and crooks and jerks they were. While their hides came off they had to listen without moving because I'd convicted them before they stepped into the office. And if they wanted to stay healthy, they kept their mouths shut until I allowed them to beg for mercy and a second chance to do better. And they usually did better.

But my using fear to keep people in line ended as soon as

I left the States. Since then, after Bull-now-S was well enough to live outside full time, I'd never had to give orders or make people hate me. Or be afraid of me like they'd be afraid of the devil.

Free of big responsibility, I was no longer so afraid of failing. Free of obligation, I was able to bury the monster devil that was Larry Tunafish. These were the best things that could've happened to me, and to clean everything up, so I'd be absolutely free, I intended to kiss off Bull-now-Simon, but not before he was well enough to be on his own. Then, just as suddenly, I wanted to believe, my mind decided that if I was going to retire all the way, because breaking the law in Mexico where I had no organization to cover me could put me away forever, I had to have something to think of. Or someone to worry about. That's when I decided to get Bull-now-Simon well and to keep him that way even if it took more years than I cared to think about. At first Bull was a hernia. Later, when he became Simon, it was—I guess you could call it psychological comfort—to know that of all the people in the world there was one who really depended on me, one person who really was my friend. Between the money that made it possible for us to live more than just good and knowing I had a real friend, I was pretty contented.

Contentment, peace with yourself, the kind that makes the head feel healthy, sort of came to me some six–seven years back, after a certain trip with Simon to Uruapan—a city in Michoacán—helped me appreciate an awful lot more the changes in him and how his changes had helped settle me down, even to the point of making me feel like more of a human being, willing to live and let live, and able, finally, to feel sorry a good some of the time for Mitch Wolf, even after what he'd done to all of us and especially to Simon, who he had scared when he was already going to, pieces by telling him, sure thing, you're right, you are going to hell. Telling him this at a time when Simon was already in such trouble with himself because he believed, really believed, that he was being punished by God for what he'd done and what all of us were involved in doing. So there were no two ways about it, Simon was gonna go to hell, and he believed this then and for years after I got him into Mexico and he hadda stay in sanatoriums for real long times.

After Simon got well and we settled down in Mexico City it was years before he went to work at the Deportivo. So my taking him everywhere kept him in sight. We developed a sort of routine. Most weekdays I'd stop into my broker's office to check quotations, then we'd go to the bank for cash or to see some tourist sight or maybe out to the zoo where we'd ride round-and-round for maybe an hour on the kids' train, which was fun. If we stayed downtown, around Alameda Park, Simon would feed the pigeons and give out fifty-*centavo* coins to lots of kids while we had our shoes shined and bought Chiclets that we'd never take. Two, three afternoons a week we looked into our *abogado*'s for a little Spanish practice with him and his secretary—the one who stood in for Joyce at my part of our wedding. A real hometown booster, she came from Uruapan and never got tired of saying we ought to visit her city and on the way there see some of the most beautiful scenery anywhere in the world. All of Michoacán was beautiful, she said—rainy, green and so beautiful, from its capital at Morelia to the smallest Tarascan Indian village, the lakes and even the volcano that shot up out of a cornfield not so long ago. But always she talked most about Uruapan, the country around it and the beautiful park where the Cupatitizio—that means "singing" in Tarascan—River flowed through.

One day when we visited the *abogado*'s, he and his secretary told us they were driving to Uruapan the next morning and they insisted-invited us to go along and spend two nights there before we'd all drive back. We would be their guests and stay at the secretary's house, which was plenty big enough, our lawyer swore, for up to twenty guests without crowding. He and his secretary understood about Simon and his funny food ways, so we could take along some dishes in a basket and whatever Simon would eat would be served. The secretary really wanted us to go along, and I got the feeling she'd be insulted—our lawyer too—if we turned them down, and to my surprise Simon said he'd like it if I said yes.

It's something less than three hundred miles from Mexico City to Uruapan. Once we got to Toluca it became mountains and valleys, steep grades, forests and rivers all the way to Morelia. Then it's through mountains all covered with pine trees and clouds and mists until Carapan, where you cut due south to Uruapan and the scenery becomes more beautiful by the mile while you go through real Indian villages with houses that have steep, funny wood-shingled roofs and the Indians weave belts by hand or make guitars, chairs or other wooden stuff they peddle from along the road and even down the middle. The scenery stayed beautiful right into Uruapan. The house of the secretary's parents—fine people—was big and comfortable and full of servants, and next morning we went sight-seeing around town and saw the plaza, plenty nice, other buildings that looked good and how this Cupatitizio River flows right through the middle of the city and at one street there are even holes in a brick wall so that overflow can spill into the street and not come up so hard against the main bridge, which isn't much.

It was raining a little when we got to the park, which the secretary called a *barranca* because it was part of a gorge. Her car got surrounded by at least fifty kids and Simon said she should allow three of them to guide us even if we didn't need them. The park—I never saw, imagined anything could be like this—green and grand, with the most beautiful flowers and plants with leaves up to more than fifteen feet high and trees everywhere all covered with fruits and flowering vines and ferns. With water going into the river right from the walls of the gorge, from fountains and springs and waterfalls and side rapids. One fountain, handmade, was maybe a hundred feet long, with a big historical picture painted all across its top and hundreds of jets in rows one over the other. There were rainbows and sprays and clouds of water, everything so beautiful we couldn't stop looking and pointing, and I was sorry there wasn't any film in the camera slung around my neck.

Finally, we came to this particular waterfall with kids swimming in the pool below it, where women and girls in their dresses were bathing or washing young kids. Boys stood on rocks or in shallow caves while they soaped themselves up good before they ran yelling from the rocks and caves and dove down the waterfall. It was a sight to see.

Now the secretary, who I was glad made us come here, pointed to a sort of big and deeper-than-shallow depression in a rock in which one of our boy guides was kneeling, and she told how it was called the Devil's Knee on account of people said that once, long ago, when the world was no more than just made, the devil came up from hell especially to see Michoacán because he'd heard how beautiful it was, a real masterpiece of a place. Finally, after he saw all of Michoacán and got to this pool and waterfall, he kneeled down on the rock—to make the depression—while he admitted out loud for the whole sky and earth, heaven and hell to hear him at the same time, how he was willing to admit that the works of God were miraculous, all right, but in this place they were the greatest and way beyond what anyone else could do.

Standing alongside me in the park, Simon liked the story and turned to tell me so. And, suddenly, I felt a sense of wonder as I realized what Simon's eyes must be seeing was something so marvelous it can never be described. Which is why I look into them at least once a day, not only to see his calm, which settles me down, but also the wonder of his believing and maybe, if I'm very lucky on some very special day, get to see, if only for half a second, what Simon always seems to see. Then, wherever I might be, you can bet that just like the devil, I'll kneel down. . . .

Maybe I shouldn't've bothered Joyce with specific questions about anything. Not immediately, when we'd just met again after so many years, and we were married to each other although we hadn't shared the same ceremony. Certainly I shouldn't bother to ask her about a burglar-alarm system and if she knew how much this real estate package was worth, give or take forty or fifty thousand. What did I expect? That she'd be happy to see us? Or that she'd welcome Simon with ticker tape? Seventeen years, almost eighteen, was an awfully long time and our coming together, the way we had—there was nothing great about it. It certainly wasn't romantic, which might've meant something to her. Matter of fact, it was downright awful.

There was nothing for me to do until Joyce came downstairs, so I stayed on the street and watched a cleaning truck pull into a driveway just opposite of me, on sort of an angle, and how the uniformed driver hurried to the back door. After several bad starts, which I heard, a gardener somewhere got his lawnmower going. When I finally located the sound I saw him working his way across the slope of a lawn toward the very end of the block away from Beverly Drive. Then I stepped closer to the curb as a colored maid in a uniform wheeled a stroller toward me with a kid in it who wore a blue wool hat and matching coat. A transistor radio hung from a strap across the stroller's pushbar. The radio was playing too loud to suit me, especially as some sort of singer with a cold in her nose was belting out something about Jesus being a soul man.

"How about turning that down?" I asked the maid as she came up to me. "People are still sleeping in our house."

The maid's eyes tried to cut me. "This sidewalk's public property," she said.

I didn't mind her look, but the way she spoke was something else again. "Who said it isn't?" I very politely kept my voice low and easy. "But if you don't want your black ass kicked from here to across the street you'll lower the volume."

Now her eyes were trying to kill me as she took in my dark glasses, the camera slung round my neck, my blue polo shirt open at the throat, my gray cashmere sweater, gray slacks and black Bostonians that I used to buy in one of the Canada stores in the Zona Rosa for only fourteen dollars a pair. Suddenly hatred twisted her lips before she flicked her thumb hard to turn off the radio.

"Thanks," I said. "But you don't have to turn it off. Just lower it."

"You can go to hell on a rocket, you white pig," the maid said. "And better pray I don't tell some brothers about you."

"Your mouth won't be big enough to hold your tongue if I put some knots in it," I said. "Which is what I'm gonna do if I ever catch you walking past this house on this side of the street. But I don't want any trouble with you or anyone else," I added. "And I don't think you want any trouble with the cops. Or me. Or do you?"

She stared at my dark glasses, my graying hair, as if she was trying to place me. Maybe she'd seen me on TV or in the movies or in a junky fan magazine. But she couldn't get by me either because I had one foot against a wheel of the stroller. Now I knew she was staring at the long, thin scar on my right cheek, which was beginning to pulse. She figured, I knew, that I'd been cut with a razor or a knife—it was a knife—and that whoever had scarred me, which had happened when I was still a kid, was lucky if he'd only been found dead. This was pretty much correct.

"Lemme go." She tried to get the wheel free of my foot. "And I don't have to walk down this side of the street."

"Fine. Just fine," I said. "Now you be careful as you cross over because that's a nice kid in the stroller. Is it a boy or a girl?"

She didn't answer me, didn't expect she would, as she wheeled the stroller to the opposite sidewalk. As I stared at her back, the way her ass moved because she was hurrying, I could see my foot in it up to the ankle and the picture got me so that I took several steps toward her before I remembered some of the advice—no, the instructions—Fred Rory'd given me. One of them was to maintain a low profile in all things. But what was a low profile? I'd never heard the expression before and Rory certainly sounded superior as he explained it was the way I was to live. Out of sight. Out of trouble. Not to say or do anything to make the neighbors, police or papers notice me.

It was a hell of a way to live. Still I was about to jog after the maid to apologize, but once she raised the stroller to the sidewalk she turned toward me, spit into the gutter and began to run so fast that the kid in the stroller started to cry.

I shrugged. Something like this never would've happened in Mexico. Something like this, if it had happened in Mexico, wouldn't've made me react this way. Here I was in the States, less than two days, and I sounded and almost acted, all the way, like the devil I'd been twenty years ago. Maybe I'd ask Tom and Milly who the maid was, sort of describe her, find out where she lived and go speak to the lady of the house about what'd happened, and why the maid'd got my back up. Really, it was all the radio's fault. But Rory, if he was here, would've advised me to forget the whole thing and concentrate harder on the low profile.

Before I went up to Joyce's—our?—house, I picked some scattered leaves and a popsicle stick off the lawn. Then I pulled up some weeds which I also carried with me. Jesus is a soul man? What kind of song was that anyway? Certainly not one Simon should hear.

CHAPTER TWO

JOYCE: Just as it seemed to say in every chapter of the book, I rested on my back, breathed deep to savor the gift of oxygen as I thought of its Creator and mine and how He was really responsible for air-conditioning too, which I'd had installed in the house almost right after I moved in, and slowly let my breath out—exhaled. The author —his book-jacket photo proved he was a serious john with a shaved head; besides, he wore a lama's robe because he'd studied in Tibet and had been initiated into one of the most secret, magical religious orders—instructed his neophytes, beginners who were studying him and had lots to learn, that we were to flood our minds with lovely colors, beautiful music and sensations, even if they were physical, so not the best kind, which is why imaginings on more elevated or spiritual levels were preferred and to be strived for. Such bathing in sensation was to be practiced often, all the time, any place at all, until good, nice thoughts resulted in "instantaneous sublimity." That's exactly how the book put it.

It put lots more, some of it you had to read over and over again to understand even a little bit. Like this. So I lifted my sleepshade, put on my reading glasses with the little flashlights built into both sides of the frame, flicked them on and read aloud. I mean loud enough for just me to hear.

"Then the psychodynamics of consciousness-alteration will enable the disciple to rise from the bed or other place of rest in so elevated a state of self-induced emotional grace that the resultant *upaya* and its consciousness-altering cognitions will influence for good every thought, action or reaction throughout the day and night, even when in deepest slumber and the disciple turns, stretches or draws himself into a fetal position that may have even held Time before it was touched by the Creator and sent forth from Eternity into countless eons and uncharted spaces."

That out of the way, I lay back, took off the glasses after I turned off the little flashlights, put on my sleepshade again and let the book fall to the floor. It was almost two months since Frederick Rory, Esq.—a legal shill if there ever was one —had shown me the courtesy of a visit, which was supposed to prove, through his *personal* appearance, how much he and certain other people thought of me. How concerned they were for me in the grief of my widowhood. Matter of fact, Rory had detoured all the way from New York before he went on to Mexico City. Now that he had come out, Rory was glad he'd made the trip because the house was beautiful, an astonishment, the end accomplishment of a talent he had never associated with me. Dirty bastard; I recognize a knock when I hear it. But seeing me in the house helped him understand all the more why the banker-tailored Joes who controlled the distribution and arbitration of industry franchises as well as broken arms, legs, teeth, necks and other forms of bad health wanted to do well by me. Busy as they were with the problems of punishment and reward, influence, patronage, juice and lots and lots of cash which could be as dangerous as dynamite in the hands of some crazy college kid, they had taken lots of time to worry about my general well-being, welfare and the future for me and mine.

Widowhood, they had decided, was an unhappy state for any woman in her sort-of-middle forties, especially for one who'd known the advantages of three hubbies and was aware, without making a thing of it, of all the legal advantages this gave them as they conducted businesses which depended heavily on a legal code that rejected any statute that might compel a wife to testify against her husband. It was imperative—Rory said I certainly understood why—for me to give up any plans I might've had for extended mourning and make immediate plans to marry a good man of their choice, a sympathetic type capable of handling a woman—me—who was having so many problems with menopause that even thinking about a single Scotch on the rocks made me drunk. A woman who hated too much, so they said. A woman who couldn't do anything with her daughter, a fourteen-year-old truant who behaved worse than a slum slut.

Maybe Rory's visit and the news of my future, which he carried like a Western Union messenger, explains why from then until now I never got past the first chapter of the lama's book. How much I read wasn't supposed to be important. How much I understood, even less. But how much I wanted to be helped, how much I believed that wanting to be helped would make it come true, this was what counted. So my manicurist—she comes to the house—said when she loaned me the book which she swore had helped her in a hundred different ways including not depending on a love life to keep her happy.

Unfortunately for me, I underwent the agony of becoming the second Mrs. Itzik Yanowitz not too long after my second husband, Winnie Dobby, had died in a sort of funny way. You see—I told the coroner, not minding the way he looked at me—for reasons I never knew, Winnie became such an insomniac that at last, no matter how tired he was, he couldn't fall asleep unless he first sat cross-legged in his pajamas. Sort of yoga. And where did he have to sit? Where else but in the open bedroom window of our seventeenth-story apartment. This helped put him to sleep for good, especially after he tipped forward. To quote more or less from the findings of the coroner's jury, "investigation revealed no evidences of defenestration." Fortunately for me, as good friends hurried to bring the news, an old sponsor who had cherished both my dead husbands as his boys—they meant this as a father–sons' relationship—had just got out of the can where he'd put in some time because my first husband—Mitchell Wolf—had told the law some awful lies about the man who loved him like a son. An ignorant jury, that actually believed gangsters were Robinsons, Cagneys and Bogarts, and did in real life what these actors did in the movies, made it possible for the trial judge to saddle Itzik with a life jolt. Still, Itzik was able to cry—at least he said he cried—when he got the news that a trustee who became unhinged in the prison exercise yard did considerable damage when he began to swing a bucket. Mitch and three other cons were rushed to the infirmary, but Mitch's head was just too caved in.

Naturally enough, after this sad thing happened, I didn't go to Mitch's funeral because his family claimed the body and they didn't want a *kurveh shiksa* at the services, I was free to marry again and Winnie, the man I'd wired to meet me in New York after I escaped from Vera Cruz, offered to go through the happy ceremony with me. Now, years-years later, as I'm resting on my back and trying to think beautiful thoughts and see beautiful images, I can't even think of something beautiful, even a small thing, because—since Itzik died —a big, ugly, evil thought's taken over my mind and refuses to go away. Had Winnie's proposal to me been *his* idea? Had he, really himself, wanted to marry me? Or had he been ordered to do the one-knee bit? In the entire history of the world, when had a pimp married one of his broads? But Mitch, who'd been a customer before he took me to Vegas—in fact he said he wouldn't go without me, even if they dropped him in the river—had married me. But not immediately. Truth of the matter, which I can stand now, I can even look back and wonder why it even hurt, maybe because it all happened so long ago, I ran away after he turned me down when I asked him to make us legal. Later, after Mitch located me in New York, in the company of a dyke and pretty drunk too, Itzik gave Mitch two shares of stock in the *old* Riviera. At first I thought it was a wedding present. Later I found out that Mitch had blackjacked the stock out of them—for marrying me. He was a good-looking guy. So, when I found out the score, I realized how I was married to a good-looking, double-dealing bastard.

No, too bad, none of this could be altered to make even some part of it into a beautiful thought or memory. But what difference did it make to me, then or now, whether Mitch or Winnie were happily married to me? What mattered is that they'd been my husbands. Although I didn't go to Mitch's funeral—so I can't say what it was like—Winnie's was in good taste, very solemn, and I behaved with dignity.

Not too long after Itzik's sentence was commuted to the seven years he'd done, and four—no five—months after Winnie was buried and a beautiful stone was on his grave, Itzik called on me with flowers, some books, some dolls and other toys for Veronica, who was three and very sweet, he said, and a gorgeous string of baroque pearls. Sitting stiff and formal on a straight-backed Sheraton sidechair, homburg on his knees, Itzik was a gray, grave man who told me how much both my ex-husbands had meant to him. He had thought of them as sons from the first day he met each of them—and I sort of really believed he'd felt that way about Mitch—and how they had always counted on him to take care of their bride, no matter what bad thing happened to them. Obligations placed on the living weren't ignored by people with decent makeups. And on one of Winnie's visits to Itzik in the pen, where he was doing time because of Mitch, Winnie had made him promise—imagine, making a man in prison maybe for life promise anything!—that if he should ever get out and he—Winnie—should die, that Itzik would marry me and become a second father to Verney, who was still little more than a baby and really needed two parents.

Two parents. With none she only could've been better off. There's a thought that hurts because it's so true.

Although I couldn't remember and didn't know of a case where a pimp, especially when he moved up in the world to better things, had ever married one of his girls, or of someone marrying a girl he'd lived with for two shares of stock worth at most fifty thousand, lots of men in associated lines of business had married and had kids. Joe Foggia was one. Pat Callahan was another. And the wop beast who married Joe Foggia's sister—I'll remember his name soon, although it really doesn't matter because he's dead, too—also had a family. But me, being of sound mind, I never intended to have kids because no one like me, or who did what I did, should. So I'd often thought of having myself fixed, but never got around to it because it wasn't a beautiful thought, I'd say. So I did what Winnie asked, because in its way it was a beautiful sentiment. That was, to get rid of my coil since it was what lots of us in the business used, seeing as it is the safest and most convenient method. But Winnie wanted us to feel married—which was something Mitch never cared anything about—so out went the coil, in went my new diaphragm before the occasions, and I never forgot to use it and to douche right after. Until that one time.

If I'd done it often without taking care of myself and then become pregnant, I wouldn't've been so disgusted and frightened. But that *one* time, believe me, just that one time, and it happened. Then I didn't do anything because I was scared, frightened, convinced that God wanted me to have a child. So to get out of it I told Winnie that I'd missed and instead of reacting as I thought, hoped he would, so that an abortion would've been *his* idea, Winnie was so shocked when I got around to mentioning abortion that he threatened to put me in the hospital—and not for a pregnancy—if I did even the smallest, littlest bad thing to—get this—*his* child. If I didn't want the baby, he did.

From the day I left the hospital with Verney, she was sick with the colic and everything else an infant could possibly have. And Winnie carried on as if I was some sort of carrier, or some kind of bacteria, and responsible for everything bad that happened to his dear, darling, sweet baby girl. It had been one big week-to-week, month-to-month, just about three-year yell-fest. And from then to now everything's combined to make it impossible for me to think of Veronica with affection, as someone who should be loved even if it's impossible to like her. Winnie used to call me an unnatural mother. Itzik began to say similar things to me because I didn't love or even like Verney, and when we could no longer avoid each other, and Verney tried to hit me back when I hit her again before she'd run out of the house—you can take every bet—I never went after her because why should I interfere with a car or truck? And where did she go? I never bothered to ask. So, as I continued to lay on my back, the only thought that made me feel better—*wait, wait until Verney and Larry meet!*—wasn't beautiful or good. Still, I actually felt dreamy thinking about it and I hoped that for their very first meeting, from which you couldn't keep me away, Verney would be more than ordinarily mean and hateful and disgusting. When she was at her worst-best, it was hard to believe she was only fourteen.

So now that I'd been awake for at least an hour and hadn't been able to think of anything good or beautiful, not even of a piece of furniture or china or jade or fabric or some painting I liked and maybe even owned, how could I possibly think of getting out of bed? Suppose the day wouldn't be just another series of disasters, which was normal for things in this house, but the kind of earthquake or tornado that's featured in movies? An average, lousy, awful day I could take, by this time my hide was tough enough for that. Besides, I felt up to handing out some lumps of my own. Today I even felt up to putting the blocks to Verney, even, for instance, after she got fired up to work over Larry and had lots of live steam left. That would give him a good idea of what I'd been living with all these years. What sort of stepdaughter he could now call his own. At last, at last he would get some of what was coming to him and was so long overdue.

Oh yes, because I remember a day so long ago, not long after we arrived at the Riviera and I was sitting poolside with Mitch, Bull-now-Simon and Feivel—poor guy, he'd really worshipped me—how Larry had come out of the hotel looking to burn anyone in his way, but all of us'd calmed him down and Bull—I just must make myself think of him as *Simon*— had gone for a pitcher of Collins and given the first one to Larry. Then, when he continued to badmouth us and I got fed up with his nastiness, real vicious, I said to him, "If I ever have kids, I'd want them to be just like you." Honest to God, I was being ironic. Still, how can you explain that Verney is as rotten as Larry? And later, after the Riviera was operating A-class, I'd wondered more than once what it'd be like to get into the sack with him? Now, just by letting him spend the night in my bedroom, I could find out. Legally too. But I'd see myself in hell first. I'd rather even touch myself first, which is a very nasty thing to do.

There, there! I clasped my hands together and made little pleasure sounds as if anticipating something I hadn't felt in the longest time and it was going to come on strong, to repeat itself again and again, with every move I made, until ass-weariness made me stop. And my mouth would be so wonderful dry-dry. Honest, I felt that way now because I could see some marvelous scenes. Get the first one! Larry locked out of his rights and privileges as my husband. Act two! Verney really chopping Larry as she told him what to do with himself, where to stick the advice he wanted her to take, the orders he gave her, giving him a sample of mouth he'd probably never heard from anyone with tits. Grand finale! While Larry stares stupidly at Verney, because he's too strung out to make a sound,

I'd approach the evil girl I have to call daughter and crack her a good one across the side of the head. Then I'd belt her with the other hand! And as if Verney's head was a Ping-Pong ball, I'd bat her from side to side with roundhouse wallops that would keep the little evil bitch from falling only as long as I continued to bust her around.

Unfortunately, the beating would have to come to an end and after Verney crawled to her room—oh yes indeed, Verney wouldn't have the strength to do anything but crawl, and painfully—I'd turn to Larry and while every one of my features registered contempt for him, I'd be daring him with a silence tougher than words to say or do anything about what he'd just seen. Because this was my house, free and clear of mortgage or any encumbrance whatsoever, and he was never to forget it. The same applied to Bull, now supposed to be called Simon. Poor guy, I'd never hated him, not really, even when he made such a fool of himself by trying to score with every showgirl in our line. But a lunatic—no matter what his name or past, either good or bad—still added up to trouble. But who would start it? Or make it? They? Verney? Or me? Most likely it would be started by Verney. That's what I hoped. That it would be started by Verney.

Somewhere along the line, the book which was supposed to tune me into peace and beauty got short-circuited, so it wasn't giving me healthy shocks. Going downstairs might. Still, that took courage—to leave the security of my bed, the feeling-safe darkness of the shaded room—and it was up to me alone to see if I had any left. First I removed the earplugs. Then the sleepshade. Nothing bad happened. No panic or nausea. No sudden thumping of my heart because I didn't know the time and it might still be morning. But certain shadows told me that it had to be past noon, so I decided to do something else that was daring. Be my own confessor and admit that my failure to get anything from the book, as my manicurist had, she swore, wasn't the author's fault. Just mine. I said it aloud —"Just mine."

My finger rested on the buzzer for Milly and as I waited for her to knock I still tried to think of something beautiful. Wasn't my bedroom a beautiful conception, founded in beautiful objects and their complementary arrangement? From the bed, a carved four-poster on the raised dais, to the matching needlepoint sofas before the fireplace, a low, graceful coffee table between them. From the oval table with its burled walnut top and Staffordshire bowl filled with porcelain flowers to the graceful rolltop desk with its Queen Anne legs and scrollwork, a piece described as unique by the Parke-Bernet auction catalogue. From the tigerskin rug to the brass chaise for which an important AID decorator had offered me double, then triple what I'd paid for it. From the heavy silk draperies to the custom-crafted bombé-front dresser, fifteen feet long and with five banks of drawers. From the Venetian mirror above the fireplace to the fine crystal chandelier that supplied the main lighting for the chamber with its dressing room, lovely bath and small massage room with its sunporch overlooking the garden. All of it was beautiful. Which was how I'd planned it, upstairs and down, every square foot of the house and gardens, so that it could've won out in competitions over most of the houses open to the public during garden walks given for charity—*if* I'd been permitted by Itzik to open the house. Still, I was able to sort of shower in the accumulated feelings of delight I'd known while I was doing over this big barn—which Itzik'd bought sight unseen a day or so before our marriage—into a house that was a standout even among decorators.

Still, my pleasure was less than perfect. I'd done over the house to help me come sort of alive again. But Itzik lived in it to do what he promised he would do when he got out of prison. Retire. Retire from everything. Not only had he stepped down and aside, not too unwillingly because he was tired, but he got pleasure in his new role as a kind of grandfather member of the board, you could call him a retired statesman, who seldom left the house and even less often had visitors. Sure, this was what Itzik and the people at his level, and those just below and above him, wanted. But I was younger. I'd had more than my share of trouble and woe. So I wasn't ready for life as a lady hermit, certainly not while we lived in Beverly Hills and weren't more than a couple of hours from Santa Barbara, San Francisco or Palm Springs. Or for that matter—Vegas. Or Hawaii. From me to you, more than once I screamed like an old drunken Irish one-beer whore, screamed at Itzik how, for all the good freedom did him, he might as well've stayed in the can. There at least he took a walk in the exercise yard.

But Itzik thought of himself as—honest, that's how he put it—a retired admiral who could keep the boat from rocking if he spent his golden years in dry dock, going nowhere, seeing hardly anyone. Until I became interested again in interior decoration there was nothing for me to do, so I tried drinking. Who could blame me? Some husband. Some daughter. Some existence. Then came the hot-flashes period of my life, the sweats and dizziness, the depressions and suddenly beginning to cry, my stomach swelling up because I was becoming irregular and I'd never realized how important regularity'd been to me, and the going to the o.b.-gyn. man for hormone shots with estrogen and other things, none of them helping me feel good or reasonable about things, people, Itzik or Verney. And I couldn't drink. One martini before dinner, some little sips of appropriate wines during the courses, no more than one straight Scotch or bourbon or vodka and my tongue would thicken, my eyes would see double and I couldn't even make it from the table to the stairs. Something bad had happened to my chemistry and the answer to this problem, on the face of it, was simple—give up drinking, which was easier said than done because of the way we lived in this house, even if Itzik did offer me an open checkbook to get started on some kind of hobby, which he insisted was the all-purpose answer to any problem. In his experience he was right, and when I at last found something to interest me, I was glad to admit he was right. Then my life became more bearable. Then I was more willing to accept loneliness, the one-drink staggers. And Verney, the all-time brat.

Miracle! After I raised myself from the bed and stood without wavering, I was able to walk as if my feet weren't being used for the first time. It was minutes past one, a little early for me, but I was awake, out of bed and on my feet, and the thought of coffee—no more—was beautiful. Why, I was able to smile at my reflection in the pier-glass mirror. I was actually in a hurry to shower and get downstairs. Imagine, to shower instead of bathe, because bathing usually took me more than an hour, sometimes two, but what else did I really have to do with my time? I felt so good I decided to touch myself, and I didn't feel guilty or think it was nasty. You see, being married the way I was and to, of all people, Larry, there were bigger nastinesses.

Some forty or fifty minutes later, what I saw of myself wasn't bad. Except for a little pouchiness under both eyes, with the left pouch a little larger, the rest of me was pretty good and firm. My midi-mini length jersey dress proved that my stomach was still flat and I wasn't afflicted with middle-age spread. I could thank the o.b.-gyn. man for these. It was a psychological lift to know I no longer had to wear a girdle, didn't need one, and the body jewelry Milly'd picked up for me at Saks made me feel as if I went out daily to make the circuit of Wilshire Boulevard and Rodeo Drive to see what the smart shops and boutiques were showing and to buy more shoes than I could ever wear before I put some money into the economy through Tiffany's, Van Cleef and Arpels, Lakin y Cie. at Magnin's Wilshire, which is sort of in the boonies, and some of the local jewelers who phoned every so often about something exquisite just for me. My pantyhose fit tightly, no ugly bags at the knees to remind me of the old one about the man who told a woman that her stockings were wrinkled before he realized she wasn't wearing any. Only my shoes were old-fashioned because I wouldn't wear the stumpy monster styles with their ugly orthopedic heels. It was still too early for earrings, so I chose a sportwatch with a bright strap to match my dress and then went to Verney's room for a large pair of frog-type sunglasses to hide the pouchiness. And who knew? Verney might be home and we might be able to talk civilly about Larry, the second of her stepfathers, and what we ought to do, I guess, to bring harmony into the house, which in the long run would cut down the problems of living with someone I'd known as a mean, evil bastard, a slavedriver who'd become my husband because Itzik was dead. Talk about laughs. Talk about the marvelous chance to get even. Talk about making Larry sorry for ever being born. This was it. But now on my feet instead of my back, feeling relaxed because I'd touched myself, did I really want—revenge? Revenge for what? For his taking us with him? For letting me go back to the States? For really devoting himself to Simon? So, what did I want?

Something that approximated peace and a little freedom, I guess, which is why I paused to move a bowl of flowers on a table at the head of the stairs and to adjust the Piranesi grouping of prison scenes which moved mysteriously every night. Face up to it, I told myself, these were just stalls to delay my approach to the door of Verney's room. This very afternoon, if I felt up to it, would see me out shopping for six, seven, maybe ten pairs of oversized glasses. Or I might phone and have my ophthalmologist bring out a selection on his way home after office hours. Meanwhile, eyes narrowed to see less of the garbage dump that was Verney's room, I found a pair of glasses, put them on and went downstairs for juice, coffee and my second meeting in about seventeen years with the *new* man of the house.

He looked good, which bothered me, especially since he resembled the fascinating louse in that cigarette ad who preferred his brand to broads and proved it for the *schmucks* who believe in all sorts of commercials more than they believe in the Bible. Taking his ease on the sofa in my morning room, he was hunched forward, elbows on his knees, the television remote control in both hands. And he was staring intently at the not-so-quite focused images of some women, one of them the show's moderator, who was—I swear—the ghost of Joe Pyne in drag. She and the other monsters with claws between their legs were especially fascinated with one guest, another woman with a face like a keg of nails and an orange wig. She was explaining how to instruct maids from Mexico, Guatemala, places like that, in birth control, which was pretty difficult, seeing as most of them were Catholic.

"I'm sorry I let them into your house," Larry said as he snapped off the set and stood up. "Some problems some people have." He raised his dark glasses to look at his wristwatch. "It's not even two and you're dressed and looking very nice."

"You've improved," I said. "Now you mix your nastiness with a compliment."

"I didn't mean to be nasty." He really seemed to be apologizing! "But for years now, as far back as I can remember for the last ten years or so, Simon and me've been getting up early. Never later than eight."

"I remember further back than that," I said for the record. "What a mean son of a bitch you were. How you prowled the Riviera like the resident ghost at four, five, six in the morning. You know"—I looked at him before nodding to indicate approval—"you've held up pretty good."

"From the neck down you look the same," he said.

Oh, he was really marinated in meanness. "Thanks for nothing," was the sharpest thing I could think of to say. "Thanks for telling me I don't look well because I don't sleep well."

"Most drunks sleep like they were dead. I know."

"Am I to understand you don't touch the stuff?" I asked to keep from spitting in his face.

"Wine, beer and the hard stuff—I can count the drinks I take in a year on the fingers of both hands."

"That's not what I remember about you," I said.

For a couple of seconds he looked at me. "What do you remember?"

"Let it go," I said before I got up to cross the room and press the buzzer.

"Not yet," he persisted. "Is that all you and maybe other people remember about me? That I was hard? And evil?"

"What else is worth remembering?" That question made me feel I'd scored some points.

He had to think. "Maybe that I took off with almost a quarter of a million?"

"That's been written off," I said. "Over about seventeen-eighteen years and split two ways—it isn't really so much."

"It's an awful lot of *pesos*."

"And even more play money. So who cares?" I rang again because Milly hadn't answered. "Dollars or *pesos*, it's been written off."

"That's what you and they say."

He sounded very nervous, which made me feel sort of good. "That's what I've been told," I said and waved for Milly, in her gray uniform, to leave. Like earlier when she came to my room, Milly looked annoyed, but that didn't bother me. "Look, I've been a widow three times. Three times," I repeated for emphasis. "So I've had enough of shock, funerals, and more or less mourning. Of getting used to new people and what they do to a tube of toothpaste." Like the book suggested when you felt stress coming on, I paused to breathe deep and slow. It did seem to make me calmer. "They know that," I went on. "And they also know how I haven't got a thing for you. No case of the secret hots. *They* chose you—not me."

"I know that," he said.

"Still, no matter what I think of you," I continued, "I let them know that being your widow wasn't my idea of the jollies."

"Should I say thanks?" he asked.

"I didn't want to marry again." I ignored him. "But I can't

convince them that I can take care of myself. That I'm not a boozer."

"One way to do that is to stop wearing dark glasses indoors," he said.

That made him laugh because he was wearing his glasses. And his camera too. But neither of these struck me funny. "One sure way for your friend and you to keep on living here is not to give me advice," I let him know. "Not even if it's good."

He thought that over for a second before he asked me if I didn't think my attitude was stupid. Like it or not, we were married. If not for better then it was for worse. Like it or not, for worse rather than better, if that was the way it had to be, would keep me alive. What Winnie did—the one thing—that put him through an open window was something I didn't want to know. Of course I knew something about how he'd begun to move up even before he met me so long ago at La Guardia when I came back from Mexico. Also, I was more and more convinced that the right people had advised—or ordered—him to marry me after Mitch's head was split like a dividend. But why Winnie'd become an insomniac—for my own good at the inquest I'd sworn he had—was something I didn't know or want to know. That some certain suspicious brokers thought otherwise, or because they wanted to keep me in the family, explains best to me why Itzik proposed. And why, before Itzik's body was cold enough to become stiff, I got paid a visit from Fred Rory, who, after he extended condolences, admired the house and grounds, and regretted that Verney wasn't home since I'd taken the trouble less than a couple of weeks ago to call him in New York about her, got down to the business part of his visit.

You see, the call I'd made on the day he mentioned was about Verney, but I was screaming how I just couldn't handle her, no one could and what were they going to do to help me? When Rory said he didn't know, I began to scream that neither did I. For that matter no one seemed to know, not even Itzik when he was alive. And as far as I was concerned the only person who could handle Verney was someone even meaner than she was, a certain son of a bitch named Larry Tunafish who I hadn't seen in close on to twenty years, the dirty evil bastard.

So I'd done it to myself was what I thought after Rory told me how I was to marry again, to Larry Tunafish no less, and how we worked out the marriage was between us, was what Juan Basqua'd told him to tell me. Whether Larry Tunafish —his real name is Tunig, that's on my marriage certificate— was to be husband as well as companion to me and keeper for Verney was strictly up to me. But even as husband, he was first off a keeper. The way Rory said that, I knew he included me in the keeping.

"Larry," I said, "listen to me."

He nodded as he looked again at his watch. "Couldn't I do that over some coffee? I know you eat supper nine, ten at night, like they do in Mexico. But you've gotta eat something during the day."

"In a minute," I said. I sat on the sofa, near him, and we looked at each other. "We're married, Larry." My lips turned down and he nodded to show how he didn't like it either. "Since that's the way it is, maybe we oughta try making the best of things? Maybe you could talk to Verney," I added. "About going to school and amounting to something."

"There's nothing wrong with that for a kid," he agreed. "Veronica could study to be a teacher. That's a nice career for a woman."

"Suppose she does?" I asked and managed not to laugh. "With us married to each other, anything's possible. Suppose she does and ends up with kids in the class like you and me and Bull?"

"Simon," he corrected me before he seemed to smile. "She wouldn't have to teach to earn a living."

I nodded. "That's for sure."

"A teacher," he was emphatic and sounded pleased with himself. "Yes. When I get to meet Veronica—or should I call her Verney like you do?—and get to know her, the right time'll come along to talk about her future. Then I'll sort of suggest."

My eyes, hidden by the dark glasses, pitied him. "This I've got to see," I began, "because it has to be one of the meetings of the century."

"Until I come out of my corner," he sounded confident. "Meanwhile, maybe I could see the house? Have you tell me all about it?" He hesitated. "Like Simon said, we didn't expect this. Didn't expect you could do this all by yourself."

"With some help from the neighbors." My tone was dry and Larry looked puzzled. "You know that Itzik married me in 1957? Just a couple of months after he got out."

"So Fred Rory told me. I was surprised."

Was Larry kidding me? It was hard to believe he'd been so out of touch. "He bought the home furnished," I said and decided to find out later if Larry was conning me about his keeping away from everything and anyone of the old days. "An all-cash deal because that eliminated any pressures certain people who worry about property values might've put on the lending agencies."

"Itzik always knew what to buy. And in what way."

How could I miss a chance to slip him the knife? "You came a lot cheaper than me," I said.

I waited for Larry to say something which would've given me a good excuse to order him out of the house. Then I would've phoned Fred Rory, because I had his number too, and told him that Larry was his problem, not mine, and if he —or they—wanted my husband to live here, that someone would have to teach him good manners. But Larry just raised his right hand, which I chose to take as an apology, something like it, and that gave me a chance to go on about how Itzik never saw this place, not even as a picture, but'd just told the right people in this part of the world to get him a big house with privacy in the best neighborhood. One set far back from the street. With a big garden in front and back and maybe a pool. So it was bought for him, we were married and came directly here, to a monster of a place furnished in motel modern and hotel-lobby discards.

"Would you like to know how the solid-citizen neighbors took to having a big operator next door?" I asked Larry who was lining up the decorators' magazines on the coffee table.

He nodded. "It's crossed my mind."

"They loved it! You just wouldn't believe how much. For blocks around they could hardly wait to get into the house. And they proved it with invitations to drop-ins, brunches, lunches and even dinners. We got more attention in a month than some hardware wholesaler, someone like that, who's made his pile and retires for some of the sweet life, gets in a year, maybe years. Larry"—I showed him my fists—"we were in."

"You're upset," he said to me, but I shook my head that we were going to talk and put the subject behind us. "And Itzik didn't go for it? People really change," he said as if he'd just discovered gravity. "When I knew him back in New York he liked parties."

"You don't have to tell me," I said. "But prison took a lot out of him. And he was older when he got out."

"Can time is tough time."

"My can's done too much legitimate mattress time," I let him know. "To a couple of husbands who didn't exactly die peacefully. Or gracefully. To a third who became my screw."

"I wonder how you're gonna classify me?" Larry asked.

"You'll find out. And soon enough," I said. "Those times I laid Itzik in New York. The times I laid Mitch before we married. Winnie, too. How do you think they thought of me? As a call girl, prosty or whore?"

Larry shook his head. "I don't know. And for no strange reason the subject doesn't interest me."

"Too bad," I said. "Because just now it does me. Enough to talk about it. Mitch was average in the hay," I began. "Winnie was always in a hurry to get to the kitchen to eat something after it was over. Toward the end he used to bring crackers and cheese on a plate and put them on his night table. I swear. And Itzik"—suddenly I was sad for him—"was a huffer-puffer. Someone who thought he was proving something important by trying to push me through the mattress."

"I've got some sad news for you," Larry said. "You're not going to rate me. You see, the room I'm in suits me fine."

"Good." I really meant it. "I've had enough of it too."

"I'm glad that's cleared up," he said with such relief it made me shiver with anger. God help me, please, did I look that bad? "So now you're in the house," he said, prompting me to go on with the story. "And the neighbors've said *buenos días, tardes, noches.* Then what?"

Any of the joined windows in the morning room offered me a nice view of the garden and I chose the one on the extreme right because it gave me a good look at the best arrangement of garden furniture under the red and white patio awning. Also, it put me next to the best of the mahogany doors with rosewood panels that we had used in quantity to do the morning room walls.

"They really wanted to know us," I said without looking at him. "Isn't a modern hood supposed to be like Errol Flynn's Robin Hood? Or one of his pirates?"

"I've never given it any thought," he said.

"They really thought we'd have them over," I went on. "Then, what points they'd be scoring when they told other people how friendly they were with one of the really big brokers and his wife who'd been married twice before—and get this—both times to boys who worked for him. For chrissakes, Larry," I turned to him, "for a little while we—I—was more popular, more of a celebrity than a broad with three tits!"

That made Larry laugh, which tended to take the edge off me because I was building up to hysteria, so I went on to tell him how a pretty good publicity agent even got in touch with

Itzik and me, and when one of the neighbors found out about this—after I asked for information on the p.a.—she offered to put us in touch with the agency that handled her husband, who was very big that year because he'd finished a blockbuster musical that was making tons of money in roadshow.

"Larry, I swear," I said after I sank into a deep wing chair at the fireplace and lifted my glasses to rub one of my eyes, "this big-time agency called us." Then I shook my head again. "But it couldn't be that way."

"I guess all I'm supposed to say here is—oh, or why not?" he prompted me.

Really, he wasn't any help. And in his quiet way, which was new to me, he was still able to put me on and over the edge. "I liked the opportunity," I continued. "Because this house was really the first home I'd had since I was a little kid, before my parents became religious nuts. And from then on, it was hotel rooms and furnished apartments. But, Larry, this was a house!"

"Every foot of it," he agreed.

Did he turn away because the restless movements of my hands, the way I knotted them and cracked my knuckles, made him nervous? "But Itzik said no dice," I said after a sigh. "He didn't even want to go out for lunch or do any shopping. Call up, he'd say. Call up and they'll deliver." I rested and played with the broad gold band of my new wedding ring. "Itzik wasn't interested in anything that had to do with people. Any people," I added, and Larry nodded that he understood. "Which pleased the people who said he could retire and die from natural causes."

Larry kept on nodding. "I'd say that Itzik and his friends didn't want the Beverly Hills cops and anyone else to get much to put into his file. Did he buy this house through Fred Rory?"

"I'd say so." I began to nod, so Larry stopped. "And you're right about his file. What was in it, Itzik said, couldn't be helped. But we weren't to do anything to make it bigger. Not even with anything as innocent as neighbors on the premises because their names would go into the reports."

"Which might make them sore." Larry continued to understand too good, which bothered me. "I get the picture. A pretty sad one for you."

Talking about the past was making me more and more disgusted with people in my present. Still, I had to go on. "So if we weren't going to be famous or notorious—I guess to some people they mean the same thing—what was the point of knowing us?" I asked him as if my question really needed an answer.

But he gave me one. "None," he said.

"So I sat in this place. Going crazy"—I waved my hands and sort of touched my hair—"until Itzik got fed up with me and my breaking windows—stuff like that. Until one day after I had a real mean fit he said very quiet that unless I wanted to be fixed up with a carbon monoxide suicide that nobody could break I oughta do something about the house instead of just criticizing the way things looked."

He didn't look shocked, not at all, and only asked me to excuse him for interrupting, but where was Itzik buried? I told him in some Jewish cemetery not far from here and how I'd put up a headstone, one I picked from a catalogue and I also chose something nice to engrave on it.

"We could go out together," I suggested. "But who knows? The cops might be watching."

"It's that bad?" he asked.

"I'm just guessing," I told him and he looked relieved. At least his mouth did. "So where was I?"

"Getting ready to decorate?"

"Yes. Why not make the house as beautiful as Verney and me? Itzik said. Wasn't that a nice thing to say?" I asked Larry, who did me a big favor by pushing his features into something that could pass for an expression of approval if you weren't too critical. "Especially about Verney?"

"You think I'll meet her today?" he asked, to avoid giving me a direct answer.

Try to think positively, about something beautiful, when a question like that is thrown at you. "Who knows?" First I felt awful, then I became angry. "I hope you're not going to say nothing like my knowing where she is? The rest of that? Because you'd better not."

"Forget I asked," he said.

"Do you mind if we keep talking about the house and how Itzik set up a special checking account for me that he called decoration unlimited? It kept me busy for years." I thought about some of the things I'd bought. Too bad I hadn't bothered with before-pictures. But I'd even torn up Verney's baby pictures because of what she was now and how things were between us. "Come on," I stood and smoothed my skirt, "let's have some coffee and a look at each other across a table."

"A good idea," Larry said. "But I want more than coffee if it's all right with you. I'm starved."

"Anything you want in the line of food that doesn't smell bad is all right with me." I paused at the door. "You really didn't know Itzik was dead? You mean it?"

Larry raised his dark glasses and right hand. "Not until Rory told me. Somehow"—he hesitated—"I always thought of Itzik as being the last man in the world to die. Sort of a rock that'd last forever."

In my wildest, far-out dreams, and I've had some chillers, I couldn't imagine Larry mourning for anyone. "People don't last forever, which is a good thing. Come on, keeper," I beckoned to him, "we'll have a wedding brunch. And Simon can join us. Simon," I pronounced his name carefully. "It'll take some doing to think of him—of all people—as Simon. Still, that'll make for good thinking and good thoughts."

"We'd both like that," Larry thanked me as we walked toward the dining room. "But he's out. Left early," he answered my expression. "So when do I get to meet Verney?"

"You shouldn't look forward to it," I warned him. "Meanwhile, I don't know where she is. It could be Tijuana again."

"What's there for kids?" he asked me. "It's supposed to be all tourist junk."

"Drugs and whorehouses," I said. "And abortion mills. I hope it's only the last she's interested in."

He stopped right there. "You're kidding."

As my husband I wanted him to sit at the head of the table, at the far end, so I pointed to the heavier armchair. "I wish I wasn't," I began. "I wish I never had. She's had two already, which must be some kind of a record for a girl not yet fifteen." I had to turn away because Larry's astonishment, his disgust, were too much. And he remained standing. "Think what you like," I told him. "But why can't I get her to take the pills regularly?"

"You can't expect an answer from me," he said before he sat and sort of tested the chair for fit and comfort. "But from what I've read, some people on the pill get blood clots. Maybe even cancer. So it can be pretty dangerous."

I removed my glasses because from fifteen feet away, which is the length of my table without leaves, I felt sure that Larry couldn't see how puffed my eyes were, and I felt that he didn't care.

"Dangerous?" I said, then paused. "In her case—would that be bad?"

He was shocked all right, but I'd pressed the floor buzzer before I started to speak, so Milly appeared with the serving cart and a variety of fruits and juices before he could say anything.

CHAPTER THREE

LARRY: I kept on getting up early because breakfast with Simon was the nicest part of my day. You see, we'd bought him a half interest in a small kosher grocery on Fairfax Avenue where more than half the customers spoke Jewish, so he was becoming very fluent. Now he knew funny jokes in Jewish and they even made me laugh because through Simon I was understanding more. We're a people with a real sense of humor. Also, there was a little *shul* a couple of blocks from the grocery and Simon told me the old men there were very nice, helped him *daven* and told him about their trips to Israel. Some of them had very good still and moving pictures. Even with the fighting they were going on a charter flight for Rosh Hashanah and Simon had also signed up. He even bought me a membership in the *shul* and signed me up for the charter.

By the time Simon would come into the breakfast room I'd be at the table with the morning papers. We took two copies of the *L.A. Times* so each of us'd have a complete paper. I'd look at the financial pages first, which were really good news this year, better than last, so we got even further ahead of the market on splits and increased dividends. Then I'd look at the TV section to see what movies were being shown at night. Simon would first read the bad-and-getting-worse news about Israel. He never looked at much else.

On this particular morning, when I went out to get the papers, two guys up the street seemed to be laughing it up about our house. One of the guys was from a tree-cutting truck. The other guy—from his truck, I guessed—was some sort of a hot-water heater repairman. There was nothing about the house I could see to make me laugh, but as they watched me, their faces in sort of nasty grins, suddenly one of them pointed to the driveway. So I walked toward it.

I could've killed someone. Because there, on the beautiful flagstone—selected pieces—that surfaced the driveway, and right at the sidewalk part, someone had painted in big red letters—VERNEY EATS IT RIGHT DOWN TO THE ROOT.

For I don't know how many seconds I was blind with anger. Then I heard the two men laughing harder and I walked toward them, saying nothing, and about five or six feet from them I stopped to look and decide who to take on first. And that's when I heard Simon calling me. Because I didn't answer he hurried toward me and I just took his arm and led him back to the driveway. When he saw the words he had to think for a couple of seconds before he decided the two men must've written them. Then he made a dangerous sound and charged them. Just in time I caught and told him how they had nothing to do with it. And as I held Simon, I warned them to get going, which they did. So I don't think they did that day whatever they came to fix.

I made Simon go to work and he did without breakfast, he was so upset. Then I got hold of Tom. Lucky he had turpentine in the garden storeroom and lucky the paint turned out to have a water base. With the two of us scrubbing for about an hour we got the sign all off. After the stones dried they looked lots lighter than those around them, so I told Tom to order up a cleaning crew because we might's well do the rest of the long driveway, which really was all beautiful stone and the finest work.

This should explain, I think, why when I saw Verney very early the next morning, and she said a couple of things to me, I let her have a backhand that cut and bloodied her lip. Then my follow-up forward swing, and kicking her feet out, knocked her off balance so that she stumbled against the stair-rail post before she fell to the bottom step, where she pressed both hands against her mouth. She was, I felt, more surprised than hurt—that was, for the time being. Still, she was making a big thing of it by drawing both knees into her stomach and yelling how I'd killed her. Suddenly she started to scramble up the stairs but I grabbed her ankles and without caring how her head bounced or her blood flowed, I pulled her across the floor, telling her all the while not to scream anymore unless one by one she wanted her teeth knocked out.

Once I got her inside the library, with its shelves filled with leatherbound books that were really photograph albums of stills of the movie actress who built this house and which some college movie departments and the Motion Picture Academy wanted, I locked the doors and windows, and switched on the overhead chandelier, the wall sconces as well as a couple of lamps, before I bent over to rap Verney again across the side of her head. This was very much less than she deserved for calling me a mother-f———. I can't even say, don't even like to think of this awful word which too many people nowadays say doesn't mean anything. Maybe to them, but it does to me. And why'd she called me that? Because I dared ask her where she'd been until four this morning? Where she'd been for about the past two days? Mo———. I warned myself to stop thinking of what she called me because something inside was nudging me to kick her insensible, and to take my time at it.

"Don't get up. Don't say a word unless I tell you," I warned Verney, who hated me as she lay up against the sofa, shaking all over, both elbows pressed into her ribs, two hands holding her mouth. I threw a handkerchief at her. "Use it," I said, "because your mother'll have a fit if you bleed on anything."

When she saw I wasn't going to kick her, Verney pressed the handkerchief against her mouth and started to cry in it. I've had my share of belts to the mouth and jaw, so I knew how she felt—lips raw, jaws aching, her head probably ringing from the knocking it took as she was dragged across the floor. I guess her ass ached too.

"That's better." I wondered if in the future when she was told to do something she'd do it in a hurry. Or would she need more lessons? "When I ask you a question you'd better answer it in a way that doesn't steam me," I advised her. "So from now on—between you and me—no lip or you won't have any." I kept on watching her carefully to see that she didn't bleed on the rug or sofa, for some sudden move on her part that deserved more pushing around. "Now just nod if you understand me," I told her.

Verney rolled away from me, but not before she nodded. She kept on crying, so I gave her time by fussing with an antique paper press that held a collection of sporting prints between a hundred and two hundred years old. Imagine people riding horses dressed like they were. Or doing other things like boxing. Then I moved toward the fireplace because you could never tell with a kid like Verney, a type who suddenly might go for the poker. I knew all right what she was thinking. What could she've said to deserve such a clobbering?

It was time to go to work, and she flinched when I kicked her in the ass, just hard enough to send another jolt of pain from her behind to her head, where all the while she was trying to make herself feel better by making over the pain into hating me, her stepfather—a thanks-for-nothing situation where I was concerned—as I squatted to stare at her with big disgust, just like she was some ugly bug. But she knew that since I could put more pressure on her than she cared to take, she'd better keep quiet, which was, I guess, what she wanted to do anyway because she ached all over and her mouth hurt so much.

"Do I have to kick you again?" I asked after I stood and raised my right foot.

She shook her head hard. I'd got through to her.

"Good," I said. Now I grabbed her left ear—it actually felt dirty in my hand—and sort of made her get up and follow me to the high-backed leather chair which I pushed away from the desk. "You've got a swollen lip and that's all, I'm sorry to say," I said after I pulled aside the bloody handkerchief. "But you deserve an awful lot more."

"And you deserve to be killed," she said to me.

Verney flinched when I made two fists. "Maybe I'll do you in first," I let her know how things stood between us. "My plea would be what you've done to yourself. Done to your mother. What you called her and what you just called me. What you called Simon because he tried to be nice to you."

She tried to make some sort of case for her rottenness by saying that he wasn't her uncle.

After I moved a lamp on the desk so I could sit on the edge, see Verney and be able to move in a hurry, I stared again at this awful girl in her awful clothes, whose face with its heavy makeup was improved because she was wearing the bloody lip I gave her. She was a mess, a living argument for abortion. Long straight hair, almost to her waist, unwashed and matted, that might've once been brown but was now some sort of red with blond streaks in it. Eyes rimmed with blue shadow and black lines that'd run all over her cheeks because of her tears. A dirty neck, filthy, her blue bodyshirt a dirty design of dirty stains, food I guess and other things like paint and dirt, levis out at the knees with two of the pockets torn more than halfway off. And her dirty ankles, dirtier feet, with soles that were actually black. And she'd given up shaving under the arms, which especially bothered me because young women in Mexico, even servants, were shaving there. And she wasn't wearing a brassiere, but that was the least of it.

Even cleaned up she wouldn't be pretty, because she looked too mickish, like her father, which was a pity because Joyce'd been such a doll and still could look like one when she set her mind to it. But Verney's eyes were too squinty, her nose too stubby, her mouth too large and she refused to wear her braces so her teeth were growing in crooked. Also, her skin was unhealthy yellow, blotchy, with lots of pimples across her forehead. Here was a kid who needed to be industrially steamed, cleaned and pressed, a real challenge to a White Tornado or that dope in armor who rides a white horse on television. Here was a kid who looked like she had been shoved back in to be made over again and right in the middle somewhere the machinery'd broken down. A kid whose mind was worse than her appearance, because that was easier to ruin, although Verney was doing her best to make it a total loss, which was what the principal of Verney's private school told me. I'd gone to see her the day before and been told that Verney was average intelligence, so certainly able to do ordinary work. But how could she, seeing as she only showed up once in a while? But Verney, like certain other crummy kids in that school, used their registration to keep them out of public schools, where they wouldn't've been stood for.

"We're not proud of it. We're concerned and troubled," the principal told me. She was pleasant, a real lady with dignity, maybe fifty-five or so, but still nice to look at. "We know that some families send us their children to keep them out of the juvenile courts on charges of truancy."

She didn't have to dress up the picture. In Beverly Hills you have to go to school until you're eighteen or graduate high school. So Verney would be involved with truant officers and courts, which mightn't've been a bad thing except that Verney was the daughter of her mother, who'd been Itzik's wife before she became mine. And there was who he was. And I was someone who'd once been. The kid was taking advantage of us.

"A school's supposed to be more than a front for a kid who'd otherwise be up against a truancy rap," I said, and wish'd I'd used the word "charge."

"But we try. Try very hard," she persisted, with the same sort of nervous movements I remembered from years ago when the help from bottom to top, no exceptions, stood on my office carpet at the Riviera and tried to convince me why they shouldn't have their heads busted. "Be assured, Mr. Tunig," she said, "we don't pass them along to higher grades. Not unless they meet our scholastic standards and pass final exams. Still, in the technical sense, she is going to school."

"Sixteen hundred a term without lunch is pretty expensive technical sense," I said.

Color flushed her cheeks, but I admired the principal, because her voice remained level. "You may withdraw Veronica," she began, and she wasn't angry. "We're not truant officers. We don't like to fail. We do do our best."

"Which isn't good enough unless you make her come to school and do the work," I insisted.

"Make her?" the principal repeated before she smiled, I guess you'd call it cynically. "You're here because we telephone immediately if a student isn't in class." She looked at Verney's attendance sheet, then shook her head. "Since the spring semester started, in February, we've called three or four times a week. It's now just past Easter. And this is the first visit you've granted us."

But I'd only been her stepfather for about six weeks, I explained, and had been busy with lots of things. Naturally I didn't go into them because I would've had to tell her—maybe—of what a job it'd been to keep Simon in the house and when he went away the whole time of Pesach, which is more than a week, to attend the *seders* at the house of one of the religious members of his *shul*, that I'd been pretty upset with wondering if he'd come back like he promised. Thank God, he did. Still, I did tell the principal that I'd only got wind of all this the other day because she, or whoever was in charge of calling, must've talked to Milly or Tom. They might've given all or some of the messages to Joyce, who'd finally the other day, when we met at brunch, got around to telling me about Verney's not going to school for weeks. Today I was glad Joyce'd slept late and I warned Tom and Milly to say nothing to her about the rotten sign we'd scraped off the driveway.

"You must admit that I took the call this morning," I defended myself as if it mattered whether or not she thought of me as a good parent, which didn't make sense at all to me. "And I called right back for an appointment."

"When someone in your household finally decided to see me," she zinged one in.

"Because I couldn't get her mother to come with me, I came alone," I connected. "Just how long's Verney been here anyway?"

Once again the principal looked at Verney's file. "She's finishing her second year as a body. But her head's only doing minimal seventh-grade work. At this rate she'll be getting her elementary school diploma when she's—seventeen?" That sort of startled her and she thought for some seconds. Suddenly she looked as if she'd made up her mind and was glad. "I'm sorry, Mr. Tunig, we'd rather not have her. Naturally we'll make some rebate."

This I hadn't expected, so I had to start begging for her to keep Verney in school at least on the records, until I, personally, had a talk with Verney. At last she agreed and promised to ask for no one but me whenever she called about Verney. So she ended our meeting by thanking me for my interest, hoping we would meet again on a more pleasant occasion and asking me if there was anything else she could do or suggest. After I shook my head and left to drive slowly toward Joyce's house—because it was hers and she never let me or Simon forget it—I wondered just exactly what I was supposed to do. About everything. What was a—father? How did a father think and *do?* Of course I could've telephoned someplace for advice—but exactly who? Certainly not my people. I hadn't seen them for about twenty years and honestly didn't even know if either or both of them was alive. Another thing: after I put Freddy Davis on a slab I decided never to think of them again. Not that I'd succeeded one hundred percent, but for all I knew, because they never even got a single card from me while I was in Vegas or Mexico, they might've concluded I was dead.

At a stop sign I put the car in neutral and rested until some *schmuck* nudged me with his horn. Little pinches of guilt—or was it sentiment?—got me driving again. No, I'd never missed my father or mother or my sisters. When I did think of them, which believe me wasn't often, it was harder and harder to remember what they looked like, the names of uncles, aunts, cousins, neighbors, even the names of some of the not-so-important Dukes and what'd got them into our gang. All of them, buried or not, were dead, and I never felt the desire, like the natives of Janitzio, to make a big thing of annual Days of the Dead, when to get acquainted again with those who'd died they brought eats and drinks and conversation to the graves of their family and friends. In some way this reminded Simon of the Jewish *Yortzeit.* So once again, to get back to the subject of Verney, what was I supposed to do about her? Who, really, could give me some working advice?

In Mexico City's Lomas, Polanco and Pedregal *colonias,* driveways made of tile and mosaic stone are common, but like I said before, the driveway of Joyce's house was of selected flagstones, which had got me in the habit of slowing up when I approached it, as if I didn't want to dirty the surface. Also, I'd been coming out of the house to tell drivers of the delivery trucks that brought us groceries from Jurgensen's, cut flowers, laundry, cleaning, other things, that they could no longer park on the driveway. They didn't like this because it meant a walk to the back of the house. Now, after the driveway would be cleaned by the crew, I was going to tell Tom that nobody was going to park on it for even a minute.

So I slowed up at the curb, which gave me time to change my mind about talking to Joyce. If she was up, talking to her would still be a waste of time because until the middle of the afternoon she usually had the temper and manners of a crazy lunatic. Still, when I saw her, I was bound to say that Verney might behave better if the house was on a normal routine, going to bed by midnight and having breakfast by nine-thirty the latest. Cover all odds, this would bring on a session of screaming by Joyce, who would tell me it was time I realized she was a night person. Also, in her bad health, the way she lived made her feel better, not much, but for someone in her condition she had to be very grateful for small favors. Don't think I hadn't made progress. Milly and Tom, who live in the garage apartment, were doing their best to help me adjust Joyce to their starting work about seven-thirty mornings and knocking off by eight at night because two day-help maids came in at four and stayed until eleven or eleven-thirty. And I'd also hired new day-help for the mornings, as well as a couple of new gardeners who were willing to work normal hours and have their work inspected, although lawnmowers and hedge trimmers still weren't to be used before two in the afternoon. That also went for vacuum cleaners. In time, as the help began to accept me as man-in-charge, they asked me for permission when they wanted to make changes in their duties and responsibilities. Still and all, they were help, not friends, no one to turn to for hard advice in time of trouble, no one I could ask into my office just off the paneled library, where I did most of my work and thinking—to talk about Verney and how to handle the bitch.

Believe it or not, it's the truth, Simon and I were in the house for six days, just about a week, before we met Verney. At least we first heard Joyce screaming and cursing, then we heard the sound of glass breaking. When I ran into Joyce's bedroom, saw she wasn't there, and followed the sounds of breaking glass and other things smashing, they led us to Verney's room. The door was locked but that didn't worry me as much as what was going on behind it, so I kicked the door hard with the heel of my shoe and the lock gave. Joyce was standing at the fireplace with a poker in her hand and Verney—with a leg broken off her boudoir chair—was systematically busting up her dressing table.

I put a stop to what she was doing by sidestepping as she swung at me with the chair leg and closing in fast to pull it from her hand before I clamped a full Nelson on her. As I shoved her toward one of the closets I could feel the way she bucked to break free and for a scary ten or fifteen seconds it felt like old times, when I'd had to wrestle Simon to control the devil inside of him. And you'd better believe it, I was glad to reach one of the closets and throw Verney inside before Simon helped me slam the door and put a chair under the knob to keep her locked in. Then, first, she hit the door with hangers and shoes. Getting nowhere, she started to scream again while she tore to bits anything she could get her hands on. Lucky for us, I found out later, the light bulb in this closet was blown and Verney'd never told anyone to replace it, so she was working in the dark and the way I figured, from my first look at her, which told me that she couldn't even've placed in a beauty contest held among rusty garbage cans, whatever she was tearing up couldn't be worth much.

After I sent Milly and Tom away, and told Simon to wait for me in the library—he was so shocked—Joyce stumbled to the bed where she stripped the filthy sheets and pillow slips before she sat on the bare mattress to cry, scream and curse Verney and me, all the while swearing that once and for all she was going to kill the girl and take her chances in the courts because no human being, no matter how rotten or guilty of you-name-it, had to endure the punishment of Verney, all monster, something worse than anything created by dropping atomic bombs on the Japs. Maybe we could block up the closet keyhole after we pumped in poison gas, fill in all around the door with concrete or bricks to make it the lid of Verney's coffin. Maybe we ought to call pet shops until we found one with rattlers or scorpions or black widow spiders for sale and they could be stuck in the closet with Verney, who hadn't been home for days—for which Joyce screamed she was going to have to go to church and give thanks—but had phoned once in a while to tell Joyce—*her mother!*—that she was reporting in to let her know she was still alive, damn it, and to stick her questions she knew where, because whatever she wanted to know wasn't any of her effen business.

The kid was a wet-sheet case. Although right off I said she belonged in a hospital, Joyce wouldn't hear of it, so I took her by the arm, made her leave Verney's room and get into the Queen-Something-or-other bed of hers, where I sat on the edge until the sleeping pill put her away. Later that day, when Joyce was sleeping out cold and Simon'd listened to me and gone to his *shul,* I went back to Verney's room with a belt in one hand, opened the closet door, moved aside quick and told the kid to come out quiet. After she did I warned her to keep her mouth shut and listen. This was the last time, I let her know, the very last time she would behave this way in the house. Or break up anything—furniture or people. I was sending Milly and Tom in to clean up the room, throw out the junk, and if I could get a glazier to come in he would repair the windows. Meantime, she was to take at least a dozen baths because there were crusts of dirt on her, she smelled bad, and if there were any clean clothes in the closet she was to wear them. Then I wanted to see her in the library.

I didn't feel like eating more than rye toast and coffee, which Milly served at my office desk, and the glazier came about eight that night. When I took him to Verney's room, the kid was gone. Out one of the broken windows. And she'd left by way of hanging-down bedsheets tied together. Too bad the sheets hadn't torn, the knots given way, was my first reaction, because she might've killed herself and that would've solved a big part of my problem. Next thought, that would've got us a lot of publicity. So I had to admit we were really hung up, and after I left Tom with the glazier and a signed check to fill in for service, plus a two-dollar tip, I got into the Imperial and headed over to the Strip to search for my stepdaughter.

The Strip was really junky, a Skid Row without missions, worse looking than even the lower end of Fremont near the Vegas depot. Also, the bums were kids, not grown men or women, and as I walked along Sunset, from Doheny down to La Rue's, first on one side then up the other, I felt like Gulliver among creepy-crawly Lollipops, because this was the closest I'd gotten to hippies, yippies or, to me, just plain freaky slobs. Most weren't no more than sixteen or seventeen or eighteen, I guess, in the worst-awful clothes I've ever seen, and not a healthy-looking one in the lot. At least a hundred times, maybe more, I must've been asked for small change and when I shook my head because kids like that weren't going to get anything they could spend from me, more than half of them, girls too—later I found out that the ones who hung around the discos to lay the rock 'n roll musicians were called groupies—told me to go you-know-what myself. Hearing this from kids embarrassed me, having kids ask me for pot or acid—even horse, which these kids call shit because they're such a filthy dirty lot—bothered me plenty. But kids—girls *and* boys —who offered to service me, that really got me sore. True, the county cops patrolled the Strip, especially where the record and hippie stores that sold astrology and Zen junk and the disco joints were the thickest, and lots of kids were being busted—even some dressed like Shangri-La monks, I guess, who'd shaved their heads and were sitting on the sidewalk while they chanted something that sounded like hairy Christmas—and I even saw a girl unconscious on the sidewalk near Clark Drive and people just stepped over her until the ambulance came and from what some people said she'd tripped out, but what the hell, they said, it could happen to anybody—and for the first time in my entire life I was for the cops and against these junior bearded nuts and their girls who were carrying infectious hepatitis along with advanced cases of syph, clap, ringworm and who knows what else. Now I understood why the Mexican cops and government was so hard on these types. And in cases like these I was for law and order one hundred percent.

But Verney wasn't there. When she came home the next day, Joyce begged me not to say anything and I'm glad she did because it was a perfect out for me. Who could go against a mother's wishes? So that was our first meeting. And from then until now I hardly saw Verney and if it wasn't for what'd been painted on the driveway, I wouldn't've cared to see her at all.

Having the ass-end of the car sticking into the street wasn't going to solve anything. So I backed out and started for Fairfax Avenue to talk things over with Simon, but the closer I got to the store which was half his, the more I doubted his being able to give me the kind of advice I needed now. What did he know about schools and education? Not even as much as me. Another thing—you can see how I was fishing for excuses— Simon might've gone to lunch, or had his lunch already, and his partner in the kosher grocery mightn't like my showing up during business to take aside Simon, for God knew how long, while I asked him to give me some pointers on how to deal with a little more than fourteen-year-old tramp who was bending her mother's mind all out of shape and giving me fits too.

Once again I turned the car around and this time I went into the house after I parked at the curb, where I killed time by going through the mail and writing checks for some bills arrived that day because I planned to run the house on a payment-on-receipt routine. At last there wasn't any legitimate thing to occupy me, so I locked the library door and phoned Fred Rory on the unlisted line I'd put in, without any extension, and Rory told me short of making a hospital case of Verney, to do anything I liked about the kid because the odds were pretty good that I'd be doing what any concerned, responsible father should do, but too often nowadays didn't.

With real relief I hung up, rubbed my hands together and took the stairs two at a time—deliberately dragging my hand across the velvet guard of the staircase, which Joyce said should never be touched—and busted right into Joyce's room where I pulled the bedcovers aside and yanked her awake.

"I know it's not even one yet," I began, "but you're gonna have to start getting up earlier."

"Is that what you came here to tell me?" she said after giving me a shove. "Now get out. Blow."

"You want me to tell the gardener to start using the electric mower and chain saw?" I asked her before I went on to lay down the law that she was up and staying up, even if it meant my setting her bed on fire.

Joyce sort of pawed at the air with her hands, because I'd let go of her, and to keep from falling, which I really think she would have, she staggered toward a small sofa when I blocked off her way to the bed.

Now—comes comedy.

First she screamed as if she was being scalded. Then she began to cry.

"What the hell do you want from me?" she wailed as she flopped onto the sofa. Suddenly she raised her nightgown, real high, up to her shoulders, parted her legs like a real bum and threw them wide. "Ass? All right, I've changed my mind. You can get in the sack with me. But in bed! It's gotta be in bed!"

I turned away, kind of laughing but still disgusted. Why, exactly, I sort of know but don't wanna talk about. "Thanks for nothing," I said to let her know exactly what her two-bit-looking offer meant to me. "Not even if you paid me."

"You bastard!" she began to work herself up to very red in the face. "To think there once was a time when I was curious about you! What you were like in the sack! You know what I think now?" she raved at me. "That you're a fag. A middle-aged, butch-type queen!"

What she thought of me—who cared? Right now it wasn't important. So I told her how Verney wasn't home and her school'd called again, which led Joyce to ask me what else was new?

"Some morning a headline'll tell us," I told her as I wondered why I hadn't taken my chances in Mexico.

Maybe Rory could've got us deported. But that would've only meant my going someplace else with Simon. Thinking it over, standing in Joyce's room and looking at her—she had once been so great. Still, it only took the truth to admit that the quick look she gave me proved how she was firm, no varicose veins and also was clean. You could tell that. But what a thing for her to do. To throw herself down and spread her legs wide like some *barrio bajo puta,* so down on her looks and luck she'd lay someone for the price of bus fare, which might be anywhere between twenty-five *centavos* and a *peso,* so she didn't have any time to dress up her act. Returning here proved that we—no, I—was no-marbles, and as I admitted full responsibility for putting us in the middle of this mess, I felt the old heat beginning to burn me up while my eyes felt as if they were going to explode out of their sockets. But here we were. And here we had to stay.

"Rory was right about you," I told Joyce after I was able to clear my throat. "Someone's gotta be here because you need a keeper and Verney needs a straitjacket. Which is what she's gonna get if I can't handle her."

"You wouldn't dare," she said. "Get me a robe. I'm cold."

"And maybe a padded cell for you too," I continued after I gave her a heavy quilted robe, very expensive. I could tell she was scared, so it was important for me to press hard. "Me around or not, that's where you'll end up too if you don't help out. And you can't help out unless you start getting up in the morning."

She began to cry. "I can't. The way she hates me makes me weak. She does," she insisted, "and you saw why!"

"Stop talking dirty," I said. "Dirty and disgusting."

"Dirty and disgusting because I don't have stretch marks?" she asked me. Then she saw I didn't know what the hell she was talking about. "Around my belly button. Do I look like someone who's given birth? Had a baby? There isn't a mark on me. And once, a couple of years ago, she asked to see the stretch marks so she could believe I was her mother. And because I didn't have any she tried to take poison. Iodine. Itzik was out of his mind."

"Enough," I said because I was feeling years worse by the second. "As of now you're up for the day."

I went on to warn her that either she dressed herself or I was gonna do it. Then I wanted her to have lunch with me. I made the invitation sound kind. Next we'd drive around—that was, if Verney hadn't come home yet. And while we looked for her we'd discuss living in a civilized way.

"Yes, keeper," she just about spit at me. "Now get out. I'm dressing and you turn me off."

"Anything I see after what you showed me shouldn't embarrass you," I said. "Not while you're dressing. So forget any ideas you have about going back to bed. With or without me."

That really triggered her and she began to curse me, even harder than she'd done in Vegas or on the way to Mexico, and at lunch she wouldn't say a word to me, picked at her tomato aspic and drank three cups of black coffee. After I buckled Joyce into the safety harness and adjusted mine, we drove out to Venice, looked for Verney along the beaches and some of the old canals, went on to Santa Monica which has some teenage coffee houses, very crummy, and once around the UCLA campus where Verney had gone a couple of times to keep the street people company, but everyone there looked like street people to me. Then along fraternity row with its lines of garbage cans spilling over into the street. From there back down the Sunset Strip where I checked some of the psychedelic stores and other kid hangouts. And finally to Fairfax Avenue with its own hippie stands, including the Free Clinic, which serviced them when they got hung up on bum sick things from between their toes to between their ears.

At last, though I hated to, we even went to Simon's grocery

and he was so glad to see us. His partner, Aaron Polchansky, was very nice and they made me take a small pastrami because they'd just received a shipment of lean, first-quality sides. A full apron around his stomach, *yarmulkah* square on his head, Simon's beard and side-curls weren't out of place in this small, very filled up—cluttered?—grocery, and Polchansky told us— because Joyce came into the store—how much customers liked being waited on by so good-natured and religious a person, especially the ladies, who were all going to make Simon a *shiddach*, but Mrs. Polchansky, who had her own proposition in mind, was going to have him meet her lady first, maybe this Sunday sometime, and we were welcome if it was arranged because as members of Simon's family we should be there.

Obviously, Simon hadn't seen Verney and I made nothing more of our dropping around than us wanting to see how things were coming along and to pick up some good things for our table.

We couldn't find Verney and about ten I gave Joyce a sleeping pill, took the rest of them with me and went to my office where Simon right off told me how he wasn't meeting anyone this Sunday or any other day. That settled, he sat down to listen with me to an all-news radio station which broadcast immediately all local accidents, fires, shootings, stuff like that, by breaking into whatever else they were telling about. So we listened to the international news of a world tearing at its own throat and reports of how people all over America were trying to kill each other in the streets and schools so that more and more people were locking themselves into their houses but then someone in their very own family might blow his top and get them all before they could open the doors or jump from the windows. These were sort of mixed up with the average local news of break-ins, heists, muggings, no-purpose-at-all a-and-b's—abortions where the mother and unborn kid both died—houses cleaned out by guys dressed as moving men and using moving trucks—drug busts that took in makers, dealers, pushers and users, some of them really little kids—and a running record of all the public and private buildings, but mainly schools, that were being set on fire by firebugs who were all kinds of revolutionaries or just plain nuts who liked to see things burn. And all the while the station might interrupt its cheerful commercials and gloomy newscast with the sounds of ambulance, fire and police sirens, which the announcers used to flash into accounts of accidents, suicides and murders in L.A. County.

"Believe me," Simon said during a commercial, "we got plenty of cops along Fairfax and they're not looking for me. They're busy picking up runaways and kids who walk around like zombies. Everybody takes pills and drugs. And lots of the kids are Jewish," he wondered.

"A lot of us were Jewish too," I said. "Or don't you remember?"

"But there was a difference," Simon insisted. "Between the good guys and the bad."

"So is that why you wear a black *yarmulkah* instead of a white one?" I asked and could've bitten my tongue off immediately because Simon looked as if he'd just taken a kick square in the balls.

Simon was frightened. Because of one, the way I looked when I said it. Second, the thing I'd said was an attack on him. And third, it was something I'd never done to him all the while we were in Mexico. But here, returned to the country which, like it or not, counted us as two of its own, I'd begun to think mean, say what I was thinking. So how soon, he must've wondered, would he be living with the old me? I didn't like it either because if the meanness got working inside even a couple of hours a day I might phone Rory and insist he do something about giving me some action, which is one of the main reasons—I told Rory when he came to see us in Mexico City—that I didn't want to go back. But Rory swore on his life that my job, very special and important, required a man no longer interested in the business, a man who would do nothing more than marry Joyce and keep her and him and her kid out of sight and out of trouble. Rory sure made it sound easy. Maybe it was, but I was busting the assignment and because I knew it, the old meanness had broken through.

"Simon, stop moving around," I said. "Sit still. And believe me as you never believed anything before—I'm sorry."

He got up to pat my shoulder. "You look very tired," he believed me. "So why don't you get some sleep and leave me here to wait up for her if she comes home? I'd call you in a second."

"And have her say again to you what she did last week?" Simon shrugged before I could shake my head. "Say it while she makes that dirty f—you motion?"

He used his hand to brush aside what I thought was so awful. "Nowadays they even show it in the movies," he said. "It doesn't mean anything. Not really."

Maybe not to Eskimos or Indians, who must have different ways of telling someone to go screw himself, I guess. We were making each other nervous, so I told Simon to leave me alone because there were lots of household bills and records that still needed going over. And I had to do something about inventorying the furniture, painting, all the art stuff Joyce'd collected, including the rugs, and having it appraised. Plus I was thinking of firing the third pool man because he was no better than the first two guys he'd replaced. I would see him at breakfast, I promised Simon, and I waved to him as he clomped upstairs. At the landing he turned, but I shook my head, so he continued climbing.

With only the radio's bad news for company, I got the small adding machine from a deep closet that held three fireproof file cabinets with combination locks, plugged in the machine at the desk, and got ready to work on current and recent bills, our current checkbooks, and those in two other locked drawers of the desk which were just jammed full of batches of canceled checks, old bills for everything and bank statements that hadn't been reconciled for more than five years. Itzik and Joyce had kept a checking balance of thirty thousand or so in their joint account, which made it pretty certain that every check they wrote was good, especially since they were friendly with someone big in the bank—*who,* is none of your business—and he would phone them whenever their balance dropped below ten. But there were times when this joker forgot to phone and just before Itzik died he was transferred to one of their foreign offices. So now, almost every week since we'd moved in, someone in the bank would call to complain that our account didn't have enough money in it to cover a just-received check for a high four figures or maybe even five. And Joyce—who was now trying to collect Fabergé eggs by the dozen, by buying them over the phone so she could fill another display case with them—didn't give a damn. Money was available, she had more important things to worry about, which left it up to me to straighten out the house's accounts if they bothered me.

Radio volume turned way down, I began to sort through checks and statements, arranging them first by year, then by month and number. Once this was finished I would try reconciling them with the books of stubs, fill in by referring to the bills what the checks were for, and by going back to 1964, figure out where the money went and, finally, come up with the basic nut for this place. Also, I'd get some idea of what Itzik was drawing above the table, at least approximately, because tax payments would give me some rough figure, so I could plan right now to establish a separate tax account because I'd never tangled with DIR men and didn't want to make their acquaintance now. Finally, when all of this was done, I intended to see if we were getting reasonable value per dollar, if household bills were accurate or padded, which may explain to you why I was firing the third pool man. He was presenting bills for chlorine and washes that were larger than those I remembered to maintain both pools at the Riviera. They were lots bigger and had to be serviced stricter.

For two hours or so I worked to bring order to the piles. I saw that Joyce spent very little you might say on clothes, a lot more on medicines and an awful lot on antiques and stuff you bought in galleries. Several times I stretched, stood to rub my eyes and cheeks because you can only ignore being tired for so long. I was going to do ten, maybe twelve more checks and call it quits, but I never got back to the desk for that since a car with one of those glass-packed mufflers pulled into the driveway. I heard laughing, some words I couldn't make out because the engine revved hard as the car went into reverse.

I had just about time to get to the center hall and sit on one of the steps before the front door opened and shut, and Verney came toward me in the semi-darkness.

"Is that you, Larry?" she asked. "Dear old Dad?"

"It's me, all right," I said. "Where've you been for about the past two days?"

"That's for Mother to know—maybe—and for you to find out," she made fun of me before she skipped toward the bank of hall switches to throw them all. The center hall and staircase got filled with hard, bright light. "When and if she gets around to asking me, and if I tell her, she might tell you. So how does that grab you, dear old Dad?"

"You'll tell me," I said. "You'll also tell me what kind of friends you've got who write the dirtiest things about you right in the driveway."

"Really?" She laughed again. "I didn't see anything."

"Tom and me spent more'n an hour scrubbing it off."

"Which means, I guess, you won't tell me," she said. "So I'll tell you to go to hell before I say good night."

"Look at you," I ignored what she said, because she was trying to rile me. "Just look at you."

"You're doing plenty for both of us." She plopped herself on a Jacobean-something-like-a-sofa without cushions, just of black oak wood, which stood against the paneled casing of the stairs, and dropped her large, soft purse to the floor. "I'm not gonna fight you to get upstairs," she let me know the score. "So if you're not gonna let me go to my room, say so, and I'll sack out here."

"I'm asking you again," I said. "Because your principal called again this——"

"She's an old snatch who munches," she interrupted.

That shocked me plenty, because it's what'd been written about Verney. "I went to see her," I continued. "And she showed me your attendance record. Some record."

"Some record," she repeated to make fun of me.

"Some record," I said again. "So when I ask where you've been it isn't only for today. But for lots of days and nights. You understand?"

She nodded. "I sure do."

When I moved to stand over her, she turned herself ass up. "And?" I asked her.

She looked up at me and her eyes were wild with hate, like a black leopard's. "And nothing," she began. "Because I'm gonna tell you what I'd tell any mother-f———."

That's when my first backhand caught her right on the jaw. Between the "f" and the "u." Then I gave her follow-ups.

"That's just for openers," I said when she looked as if her head was clear enough again to understand how she was to march into the library. But she called me that name again, this time with all the letters said, so I gave her more lumps, which didn't worry me none because she was far from being a hospital case. Then, when I began dragging her by the feet I did tell her, just once, to do herself a favor and say nothing.

For more than five minutes I stood beside the fireplace, swinging the poker I've already told about, just shaking my head whenever Verney looked toward the door, to let her know how trying to get away would be bad business—for her. So she shivered against one of the cabinet doors under the recessed bookshelves filled with those old picture albums that look like books, and hated me hard. If it made her feel better, it didn't hurt me none. Name your bet, fix your odds, I knew that never before had she got belted around so hard. So she hated me and was afraid, too, because I hadn't looked sore or wasted a motion when I worked on her.

"What I called you wasn't cause to hit me," she said at last. "It's just sort of against-the-Establishment dirty talk that really doesn't mean anything."

"You won't use it when you talk to me," I told her. "Besides, I'm only interested in things that mean something."

"You really sound like old fart Itzik," she continued. "When he used to bawl out my mother for her screaming dirty things back at me. He was a fine one to talk, that old, broken-down murderer."

"You must really want to get beaten up," I said. "But maybe that'll improve your appearance."

"Hitting me because I called you that thing." Like a bug she crawled away from the wall. "But what you said to that maid the day after you got here is all right?" she said. "I guess in your book it's all right to be a racist."

"I'm not a racist." I wondered how Verney'd found out about my run-in with the maid, who I never saw again. And I wondered if Milly and Tom knew. "Did she also tell that I apologized?"

With a hand still at her jaw, Verney licked her lips because they were still swelling. "You insulted her," she told me. "Tried to make her feel inferior when she's got lots more soul than you."

I put the poker back on its stand and helped Verney into a chair. "Anyone's got more of a soul than me," I told her after I sat again on the edge of the desk. "But having a soul doesn't give its owner the right to play music so loud the whole street's gotta hear it. Is that where you've been?" I asked. "To some kind of race relations convention?"

"Shit, no. I'm one kid who doesn't think black is beautiful."

I let it pass. "So where've you been?"

"Wait until my mother hears about your beating me up," she said.

"I can arrange that right now," I told her. "And after one —I drag you upstairs by one leg, and two—give you the shellacking of your life right in front of her bedroom door, for three and for sure—you'll be a picture that'll tell her more'n ten thousand words." Saying it that way made me feel good. "Just say the word." I made myself sound anxious. "Just say —go."

That made her think a bit, before she tried to scare me by saying she'd call the fuzz, which gave me a chance to point to the phones on the desk.

"Do it," I called her. "Of course the cops'll ask me why I knocked you around." Then I went on to say that I'd tell them more'n enough to get her sent to Juvenile Hall because whatever happened to me would be worth it just to see her booked as a juvenile delinquent. Then I would get a lawyer to go in as a friend of the court to see that she didn't get probation or a suspended sentence, but a real jolt in the reformatory. The more I spoke it, the better it looked. "If you want me to call the cops just say so," I said. "I'll even tell them whatever you want me to."

"You'd rat on one of us?" she asked me.

"You're not one of us," I let her know. "We never had room for your kind."

"I don't believe you'd turn me over to the pigs," she said, but her eyes told me different.

"Try me," I kept the pressure on. "Take a chance."

Verney got up to limp toward a bull's-eye mirror. What she saw she didn't like because even in littler size she was a mess. "Seems to me that since you got here you've taken over," she said. "And I don't like it."

The kid moved restlessly—touching her mouth, scuffing her feet, hitching at her pants and wondering, I guess, if I meant it about putting her on ice, if I was really worse than she already knew, especially since I seemed very anxious to involve the cops.

"I had a business appointment," she said.

I indicated her filthy clothes. "Dressed like that?"

"Dressed like that," she repeated. "I'm gonna be an actress."

"Come again?"

"You're not deaf," she said. "I'm going to be an actress. Or a singer. Maybe both."

"For the sake of conversation, I'm going to say—I see." But my voice told her I didn't.

She'd thought it all out, she began. As Verney talked she moved to stand next to an antique globe of the world that she began to whirl around. What was the use of her going to school where she was all hung up with flunking everything? But this wasn't really her fault.

"Go ahead, ask my mother," she pointed overhead. "Go ask her why I hadda go to private schools."

I didn't have to, because Verney went on to tell me, and the more she talked the more I could've told a child psychiatrist that was important. Instead, I was going to call Rory and tell him what had to be done with this kid. Which made me think it was inconvenient to phone across the country for answers to my problems, so I would have to get permission to speak to some middleman close by. Someone like Harry Freund who'd been our friendly drop when we operated the Riviera. At that time his front was Hollywood talent agent. Now he was living in Italy where he was pretty big in producing Hercules-type movies, Joyce told me. Not that I'd be bothering a man with every problem, but this kid was too much.

"Go ahead," I gave her a straight line. "Why did you always go to private school?"

"Because they didn't want any public records on me. Look, Larry," she appealed to me, "I was just started in parochial school in New York when my father"—she gulped hard, shuddered and shook her head fast—"when he died. He sent me there, I guess, because he was Catholic."

"I hear nuns are good teachers," I said. "And don't stand for fooling around."

"When we came out here, I think—but I'm not sure—that Joyce tried to put me in a parochial school. But the kids' mothers—the narrow-minded cunts—wouldn't have me contaminating their kids with my background."

"I see," I said, and did. "I'm not gonna warn you again about your language."

"That seems to bother you more than what's supposed to've happened to my father," she challenged me. "How he fell out of a window." That made her laugh in a way I didn't like. "And then coming out here and not being wanted in a school whose religion is supposed to be all love. Because of my mother and Itzik—who made things worse because he was also a Jew."

"I'll let that pass too," I warned her. "But Simon mightn't."

"He's a lot nicer than you. He wouldn't beat me up like you did."

"He's not supposed to take care of you." Only after I heard what I said did I realize how funny that sounded coming from me.

"I'll let that pass," she told me and scored some points. "So I had to start off in some crummy private school with the kids of other crooks and heads and psychos and stiffs like that." Suddenly she clenched her fists, took a couple of steps toward me before she stopped and began to shake like someone kicking it cold turkey. "Don't be so stupid!" she screamed at me before she made a face of pain because of her mouth and jaws. "I can't read! Not good!"

Tell me, how did she expect me to believe that?

"I can't read," she repeated before she tried to lose herself in a deep wing chair where she cried a little because her lips were swollen and they hurt, but not as bad, I'm sure, as her insides because of what she'd confessed. "I can't read *Seventeen* or *Time* or *Life* or even *Modern Screen* without tripping over most of the words. I can't even read *Groovy* and that's no class at all." She pointed at me. "Now you listen hard."

"I am."

"Tell this to Joyce or anyone else and I might kill you."

Verney looked like she could, so there was nothing to say except that if she went into the kitchen I'd do something about fixing her mouth. And she could take my word how I'd tell no one who might hurt her. That's the best I could promise. Meanwhile, we'd just leave it that I'd slapped her a couple of times because of what she'd said to me, which was absolutely true. What I couldn't believe was her being unable to read, so I told her so.

"Try harder," she said.

"Even I can read," I said. "And I didn't go to school much."

But Verney said that me and her mother were taught different, there was no other explanation. We talked while she mixed hot and cold water and dabbed at her face with a clean dishtowel made of terry cloth. That got some dirt and tears off her, but now you could better see the lumps I'd given her.

"Simon told me he can even read Hebrew," she said.

I nodded. "And he's learning to write it real good."

"So why can't I read?" she asked. "Meanwhile, if I can't read, what's the use of going to school?"

"To learn." This early morning I sure sounded funny.

"So I can get a job in some office?" she asked after she put the towel on the sink. "What office? And doing what?"

That's what most cons ask after they get outa the can. Sure, there was lots of big talk in pep sessions about having paid their debts to society and going into it with clean slates in their left hands, diplomas in their right that said how Number So-and-So had passed a carpenter, sheetmetal or die-stamping course. Big deal. Who wanted trouble? Probation officers and cops and social workers around? Who wanted to run the risk of having the petty cash pinched, credit cards missing, the safe worked on, some of the inventory stolen? Who in his right mind wanted to take a ten-to-one chance that the check-writing machine, ID cards and company checks wouldn't disappear? Who in his right mind wanted his insurance rates raised if he was lucky, canceled if he was unlucky? Verney'd said an awful lot: what legitimate operation would want her on the payroll?

Even Polchansky, a nice guy, got more reasonable when I talked to him about buying in for Simon rather than having him work as a clerk. And I shut my eyes, accepted everything Polchansky told me about volume, gross, net, inventory and goodwill because it would make things easier for Simon, me and everyone else. Rory told me after I asked and he found out, that everyone agreed it was the best way for Simon, especially since everyone who should know knew he was now a nut on religion, so he was harmless. But what did Simon have to do with Verney, this dumb kid, who if she got a job in a legitimate operation could only hold it down until the second the boss found out who she was? Before he fired her the very next second, would he think for a minute that like everyone else she had nothing to do with choosing her parents, had no record, and deserved to be treated like anyone else until she did something bad? There was little chance of her getting such charity and it was sad because on top of this, Verney, dumb kid, was doing nothing except prove the old crap about blood telling, heredity and all the other reasonable excuses for not taking chances on bums.

"So that's why you want to be a singing actress?" I asked. "Because nobody cares about you?"

"We're not connecting," she said as if I was so stupid people just had to pity me. "Nobody cares about what they were before they became stars." She pointed overhead. "My room's full of movie magazines that tell all about big stars who were pro-lays, convention party girls, that sort of gash. Some of the newest, biggest box-office studs were in reformatories. Some of them were fuck for faggots. Some were even in prison."

"Look at what I didn't know," I said. What was the sense of warning her again about her language, which for her was natural?

Telling me this excited Verney. "Some've been strung out on drugs," she went on. "Some still are. Some've even had illegitimate babies. Right now I mean! Some are still fags and dykes and shoe sniffers. And nobody cares. It's not like when you were a kid and went to the flicks."

"I never liked the movies," I said. "These magazines"—now I was the one who pointed—"really have stuff like that?"

She laughed. "Would reading be believing?"

"At least that it was in print," I hedged. "Things've really changed. I mean about no one caring."

She looked pleased that I sort of believed her, so she went on with some ideas really impossible for me to believe. That in show-biz if the word got around how her father'd been a hood, that her first stepfather had been a top-top organization man and how I was pretty hard and important in my time, these would make her glamorous.

"You're crazy," I said.

That didn't bother her because she shrugged and told me I could keep out of the picture if that's what I wanted.

"Can't you just see the headlines about me in the fan mags?" Verney moved her hands as if she was framing a poster. " 'Starlet's Mother Was Star Party Girl.' " She breathed deep, as if inhaling something that smelled good. "My agent says it'd be the greatest publicity."

"What agent?" I asked, to keep from belting her again.

She moved to keep a big table between us. "You don't know him."

"Must I know him to ask who he is? If this is his idea, I don't like it."

"Which proves it must be good. Are you gonna let me be an actress?"

"Who'd want to look at you? Or pay money to see you?"

"You'd be surprised," she said. "We've been working on it all day," she was serious. "Even taking pictures. They're gonna start me off by making me a centerfold chick. All skin. So we worked at a place with a private beach."

I had to sit. "You posed for pictures with no clothes on?"

"They're not beaver shots." I didn't understand, so she explained. "Those concentrate on the hair down there. Which is why the photog helped me shave. After, he said I looked like a nymph—a sea sprite. And that my slit was beautiful."

I forced myself to remain in the chair, to not let go of my knees. "You took off all your clothes?" I was very deliberate. "Shaved your hair before you posed naked?"

"I wasn't cut by the razor—if that's what you're worried about," she said.

"Good," I told her. "But if they helped you shave down there, how come they didn't do you under the arms?"

"Because that makes me look and feel funky. You don't understand," she read my expression. "But that must be because you haven't made the scene lately."

"The chair I'm sitting on is gonna knock your head off," I said. "Make it? Why would I make it with the stinkers I've seen on the Strip? Kids who look and smell like unflushed toilets?"

"You're something. Really the end," she sneered at me.

"Mouth shut," I warned her. "Because I'm gonna say it again. You're crazy. Straitjacket crazy. So I wanna see the people who put you up to this. The con merchant who calls himself an agent. The photographer."

"Why?"

Suddenly I was yelling, didn't want to, but couldn't stop. "Because I want all the pictures and negatives! Who's the photographer?"

"You're going to ruin my career!" she yelled back.

I made myself move away from her, to the swinging doors of the butler's pantry. When Verney started to back out of the kitchen I raised both hands as a signal that she'd better stop.

"We've gotta do something about you," I said, very slow, very patient. "Whether you like it or not."

"Just leave me alone, creep." That's what my patience got from Verney.

"Dirty-picture posing isn't gonna make you an actress. Or a singer," I went on. "Still, if you think that becoming an actress is gonna help solve your problems——

"——split this house and you'll take ninety percent of them with you—

"——then I'm all for your becoming an actress or singer."

Her mouth opened wide, like a fish, and her eyes told me she was confused as well as surprised. So I nodded once, twice, and she still shook her head because she didn't believe me.

"So why'd you beat me up?" she asked.

"Because of what you did yesterday. The day before. The weeks and months before," I said. "And for what you said to me. Because that's no way to become an actress."

Verney seemed to consider what I said. Then she tilted her head. "Maybe you'd rather I laid my agent and the photog rather than let them put together a picture layout? Is that how they did it in dear old Mom's day?"

I decided to talk rather than do what I wanted to. "Forget about other days." I made myself ignore her dig at Joyce. Even if her mother'd been a whore, a kid who wants to show respect should never mention it. "What do you expect from those pictures—which must be downright ugly if they're not outa focus? Where would you find some magazine dumb enough to use them? Or haven't you heard of contributing to the delinquency of a minor?"

"That's a laugh," Verney said. "Coming from the kind of background I have—natural and stepfathers to match"—she raised two fingers to show she included me in the count—"I suppose that isn't some kind of crime?"

For one of the few times in my life I wished I'd had a real education. Then I could've told her off like a judge or lawyer who wouldn't've let Fred Rory serve his summonses. And as I watched her watching me, while she waited for me to say something, both of us knew she'd taken the round. And maybe the match.

There was nothing to do now but stall. "We'll talk about that later, Veronica," I said. "After you've got some sleep. I'll call your school before they call me. And tonight—you and me—we'll go somewhere for dinner. Anyplace you say and we'll talk. Because if acting'll keep you outa trouble, I'll be the last to fight it."

"You really mean that?"

"All the way," I swore. "But if you're gonna be an actress I'll expect you to become one. By the way, can you sing?"

"Not good," she said. "But that doesn't mean anything anymore." She looked at me for a couple of seconds. "What about school?"

"I'll talk to the principal," I said. "We'll work something out about your reading. Your acting. And also about your teeth. Because"—I motioned for her to keep quiet—"you haven't worn your braces for a long time."

"I hate them."

"So your mother told me. Still, an actress has to have good teeth," I pointed out. "Even if you put caps on crooked teeth they don't look good."

Off the record, I'd never let anyone with teeth that were yellow and dirty and crooked eat me.

CHAPTER FOUR

VERNEY: Things that've happened in the past don't bother me, which doesn't mean I forget them. I just say the past bothers me if I'm trying to score points with Larry or Simon, who've moved into my life like more braces in my mouth, or to hurt Joyce with words and memories I bring up. Really, I'm one of the now-kids, so that's how I'll begin. With today's score.

My mother hates me. I see that as good. But Uncle Simon and Creepy Larry are up-tight about how I should love her. That's bad. Dismal. Love's never been my bag and anyway I'm a free soul as long as Joyce hates me, which might also lead to her busting a gut. That could be very good. And she seems to hate me more since Larry told her how he was gonna sincerely help me have a career. So it would be a disaster if she started loving me. Because then I might be forced to consider some straight reactions—like shouldn't I force myself to think of her with affection? Shouldn't I think of connecting up with her like when I was first born? That sure could crap out my career plans, which I'm very serious about.

To prove what I'm saying about how serious I am about my career, we've gotta go back some. To when after Larry beat me up good for calling him a mother-fucker. Which he is, especially when he undignified me more in the kitchen by examining my arms and the backs of my knees, even between my toes—which gave him the chance to insult me more by saying how they stank—and looking at my eyelids for needle marks. He found none because I was clean and never went near that or anything else because I actually saw how a kid died from an overdose. It wasn't pretty and it scared me enough, lots more after they found his body, but the fuzz never found out anything else. Still, when it comes to mind it gives me the trots. So, because I was clean, Larry got more friendly as he walked me upstairs and said we'd work things out positive.

I slept pretty late and couldn't move when I woke up, I was that stiff with lumps and bumps and bruises all over me. Then I really hated him. But I made myself stay quiet when he came in, turned on more lights, looked at me and said nothing except I wasn't to get outa bed until he had the doctor over who he had called hours ago. Which shows what kind of very special creep he is. Afraid of nothing. Not scared that my pediatrician and me might report him for child beating.

So while I lay back in bed and thought over about maybe I oughta call the fuzz—and what Larry'd said about not caring about anything as long as he put me too in deep freeze for a long time—Simon came in from work. Actually came home early to see me. He just shook his head and said nothing while he straightened the bed and covers. Then he asked if the doctor'd been over yet. I said no and Simon said I'd be all right, to rest, try to eat something because Milly'd told him I'd had nothing all day. Then he went out and about fifteen minutes later came back with Milly. You know what? He'd had Milly open up one of the other bedrooms and he carried me there and put me in a clean bed. Then he asked Milly if she minded having some of the day-help clean out my room, which I must admit looked and smelled like a pretty dirty cave. Milly said she'd take care of it and told me I oughta have some soup. So I said okay.

And while I'm having my bouillon, who comes in but Joyce. And she too looks at me and says nothing until suddenly she points at me and begins to laugh like a very sad wig who's flipped out and's glad of it. Then suddenly the bitch begins to cry like she's real sorry for me. And then just as suddenly she begins to curse herself, me, Larry, everybody and everything. And she tears outa the room, still crying. That's life in our Peyton Place. Where Milly and Tom know not to interfere between us no matter what they see or hear. Any way you figure, if I can make my career work I'd be able to blow this asylum. Of course there'd be other advantages about making it to the top.

For example, then I could spend the rest of my life putting people down and making them love drinking my piss. So to be able to get there and have it happen I mustn't think of what might be good for my soul. Even less of what's good for other people. Only of what's good for my career.

Like only taking the lock off for the rightest people—man or woman, straights or bents—and only at the very-very right time. Because, honest, believe it—it never really grooved me. Besides, I don't like being chewed on or aborted in Tijuana because no local would touch me, although it didn't stop the four or five docs I saw before I tailed it to TJ from stringing me out for being a little jerk and not knowing enough to protect myself. So now I'm taking pills and I've got a diaphragm. The case is very nice. And while my pediatrician came in to take care of me from the beating up, he spoke to Larry about having one of those machines put inside me. But that would make me feel, I guess, like a robot. So as long as I can dig my juicies by playing solitary, which sure saves a lot of time, eliminates disappointments and keeps you from getting an assful of ants, gravel, fleas, sand, poison oak or something worse, why bother getting stabbed by some raunchy stud who mightn't even know your name? Who right after he rolls off and while he's drying off his wet cock on your dress or something else you're wearing, looks down at you all smuglike because he wants you to dig for sure, bird, how he's done you the biggest favor since the world began? You're lucky if you don't get crabs, ringworm, trenchmouth, hepatitis or some kind of mysterious discharge that only doctors in those crappy television series can cure. Another thing. If the hairy ass is lucky enough to make a chick pop, he gets very big ideas, like he starts believing how her whole life now depends on him. Like his granting you a royal boot in the ass should fill your peasant crotch with rockets. And you're supposed to give him presents and best wishes while he's sniffing other Honda seats and poolside chaises for new stuff to make it with.

Now if you've been made promises like lots of kids and groupies have while you're laying or eating—or plating, which is what English types and kids who've made the scene there call it—no matter how hard you've been sworn to—it's just too bad. It figures. Everything is bad for losers. Everything is turned off for bummers. Which is why losing and bumming and getting strung out isn't gonna be my ultimate life-style.

Especially if I'm gonna have a career in show business, so much of which is a suck. Like more than anything else, only big winners count and that's what everyone including me and Simon and Larry wants. But not Joyce for sure. So once I'm that—a big winner—the first order of business'll be losing everyone, sending them on their way with a kick not a kiss, and if Larry or Simon or Joyce—especially Joyce—or anyone else bothers to ask me how, when and why and where's my gratitude?—I'll just give them the score. That most everybody's gotta go through life on their knees while they're sucking. That very few don't have to. And if they don't like it they can just crawl out of line and let someone else move up for anything my kind and me might care to give. No promises. Just if I felt like giving.

No, I didn't dare like anyone, least of all Joyce. But as a smart puss I was gonna play along, sort of give in slow, so Larry—I've gotta be very cool about him—and Uncle Simon wouldn't get suspicious of my too-fast turnaround and they'd go on thinking they were sort of scoring big points on my psychology. That's how I'll buy time. Because in this business of entertaining the public all a kid needs is one big break. The rest is bonanza.

So for about more than two months now I'd been filling the part of Little Miss Grudgingly Cheerful, smiling a little more every couple of days or so, sort of cooperating more and more. First thing I did more'n a week after Larry beat me up, when I felt better and not black and blue, was to tell the creep how I felt ready to do anything he told me. So the next morning I came down to breakfast with him. I wore clean denims and a sleeveless, but I raised both my arms to show him how not only had I showered, brushed my teeth and put on the lousy dentist's brace, but I'd shaved too. He just nodded. Then Simon came in and, without being told, I apologized for the way I'd acted.

"Honest," I began, "I never meant those things I said. Not really."

"It's all right," Simon replied, really shaken because I'd hold of his right hand and was squeezing it like he was the most important soul-saving priest. Correction—rabbi. "Nobody's perfect," he went on. "We all make mistakes. I shouldn't've asked you to call me uncle."

"You shouldn't've had to—Uncle," I said real quick. "I should've done it by myself. Without your having to ask. Because a kid would be lucky to have someone like you——"

That's where I stopped because Larry the Hawk alias the Creep was watching me. I was coming on too strong to be sincere. So I let go of Simon's hand, bit my lips and sort of ran toward the powder room with a hand to my eyes. Now, however, because in this case the truth is lots better than a lie, I've begun to like Simon because I never get the feeling he's rating me. Even though my gig is to look out for myself first and only, if I had to think of someone else, the only person I can think of is Simon. And not even of him every day. He's a nut, but a nice kind, and Milly and Tom are just gone on him, so Milly's knocking herself out with studying a Jew cookbook that tells all about kosher stuff and kitchens—and she's going to fix one up in the guest house—which might be fixed up anyway for Simon to live there by himself, like Milly and Tom who live over the garage. Simon is some sort of senior guru to Milly. But she's got her angle too. To her Sammy Davis is the greatest and maybe she'll get to meet him through Simon because they're both Jews. It strikes me as kind of far-out, for a gorilla to change into a guru, which I mentioned to Joyce because I thought it was pretty deep thinking. But she wrinkled her nose as if what I said smelled bad. So the hell with her now more than ever. Still, of the three old-time weirdos in our house, I like Simon best and made up my mind to operate through him.

Another thing, I've gotta be careful about Milly and Tom. I'd be crazy to think they don't know what's been going on with me—Tijuana and everything. And Tom did help Larry scrub off what some jerks wrote about me on the driveway. Not that Tom or Milly look at me funny but you can't tell about niggers. They've had hundreds of years of practice in not showing their true feelings to us, so I've gotta be very careful they don't decide to sell me out. For a kid my age I've got plenty on my shoulders.

Especially since there's been a big operation going on involving me, so much at one time that I'm pooped out and sleep like a stone. Still, so many things're happening to me because Larry's being in charge has to make it a real groove. For example, to go back to the morning when I'd come down clean and shaved and apologized to Simon, we had breakfast after I returned to the table and conversation was real easy, with Simon telling us all about the store and some of his customers. Stuff like that. Then Larry drove Simon to the Sunset Boulevard bus stop where he got lots of looks from the maids who were waiting to be picked up and taken to work. Some of the women he recognized and he touched his funny little skullcap and they liked that because he really meant the respect. Then we drove to my school and had an interview with my principal—Mrs. Cannon—and right off Larry let her know hard how I was there first to learn reading and writing and spelling. Nothing else mattered. Since school was gonna be out the middle of June, she was to go out and hire a special summer teacher for me alone and she could spend up to a thousand a month on her. It took a little while for this to get through, but when Larry wrote her a check to prove he wasn't playing about reading or bread, the old kooz began to believe him.

"I'll help any way I can," she said after Larry turned down her offer of having me study at the school this summer because he wanted me to work at our house. "However, could I suggest an additional subject?"

"Must you, Mrs. Cannon?" I asked in a way that was real polite for me.

Larry's eyes told me to cool it, I did, and Cannon went on to say how she had a teacher in mind, someone special, who could also work on my elocution because if I was going to be a singer or actress I might's well learn now to speak right and make myself heard. Larry agreed. So it's now time to introduce you to Mrs. Beverly Droutswood, widow, former WAC with the rank of major and a real tough bitch of a drill sergeant who came by every school-morning until the term ended to take me to school and was helping me a lot. Excuses weren't part of her vocabulary, so from nine to one-thirty all summer in a little room fixed up just for the two of us, she really worked my ass off between books, exercises and swimming which she said was good for expanding breath control. Surprise and good news—although I didn't want to let on, I began to feel better, go to the can more regular and week by week I was reading better. My spelling, penmanship, even writing things out, improved too. Mrs. BD didn't care what I read as long as it was something she gave me—that was the only joke she allowed herself—and I was supposed to read at least an hour every night after I did my Canadian Air Force exercises.

Right off I learned that Mrs. BD was all business. After she chewed me out a couple of times while she made me stand at attention, made me work later to make up for fooling around, goofing off or not doing assignments the way she liked, and I couldn't get Larry or anybody to listen to me, I surrendered and did pretty straight out what Droutswood told me. In her book the only way to do anything is on your feet. I wish I dared tell her, maybe so, but that could make them awfully sore.

Lunch now for me was no more frenchies and Coke, but solid protein and lots of milk because the pediatrician said I was too skinny and he didn't give a damn about how Twiggy and Mia Farrow looked. Then Larry would pick me up for the professional part of my day, which never ended before five-thirty. Wow, what we covered in those three hours! Man, we flew! Here too, I've gotta—no, I got to—or better yet, have to—go back a piece before we catch up to right now in August.

Right after Larry and me saw Mrs. Cannon and she spoke to Mrs. Droutswood on the phone and arranged to meet her so that both of them could come to our house that night for a meeting of square minds, Larry made me take him to the office of my agent, whose name I won't even mention—the kink. When my agent said he had some important business to take care of and we weren't part of it, Larry took charge right off by taking the phone off the cradle. When this dumb cat stood up to tell Larry how he and me wasn't welcome, he sort of squealed in the middle of a word because Larry was standing on his feet, with one hand gripping the dumb-dumb's belt, the other made into a fist which was pressed into this guy's balls. The creep was terrified, said he'd do anything Larry said, so when Larry pushed him into his chair, he phoned the photographer—whose name also I won't mention—and he was in his studio.

So with the scared-shitless agent sitting between us, Larry drove to a crappy little building on Melrose near Crescent Heights. Before the photog could say anything Larry began the conversation by giving him a good shot under the heart. Now he wasn't in any condition to talk, but he could still listen as Larry—who now had him by the ears as if he was a Dumbo—said how he wanted all the negatives, all the prints he'd made, and what could happen if he decided to go square and turn over a certain pervert with a camera to the cops for corrupting a juvenile. Never before did I see anyone so scared. And before we left with the negatives and the prints and me feeling the couple of looks Larry gave me—real Bogarts—he gave it to them right in the nuts, then told them how their pain was to keep'm remembering to forget me forever. Believe me, I was pretty shook myself but grateful now for sure that he hadn't let himself go on me. If there were any doubts in my mind about how mean he could be, they'd been blown. Like some sort of machine he was able to be evil just by switch-on. And he didn't look much worse when he worked on you than when he was smiling.

"How about some lunch?" Larry asked after we left the photographer's place.

That was the last thing I wanted because, suddenly, my jaws and mouth hurt all over again. "Aren't you afraid they'll call the cops?"

"They'll do nothing," he said. "Curse me a lot. Even think of getting even. But they won't."

"Why not? I'm sure they both know psychos."

"Because tomorrow they're going to be worked on again," Larry said before he stopped, took a little notebook from his pocket and wrote in it with a gold pencil. "Just something I mustn't forget. Not to splash too much acid on the camera artist." That made him smile, made his eyes really laugh when

I shuddered. "We don't want any trouble with them," he patted my hand. "So one more visit should be plenty. Of course," he asked me, "you're not gonna phone either of them?"

I shook my head long enough for him to decide I was obeying orders. He ate pretty good at McDonald's because I just didn't want to sit in a restaurant. And he said nothing when I pushed everything aside. By now it was almost three, so he said it was time for us to go see someone named Phil Hammschlager, the president of Public Associates and Hammschlager, which struck me as a pretty big-head way to tell the world who was boss of the combo. It was also the sort of name no one would've used before Humperdinck.

The offices were on Wilshire Boulevard, not in Beverly Hills or Westwood, but near the Ambassador Hotel, which pretty long before I was born used to be a boss place. There were good stores on the street level, big business offices above them, but not show *dreck,* so I couldn't figure what PAH could do for me. My stomach was beginning to feel loose, but not in a nice way, so I concentrated on settling it down and on our way up in one of the smooth elevators, with music for senior citizens to fly by, Larry told me how this was probably one of the most expensive buildings in the city, where a tenant had to sign up for a minimum of ten thousand square feet, with at least two thousand for reception, and all the decoration done in complementing modern so that one suite of offices didn't jar with another. Because I was supposed to be impressed, I nodded as if all this information had hit me square-on.

The double glass doors said that PAH had offices in New York, Washington, D.C., Chicago and San Francisco. There were also offices in London, Paris, Rome and Tokyo. The reception room was all bright colors, Plexiglas and chrome modern, very outer space, and I wasn't exactly surprised to see Joyce waiting for us behind a big pair of shades. She looked uncomfortable on a low orange sofa that wasn't any more than a shelf with a back attached. What did surprise me was to see her looking so good, up and down, so boss she could've been part of a fashion photography session. That griped my ass, so my stomach got more upset, which made me ask if there was time for me to visit the can. Joyce only said she didn't know after Larry spoke to the receptionist, a tony straight whose eyes slid down her nose as she cased me in my clothes. Still, she handled Larry with respect. I forgot to say, this morning he was dressed like a probation officer, or maybe like the banker character in *Beverly Hillbillies.*

"Glad to see you got here," Larry said after we joined my quote-unquote mother. "And things're straightened out at school and for the summer." Then he looked around and raised a hand to indicate the whole *schmeer*. "What do you think?"

"For a hospital operating room it would be very cheerful," she said.

That's when I let her have it where it would hurt hard. "I like this better than our house," I said. "This is with it. It's now. Not Sunset Boulevard." By that I meant the movie which I've seen three or four times on TV because the old nuts in that house are creepier than anything in *Dark Shadows,* which lots of kids groove to while they're on acid or grass. They say the combination is the greatest. "Sure," I went on, "the decorator who did this place could do something with our tomb and vaults."

Larry grabbed my wrist and moved me to the left of him, so that he sat next to my mother and between us. "The kid's had a long, tough day," he explained to her. "So forget it."

But Joyce wouldn't. "Every day I curse myself for not having used Saniflush that one time." She didn't look at me, but at Larry. "And I mean as a douche."

That belted me. Damned satisfied with herself, Joyce moved to sit in a chair with her back to us. There she concentrated on colors moving up and down and every which way in a colored glass tube about three feet high. I told Larry that it looked like a working intestine, so he squeezed my wrist harder, his way of warning me to shut up. Right then, because he'd gone to work right away on helping me with my career, he could stop me from saying most anything. But not from thinking. So I filed a silver dagger to use some other time, maybe when the moon was full, on a very particular witchy bitch. Meanwhile, it would stay hidden. And long and sharp.

Before anything else could foul up our happy, silent-majority family group, and before I could ask again where was the can, the buzzer sounded on the receptionist's desk and ten–twelve seconds later the Chinese-red door opened and a neat-looking secretary, more with it than the receptionist, came out to say hello and escort us if you please into Mr. Philip Hammschlager's office. For a guy who ran such a ship he was too fat, didn't look very big or bright, and he had little-dog-lost eyes—later that night Joyce insisted he was wearing pancake makeup—and the rest of his face and head seemed to be made up of nutty putty. If you didn't like the way his mouth or nose or even his ears or something else looked, he could take it off, mold it right in front of you and put it back. Man, does that suit you better? *Nyet?* Okay, we'll try again. Or maybe we can just rearrange the lights or fit *you* with correct-type glasses to make Philip Hammschlager look like a beautiful person. Also, most of his head was polished skin, actually looked waxed, and the little strands of hair up the middle were combed as if they really mattered. But what I liked least about him was the way he kept wetting his lips, as if he—more'n anyone else—liked best the taste of the tears he'd just shed, or whatever crap he was pushing hardest right now.

Right off, after he stood up to bow to Joyce and extend his right hand, without letting us touch it, to Larry, then to me, he let us know in a soft, humble voice filled with that other popular spread—purest bullshit but pasteurized and packaged to please the most discriminating square—that he was seeing us because of Fred Rory.

"I represent institutions," he said in a voice that sounded

like someone who's just got an important direct message from God, so now because he's experienced a most righteous high, he only says the holiest Establishment prayers. "Long ago, I had individual clients. But that was long ago. Very long ago. Before time began."

How was that for a rap on our skulls? What a perfect put-down of us. I looked at Joyce. She was still chewing her lips. That's all you could see of her face, really, behind her glasses. Larry just sat there, both elbows on the metal arms of his chair, his head moving slow as if he was panning out what the fat *schmuck*'d just told us—that we were wasting his time which might be worth as much as a million a minute. The man was a definite *yuch,* and I began to like his furniture even less than *yuch,* especially his desk, just a big Plexiglas top on flat chrome legs. No drawers or anything. With the only thing on it a bright red phone and a box of colored buttons, to let everyone know, you can be sure, that he was the kind of plastic cat who only took very hot-line calls. What this meant for other people, Larry didn't care. And pretty quick I caught on why. PH's taking Mr. Fred Rory's call put him and us, his clients, in the sig-alert class. Still, Hammschlager didn't really like having to see us, that was plain. And Rory's telling how I wanted to be a singer-actress, which meant, according to Larry, that I needed a talent agent, publicity rep, material writers, acting and singing coaches, and a good electronics engineer to give me a voice if I didn't have one—the whole pro bit that costs big bread—had sort of bent his mind. Which might explain why a couple of veins in his forehead were throbbing like hard-ons being kept out when they wanted in.

"Fred Rory didn't say you'd represent our daughter," Larry finally decided to say something, and hearing myself called daughter—Joyce and his—gave me the funniest feeling until I was able to think CAREER—all in great big colored capitals with fireworks going off around each letter. That straightened things out for me, but it was a close sweat. "What he did say"

—I was able to hear Larry again—"was that you'd steer us right. That someone in your office would line us up with the best people."

Hammschlager's veins relaxed as his eyes became out-of-sight kind. "Exactly what I told him I'd do," he said. "And I will. Although I've never had so young a responsibility. But of course I wanted to meet the future star—so unaffected in her sleeveless shirt and denims—and her parents." He wet his lips again before he turned to Joyce. "I knew Mr. Yanowitz," he said. "A fine gentleman."

"That's what we all thought of him," Larry answered for us. "There was an agent out here about sixteen–seventeen years ago that I knew real well. Mr. Yanowitz too."

"Oh?" Hammschlager said hopefully. "Maybe you'd rather put this in his hands?"

"Not really," Larry replied. "He's living in Rome. No, we'll do what Fred Rory advised. Let you work things out for us."

"It'll take some days. Maybe a week, even two. Possibly a month or more. Meanwhile, you might think of an appropriate wardrobe for Veronica." Hammschlager shook his head just once after he looked at me for no more than a split second. In his arithmetic I added up to zero, or less. "What sort of budget do you have in mind?" he asked Larry.

Larry signaled Joyce and me that the interview was about over. "Get the best," he said before he stood up. "Schedule some appointments for us with the people you think can do the job."

"Of course," Fatso made like Buddha. "If I'm not at the discussions, someone above the line from my office'll represent us. And more importantly—our young star."

"Good," Larry sounded a little bit satisfied. "Your man can tell me what they expect costwise. The top figure. For working with someone absolutely without anything going for her, no talent—if that's the case."

Hammschlager liked Larry's agreeing that he wasn't required at the next career conference. And he raised both hands to keep me quiet because Larry's remark—which really wasn't necessary—about maybe I didn't have any talent made him sad. But it also made sense. So he told Larry that he'd be called direct.

"But not before you or your man call me first," Larry made that plain. "So I'll know something about them besides their names."

"I see that we'll get along," the Poor Soul behind the big, far-out desk said, and this time he shook hands with Larry.

So we thanked each other for meeting each other and said we hoped to see each other again, real soon, and then I got some idea of why this wig was supposed to be one of the best around. Because like she was an experience, he grabbed Joyce's hand and told her how he'd heard about the house, how she'd done it, that some very big antique dealers and decorators whose judgment he respected said the house had rooms in it good enough for books and museums, and he hoped he would right away soon be invited over to see it for himself. Man, he was creative.

Joyce couldn't've looked more flipped out if she was wetting *me* down, and the way she stuck to his hand had to be seen because you'll never believe me that right-on she looked ready, willing and anxious to go down on him. That made me a little sore, so I almost missed the pressure the good, dear man's hand gave me in the middle of my palm, which signaled me some very significant information. Like maybe he was hung up on kids who were still built like little kids, which made him a kind of special Dirty Old Man. The pressure was there, all right, like his look just for not even a second, but it told me what to say.

"Thank you, Mr. Hammschlager." I made it sound real grateful. "Can—may I write you a note about how I feel?"

That made him smile like he was grooving on pure purple wedge. Then his eyes seemed to become wet. "Nowadays kids aren't supposed to be grateful," he said directly to Larry and Joyce.

"I'll prove that this one is," I said.

Then I wiped out my shades and put them on quick to keep Larry or Joyce from seeing my eyes. Maybe they'd think I was overcome with emotion, but whatever they thought I didn't want them to see how I'd figured Phil H. as being *intimately* important to my career. Naturally, talent would help if I wanted to be an actress, but it really wasn't necessary for a star.

We didn't rap in the elevator because other people were riding with us. In the lobby Joyce said she wanted to do some shopping by herself in Bullock's Wilshire, for something she called Bum birds, I think. So no thanks, she'd rather take a cab there and home. What was nipping her nipples I don't know, because only minutes before in PH's office she'd been on a high. But that's the way it is with psychos who wrap their minds around their emotions. God, I hate her, because just before the cab pulled away, she lifted her shades to give me a look like I was a hundred-plus Wasserman. So without Larry seeing I raised my right middle finger and jabbed up, but it didn't make me really feel better, especially since I was doing some hard skulling at the same time.

This was no time for mistakes. So now, only a little while later, I had to ask myself—had PH really pressed my palm? Maybe it would be wise to wait for a real strong signal that he was a Dirty Old Man. If he didn't move, I wasn't hurt. If he did, his message would clue me in on some good move.

Meanwhile, I went to school regular. Got all this special attention. Was beginning to learn things I should've learned years ago, I guess, which made me feel lots more confident and lots less inferior. It also got me promoted to the upper seventh grade. And Mrs. Cannon said that if I did well during the summer months with Mrs. D., she was going to combine my seventh-grade work with some eighth-grade stuff. That made Larry feel good and Uncle Simon was so happy with me that he bought me a real old Mickey Mouse watch, one of the first ones from long before I was born. And he and Larry had it mounted inside a special gold case to hold the old one. Then they had it put on a wide alligator strap with three gold buckles. It was creative. Joyce congratulated me but bought me nothing. So up hers now and tomorrow and forever.

Because PH had to go abroad for a couple of months to take care of some business things—there were pictures of him in *Time* and *Newsweek* sitting in important bank offices, places like that, in Zurich and London and Paris, and Larry read us a piece on his part in an international image campaign the *Wall Street Journal* thought was important enough to put on a front page—Larry said he wasn't going to make any big moves until the mastermind got back. Meanwhile, to prove how he wasn't kidding me even a little bit, Larry said we ought to do something about giving me an appearance and he told me to go through the mags for kids and pick out the way I'd sort of like to look. So I did. I still thought I was the Mia Farrow–Liz Minelli type, with maybe a little bit of Nancy Sinatra and maybe Diana Ross. Except I didn't want him to think I wanted anyone to think for a second I might have some soul blood in me. Being the legit daughter of a pimp who married one of his whores is enough good luck for anyone.

Once I did what I was told, Larry talked things over with Joyce because he wasn't gonna do anything without her. With her along we went to the good stores and got me a new haircut that made me look pixie, a facial to start cleaning up more of my skin, a new wardrobe, mod but not wild, with lots of boots —all heights—that I could wear even during the summer. And Larry promised me a couple of fun-fur shorties for the fall. Sometimes Joyce—who was getting up now as early as eleven in the morning—would go into the library or Larry's office and scream at him how she wasn't standing still for his planning to spend a hundred thousand on me—which is what a year's budget might come to. But Larry said it was worth it because we would be buying the best and if at the end of a year nothing was happening, maybe I'd want to consider being something else.

And with all this, some personal important things were breaking wrong for Larry.

Let me explain. Think of a guy onstage, maybe like on the Big Square Ed Sullivan Show, which, irregardless how you dig it, means you're right-on with your career. And this guy is juggling lots of plates. This is his big chance to score. But just then he becomes the target for a fly that tries to make it up his nose or right in his ear. Bad off, sweat begins to drip into his eyebrows. What else now but he develops an awful itch somewhere, and he gets a cramp, the first in his life, in maybe one, maybe both legs. Meanwhile his underwear shorts creep up his crotch. Man, he's just gotta do something. Swat the fly, wipe his eyes, scratch or massage out the cramp. Or do something about his crotch. Exactly what? Which what'll keep him from dropping the least number of plates? Or, if none of these happen, just by thinking about a fly, sweat, the itch or cramps, the juggler might still lose control of the plates. It's a sad scene.

So Larry was not only tooling up to handle my career, he was juggling hard to keep his own, Simon's too, from breaking up. That it didn't happen was important to me, if not to Joyce, because without him, or them, I was right back in Nowheresville, a place PH would never bother rescuing me from. You see, while PH was abroad, Larry'd made some inquiries about him and through Fred Rory he learned that if PH looked like Old King Cole or the Poor Soul he could give it to you right in the jugular, like he was Dracula, the Wolf Man or this Nostradamus, Son of, who's so big in those Mexican horror flicks which show on Channel Eleven's Chiller on Sunday afts. So Larry warned me to be very careful in anything I said or did. I wonder if Larry felt the pressure in my palm? With him anything's possible.

Excuse me, I got sidetracked. So right about the time Larry

was interviewing a couple of phys-ed instructors to work with me during the summer weeks when Mrs. D. was taking time off to go to Hawaii for some sort of old WAC reunion, he got a call from a Man From Fuzz in Beverly Hills who invited him and Uncle Simon to visit the station where a certain captain of plainclothes pigs wanted to have a friendly rap about their appearance and residence around here. And how they intended to occupy their time for fun and profit. Because Larry was already busy juggling lots of things more fragile than Joyce's Sèvres plates—whose cost is beyond belief and which are firsts on my destruct-list at a time when it'll do my insides the most good—he took the call in the library, where he was being stomped on from a field snoop from Internal Revenue who was trying to take Larry's hide to make his reputation, I guess.

Right off he told the IRS creep that he'd have to adjourn their talks. And that night, in the dining room, Larry told Joyce how he was fed up to the teeth with calling Fred Rory and he had to have someone near, say within fifty miles, to talk to when he had to, especially when things were bound to start moving soon for me, which meant publicity and blowing what Larry called our low profile. So I could see that the phone call from the BH pig meant he had to put an extra plate in the air and keep it there along with the rest while he worked up a bigger sweat to make everything come out happy ending.

Meanwhile, he told Simon and Joyce—who was fit to be nailed because I was getting so much attention—how he was having trouble keeping his cool with the IR weasel, seeing as how he seemed to want Larry to pay all by himself for a whole regiment, at least, in Vietnam. Can you believe it, this animal wanted Larry to account for every month of the seventeen years since he and Uncle Simon had blown Vegas, because he wouldn't buy how in all that time they hadn't received a dime's worth of bread from the States. Of course Rory had helped Old Larry along by sending someone over to the six, seven, maybe eight meetings Larry'd already had with the tax ape. And Larry liked Mike Loesinger—the accountant-lawyer who was also at the supper table with us—so much that he was hoping Rory could fix it for him to be his juicer and Dear Abby. Especially since Harris Crowder—the IRS secret agent who looked like a very bad before-picture for a cheap hairpiece ad—had let on that he felt Larry and Simon might owe taxes on—get this!—about a quarter of a million dollars! Owe taxes for almost seventeen years, which with interest penalties might add up to more than that much bread!

"It took until yesterday to get him to say right out what he had in mind," Larry said while us guys—me in my dental braces and a dress, stockings and shoes, Larry, Simon and Mike wearing shirts, ties and jackets because of Joyce who said she'd only allow civilized people to sit at her supper table—listened. "So I was glad that Mike was especially here today to ask Crowder for specifications."

"Specifics," Mike corrected him.

Simon, who was only having tea and pumpernickel toast, sighed in his beard. "He sounds like a very rotten type to me," he said.

Joyce tapped the side of her water glass with a demitasse spoon—oh she's the elegant bitch—to signal Larry not to answer. Then, flat out, she told me to get upstairs and practice reading or reciting or getting to bed early. Or even brushing my teeth. I knew what I wanted to tell her, but that might've been exactly what she wanted, I figured, especially since she controlled the cash around here, at least the big chunks. So, in a way that might've got me a merit rating with Mrs. Beverly Droutswood—I just know she's a bull dyke—I asked to be excused. Spoke it in my best voice and pronouncing. Next I said good night to everyone, shook hands with Mike L. to see if he was going to give me some pressure, kissed Uncle Simon on one of his cheeks—he smelled of all sorts of good things and cream cheese—and went to my room.

First I locked the door. Next I got undressed to the skin

and took out from the very bottom of my bottom dresser drawer the makeup kit for tits which I bought for seven-fifty. It was advertised for intimate evenings at home, but at the right time I was going to use it someplace else. Not with Mike L., who just shook hands. But with someone who did. The kit had something called a blusher to make my boobs stand out, it seemed, apart. I wish I had Joyce's pair. She doesn't deserve them. Then I worked with the frosted cream to touch up the tops of my boobs and then—this is wild!—I used the rosy-red pink liquid gel on my nipples. Honest, they were now standing up maybe half an inch.

Now I was feeling very very good and I got into bed with the book I also kept at the bottom of the drawer which told all about positions—with pictures of real people yet—and other things birds could do to really wing their studs. Because when the time came I was going to send Mr. Hammschlager around the world, which struck me as kind of bright since that's supposed to be basic international dolce vita. All of this got my imagination fired up so I put everything away, got back into bed without that awful brace in my mouth, and practiced dramatics and elocution by saying, "Oh, Phil! Phil! I never knew anyone could mean so much to me!" What *basura,* which Uncle Simon says means garbage. But pigs and goats like *basura,* so it might be just the right diet for Old PH.

You see, on my own I was thinking lots about my career. Times've changed since Creepy Larry was the Establishment in Vegas and everything he did and ordered was planned. Nowadays things're different. It's all playing dirty, kicking hard and foul, electronics and luck for us kids. Talent's for squares. So here was Larry planning my career like it was still yesteryear, the long ago of "Greensleeves." Very carefully. A solid head interested in digging a foundation before he started to build up. Who knows? Maybe that's the way he even cooled his victims? Because I'm sure he's got a killing or two in his score. Sorry to say, honest, I guess Uncle Simon has too. Guess my *real* old man—the window sitter—must've had a couple he could call his own. But all that's history, and Larry's way of doing things for my career struck me the same way, as dead history.

So like a cooperative type, I was going along because there was nothing else to do right now. But at the right time what I'd learned from the book, my tit makeup kit and a little lipstick inside my pussy—like that creep photographer wanted me to do when I came around for our next session, which was to be color but never was—might speed things up with the just right Dirty Old Man. Or men. Which led me to think of maybe DOM Phil Hammschlager, or maybe my pediatrician, could get Larry to okay a silicone job for me. If I had one or both of my victims psyched out right, that sort of conversation—with me being very coy and blushy—could really rip their minds. Then if Larry said okay, after it was done the makeup kit would be that much more kick.

Now I practiced putting in and taking out my diaphragm, which made me feel so goopy good that I felt entitled to some sort of kicky reward. Especially since I was playing things cool and not talking at all about my career, not even to kids I met once in a while who also were doing time at Mrs. Cannon's. Not that any of the beasts and brutes there would've believed me. But what do you expect from nowhere zonks whose idea of all-time balling is to run away from home to a commune somewhere and get so stoned it becomes impossible to do more than vibrate like they say they do in *Barbarella?* The word's out that it's supposed to be a funny flick, which I'll have to see. Anyway, that's not my scene. No longer. Larry said and Uncle Simon backed him, that if I fooled around with shit, any kind at all, I was through. For them that stuff's a real turn-off. So I had nothing in common with the cutouts around me, which helps explain, I guess, why I treated myself to a session of rubbing, which may strike you as a pretty awful way to act. But I don't have outside friends I can really rap with, don't know anyone I can tell about my highs, so I had to share my feelings with my inside friends—me and myself—and both of them wanted to feel tingly.

Does anybody know the name of that lousy queen who tried to fuck up Snow White so she wouldn't be the fairest in the land? Could it've been Joyce?

CHAPTER FIVE

SIMON: Until we heard Verney slam the door of her room, nobody said a single word. I guess she slammed it hard to let us know she wasn't someplace she shouldn't be. Then Larry started right in.

"Who wants to cream us?" he asked nobody in particular, but Joyce and me and Mike Loesinger all heard it as if he was asking each of us alone. "Why? After so many years, when during all that time nobody said anything, how come this revenue joker wants to hit us with paying taxes on money he says we stole?" Now he looked directly at Mike. "How come?"

"Because taxes must be paid on embezzled funds," Mike began. "Also on blackmail money, extortion money, kidnapping money," he told us. "It's all covered in Section Sixty-one of the Internal Revenue Code, which says that gross personal income from whatever source—even those not listed—is taxable. So you"—he pointed to us—"come in under the unlisted items."

Larry's hands tightened on the arms of his chair. "Then you believe he can hurt us?" he asked Mike.

"Yes," Mike said right away. "But first he has to prove his case and I'd say he's fishing without bait or a hook. So I wouldn't worry."

"That's easy for you to say," Larry told him. "Suddenly I seem to remember lots of old history where the feds put some of the biggest people away for not paying taxes. Taxes they got from—you name the action. So I'm worried."

Mike smiled as he wagged his hands for Larry to relax. "Which is quite natural. What bothers me more is your not filing returns for almost twenty years—1951 right through to 1968. Which is now. Which also means the statute of limitations doesn't apply because neither of you ever filed a return." He let this sink in before he told us what part of the code covered that. "Still"—he went on—"after five hundred and ten days, say eighteen months, the first twenty thousand of ordinary income's exempt. So I think you're safe."

"We paid taxes in Mexico," I said.

"Still, you should've filed U.S. returns even if you had no income to declare," he sort of scolded me and Larry. "But that can be smoothed over once I make up all the returns."

"It's a lot of work," Larry said. "And I'd have to go back to Mexico City. But you'll get paid."

"I don't want you to think I'm interested in generating fees," Mike said in such a nice way. Now he thought again and we remained quiet. "It's a nuisance, that's all," he said in a way there could be no arguing with him. "And I'll find out why. Of course"—he pointed first to Larry, then me—"you'll pay taxes on that letter of credit deposited to your account in Mexico."

Suddenly Mike put a hand to his mouth as he looked from Larry to Joyce, but she only laughed and said she was accustomed to being bought, sold, traded or just passed on. Besides, Larry'd leveled with her and told her she could have a third or even more if she wanted, as long as she would shut up and stop yelling how Larry intended to ruin her by spending a hundred thousand dollars on Verney's career. I knew all about this and I'd even told Larry that if Joyce took him up, naturally fifty thousand must come out of my share. So I hurried to tell Mike he hadn't said anything he shouldn't. And Joyce told Mike she was flattered. Seeing as her first husband had demanded about fifty thousand to marry her and now almost twenty years later her fourth husband'd been given six times as much for going through the ceremony. She was, she said, a very good example of how the right sort of antique can go up in value like crazy. Still and all, it was a little rough on Mike and all of us for a couple of minutes.

It was Larry who brought us back to the principal subject. "I can't get it out of my nose," he began, "how something stinks very bad. The way the tax people and now the cops're bothering us." He shook his head harder before he lifted a finger to me. "What do you think?" he asked direct.

"Maybe that we should go back to Mexico," I said right away.

I had no ideas about these things and didn't want any. Not when I was having my head busted by other ideas. Like God couldn't be doing this to me, to us. Not after so many years of praying. Of living good. So this trouble had to come from something not good, not holy. Which is why I wanted nothing to do with it. Unless—I couldn't help thinking it although it made me feel awfully rotten—God didn't like Larry marrying a *goyeh*. But what could Larry do? He did it for me. That I know. For himself, he could've said no and lammed and maybe no one would've been able to find him. What stopped him was me. I'm not so fast anymore. I just want to be let alone. I'm very afraid of things and sometimes I do things that can hurt people. But God wants me not to do anything anymore to hurt anyone without Him first telling me to. If God has an enemy and He tells me to fix him, do even worse, I'll do it. But God—in all the time He's been speaking to me, not exactly with a voice but with special feelings—has always been upset or very mad at me when I hurt someone now that I'm reformed. I mean in the heart and the way I live. So if someone bothered me, what God wanted was that I should run away from the bad person. But sometimes I couldn't. Then I would have to suffer. Pray lots and cry.

For a long time now, Larry and me, we've been very good. So why God should suddenly put such a burden on him is something I don't understand. Job was a very religious man. A *tzaddik*. Larry isn't. Still, if I don't understand everything about God, who is so conceited that, like a fool, he can say he does? Right now—to make things easier for my friend who was also like a father and brother and all sorts of other good relatives to me—I had to not do anything to bother him.

"My friend Simon doesn't say much but what he does makes lots of sense," Larry said to Mike. "But we can't go back."

"I'm not keeping you," Joyce broke in. "Don't stay account of me."

Larry looked at her and I didn't like his expression because it meant he was thinking of her—very suddenly—as someone who could've fingered us to some certain wrong people. First, why should that rotten, *goyischer* tax guy be bothering us? And why, just when he got around finally to telling us why he was bothering us, should Larry get a phone call from the cops to come in for a talk? And to bring me along? The right way should've been that as soon as we got into Beverly Hills, maybe even right at the airport, before we even got into the cab, the cops should've been all over us.

Too long a time had passed by. Once or twice, maybe even three or four times, Larry said to me, and I said to Larry, how wasn't it funny the cops hadn't bothered us right off? That nobody or nothing had bothered us? Sure there were problems with Joyce—poor thing—and Verney, which is why Larry was brought back. And why Larry brought me along. Now these were very big problems, Joyce and Verney. And because Larry was going to help Verney amount to something, which meant she had to be noticed by outside, the kid was going to be connected up with us. This, it wasn't past me to figure out, might be something certain big people didn't like or want. Which explains the reason why Larry wanted someone close—like Mike Loesinger instead of Fred Rory—to be the middleman to talk to the certain big people and get them to go along according to certain rules agreed on by everybody.

No, I didn't like the way I was thinking. It was the old way. I never thought I would have to think that way ever again. But not thinking didn't mean not remembering. And now, because Larry had to—I had to help him. Whether I liked it or not, even if it scared me sick, I had to remember. And to think if thinking would help my Larry.

"Let me say something," I broke the long silence, seeings as Larry didn't want to pick up on Joyce's telling us to get out if we wanted to. "All of this coming at exactly the wrong time could mean one of two things."

"That it's a coincidence?" Mike suggested.

"A coincidence," I agreed was the first thing. Like Larry, I also liked Mike right off. A nice man, maybe thirty-five or a little older, with a wife and children. And if he isn't *frum,* he is conservative and doesn't belong to a reform temple from which, I've been given to understand by customers who come into our grocery, the next step is to become a Unitarian. Once, long ago, for that sort it was Christian Science. I spit when I say the words aloud. Now it's Unitarian, which I must find out what it is and if I should also spit on that. "But second, it could also be that the people who don't want us to go outside are giving us a little heat so we'll rush back to the shade where it's always cool."

"Or three," Larry interrupted me to look right at Joyce, "that maybe someone in this house who doesn't like some new things that're happening around here is trying to finger us."

"Finger you?" Joyce said as she pushed back a little from the table. "You, personally"—she pointed direct at Larry—"I'd like to heat a long spear and shove it up your ass until it comes outa your mouth. I never ratted on anyone. You know that, you miserable son of a bitch. That's why you let me leave Mexico. Or you've forgotten telling me that when you said okay?"

Some supper. Some night. Larry apologized and said he shouldn't've tried to top me. Because maybe there was something else I wanted to say? But I only shook my head and also apologized to Joyce, because I was going to say something more. That if she didn't want us in the house or even in the country, she should never think of doing something bad when all she had to do was to tell us direct. So she told me too—to go to hell with my keeper—and left the table. So that left the three of us sitting there—Larry, me and Mike—and it was some minutes before Mike cleared his throat and said we needn't worry about anyone finding out about this and he, personally, was going to phone Fred Rory and explain that someone had to be close by us because of what'd happened. So he asked to use the phone and while he went into Larry's office to place the call, Larry and me just sat at the table, he with his lips very thin, his scar getting red, just staring at the tablecloth.

Then Larry began to talk to me in so low a voice I had to strain to hear him, until finally I got up and moved to sit next to him. And he was sort of saying what he would like to say and do to Harris Crowder. How he thought that this might be someone's idea of a joke—to have the Revenue fasten on him—and how he would like to make the joke backfire, if it was a joke, by breaking Crowder's head, getting out of the country before he was booked and leaving Crowder as a mess for someone to mop up. Maybe that'd give them a laugh. Also, what bothered Larry was how in the world could there be legitimate taxes on illegitimate money like strong-arming, protection, especially on blackmailing and kidnapping? It just didn't make sense to him.

While Larry was asking me this last, Joyce had come back to the dining room because she said like it or not she was involved with us. So she also heard as she sat down again at the table how Larry asked if the government, which was supposed to be an honest one for honest people, couldn't see anything wrong with taking its cut of racket money? And was there some special section in the new tax-return form to report hot money, graft, cuts from blackmail, maybe a kidnapping, stuff like that? This made Larry laugh a little because he said he'd like to see such a funny tax form made up and sold to people.

This led Joyce to laugh a little too, and she told us a wild story that'd happened in Brentwood, which is a good residential neighborhood not far from Beverly Hills. It happened about 1961 or 1962 and also involved the Revenue. Seems that this operator, an intelligence agent for Internal Revenue, got assigned to do an audit on the return of this vice-president of a private finance company, the kind that advertises mostly over radio and TV to tell people to come in for a friendly loan that in the long run won't cost more than maybe an arm. So this agent gets the idea of giving up his salary job for one high try for the big money. So what does he do—but when his vacation time comes up he goes out and kidnaps the ten-year-old daughter of this company's vice-president and holds her for four hundred thousand. And he got it and they got their daughter back. Then he goes back to work on his job. About a year later, this agent's wife finds out he's got a girl friend. First she sues for divorce. Next she goes to the cops, gets immunity and tells all. So they nab her husband, try him for kidnapping for ransom with bodily injury—seeing as he'd done some bad personal things to the little girl—add some other charges like burglary and a jury gives him the death penalty. But he was still on Death Row at Quentin because the law and the family were still trying to work out a deal with him—his life for the money which was never recovered and everyone thinks is hidden in a Swiss bank.

This was a pretty terrible story, to which Mike also listened when he came back from his telephoning, and he starts to tell us what he described as the cherry on the sundae to this story.

Because the four hundred thousand had to be cash, the father of the kidnapped girl, her two grandfathers, a couple of uncles who are also pretty rich put up the money. Then when all these people filed their tax returns for the year, they deducted what they'd put up for the ransom as being money stolen from them. But the government said that was a no-no. They weren't really forced to pay the ransom. They had paid it willingly, so that meant they couldn't deduct it. The case was still in the courts.

This shocked me, didn't make sense to me, to Larry, even to Joyce, even to Mike. And I especially remember saying this wasn't an honest way for the government to act. What was worse it showed the government had no heart. Maybe the mother and father and the whole family should've not paid the ransom and let the little girl get killed?

We sat around thinking because everyone said what I'd last asked made sense. Then Larry wondered if Mike oughtn't to find out who Crowder's bosses were, right up the line, and see if maybe one of them had once known us and was now trying to get even for something we might've once done to him, a relative or a friend. Which might explain why Crowder—a small-time bastard if there ever was one—had dared park in the driveway every morning, even though he'd been told not to, and how every time he'd become snotty, really angry, when Larry told him to put his car on the street. But he did as he was told—until the next time he came.

"Crowder"—Larry had to say—"from the first second the delivery doctor could see how he was born with a prick in his heart. And still he let'm live."

But Mike only laughed because he had good news from Rory, who'd been a little sore at being waked up. Still, Rory'd said he had us on his calendar to talk to in the morning and tell us that Mike Loesinger'd been approved as our representative. This made us feel better, we shook hands all around and over the expensive tea served at supper we talked and Mike told us not to worry because the Revenue was just fishing. Meantime, he'd try to find out where they got the lead. But he was pretty sure the investigation could be squashed.

"But suppose you find yourself up against some honest type who just likes it fine living on his salary?" Larry asked. "Then what?"

"He can always be put on something else. So don't worry," Mike said again.

Then he went on to tell us why we shouldn't worry about our meeting tomorrow morning with the Beverly Hills cops. We hadn't done anything wrong, we'd been let back into the country and he'd try to find out why their sudden interest in us. So we were to go to the station which was in the city hall, just answer questions politely and stick only to the truth— that I'd come back with Larry because he'd married Joyce and a husband should be with his wife. If someone thought a proxy marriage was funny, Larry should admit it was, but they both wanted to get married right away and Joyce wasn't feeling well enough to travel and coming back to get married would've cut into the time it took us to close out our affairs in Mexico. That and nothing more. If we didn't like the questions we should ask to have the rest of the interview before our attorney, who was Mr. Loesinger. Meantime, we were to believe him—everything would be all right. When Mike left I felt better. But Larry went back to his office to mope and I sat with him until Larry asked me if we should play some pinochle and he took me for three dollars which made him feel very good because I usually take him.

The next morning after I finished my prayers and put away my *tefillin* and *tallis,* I phoned Polchansky to let him know I mightn't be in the whole day and if he called the union for a man, I'd pay. Polchansky told me to forget it. He could manage. I think he was specially nice because of the widow his wife talked about almost every day. From a couple of customers who like to gossip, I found out she was a relative, not badlooking some people said, and with a nice house in Carthay

Center which used to be very fancy and still is a nice place to live. Also, she's a piano teacher. So I thanked Polchansky, said I'd do him a return favor and sure enough he said that the favor he wanted from me was to meet his wife's lady friend. But he still said nothing about her being a relative.

By the time I hung up, Larry was waiting with his comb at the head of the stairs for his barber routine on me. I hoped my eyes didn't look worried. Because he said nothing I guessed he felt I could carry my end of things. Larry was already wearing his camera and I asked if he was going to the station with it. He nodded yes. You see, Larry doesn't have any film in the camera, but he always wears it on a strap. In Mexico, which is full of tourists, they're always taking pictures. Who could tell, by some accident Larry felt he might find himself in one? So he got the camera and if he was in a place where people were taking shots, he'd make as if he was taking some himself. That way he blocked off his face. Here I didn't think it was necessary. But I guess the camera had become a habit with him.

At the breakfast table he gave me my copy of the *Times* and I turned to the news of Israel—a country of which I'm very proud—to see how they were doing against Egypt and the rest of those dirty Arabs. Can you imagine a people so rotten they have arithmetic books for children in their schools with problems that if there are five Israelis and you kill three, how many are left? They're not even human beings. What upset me a lot was the way the United Nations and this country too couldn't seem to understand how Israel just wanted to be let alone to live quiet, like us, but the *momzerische* bastards around her—and Larry and me—won't allow it.

Still, the Israeli army, navy and air force was giving them what for in spades anytime they had to, and this made me feel good because even our generals were saying that Israel had the best soldiers and fighter pilots in the whole world. So how else could I feel but glad and proud? Still I was worried. Such a little country with so many enemies around it. Including the miserable Russians and from only God-knows-where-they-came

—suddenly the Chinks too. Maybe God was keeping Israel on its toes so it shouldn't be surprised by anything the murderers all around her did. This is what I hoped was true. If He wanted to, God could also be a trainer.

I said good-bye to Milly real nice while Larry gave Tom instructions what to do while we were gone. Then Larry drove us to the police station where we had to put money in the meter to park on the street, and had to wait maybe ten minutes before we went into the office of the cop who wanted to see us.

He was younger than us, not much I'd say, and he didn't look like a bad type. By that I mean not the worst type of cop, because I don't like them but I like even less the way Verney calls them pigs which she got from the Black Panthers she met when she was running around with a bad crowd. Black Panthers are rotten anti-Semites. Of this I have proof because some of the *shul* members who belong to the B'nai B'rith's Anti-Defamation League showed me copies of their paper, which is also called *The Black Panther*. They also showed me copies of other anti-Semitic papers and printed stuff coming out of Glendale, which is close to Los Angeles, and stuff from El Monte where the American Nazi Party is holed up. I must go see both these cities because I don't understand how respectable cities allow such stuff to be printed and sent from them.

The detective cop—I get sort of carried away when I start thinking and talking about anti-Semites, so, to get back to him—he was polite, gave us chairs and told us we could smoke. If we didn't have cigarettes we could take some from the fresh packs on his desk. We didn't take any but thanked him. He saw we were anxious to get down to business so he told us the talk was informal. No secretary to take notes or anything. We could have our lawyer come in if we wanted him. Then we'd set up an appointment to talk another time. Larry thought for a second and asked if at any time we decided to ask for our lawyer—what then? Without even hesitating the cop said yes.

So we began, and right off he asked us how we liked Beverly

Hills and he knew all about the house which was quite a famous place inside and out. Then he asked us what we were doing with our time and Larry said he was managing his wife's property and income. Had the cops heard that any of it wasn't legit? He said no and turned to me, and I said that Larry'd helped me buy a partnership in a grocery and both of us hoped he wasn't going to make trouble for Mr. Polchansky, who mightn't like having to find out who we once were, which the captain knew was a pretty long time ago.

Like I said, I've met lots worse cops. And he said he wasn't about to cause us trouble if we didn't make any. To that Larry said it was the last thing we wanted. Then he asked how we got along in Mexico because he'd heard how for the first five years a foreigner isn't allowed to work or go in business. And I was glad that Larry'd thought this might be asked and Mike had told him to just say we'd gone into the country with money of our own—about twenty-five thousand apiece—and with the interest we got from the money plus a little card playing, horse bets and going into the market with lots of luck, we'd got along. Then I'd gone to work and once in a while Larry had helped people meet each other and if the deal'd worked out he got paid. But the only deals he was interested in was those that could be talked about in broad daylight anyplace at all. That's how we got along. And that's how the interview ended.

When we left the city hall I felt pretty good. Larry didn't. He said it'd been too easy. We stopped in a coffee shop for cold drinks and while Larry phoned Mike, to tell him how things'd gone, I began to worry too. Suddenly Larry came back and he was all smiles. He'd just talked to Mike on the phone and we weren't to worry no more about Revenue and tonight he'd tell us why. This was very hard to believe, even though I'd prayed specially hard this morning and somehow'd got the feeling I was being answered. Also, before I came down from my room I'd looked at the poster of Super-Yid which Verney'd bought and framed for me in very nice wood. Such a funny poster, it came out right after the Six-Day War and showed this Chassidic *yeshiva bucher* coming out of a phone booth. He is wearing his high, broad-brimmed black hat—a *shtreimel*—also glasses, very long and beautiful *payess,* a caftan and black shoes. Also a white shirt collar. No tie. But under the caftan and over the shirt he's wearing a blue and orange Superman suit, and in the shield on his chest which is sewn to the suit is the letter *Shin,* which stands for S, which stands in this case for—Super-Yid. Also, in the pocket of his caftan is a Jewish newspaper, and because he's holding his caftan open to show the Superman suit, his right middle finger is stuck out in the up-yours signal. For him I don't exactly like that, still it's a very funny poster and lots of stores on Fairfax and all over the country, I'm told, sell it.

Pictures of people, you know, camera types and even paintings worry me because they are against God's law. Still, in Israel the biggest leaders let their pictures be taken and they have picture galleries, too, I've read. So maybe God's changed His mind and it takes man a long time more to catch up. Anyway, we're too smart to worship idols.

To go on, when I happened to mention how much I liked the poster at the table one night, four–five days later, Verney gave me this package all gift-wrapped to her Uncle Simon and they made me open it right there and it was this framed poster of Super-Yid, so kind and nice, looking like a serious student but he could also in a second be like Clark Kent who became a Superman fighter like no one ever saw before. Looking at the poster, which now hung on a wall where I could see it from my bed, always made me smile, even feel good, and lately, as we became better acquainted, I'd started talking to him and just the other day I had a feeling he was hearing me, listening, and if I dialed the number of his pay phone he'd answer. Meanwhile, we talked in our heads and this morning when I told him I was so worried about the rotten tax man—and going to see the cops who might bust us—he seemed to smile more before he told me not to worry because everything would be all right, trust him.

"It wasn't much of a session," I said to Larry, who suddenly was gloomy again. "Nothing at all."

"I'd like to believe it," he said to me. "That cop also asked questions about money."

I touched his elbow as he started to unlock the car door. "Larry, he could've asked us about lots worse things." I looked around, there wasn't anyone near us, still I spoke low. "I'm responsible for a couple of dead ones, Larry. And he didn't ask anything even close about them. Stop worrying. It's your nature to worry," I went on. "So worry about the things that need them. Like when is this Hammschlager coming back and how's he going to see about helping Verney?"

Larry just looked at me, shook his head and held the door wide for me to get into the front seat. I opened the lock on his side and he slid into his seat and said nothing until we were at Fairfax and Melrose, just a long block and a half from my store. Then he asked me if I wanted to be picked up later and when I shook my head he just told me not to worry about anything because he'd already collected flight schedules of every airline leaving Los Angeles. So maybe it might be a good idea for me to step into my store for a minute and tell Polchansky that I wouldn't be in for the rest of the day. When I asked why, Larry said he wanted to go downtown with me and get passports. He looked so serious and upset that I didn't hesitate for even a second and just told him to start driving there and I'd call Polchansky the first chance we got.

"We're going to get real passports," Larry said after he thanked me. Next he looked at me and laughed. "Once we take passport pictures you'll have to keep the beard."

"I'm not doing it for any government. Just for God," I told him.

Larry tapped himself over the heart. "You know I've got a picture of you without a beard? It's pretty old," he answered my sound of surprise. "And I don't like to look at it because Mitch's on it too." He thought for a bit. "I've just never been able to cut him off the picture."

It must've been taken long ago, at the Riviera. "Can I see it?" I asked.

"When we get home," he said. Then he hesitated and again —for a second only because Larry is a careful driver—he turned to me. "We're liable to leave this country in a hurry, Simon," he gave it to me straight. "Which means that after we get real passports I'm gonna scout around to have some phonies made up. Different names and for you, Simon, it's just gotta be a different picture. It must." Again he tapped his jacket and I realized he was touching his wallet, which he carried in an inside breast pocket. "That's where the old one'll come in handy."

Now I didn't answer right away, didn't answer at all because what Larry said meant I might have to shave off my beard and *payess*. But this is something I could do, if I had to, with a special acid and a thin wooden stick. At last, when I could speak again, answer him direct, I said that if things seemed so bad to him, maybe we ought to keep Mexican tourist cards handy? But Larry said he'd found out that our *Inmigrante* papers would get us back in and he'd never given them up.

Downtown L.A. is a real nothing and I couldn't smile when the photographer asked for one because I'll always feel funny about pictures. At least until my heart tells me it's not a sin. But passport pictures are never supposed to look good and while Larry helped me fill in the passport application and showed me that he had both our birth certificates, which made me more unhappy because I realized now he was really worried and'd thought a lot about maybe we would have to run, I wondered, after we got through with this, if Larry would drive me back to my *shul* because I had a lot of praying to do, a lot of big favors to ask from God.

One good thing about Larry, he knows when not to suggest

something else for me whenever I tell him I want to do certain things, so he let me off at the *shul* and when I came home that night to Beverly Hills after nine o'clock he said I should come into the dining room to sit with Joyce and him—not Verney, who'd gone to the movies with Mrs. Droutswood—because we had not to let on that we were worried and thinking of running. This was a secret only for us.

Lucky for me, Joyce was in a good mood for her and she listened quiet while Larry now said that he'd thought it over and decided the visit to the cops'd been a breeze. Also, more important, Mike Loesinger had passed by to bring some very good news. He'd gone to see certain people at Revenue and told them to put up or leave us alone. If they had charges to go ahead and make them. Otherwise they were to leave us alone because citizens had rights and we were in a position to get some very high-priced talent to represent us and maybe make things very hot for guys like Crowder and even people over him. To me this seemed like pretty unnecessary tough talk until Larry explained. Mike'd already gone into the matter of the two hundred thousand and there was nothing wrong. How could there be when all Larry had done was clean out the Riviera account from the Vegas bank and a couple of days later put the money into a Pittsburgh bank? The deposit slip had been marked transfer of funds from the Vegas bank. And the name on the deposit slip was Larry's.

I became very pale, looked as if I was going to faint, so Larry helped me to my feet and got me outside for a couple of times slow walk around the swimming pool. While he walked me around he told me how just before I'd got too sick to be bothered with things, Itzik and Foggia and Callahan, a couple of other people, had come out and arranged for skimming to start in the casino. At least a hundred grand a week just disappeared off the top, sometimes more if there was big action. In just about six months at least two million was in certain private pockets, which could explain why nobody had said or done anything about the two hundred thousand Larry took, seeing as it was only just about ten percent of the take, a little less, to which Larry and me were certainly entitled.

This skimming was news to me but I understood right away. Nobody wanted an investigation especially since the dropping of Joe Foggia had blown some other things wide open when right off Mitch became a state's witness. Larry, who knew so much about other operations besides the Riviera, clearing out fast and taking the microfilm which might've been got at by the wrong people, proved he was still on the right side. All in all, Mike said, Larry and me were to stop worrying about Revenue. All the past returns would be made up. If there were penalties they would be paid. Still, Mike was going to nose around, see if he could dig out the tipster. If and when he did, the next step would sort of suggest itself.

Tell me now—how could anyone with an open mind say that we weren't being looked after by Someone Who was wiser and smarter and stronger than everyone? Believe me, when I went to sleep that night I waved pleasant dreams to Super-Yid and made a joke. I asked him if he was stronger than Samson.

So I put out the light and thought I'd fall asleep right away, but this time I couldn't. So I lay there in the dark—really not so dark because I burn two night-lights in sockets on either side of my bed and two across the room—and began again to worry. If Mike had brought Larry such good news, how come he hadn't said anything to me about not bothering with passports? Maybe because we'd already made the applications. All right—so why didn't he say something like we'll forget the phony passports because we won't need them? And I didn't exactly want to go back to Mexico. Israel. That's where I wanted.

You see, since we got settled here and I joined my little *shul*, one of the men there, a fine person, lent me his scrapbook he made up from articles about Israel in *Time, Life, Newsweek* and *Look*. Also from the *Jerusalem Post* and the *Jewish Chronicle* which comes out in England. The scrapbook was all about things in 1967 from before the Six-Day War right up to now. This man was a real scholar, so every article had in it the name of the magazine, the date and even the page. When I showed Larry the scrapbook because I wanted one like it, he spent maybe a whole day writing down the information about dates and pages. Then he told Tom to go to secondhand magazine stores and buy what he'd written down. The *Jerusalem Post* and *Jewish Chronicle* articles he Xeroxed, and the next thing he did was buy me subscriptions to all the magazines and these two papers. Xerox is a marvelous invention. I think—no I'm sure—Larry and me own a nice block of it which he bought on a good tip. Larry helped me put all my articles in two nice books, one for each year, and from then on, taking care of the 1968 scrapbook was my responsibility, he said. But he made it a point to read every week what I pasted in. He was proud too and said how niggers must be very stupid to feel sorry for Arabs seeing as it was the Arabs who'd been the raiders from way back of nigger villages to get slaves and sell them. Of course he didn't say this where Milly or Tom or the day-help could hear him. Sometimes Larry surprises me with the things he knows.

So it was Israel I kept thinking of. And although I'd put down a deposit for the tour from my *shul* I didn't see how Larry or me could go. Still, I'd bought some guide books on Israel in the Jewish bookstores on Fairfax—they also sell lots of books in English—and I liked to read them. Believe me, I'm real glad the Israelis got their cemeteries back when they licked the Jordanians. You know what? Sometimes I make up that maybe one of my grandfathers or maybe grandmothers, who I never saw because they were left behind in Poland, might've changed their minds and gone to Israel when it was still Palestine and been buried in the old cemeteries around Jerusalem. And how me—an Israeli fighter—was one of the first to bust through the Mandelbaum Gate and into the Old City to head on the run right for the nearest cemetery, throwing grenades and using my submachine gun on all kinds of

Arabs, from Egyptians to Syrians, and how I killed a whole lot of them right on the graves of my grandparents. Then it would be in all the papers and my family would find out where I was and get in touch with me and they'd be so proud of me for being a good hero that my father would say I was his son again.

Because I will never forget one night in Vegas when Mitch got drunk. I undressed him for bed and he started to tell me how when he went home to get his clothes and go to Vegas with us and Joyce, how his mother and father tried to stop him. But Mitch had to go, they didn't understand that it was an order from Itzik. Suddenly, Mitch's father, who was sitting in his place at the dining room table, picked up a knife and cut his vest before he tore it. And then he closed his eyes and began to recite the *Kaddish*—the prayer for the dead. Mitch's mother screamed no, but he kept right on, louder now although it was still a whisper—*Yisgadal v'yishtabach v'yispo-ar v'yisroman v'yisnaseh v'yishador*—Mitch didn't want to say no more and when he began to cry, because to be alive and have the prayer for the dead recited on you is a terrible thing, maybe the worst in the whole world, my hands, my feet too, became cold as ice. And once before I left New York for Vegas, Mitch told me what his father'd told him. That my father had gone to *shul* to say I wasn't his son. But at least he didn't say a *Kaddish* on me, for which I'll always be grateful to my father.

Thinking this must've made me feel better because the next thing I knew the alarm clock was ringing and it was six-thirty. So I got up, cleaned up, like a religious Jew's supposed to, put on my *tefillin* and *tallis* before I faced east to say my prayers and thank God for taking such good care of us for such a long time. And I hoped He would go right on being good to us. Then I promised Him to go to Israel as soon as I could. And I'd do everything possible so Larry would go along.

Polchansky was glad to see me and didn't even look a little bit sore about yesterday. After we took care of the morning trade I swept the sidewalk again, marked down sale items and unpacked crates. Then I marked the prices of cans and boxes, then I stocked the shelves. Next I decided to clean out one of the showcases and I made it shine. By this time it was two o'clock and Polchansky said I should eat something. I wanted to make a sandwich in the store but he said he had to have a rest from my working so hard, which was making him nervous, so I should go to Gold's Delicatessen, sit down and eat like a person.

Gold's is only about half a block from our grocery and in between there's a bakery, a drygoods store, a record store, some other kinds and two bookstores. That's on our side of the street. One of the bookstores has the most beautiful brass candlesticks for sale. Also Torah crowns and breastplates for the Torah made out of genuine silver. For some time now I've been thinking of buying a crown and breastplate to bring home and put in one of Joyce's cases. But I thought I ought to talk to her about it. I guess I was afraid to. Then I also thought that if things worked out all right, and we didn't have to run away and we could take a trip to Israel without being chased, if I shouldn't show my appreciation by donating a Torah to my *shul*? That would make a wonderful gift and I could afford it. So I went into this bookstore to buy a new *yarmulkah* for *Shabbes* and I also asked about prices for a crown and breastplate, what a velvet cover for a Torah cost and finally, how much was a Torah itself? And how long did it take to make one because it's all done by hand and there can't even be a single mistake in it, nothing erased and the man who writes it has to be very very holy and is supposed to say a prayer before each letter he writes down. I got some facts and figures, paid for my *yarmulkah* and left it there to pick up on my way back from Gold's. Now I felt hungry. But there was a crowd across the street from Gold's, with a lot of motorcycles, maybe nine or ten lined up at the curb, and the crowd seemed to be very excited and angry about something. So I crossed over.

First, there's a hippie bookstore across the street that sells all sorts of posters, some of which are funny, some are dirty, and lots of books that I don't understand and all sorts of junk to do with fortune-telling and astrology and black magic which I don't believe in for a second and is also a sin. Next to the bookstore is a hippie place that sells love oils, crazy jewelry, secondhand clothes and old beaded pocketbooks, other things with beads and all sorts of funny glasses and hats that hippies like. But these don't bother me at all. To many people I must look like a strange cat myself.

What did bother me and the crowd, even more angry now, was that one of the motorcycle riders—I found out—had set up a platform. And all around the speaker on the platform, like a bodyguard, were other guys from the motorcycles and their girls who were also guarding. Also other young kids were with them. On the platform was a couple of flags in holders which an upset man I asked told me was from North Vietnam and the United Arab Republic, which you know is Egypt. What was also upsetting this man and other people around him was that with these motorcycle roughnecks and their girls there were some hippie types. Also some student types. Also nigger and Mexican types—in sort of uniform military jackets even though the day was warm and with black and brown berets—every one of them in dark glasses and trying to look very mean and hard. There were even kids from Fairfax High, which is just a couple of blocks away. And a middle-aged woman near me was red in the face with anger as she told the people around her how one Jewish Fairfax girl she recognized —see, there she's doing it again!—was sticking her tongue in some nigger's ear and laughing every time she did it. This girl was from a good home and when the lady called out to the girl how she was going to tell her mother and father what she was doing, this terrible girl made her lips move so that everyone could know what she said. Which was—go fuck yourself. Another woman remarked that lots of girls were saying this and worse to older people.

And all these types were sympathizing with the speaker, a boy who looked Jewish. When I asked the man who was so angry what was this Third World which the young outcast was talking about, what did it mean, he said that according to these dopes Israel was a tool of American imperialists who were keeping people all over the world in slavery. This was because America and Israel treated Third World countries like colonies.

This made no sense to me. How could a Jewish boy say Israel was a bunch of murderers and stabbers in the back because they won the Six-Day War and grabbed places to make the country safe? How could he say that Nasser and that king of Jordan Hussein had told the truth about American pilots painting Jewish stars on their planes and flying out to bomb the Egyptians and Jordanians and Syrians who were fighting to free themselves from the chains of economic slavery put on them by America and Israel? How could anyone with sense believe such crap? He was a terrible boy and I was shocked to hear him say it was time for the people in the Third World —which I still don't know or understand what it is—to rise up everyplace, especially in the streets and schools, and carry the battle right to the enemy—who was us! That's why they'd come right into this up-tight Jewish neighborhood to show they were braver than we were because they didn't have the United States, its organized churches and public opinion, its pig troops and police behind them when they showed up to challenge us with ideas in words and if we wanted it—ideas in fists.

"With fists!" this speaker shook his right one at us. "With our blood if it's necessary!"

"So Jewish people don't have a right to live?" a man with a shopping cart and an accent asked this boy. "The United Nations said different, thank God."

"Your communist Russia helped smuggle Jews into Palestine from Black Sea ports and every other way they could when England and this country didn't want any there after the war in 1945," a nice man in a suit, who looked like he might be a lawyer or something, spoke. I could see how the speaker looked down on him, not liking what he said because people were listening to this man, not the speaker. And I was too because this was very interesting to me. Imagine, Russia helping Jews. "Yes," I heard this man go on, "in 1947, for maybe nine or ten months, Gromyko, who was high in the Russian government even then, pleaded the Jewish cause with its war allies. And Harry Truman wanted to go along. But our State Department didn't."

Suddenly this man was interrupted by a tough-looking nigger in those big dark glasses. "What's your point, man?" he asked really snotty. "We're not here to talk about the past. It's now, man, now. The relevant time. That's the history that interests us."

The man didn't even try to answer this nigger, or the speaker on the platform, a miserable type who was probably the kind of kid to've made a good Nazi because he would've turned in his mother and father to the Gestapo and taken a shower with soap made from them. But I was interested in what this man had to say, so were other people, and we told him to go on. Some of us, including me, took out pads and pens to write down some of the things he told us, even the names of books. So it was interesting to find out that our State Department didn't want Israel to become a country because it would go against our policy with the Arabs. That even John Foster Dulles, a *goy* if there ever was one, who was later on Secretary of State but was then a member of the American United Nations team, was also against Israel. And he teamed up with the Arabs to say that the United Nations had no right to deal with the problems of making a Jewish state. But Russia and most of the nations it controlled voted against this and they won by one vote! Twenty-one to twenty!

Then, because Truman saw how things were going, and that Russia might come out the real hero of the Jews, he finally told the State Department to get in line or else. Even though they finally knuckled under, they managed to trim down the size of the future little country before it was born. By hundreds of miles. So at last, at the end of 1947, because Russia, the Czechs, the Polacks and two other Russian countries whose names I can't remember all voted for Israel, the resolution to make it a country squeezed through by the two-thirds majority it had to have. But because the English refused to cooperate in Palestine and let the Arabs send soldiers against the Jews—the American delegates to the United Nations said see, it won't work.

Still, on May 17, 1948—I wrote this down—Russia was the second government in the whole wide world to recognize Israel as a new country, right after we did, two days before.

Like I said, what this man was telling us was so interesting that people were listening to him rather than the jerk-off kid on the platform, who was shouting louder and louder but not getting the attention of most of us. And then the trouble started. You see, a woman, who must've been about fifty, pushed her way to right under the speaker's stand. Suddenly she pushed up the sleeve of her dress and people were shocked —me too—when we saw the tattoo numbers on the inside of her arm. Next she began to scream at this speaker how he was worse than a Nazi because he was a Jewish boy who'd become one. So she spit on him and everything he said and the kind of people he was speaking for.

It happened. I saw it. This Jewish kid on the stand, with his rotten mouth, starts laughing at her and he says that being Jewish doesn't mean he has to be an imperialistic Zionist who is kissing Johnson's ass. At this the woman, who was screaming at him, reached into her grocery bag for a can of something to throw at him. Too bad, it only hit him on one of his arms. Now one feller in a beret, a brown one, tried to get at the woman but I got him by a shoulder and held him, all the while telling him to lay off because the kid on the stand deserved to have his tongue torn out. Then what do you know? A motorcycle-type joker pushes up to me and tells me to take my Jew hand off his brother.

I didn't understand, because they didn't look at all related. Still, I did. Then this motorcycle type spreads his feet, puts his fists on his hips and tries to look hard at me after he took off his dark glasses and handed them to some girl with little flowers painted on her cheeks who is all excited now because she thinks maybe she's gonna see some real bloody action. And this guy, who has mean eyes and a mean mouth, looks at me—we were both about the same height—and he sneeringly asks me if I'm one of those tough hypocrite rabbis who thinks concentration camps for Arabs are right as long as we're the guards? Or maybe I'm someone who thinks the whole world has to be afraid of a Jew because he's got all the money?

Now I can't say I wasn't flattered to be mistaken for a rabbi. It's happened before. In Mexico City and even here. But this joker meant it like an insult—like he meant the questions at me which aren't true—so when he started to touch my *tzitzit,* while he told me I oughta be neater if I was a rabbi, I told him to lay off if he knew what was good for him. Then he looked at me as if I was a nothing and—I swear it happened —he spit square in my face. And as I felt his spit on me I also felt that I heard the voice of God ordering me not to do anything even if this was the worst thing to happen to me, to Larry, in a week that'd given us nothing but aggravation and bad memories from the old times.

Suddenly he hits me a pretty hard shot in the belly. But lucky his fist landed against my belt buckle and the next instant another voice drowned out God's, and it seemed to come from the mouth of Super-Yid. And I remembered how in the old days when I was working over a Puerto Rican kid or some nigger with a ducktail haircut, I used to reach out real fast. With my left hand sort of grab the ducktail between my fingers while my palm sort of supported and held the back of his head. Then I'd land the right.

Which is what I did to this motorcycle type because he had long hair too. So it was easy to get hold of and hold him while I let go the right and felt his face explode against my fist.

CHAPTER SIX

JOYCE: My house has an impressive master suite. Both bedrooms, each with its own fireplace, are about twenty by thirty. Both bedrooms have fine parquet floors, elaborate baths, dressing and exercise rooms. Mine also has the sunporch. Between the bedrooms is a common sitting room, also with its fireplace. By the time I started to do over the house—and without discussion—Itzik and I understood we should have separate bedrooms. It was kind of him to feel that way, so I wanted to please him one hundred percent when it came time to do his room.

No question about it, he hated the sketches shown him of what was to be his Empire bedroom with red and gold silk-brocaded wallpaper to establish, the decorator said, the room's Napoleonic purity. I must say Itzik did laugh good-naturedly as he pointed to the sketch of the crystal chandelier, the sleigh bed with ormolu detailing and white chairs in their wine-red mahogany frames. Also he laughed at the little dressing table and the marquetry desk which he said was downright ugly.

Plus he didn't like at all the heroic portrait the decorator had *schlepped* over, about five by eight feet of some French officer or nobleman in a blue and yellow velvet suit, maroon sash, white cape and stockings. Definitely not for him, Itzik said. Certainly not for ten grand. Not even for ten dollars or ten dimes. Or as a gift. Next, did we really expect he'd sleep in a bed that looked like a jingle-bells-one-horse-open-sled?

Then, because we'd put a lot of work into planning the room, Itzik said if the house was English, why shouldn't we do an English bedroom for him? He liked red and the idea of a fancy bed—something like the one Charles Laughton slept in when he played the king who was such a good wrestler and had so many wives—appealed to him. All right then, he decided for us, the room was to be English, and red, but it'd better not look the least bit *faygel*.

So we planned to make the most of the bedroom's classic Adam fireplace, good dadoes and panelings, and the classic Greek moldings with their carved acanthus leaves. So, because Itzik said he liked red, the decorator thought we should do the walls in a complementing light Wedgwood green because he knew where to get the most marvelous Chippendale canopied bed. Then we could do the bed hangings and draperies in red damask. Situated room center, between two windows, it would be stunning. Two other pieces he had in mind were a good Chippendale chair with solid arms and a broad needlework seat, just the right size for Itzik when he worked or read at the compartmented Chippendale desk.

This sounded better. Itzik himself chose the Persian rug because he liked the reds, and he went wild over a reproduction of an American highboy that's in the Metropolitan. It's quite tall, with seven banks of drawers, an exquisite shell carving within the scrollwork, and the japanned decoration is gold on black lacquer. Gorgeous.

Now it was Larry's room and he didn't feel at all squeamish about sleeping in Itzik's bed because, he said, Itzik'd died in the hospital. And most of the furniture in the house, hadn't it belonged to other people now dead? Even the original owner of the house was dead. So why make a thing of a bed? He too found it a kick. Personally, I'd always thought it a little too much.

To go through the common sitting room into Larry's didn't strike me as right. So I went into the hall. There I straightened the Piranesis and stood at the head of the stairs until the second chime of the big clock downstairs faded away. Now I listened for other sounds, maybe Verney moving around. I can't get myself to trust that kid. But I heard nothing and only hesitated for a moment before I knocked gently on Larry's door as I opened it to enter his room.

"Who's there?" I heard him ask as he moved to turn on a bedside lamp. Then he actually put on glasses as if he was going to read, but took them off when he recognized me. "What's wrong?" he asked. "Verney?"

"No," I said. His pajama coat was some light broadcloth and didn't look the least bit rumpled. "Mind if I sit? I can't sleep."

"Be my guest," he said. "Mind if I don't get up?"

While Larry pushed back the hangings, fixed his pillows to help him sit up, I turned one of the crewel barrel chairs at the fireplace toward the bed.

"That's a pretty outfit," he said about my peignoir and nightgown. "Very nice."

"Thanks. I'm nervous," I explained my coming into his room, which I seldom do. "You know, waiting for Simon's plane."

"Which isn't due until the afternoon," he said after he put away his glasses and sat with both hands clasped behind his head. "If it's on time."

"They never are," I said. "At least I guess they never are when they come from Europe."

"Israel's in the Middle East," he corrected me.

That made me a little angry. "I know," I said. "But the plane does make a European stop." Larry nodded an apology, so I decided to keep talking. "How do you think he'll be?"

"That's why I wasn't sleeping either," he admitted. "So I'm glad you came in."

I nodded, thought a little, then nodded again. "It's better that way."

It was Simon who'd made it that way. Poor *klutz,* not that he intended to, but Simon really blitzed our covers when he hit back. The next second after he dropped the goon with his nose and jaw broken, besides some teeth gone, the goon's goons jumped him, which was a mistake because that turned him into a runaway truck who rushed the speaker's stand and turned it over with his bare hands. Throwing killer rights and lefts as he yelled how he was going to wipe out all the *pogromchiks,* he worked his way to the motorcycles which he knocked over, every one. When one of the cyclists swung at Simon with a tire chain to catch him an awful crack across the back, he flung himself on the guy with the chain, twisted it loose by almost breaking this guy's wrists, and really began to use it good while he yelled now how he was going to slaughter all the Philistines and Arabs and enemies of God. Meanwhile, while Simon is making like Samson, I guess, people in the crowd who'd been steamed up because the meeting'd really been held to work them over, maybe even beat them up for being Jews, tore into the hippies, the cyclists, the blacks in their black berets, the Mexicans in their brown. And they also went after their girls, just anyone who seemed to be on their side, so by the time the cops arrived to break up the riot and arrest Simon along with about forty or so other people on both sides, it'd become a massacre against the outsiders. A couple of ambulances had plenty to do, but most of the badly hurt were on the other side, especially the goon Simon first laid out and the guy who'd hit him with the chain.

Like everyone else the cops took in, Simon was booked for misdemeanor assault, but at least a hundred people who went along to the Hollywood station protested his arrest. Some of them were witnesses who swore how the bum who was all busted up had spit on Simon and hit him first. So what was wrong with the cops if a man couldn't defend himself in a free land? Or were they also for Hitlerites?

In a routine booking, the cops took his picture and prints before Mike Loesinger was able to arrange bail, which in the end amounted to a hundred and ten dollars. The ten is for an educational fee, Mike told me. As soon as Simon sets foot the next day outside the municipal court where he'd been given a trial date the end of October, he's surrounded by all kinds of reporters and photographers who want to interview him. So he tells his story just as it happened. Explains how badly he felt that people who weren't bothering anyone had to stand for listening to a bunch of snotnose anti-Semites deliberately come to rough them up in their very own peaceful neighborhood. For the man who'd hit him with the chain, he didn't feel too sorry. But for the first man he hit, who was still in the hospital, Simon felt bad. But the man had spit on him, hit him and worst of all made fun of his religion. One reporter called Simon a modern Maccabee. Another a reincarnation of Bar Kochba, who was some sort of fighting king of Israel. Both of them gave the public our house address.

At home Simon was moody, so we let him go to his room before we sat down to watch him on TV newscasts that night on every station. If you saw him, you know how great he came across. The things he said sounded dignified, reasonable and you felt that Simon was sincerely sorry he'd hit anyone. And he looked intelligent. Old-fashioned but intelligent.

The very next day, from eight in the morning, there're platoons of reporters at the house, television trucks all over our block, and Larry's out there telling them to keep off the driveway, ordering them to blow because Simon wasn't going to do any more talking. Just then, who shows up but Polchansky who identifies himself as Simon's grocery partner, so the reporters start interviewing him. In four or five minutes of tape time he told them—and indirectly some millions of people in Southern California—that Simon was his partner, a fine man, religious, kind, very popular with their customers, a credit to the community. For two days now their store'd been filled with people all coming to see Simon Bronstein and congratulate him for dealing with anti-Semites the only way they could ever understand—by breaking their heads.

If that isn't enough to bring out the neighbors to make the block we're on look like the first stages of a disaster area as they crowd our sidewalk and front lawn, which is making Larry lose his mind, a delegation or committee—call it whatever you like—shows up from Simon's synagogue. Believe it, they're carrying a Torah and singing songs. There's more. A couple of men actually dressed like Super-Yid—Chassids, I found out—are singing and dancing all around the Torah and clapping their hands as they come up the walk to the front door to honor Simon, their hero. By this time the Beverly Hills cops come on the scene, uncertain what to do. Also some cars of the California Highway Patrol, who're just as confused, especially after they see maybe twenty students from a very religious Jewish rabbi college march up to our front door to announce how they want Simon to speak at their college and they're ready to help him form a regiment to protect Jewish neighborhoods in Los Angeles as well as synagogues and religious schools, some of which'd had swastikas and dirty signs painted on them, besides having their windows broken and other damage.

It didn't end there. Suddenly, Verney—living proof I didn't live right because she's so wrong—comes rushing out of the house in what I guess she thought was on-camera makeup, the lowest-cut dress she's got and no bra. Bending over as often as she can, she announces to the whole wide world that Simon's her uncle. Which made Larry and me relatives. Stupid us—we tried to explain to people who didn't care that Simon wasn't Verney's real uncle. That she just called him uncle as a sign of respect.

"Respect!" Verney screamed into four or five hand microphones before she did everything possible to fall into the cameras, "I love him!"

Now she's surrounded by reporters and cameramen, who're zooming in on her goodies, while she goes on to tell them how she loves Simon more than anyone in the world. Because of Simon she'd stopped being a dropout and was now back, studying harder than ever before in her life as she also prepared herself with Simon's blessing and encouragement to become a singer and actress. All this time, with Milly helping me, I'm trying to drag her indoors, all the while begging Larry to help me, but he seemed to be paralyzed, until some reporters ask Verney if I'm her mother and she screeches yes and reaches out toward Larry to introduce him as her father. So then they about knock us over with questions about Simon while Verney is mugging it in every shot they're taking.

Wait, there's more. Like Indians or the cavalry that's just snuck through the pass, we're confronted by two gangs—blacks and Mexicans and with signs yet—who've come here for a demonstration of Third World solidarity. While the cops're trying to move them out without force and are getting nowhere, suddenly there's still more action because about a dozen American Nazis in uniform, with Nazi and American flags, come goose-stepping around the corner to picket the Jew house. For a couple of minutes we're saved because the Nazis see the blacks and Mexicans in *their* uniforms, so they start chanting hate slogans, calling them savages and telling them to go back to Africa and Mexico because the country's main problem was too many mongrels, which sort of reminded a few of them that they'd come here originally to get in their licks at the Jews. So every so often they'd chant that Uncle Sam had no room for Uncle Ike. Top bit for this routine was when one of them puts on a phony Jewish nose and starts waving his arms around in a bad imitation of a peddler. Which brings all the Jewish groups together—even some of the neighbors and Larry—and they want to charge the Nazis, but they don't want any help from the blacks and Mexicans.

Now, while I'm holding on to Larry and Verney at the same time, and Milly and Tom are calling trash the blacks who're yelling for them to throw off their shackles, liberate themselves from the Man and come over to their side, other people who live all around us are demanding that the cops clear out everyone. Meanwhile, some of these good souls are blaming us for what's going on. So they want us arrested for creating a public nuisance.

There's more. Because who comes tearing down the street but the maid Larry had trouble with the day after he got here. Pointing right at him, she starts screaming that our house is racist, which gets all the blacks together, some of the Mexicans too, especially after the lady this maid works for rushes over to order her right home immediately. At which the maid calls her a honky, tells her to go screw herself and marches over to join her black brothers, which makes them cheer louder because she's become so beautiful. But she's there for only seconds before another woman runs up to offer her right now fifty a month more if she'll live in, plus her very own large-screen color TV set and her room redecorated any way she likes if she'll accept and leave with her immediately. So the maid does, which blows the mind of the former lady she worked for, but nobody gives her much attention because suddenly a fire truck comes sirening onto the block to put out the fires set in garbage cans in the alley behind the houses across the street.

By this time Lexington's getting filled up with smoke, sheriff's cops show up in riot helmets, with more bull horns, and a traffic jam forms right on the corner of Beverly because two rubberneck busses are trying to turn into our street. They can't go forward or back up because traffic's piled up all around them. Now there're photographers on tops of trucks, even in the trees. The cops still don't want a riot and are only trying to get people to go peacefully, but this is only creating more trouble as some of them become passive and sit right down anywhere. Suddenly bottles are thrown, so everybody is up again and more cops come pouring in. And all the while Verney is chewing any microphone she can get her hands on, Simon's locked himself in his room, and Milly, Tom and Larry're banging on the door because he's crying so hard. Just about then windows started to break in our house and those around us. From then on with the cops moving in on everyone it became a real freak-out happening.

Yet there's even more. Lots worse. Because starting with the eleven o'clock TV news that night and a couple of hours earlier on radio, I can't guess how many millions of people around Los Angeles found out who Verney's Uncle Simon really was. So, naturally, who we were.

A routine check of Simon's fingerprints, which'd been sent on to Washington by whatever new machines the LAPD uses to get immediate information, showed that in the FBI files there were his prints from the time he'd been an Amboy Duke and the whole gang had been pulled in on weapons charges, a roust which took place some time after a high school teacher'd been shot and killed in his classroom by someone with a zip-gun. The cops suspected somebody in the Dukes, they were right, and when one of the kids who killed the teacher squealed on the other, still another member of their gang—Crazy Sachs, who used to be controlled by my first husband Mitch the way Larry controls Simon—pushed the rat off the roof of an Amboy Street tenement. That decided the cops to put all of them on ice. Mitch did time, Larry got two years and so did Simon. From then on, the cops had files on all of them, seeing as they became strong-arms for Itzik when he was a garment protectioner, among other things. Later they'd gone to Vegas and operated the Riviera for him and his people, until Mitch'd become implicated in a killing and to save himself from murder-one fingered Itzik as the hit-master. That's why I left for Mexico with Simon. Both of us were part of the baggage Larry took with him.

It worked out that Simon was the only one of us with box office and we had to call the cops and demand they put some men in front of the house to keep people and reporters moving. But that was hard, seeing as they were interested mostly in Simon, who got most of the ten to fifty or so letters delivered daily. Most of them congratulated him, some asked him to speak before their groups or to send lots of cash to support their noble causes and some were poison pen. Some sent to us were poison pen. The others, mostly from civic groups or just plain people with civic minds, ordered us to sell and clear out immediately.

Yes, there're all kinds. Especially some who're supposed to report the news for the local TV stations. The worse of the lot was a prime-time bastard who thinks he invented the American flag, actually wrote the Declaration of Independence and the Constitution. Those were his, but the Bill of Rights was the work of a bunch of communists. Always talking very big patriotism, when he addresses the camera he stands sort of sidewise and wriggles his eyebrows like danger signals while he pitches good citizenship at his dumb listeners, which, as he sells it, is to kill everyone who doesn't agree with him. So he goes on in rounded tones about the Mafia coming into Southern California, right in the best residential area, and how would any good citizen like having the Cosa Nostra right next door in a million-dollar house? Mind you, he hammered this home for almost a week—a million-dollar house. Which is almost a half-a-million-dollar lie. Mike told me not to mind this nut because the only people who take him seriously are other nuts who think he's good for their constipation. Besides, everything he says always sounds like he's reciting the-boy-stood-on-the-burning-deck. Some newspapers were unfriendly, but only the local Hearst rag and some Orange County sheets gave us the full Mafia-is-coming! treatment. The funniest, in a sad sort of so-what-else-is-new? way, was the underground paper out of Watts which called Simon a secret recruiter for the terrorist Israeli-armed Nazis. I guess you can only be so sane or good, but there's no limit to how evil or insane a person can get.

Meanwhile, Mike Loesinger just about lived at our house which made things rough at his. I phoned his wife and invited her and the kids to stay with us, but she sounded scared, so I felt sorry for her. Still, we needed Mike. After he went to his office to take care of morning routine he'd start making and returning calls of certain people, including Fred Rory, who were blue from screaming that Larry'd been brought back to keep things quiet in my house and look what'd happened. Who needed to know about Simon and Larry and even me—except them? But now the whole world knew. People supposedly on your side can be beautiful too.

Simon wouldn't go to the store, Polchansky had to get a union clerk, which made him call every night to beg us to make Simon come back because every customer wanted him and business was great. Then there were phone calls from people in Simon's synagogue, even his rabbi, offering to do anything for him. And how do you handle a well-dressed woman, real soft-spoken, who introduces herself as a piano teacher and says that mutual friends've been trying to arrange a meeting between Simon and her for a long time? Besides, she's carrying a big bouquet of roses which she wants to personally deliver to her fiancé.

After her visit I laughed too hard, too long. Suddenly I'm crying at the same time, a really big hysteria, but there was good reason. After Itzik died, his body was taken from the hospital to the mortuary, to which I didn't go. Sure there were lots of plainclothes cops in front of the hospital, the funeral parlor, even at the cemetery. And for all the good it did, they could've spent their time taking pictures of each other and sizing up reporters through their binoculars. Because no family people came. I told Fred Rory to pass the word along—no flowers, no mourners. Everyone was to stay home. I went to the cemetery to see that Itzik was prayed over properly at the right times. So his funeral was so quiet, so uneventful that the only news value it had was in no one except me being there. That's tough material to work with, so the coverage was thin. And I did this all by myself, which you would've thought would teach certain people something.

Namely, that Joyce could take care of herself. But no, they had to send a keeper. Larry. And five months after he arrives he's made a complete nut of Verney and turned the beautiful street I live on into carnival alley. Which explains why I went upstairs after Milly helped me get rid of Miss Piano Teacher without letting her in the house—although Milly did take the roses—feeling at least like an eighty-three-year-old old man with the shakes.

Lucky for us that Mr. Polchansky found out right away about the weird lady with the bouquet and comes over alone. And lucky for us I'm coming downstairs when Tom answers the door and Polchansky begs me to listen because he has some good suggestions—he swears—to help Simon and incidentally all of us. Too tired to scream for him to get lost, I told Tom to let him in.

As Polchansky sat on the edge of a sofa in the living room he kept looking at the seat of his pants to make certain, I guess, he wasn't staining the cushion. Even though he wasn't anyone, his awe of everything made me feel good until I got the wild feeling he was pitying us. You know, little people little troubles, big people big troubles. And I could swear he was telling himself and probably believing that he wouldn't change places with us. Before I could become more upset by thinking about what he was thinking, Larry came in and Polchansky got right down to business.

"He's all right?" he asked us.

"If moping in his room, saying nothing, is all right, then you can say he is," Larry said.

"I miss him," Polchansky went on. "Everyone does. The whole neighborhood. I can't tell you how much he's liked." He paused to look at Larry. "The other day a paper did a miserable article about all of you."

"We saw it," Larry said.

Polchansky scratched both ears before he coughed into a fist. "Did he really have the reputation of being one of the hardest hitters in Brownsville? I mean with his fists. This I got from a customer who years ago lived in Brownsville." Then, as Larry's face began to redden, Polchansky raised both hands to show he was sorry. "My missus wants to apologize for her younger cousin," he said to change the subject. "She's a good woman, really. Too young to be a widow. Very sincere. Very moral and missing a husband, which sometimes carries her away."

In that sweet lovable way of his, which'd always made him everybody's favorite, Larry snapped his fingers at Polchansky as if he was some sort of not-quite-housebroken dog. "If you're here to discuss a *shiddach,* you've taken too much of our time already," he said. "Simon doesn't want to marry or even see anyone. So I don't know when he's going back to the grocery. Don't count on him."

"That I've figured out for myself." Polchansky really was unhappy. The way he sighed proved it. "But I came here to suggest something that'll be good for Simon whether he comes back or not. And he can sell his half back to me and make a good profit if that's what he wants. Listen, please, Mr. Tunig" —he gestured to tell us he was getting to the point—"Simon should take the trip he talked about every day. He should visit Israel."

"You must be kidding," Larry said.

Polchansky wasn't. Simon had signed up for the charter flight which his *shul* was taking with other orthodox *shuls* to go to Israel for Rosh Hashanah and Yom Kippur. These are the holiest days, especially Yom Kippur, which is Simon's Day of Atonement. I wish it was Larry's also. All told, the charter group was going for just under four weeks, so they could also do some sight-seeing. If Simon went on the trip it would take him away from people who were doing their best, knowing or not, to make him unhappy, seeing as they were bothering him, and us, with the past, which in Polchansky's mind didn't bother him personally at all. As Polchansky explained it, all he had to do was drive along Doheny Road to think right away of Teapot Dome. All the connivers had been very important men and big business in and outside the government, and he doubted if any gang at all had ever been able to get away with so much. But no one'd ever suggested changing the name of the street. Or along Wilshire Boulevard, named after a man who invented a quack cancer-cure machine which made plenty for him and also might've been responsible for the death of gullible people who might've been saved if they'd gone to ethical doctors, who were also becoming harder to find today, seeing as patients interfered with their reading the *Wall Street Journal*.

Another thing, Simon's case wasn't supposed to come up before October 27, so he'd be back in plenty of time. But right now Polchansky was willing to take bets that nothing would come of it, seeing as the morning paper told in a little piece that the bum whose face was broken by Simon now refused to press charges because Simon wouldn't either.

"Send him," Polchansky pleaded with Larry. "It'll get him away while things quiet down even more. Best of all it's what he wants to do more than anything else. I know," he insisted. "And don't worry"—he wouldn't let Larry interrupt him—"Simon'll get the best of care. All the way. I could bring a hundred people here who'd be proud to sit next to him going, and there, and coming home."

"Don't bring even one," Larry said. Then he also said he was sorry, because Polchansky made a lot of sense. "What about it?" he asked me.

"He hasn't got a passport," I said but nodded to show I also thought it was a good idea.

But he had, Larry said, and signaled me to hold up because he would explain later. Then he asked Simon's partner to sit while he went upstairs to ask Simon if he'd like to go. Milly served Polchansky a glass of wine, some biscuits, and he listened attentively while I told him something about the history of the house, which made him say he was sorry now that he couldn't remember ever seeing the old star in a movie although he was old enough to.

In about ten minutes Larry returned with Simon, who actually beamed. It looked as if he would pump Polchansky's arm out of its socket and he hugged Larry and me for saying he could go to Israel. Would the police really let him? Larry said yes, especially since charges were being dropped. He also said he was sorry that business made it impossible for him to go with Simon, since he was also signed up on the charter.

Much later that night, hours after Polchansky left, many things were decided, including Simon's moving into the guest house. As a bachelor he appreciated living with us, but he did want to entertain on his own some of the people he'd met. And he wanted to entertain us too. In the guest house he could have his own kitchen, stop bothering us, buy things he liked as decorations. That agreed to, I wanted to know why they'd got themselves passports and not told me. They were entitled to privacy, but if they had ideas of running out on me—and they could go to hell with my blessings and my paying for their transportation if they wanted to know the truth—simple decency should've made Larry tell me. Certainly the three hundred thousand they'd got entitled me to that much. He knew I'd never talked about him in the past. So why should I now? Or in the future?

"Because we change," he explained. "Just look at Simon. Or me. Even you."

I let it go. Only later I realized he hadn't told me anything. But he no longer had to. I knew enough to become more watchful and say less. Also, I'm happy to say, Larry's biggest problem was with Verney, who wanted to quit school and go to Israel with Uncle Simon. When he turned her down she began to take the house apart, so it was like old times and Larry had to belt her a couple before she screamed surrender and promised to be good. Still and all, I asked him, when was Hammschlager going to start on the kid's career because I was anxious to see how far nothing could be promoted. That made Larry kick me out of his office with the suggestion I take Simon shopping for his trip.

The day after, Simon left with promises that he'd write every day and our promising to do the same, Larry took off for Mexico City with Mike to straighten out the delinquent tax returns and I got very busy with the work already begun on the guest house, which I was doing as an English cottage. Larry was gone about a week and my only problem was with Verney who was giving everyone big aggravation because Hammschlager was back in town and too busy to talk to her or even me. Because right is right and I don't like to be pushed once I'm involved, I put it directly to Larry after he got back that if Hammschlager was too big we should think of bringing in someone else who wouldn't brush off the kid and us by promising a lot, leaving town and always being out when we called.

Larry agreed and got Verney on track by telling her how disappointed Simon would be if she copped out. Then, as if he was determined to foul things up for me, he got Verney interested in Simon's cottage. Now I had a pest on my hands.

The days we had cards from Simon things seemed to go better. Nevertheless, no matter how hard we tried, there was no possible way of having the cottage ready because plumbing was the worst problem, seeing as the guest house had never been built for long-term occupancy. Still, day by day in every way something got done, so my disappointment lay in not having the cottage finished for me to get Simon's reaction if he could've been taken directly to it when he got back. Now the pleasure wouldn't be so great for me.

Although Simon was only gone for not quite four weeks in all, Larry missed him right off, especially when he was in Mexico City and there was so much he began to remember that he worried day and night about Simon's getting along.

"You'd feel better if he just couldn't make it," I had to say. "If he had to be sent home on a hospital plane."

That made him more upset than mad. "I swear it, Joyce," he told me, "I'd like to wipe out the past two months and start all over again."

"Which would've meant Simon not going to Israel?" I asked.

That corked him. Then, very quiet, he asked if I wasn't worried about Simon, something happening to him, maybe some Arab nut throwing a grenade at a bus Simon was on, or the bus hitting a landmine? Both of these had happened to other busses. Also, look how Simon had turned on Super-Yid and thrown him out of his room because he said Super-Yid had to be the devil, seeing as he'd made him disobey God's voice. This didn't make sense to me, but Larry's worrying got me to see him as human, so I began to pray a little for nothing to happen to Simon. That way we all took an interest in writing him, and getting his mail, plus the work on the cottage even with Verney in the way, made things run lots more harmoniously.

Larry's worst attack of nervousness started the day before Simon was due back. But all of us were and this night I couldn't sleep as all sorts of things—from material swatches to English cottage chairs and the choices I had to make between Welsh dressers, plus four sets of dishes for his kitchen—were competing for attention in my mind. And as I looked back on the weeks Simon'd been gone, I had to admit that sometime during his absence we'd begun to function like a household, if not a family, and more and more I thought better of Larry because I wished I had a friend who felt so deeply about me. Someone I could feel that way about. Which may explain why I was so restless tonight, why I decided to enter Larry's room and talk to him. There were times I did that when Itzik was alive and toward the end it was as if I was talking to an uncle, sometimes even someone closer.

"I've been wondering lots tonight," I told Larry. "One curious question in particular."

"Namely?" he asked because I'd hesitated.

"Whether there's ever been another hood who got religion like Simon? I mean a Catholic or Protestant?"

That made Larry think too. "I don't know and don't care. Simon's Simon."

"You're telling me," I laughed. "Even today I got mail from a neighbor."

"You should've torn it up without reading it."

"You're wrong," I said. "She was one of the people who said welcome when we first moved in. She still wants to be friendly. How she found out he's gone to Israel, I don't know. But she wants us over for a visit after he gets back."

Larry shook his head. "Forget it."

"I came in to be friendly," I said. "And you're knocking me down. Can't you feel good when people around here still try to be friendly?"

"If I felt good about getting killed, I might," he said.

That froze me to the bone. Made my tongue cold iron. I wanted to speak but couldn't, and that made him look kinder.

"I didn't want to bother you," he said, "but very soon after Simon gets home we're visiting a vineyard up north."

It was one of the biggest efforts of my life to speak, but at last I managed. "They want to see us?" I asked very slowly.

"Me, Simon, you. And Verney." Even the shadows couldn't hide his worry. "Fred Rory'll be there."

"And Mike?"

"Fred Rory," Larry repeated.

I couldn't control my shivering. "I'm very cold," I said. "Can I get into bed with you?"

Larry thought about it for a second, no more. "Get in," he said.

The bed was a little narrower than a double so I had to lie close to Larry. Back to back. When I felt how warm his calves were I put my feet close to them. Finally he reached out to turn off the light and I got the feeling he was worried but not afraid. Then he whispered for me not to worry, everything would be all right, that a meeting might be best for all of us and it was good to get this over with right now, at the beginning, rather than some time later when things had gone so wrong they could only be corrected by wiping out everything in the problem.

"It's all Verney's fault," I said. "Everything began to go bad after she got your promise to help her."

"She's got nothing to do with the way things are," he objected. "With the kind of people around today. So go to sleep."

"No," I said. "Not yet."

"You're thirsty?" he asked and started to get up.

I pulled him back. "Don't ask me why I'm asking," I told him. "But don't you think it's time we really felt married?"

Did his shoulder lift in a little shrug? I don't know for sure. I didn't care.

"If that's what you want," he said.

"If you don't mind," I said, real tender-gender.

"No," he told me, "I don't mind."

I wish he'd sounded more excited. More romantic. But at my age, in menopause, although my gyn. man says I'm just about through the ordeal, I wasn't going to make too big a production about attitude, at least not to him. Also, it was late and he could be tired. Besides, I didn't exactly know what exactly to do, seeing as I didn't want to appear too professional.

CHAPTER SEVEN

LARRY: We made Western's morning flight to Sacramento—Joyce, me, Verney and Simon. An hour later I'd rented a car from a local u-drive operator at the airport, just like I'd been told, and drove more than fifty miles on Route 50 into the next county. We stopped at Placerville, then went on until we came to this little town, where I went in alone to the sheriff's substation and introduced myself to a deputy I'd been told to ask for. Once he was satisfied with my identification we shook hands friendly and he made me have a Coke while he telephoned Mr. Basqua's place. About five minutes later the deputy got into his own car—not one of the sheriff's—and we followed him another ten miles or so until we came to the Basqua Winery, a very nice place with a wine barrel the size of a truck outside the visitors' building. It was time to thank the deputy again and he said it was his pleasure because Mr. Basqua was one of the county's most prominent citizens, so anything the law could do to keep creeps from trespassing or bothering him were services he deserved.

While I got Joyce, Simon and Verney into the building's

tasting and hospitality rooms which led to the wine cellar, the deputy made another phone call, then came back to tell me that one of Mr. Basqua's men would be down for us in about forty-five minutes. This allowed time for a little tour given to special guests before Basqua's man arrived to drive ahead of us for maybe two miles through beautiful trees and vineyards, past a marker that told us an old gold mine was here, right next to a stream filled with stones to make little rapids. Finally we slowed up because the car ahead of us did, right at a caretaker's house, which controlled two of the largest wrought-iron gates I've ever seen. When we were through, the rest was simple. Just to keep driving up the shaded brick road to the hacienda.

Joyce wanted to make easy conversation as we unpacked in a guest bedroom, so she stood at the window and oohed over the view of vineyards all the way to the foothills and, most of all, about the clear sky absolutely free of smog. Standing next to Joyce, admitting that what I could see of at least a thousand acres was great, I couldn't help but think how Juan Concepción Basqua'd really made it. Three years before I was born, in 1924, Johnny Bucconeri decided to get out of Detroit and the heavy action that'd cost him a brother, two cousins, a brother-in-law, some good friends and associates. He'd won the action, made his point. Still he sold out at about thirty cents on the dollar, which was a real bargain for the buyer. But that made him glad, Johnny let people know.

Right after he made the sale, paid taxes, bought a letter of credit and attended to loose ends, he left for Arkansas where his name was legally changed to Juan Concepción Basqua. Then his four daughters, wife and he got back on the train until the last stop. San Francisco.

Thanks to Prohibition, a couple of months later Señor Basqua moved his family to a vineyard he'd bought at a give-away price. Then the vineyard was about half or less the size of now. Since then, mostly during the Depression and right through the World War, he'd grabbed up property, lots of it taken from the Japs all over California after they were shipped off to the what many people now call concentration camps. Came boom times and he sold off maybe half his holdings for tract house developments, shopping centers of which he always took a piece, schools, some people say at least twenty miles of freeways all told, stuff like that. But he also donated two big parcels to cities. One for a school, the other for a hospital. He also bought a lot of the hospital's equipment and paid for the school's playground and twenty school busses which he kept exchanging every three years. Naturally, while he was becoming a big wheel in the county, he was also becoming one of the richest men in the state. But right from the start, how could he miss when he could get all the stoop labor he needed for the vineyard for next to nothing? And after the Depression started, he could've had it for about nothing? But there was something else. Basqua staked a college professor of agriculture while he invented a better grape brick.

On every dollar Basqua took in he kept books, paid taxes, spread around the right amount of juice and charity, and banked heavy millions up to the end of 1928, which was just before the country fell on its ass. By that time Basqua had maybe ten–eleven million, not a penny of which was lost in the market or banks. You see, starting in January, 1929, his study of economic conditions and believing every word in *Babson's Reports* convinced him to get his money out of the market. Also out of deposit in banks and into vaults.

From what I understand, lots of big people lost theirs in the crash and when some of the people he'd sold out to, as well as other hyenas, heard how Johnny Bucconeri was now some sort of multimillionaire rancher in California, they tried to put a heavy arm on him. It got them nowhere. How can you touch a man the law's interested in protecting? A man who could round up a couple of hundred vigilantes to run people out of the county if they were lucky enough not to get killed for being squatters? California could be mighty rough on Okies and Arkies and communist agitators. So Basqua would just let it be known that the people bothering him were all three.

Then it occurred to somebody with a brain in the East—maybe Costello himself, seeing as in 1929 he got Adonis, Capone, Frank Erickson, Bugs Moran who really hated Capone for what he'd done that year to celebrate St. Valentine's Day, and some other big people to agree they were in business, and killing'd given them bad names and worse publicity—to realize how Basqua deserved everything he had. Why? Because he was smart. Two more things—he wasn't bucking anyone for territory and he'd even got the law to defend him. So it would be very stupid to kill off a man who'd really studied the country, understood its machinery, and was making it pay healthy dividends when everyone agreed it was very sick, maybe even dying.

After the first apes who tried to cut into Basqua were found permanently out of breath hundreds of miles from his place, certain thinking people here and there put the word out to let him alone. Not only was he too tough to touch, most important, he was smart and needed. Muscle was cheap. Brains came high. And Basqua had the kind our people had to protect for their own good.

"You're not worried, I hope?" is what I asked Joyce who was putting some of her things in a closet.

"Let me show you how much I'm not worried," Joyce said as she reached into a piece of her matched luggage for two nightgowns to show me. "Which should I wear tonight?"

"They're both pretty." I was glad I could make myself sound pleased. "So maybe—no, you might's well wear neither."

How she loved that. Since the night before Simon got home, when I let her into my bed and she invited me to go the whole route, living with Joyce'd become lots easier. No one has to tell me how up to then she and maybe other people in the States kind of got the idea I'd gone gay. What they probably never stopped to figure was how I never liked paying for it, wasn't going to mix it up with native amateurs since that can get you killed by their relatives, and staying out of sight eliminated lady tourists. Besides, like everyone else who's living, I was growing older, slowing down, no longer burning so hot about most things, so needing it less. Which is why Rory's coming to see me in Mexico City with news of my being picked as Joyce's husband bothered me on lots of counts, one of the most important being how I'd have to service her. And she was one of the last people in the world I could stand laughing at me. So you can understand how relieved I first felt when Joyce said she wanted no part of me. And when she asked that night, what made me feel best was being able rather than the actual. This was something she'd never know.

We agreed to keep our separate rooms and in the week since Simon'd been home she came once into my bedroom and once I paid a courtesy call on her. Joyce said she liked my style, so now both of us walked through the common sitting room because the door on her side was unlocked. But we also knocked first.

"Larry"—at last I heard her—"what were you thinking of?"

"Something very important," I told the truth. "How you'd look in those nightgowns," I lied.

The next second she had both arms around me and her head was tilted back for a kiss. She got one and the tip of her tongue in my mouth had a nice flavor.

"Too bad we have to go down now," she said. "I'm in the mood for a matinee."

"Your mood'll have to keep," I said as I patted her ass. "We're expected right down."

"The don?" she asked, sort of put out.

"I hope you didn't mean that in the family way," I warned her.

"As far as I'm concerned he's Mexican, or Spanish." Joyce liked my joke. "And from what I've seen of this room and a little else, I want to see the rest of the house."

"Hacienda," I corrected her.

"Hacienda," she repeated, then suddenly looked sad. "Itzik used to make a joke out of that word. He'd say he was going to move south of the border and buy a Mexican"—she slowed down to pronounce the next words right—"*heisse-yenta*. It wasn't much of a joke," she said, "but I usually tried to laugh. Especially after he began to feel bad."

"That was his sense of humor," I said. "Not very good. Which brings up something I've been meaning to ask."

"Yes?"

"Did Itzik ever mention us? Mitch, me or Simon? Shimmy or Feivel?"

"Never."

"You're sure?"

"I'll swear on anything you say," she was serious. "From the first day he came to see me, when he talked some about Mitch and more about Winnie, he never mentioned them again. And he never once talked about you or Simon."

I let go of her. "Which reminds me—"

"Yes again?"

"Simon's making a big thing of our not going to his plot," I said.

Joyce looked into a full-length mirror to smooth her dress. "We'll do that. I promise. Soon after we get home."

We found Simon and Verney outside at a little stand before a large cage Joyce called an aviary. It was taller than the tree inside it, which I'd say was over thirty feet. The cage was filled with birds, some of them very beautiful, and Simon and Verney were picking them out with the help of the colored pictures under glass with their Latin, Spanish and English names. Verney said it was real neat. I picked out a couple of birds from the pictures, Joyce also, then we noticed a servant standing near us. Like others we'd seen, he was dressed in a good charro costume, the real thing, not what nightclub musicians or dancers wear. Very *por favor* he told us drinks were being served in the tack room. He didn't ask if we wanted a drink, just told us where they were and seemed to know we'd follow him up the path. Joyce looked a little scared so I took her arm, and with Simon and Verney behind we followed the servant, and all the while compelling myself to talk, to point at this and that while I said things about the weather, flowerbeds, a big bronze sundial and a tile chapel like those you see all over Mexico. A pair of little brass cannons and a carved stone watering trough filled with flowers were really nice.

The servant stepped aside and Joyce exclaimed when we entered the tack room which was about half again larger than her living room, which's a good fifty feet. Since we moved into Joyce's place I'd begun to learn something about things, so Joyce didn't have to tell me how great this room and the rest of this was. The floor was random-width mahogany planking, tongued and grooved and pegged. One wall was of old red brick with light whitewash. The ceiling was about twelve feet, I'd say, with fine dark beams shaped by hand, and the fireplace in the brick wall was walk-in, with the sort of highback benches they have in old costume movies whose plots call for classy inns or castles. There were brass bridle badges on one section of paneled wall between the windows covered with Spanish shutters, hundreds of them for sure, and the chairs and sofas were leather and wood, with nothing bulky about them. A saloon bar with a polished brass foot rail was off in one corner with an antique brass slot machine near it. There also was a beautiful wheel of fortune that Joyce said was unique. A pool table near the bar wasn't in anyone's way.

I've told how Joyce exclaimed when we entered the room, then we both groaned a little because the entire effect was spooked by our noticing Fred Rory at the bar, who called us *amigos* and said it was good to see us as a married twosome.

"Let's get a real look at you," he held out his arms and hurried toward us. "Simon, Verney, Larry," he mentioned each of us and made a thing out of kissing Joyce's cheek with a big smacking sound. "You make a nice family group."

I'd never liked Rory. Long ago, when we were first getting started, his uncle was Itzik's personal attorney, had been for a long time. From what I was given to understand, the uncle looked the way movie studios expected people from Boston to be—with class written all over them. How he took on Itzik and some of Itzik's connections I never found out. But after he died, his nephew—Fred Rory—took over the practice and whether or not you liked Rory, some plus-things had to be said for him. Among them were that he looked like a man with the best ancestors. He was smart, worked hard and forgot nothing. Also, he represented some of the biggest.

Still, I remembered Rory as someone who'd come to Vegas as Itzik's guest after I was phoned to give him the super red-carpet treatment. The charges which were to be put on Itzik's bill would tell how well I'd taken care of the young lawyer. Lucky for me Harry Freund drove in that same weekend with two starlets—are whores ever called anything else in Hollywood?—and both of them were more than willing to ball the very important visitor who'd come west to see how the natives did it. One of them—a really imaginative chick—now got about a half million a picture, which had to be turned over to her on the first day of principal photography, plus a percentage of the gross collected right at the box office. It made me laugh, Joyce too, because she couldn't do anything but wet her lips, which was the extent of her acting, but I guess the hot-shot johns who wear Bunny Club tie-tacks, swing their Bunny key chains and serve drinks with tit-shaped cubes think she's the greatest. There sure are an awful lot of Anaheim swingers in the country.

On one of the nights I saw Rory in Mexico City—when I went to his suite at the Maria Isabel because I didn't want Simon upset by anything he might have to say—he got pretty sauced up and just as confidential. After he told me about the starlet now a star, who I'd never ever thought of because I saw few pictures in theaters, he suddenly began to bawl how she'd been the most marvelous lay of his life. So he'd got rid of the other broad to be alone with the greatest hump since it was invented. And at that time she was more beautiful, a hell of a lot fresher and she'd done everything for him—things he didn't believe possible—not because she was told to, she wanted to. Why? Because she liked him, so that he'd actually thought of marrying her. In Vegas it could've been done in five minutes, then he'd have all her goodies forever, with nobody else sharing. But while he was patting her head because she was nibbling away at him so specially, he got to thinking it could be a disaster to marry someone who might actually be a part-time whore and had learned what she knew through lots of practice. Besides, before she got down to sending him first-class around the world, she'd already said enough to make him realize she was career crazy about the movies, was going to use screwing better than anyone else to get her places, so she wouldn't think of going east of the city hall. And the practice wouldn't allow him to move west.

So he'd gone home, never able to forget the broad, even after almost twenty years. When he finally married it was to a girl with more family than looks, who at the very first time turned her head aside, bit the knuckle of her left thumb and acted like she was being sacrificed. And she still was doing that. There weren't any children to pay him off. And with all the big-shot laymen and priests she had in her family, he didn't dare even think of divorce, let alone mention it. So memory of the past, how he lived today and how he had to live until death did them part were enough to keep him crying until that happy funeral day, which in a way was my fault because he'd met Harry and the girls through me.

The people most intolerant of people who drink, smoke, jerk off, shoot dope—name it—are the people who've quit. Drinking used to be my monkey, so I'm especially hard on drunks who talk too much. Besides, the way he told me about his wife, how she was built, which I think should be private even if what he said about her was true, made me like him even less.

But he was important. Only someone who rated would be here. And the way he moved behind the bar gave me the feeling that this wasn't even close to the first time he'd been Basqua's guest.

Rory dismissed the bartender and made a big thing of giving Verney a little sherry. After she took it and nudged me to move away from the bar, she whispered if I didn't think he was a big, gabby prick? I warned her not to ask again. Back at the bar I smiled at Rory and snowed him how I'd taken an antihistamine for some sort of allergy, so even the smallest drink would start me snoring. I took some soda on the rocks and Simon had the same. Joyce did too, which made Rory laugh that since we were the straightest family group he'd met in years, he was going to join us in the simple life.

Because I didn't know what else Rory might remember and start talking about, I kept my hand on his arm while I asked how he'd got here, what did he think of the country and this place, what the weather was like back East, when was the last time he used the subway, was it true that come night they had cops riding every subway train in the city, with more cops on every station platform? Even what he thought Humphrey's chances were against Nixon. Not that I cared about politics or ever voted in my life, but I thought this might keep him talking the longest about something that couldn't hurt us. It did. He started off pretty good on how the country should've elected Goldwater because Johnson, that son of a bitch who'd gone around thinking the country was his spread, with us citizens as his hired hands and the army as his gunslingers, had done all the things bad in the war that Goldwater would've done good.

Red in the face and no longer caring about anything but cursing Johnson and Humphrey and all the nigger-loving Democrats he had to ride with on the commuter trains, Rory leaned across the bar to shake my shoulders and give me a good smell of his Sen-Sen breath. And he only let go of me when Juan Basqua was almost at the bar.

"Let's not talk politics yet," Basqua said as he lifted Rory's hands off my shoulders. "Not until we get acquainted." He greeted us with a smile a lot more genuine than the caps on his teeth. "Let me see if I can pick you out without introduction," he said.

We sat on bar stools, Rory wiped at his sweated-up face with a bar towel, and Basqua walked up and down. He was a handsome seventy, I'd say, just middle height, standing very straight, thin, with black and silver hair cut sort of short. He wore a short whipcord charro jacket, matching pants, polished cordovan boots, a white shirt and maroon string tie. No jewelry except a simple marriage ring and this big belt buckle that had to be gold. His complexion was the refined brown of people you'd accept as Spanish aristocrats. So with his dark brown eyes, a thin nose and mouth, and little ears close to his head, I could see him as the handsome grandfather of Zorro in a TV series. But his eyes impressed me most. They were intelligent. And when he spoke it was with the voice and pronunciation of someone just as good as Hugh Downs, who I like to listen to mornings.

Like anyone who's smart, he knew exactly when to end the game he was playing with us. So he said Simon had to be the man with the beard, Verney had to be the pretty teen-ager, Joyce had to be the beautiful lady in the tailored dress. By the process of elimination I had to be Larry. That was it because right then a servant came in to announce dinner. It was only five but Basqua explained he liked to eat early. Then if he stayed up late he could enjoy a light supper.

His dining room table was longer than Joyce's but narrow just like they are in Mexico, and Basqua told us something I already knew—that narrow tables made it easier to pass things across. What surprised me most was Rory not being at the table with us, which Basqua explained very simply. He wanted to be alone with us, to see us as a family, because his wife was dead and his daughters were married and living abroad. Two in Paris, one in Majorca and the other at Estoril, which Joyce whispered to me were in Spain and Portugal. But I knew where Majorca was.

"It's nice to visit them," Basqua told us after he let me know two more guests were arriving next day. "So twice a year I go abroad for a month or six weeks. It's always a temptation to stay longer. But I like my home, my vineyards, this area," he continued, "even if some people think it's too dull, too quiet. However, quiet isn't dullness."

Basqua let that sink in and nodded after I shook my head to let him know his message was received and understood. Then he changed the subject by turning directly to Simon to assure him again that everything to eat off before him was brand-new and how he'd flown a Jewish cook from San Francisco to fix his kosher meals. Now he expected something in return—for Simon to tell what his trip to Israel was like. Which was all Simon needed to make him talk his head off how he'd blown the *shofar* at the end of his congregation's Yom Kippur services at the Wailing Wall. How he'd gone everywhere, even to the Golan Heights where he'd said *Kaddish* for the dead Israeli soldiers. How his heart broke at the memorial dedicated to the six million Jews murdered by Hitler. How he screamed when he saw what the Arabs did to the old Jewish cemeteries, and how in one of them, on the Mount of Olives, he'd found eight Bronstein graves and three named Waldbaum, which was his mother's family name. He didn't know if they were relatives, there was no way of finding out, but they were the same name, they might've been *landsleit*, and the graves had to be restored. So he'd pledged ten thousand dollars to do it, and other graves were to be fixed up if there was money left over. He'd pledged another five thousand to plant trees, another two for the Hadassah Hospital and a couple of thousand more to *kibbutzim*. All told, about twenty thousand. Plus another five for a Sefer Torah he wanted to donate to his *shul*. Since he had the money, he told me to tell Mike to prepare the certified checks. I hadn't argued.

"It was the most wonderful experience of my life," Simon said. "Which is why I want to go back again and again."

Basqua nodded. "You should."

"I will." Simon was excited but he motioned for me not to worry because he had control of himself. "Just before Passover there's an *oleh-b'regel*. That means a walk to Jerusalem by thousands of people. It takes three days. Before I die I must be one of them."

"Maybe you should go to live there," Basqua suggested.

Again Simon gestured for me to keep out of it. "I'd like to," he said after some slow shakes of his head. "But I'm not going alone. So I'll stay here with Larry. Maybe, God willing, he'll go with me next time. And you know," he added, "I'm beginning to feel less guilty about myself, even though I know I've been forgiven. I was a hood. But governments in the United Nations are supposed to be civilized. And they're not."

So we got through the dinner without incident and Basqua made Simon his friend for life by saying the next time there was a drive for funds Simon should let him know immediately because he wanted to make a sizable contribution. We had coffee and liqueurs in Basqua's library, a room filled with real books. After Simon and Verney went to their rooms we sat with Basqua, who'd ordered a fire started. Nothing was said for maybe ten minutes. We were thinking, he was smoking a cigar and also thinking, I guess, how to get going with us.

"We have to begin somewhere," he said at last. "Personally, I'd rather begin by saying how I've always admired you for destroying the microfilm than by repeating what some people who knew Itzik Yanowitz think of you."

"Which is exactly what?" Joyce asked.

She sat next to me, close, and her hand was cold in mine. "Start with the worst," I suggested to Basqua.

"As you say," he agreed. "Well, it's their opinion that it's your ambition to become a feature story in *Life* or *Look*."

I wanted to laugh but settled for a smile. "Who'd want me?" I asked.

"Any editor if you'd boost circulation," he said. "Now we've had people—some I once knew—who've made these magazines.

But they're not our breed. Our breed," he repeated for emphasis. "Am I understood?"

I kept squeezing Joyce's hand to make it warmer. "To the letter," I said.

"Good," he said with a little gesture of salute. "Very good." He paused again, looked at Joyce and stood to stir the fire after he squeezed some sort of oil onto the logs to make colored flames. "We're still in preliminaries," he said, "although I think I can assure at least one of the men who'll be here tomorrow that you certainly don't want public attention. So, now a question from me. Did my invitation frighten you?" he asked us.

"When Larry told me about it I got the idea it was an order," Joyce told him.

"I'm sorry," Basqua said.

"But not so much now," she added.

That made him look happy again. "And you?" he asked me. "I know it didn't frighten Simon or your daughter," he went on. "But you?"

"I'm shaky," I admitted. "Because you said it tonight. Quiet isn't dullness. And we sure haven't been quiet."

"Or dull." He smiled before he tapped the long ash from his cigar. "I wish I could say otherwise," he said to Joyce. "But I don't think your daughter's talented or particularly bright. Still, from what I've been told, both can be assets in what she's chosen to do."

Joyce looked at me and knew she could say anything. That we were here to level. It might get us killed, but not being honest with Basqua was a quicker way to make sure we were. So she still made me hold her hand.

"I don't want any of it," she said. "I think it's crazy. No matter how she behaves now, she was an awful awful slut. I think that shocks you, Mr. Basqua?" she asked. "But you told us to be frank."

"In everything," Basqua agreed. "So if we can improve your

relationship with Verney, things are bound to go better." He looked directly at Joyce until she nodded, which told him and me enough. "Now this brings us to Larry promising to help Verney. His promise involved Fred Rory after the fact. He involved Mr. Hammschlager, who hasn't made a good impression on you."

"He snowed us, Mr. Basqua," I said. "Or am I wrong?"

"He was out of the country," Basqua avoided my question. "Now he's back."

"We know," Joyce said. "And I'm glad we didn't stand on one foot waiting for him to return Larry's calls. Even a couple of mine."

"He wouldn't unless I approved. And I hadn't approved," Basqua told us. He drew on his cigar, blew a ring, then put it aside. "But if I'm satisfied with our discussion tonight and tomorrow, things'll start."

I began to breathe easier because what Basqua had just said meant there might be tough talk, even threats, but no cut-off action. But Joyce didn't get it, or if she did, she still had to make a thing of how we still had sight-seers on our block. How tour busses now passed her house very slow.

"That'll stop," Basqua assured her. "And you should thank Veronica. Why? Because," he answered Joyce's look, "her silly—all right, stupid—ambitions can make life better for all of you." He was about to pick up his cigar again, then changed his mind. "She might even be of service to other people you'll never meet."

"Verney? Of service?" Joyce didn't believe what she was hearing. "That girl never did anything good for anyone. And that includes me."

Basqua's laugh was real pleasant as he motioned for Joyce to relax, which she didn't do. "Through Verney we'll find out just how much of you, and us, the public is ready to take. And that's a very big service."

"What you've just told us has given me a very big headache," Joyce said as she got up and sort of pushed my hand aside. "Could I be excused? I'll find my way up," she said to us, and especially me. "So, good night."

We sat quietly after Joyce left and when at last I looked at Basqua to see how he'd taken Joyce's walking out—really on him—he shook his head for me not to worry. He was a father, had been one for a long time, so he understood how a mother felt whose daughter was rotten.

"Juan," I began. "I'm sure you know about Verney? All right then," I went on after he nodded. "We've got to get the kid started on her career. Unless we do I'll take bets that she starts popping. And no matter what Joyce says about Verney —I've got the feeling that would kill her."

"It probably would," Basqua said after a second. "And if she wasn't one of us—I'd say let them both die."

I had a very sick feeling that I was standing with a man who, when he was Johnny Bucconeri, could've fed people into an oven if he had to. Now, as Basqua, he could order the stoking up of a lot more ovens, even press, if he had to, a red button that would kill a million people. And he seemed to understand how I felt because he began to speak very slow, very calm and warm, how we had a right to live as much as the next man, especially if we stopped belting him around. How all the talk of paying a debt to society was crap, as I'd probably figured out for myself. How with things going as they were, with more and more crazy kids wanting nothing from us but drugs, and less and less people wanting any of our other stock, this was a golden time for us to split the so-called crime-syndicate scene. There were plenty of legit valuables lying around just begging to be picked up.

"You're heavy in the market?" he asked me.

"Sort of," I said.

"You've ever read Eliot Janeway?" When I shook my head, Basqua sighed. "He's a very bright man. So listen to me because I'm listening to him the way I used to listen to Roger Babson. Sell out as soon as you get home. No questions," he went on. "Pay your capital gains and put the rest of the money in the bank until I tell you to move. At the right time you'll buy back and probably double your holdings."

This was drastic stuff. "You're serious?" I asked.

"I'm never anything else about money. There's an election coming up," he said. "I don't think either candidate is big enough to handle the war, smog, garbage and the kids. With no place in any city safe. So they'll panic and when they do, we'll be the handiest scapegoats. And one particular thing they might do could give us the kind of trouble that thinking about makes my head spin."

"Like what?" I asked because it was obvious he wanted me to.

"Like passing legislation that money made in organized crime can't be put into legitimate business ventures," he said. "So hope and pray they don't get around to it before the bottom falls out. And it will, Larry, it will."

"All right," I said, "I'll get out. Meantime, would I be way off if I figured that we're not in your problem book?"

"Not even near it. Or on the same shelf. Or section of shelves," he told me.

"Thanks," I said. "Since we're part of a pilot project, I want to know more about what we're—I'm—supposed to do. But could it keep 'til tomorrow?" I asked. "Suddenly I'm tired and too tired to think."

So we said good night, but seeing as it was only past ten, Basqua told me he was gonna read for an hour. But we made up to meet at eleven, right after late breakfast, when we'd split into two parties. Joyce, Verney and Simon would go on a tour of the vineyards while Basqua took me around alone.

In our room Joyce still complained of a headache, so did I mind not? I made like I did, which started to change her mind. This gave me a chance to play hero, so I said it'd keep. Before Joyce got into bed I got her to take some aspirin. She thanked me by saying that if she woke up during the night and felt better, I was going to find out how much. News like this tempted me to say she should also take a batch of sleeping pills.

CHAPTER EIGHT

VERNEY: Really, I should've worn a granny dress because it felt so old-fashioned being laid by someone using a cundrum. But then Mr. Fred Rory was a conservative straight. And are you ready for this? Imagine him turning away while he slipped it on. Such modesty. Still it gave me time to take the braces off my teeth and wrap them in my dress. For my first experience with the social-security generation, he wasn't bad. But that doesn't mean he was good. Matter of record, although I'd warmed myself up, he never came near tripping my switch, which I wouldn't've minded because we were doing it sort of out-of-doors and it was pretty cold. But because I didn't want him to feel let down, frustrated or out of it, you should've seen and heard my blue acting, the way I wriggled and moaned and made like biting him. He couldn't help but believe he was scoring right on target, which was good for him as well as me. So my performance, all porno theater, kept him hard after he was through, which made him feel great even while he became modest again.

Then reality. He turned toward me again, kneeling sort of

and looking kind of dumb, confused, even shivering a little, not exactly knowing what to do because you just don't throw something like that away anywhere in Basqua's ghost town. This little decision scene ended when he wrapped it in a handkerchief that he stuck in his pocket while he told me he was going to wash and keep it as a souvenir of a sweet childwoman who'd made him so happy and proud. This gave me the perfect opportunity to thank him and say—now that we'd got through to each other—how I expected to be more than a good-time memory to him. Because I expected him to do what he said, which was to get sincerely in touch with this big star I don't think's so great, but that doesn't matter. Mr. Rory said he knew her before she was famous, had basically done with her what he'd done with me, but not on a falling-apart horse blanket in a pretty damn-cold cave. With her it was in a very nice suite at the gambling joint Larry'd once run with Bull, long before he became my Uncle Simon.

"Yes," he'd told me as we drove away that afternoon, right in the middle of lunch because the two men who'd been at the table had just about flipped out at Larry, Joyce, Simon—even me, "yes indeedy, I've a great idea. Libby Dorne, who most men say is a great idea." He laughed at his joke, seemed disappointed that it didn't amuse me, so went on. "I knew Libby when she was just getting started. Knew her as well as a man can ever get to know a woman." That made him take his right hand off the steering wheel. Then, faking the sympathy bit, casual-like he dropped it on the inside of my left knee, where he patted a couple of times. "You understand?"

Sure I did. I was riding in a station wagon with a Dirty Old Man, but I still was pretty shaken up, almost wigged out, because of the small war that I'd left behind at Señor Basqua's king-size dining room table. We'd all got back to the hacienda around two o'clock and just about three went to the dining room for late lunch. And there were those two men standing near the sideboard, oinking very hard at each other, laughing a lot and slapping each other's back when they weren't wiping at their eyes. Once in a while they turned to Basqua, who stood near them with his hands clasped behind, also smiling and laughing, and they'd say something which might also make him laugh harder, but always like a gentleman. Both men were more'n sixty, I'd say, sort of chunky the way truckmen or stevedores who move heavy things get to be, I guess, and they had lots of chins and loud ties. Then as one of them noticed us with Fred Rory, he grabbed the other man's arm and both of them stopped laughing as if we were giving off very bad vibes. This made Basqua turn around and say hello before we were introduced to Marty Grobbernasch, who was taller, and George Atkinson, which I knew right off wasn't his name because he looked hard Italian and had that kind of voice—hoarse and tough.

They were ice cold to Joyce, sort of brushed me off as bad scene, were surly mean to Rory and you could see plain-out how they hated Larry and Simon so much they wouldn't even touch their hands.

Fireworks started right after the entree was served and Mr. Basqua dismissed the help. Grobbernasch told Larry how he'd hated Uncle Itzik for the longest time, ever since Itzik did something to make Mr. and Mrs. Fat Dovel disappear in spite of one, their being his closest friends and two, Fat Dovel being one of his closest business partners. And Atkinson growled how he'd been related to a Mr. Joe Foggia, also a partner of Itzik's and supposed to be his boss, and how Itzik had helped do him in, which was why Itzik'd done time, but not nearly enough. I knew Itzik had been in for something to do with murder. Now I knew that the victim, Mr. Joe Foggia, had been one of the most important people around, a Mr. Untouchable, so most everyone thought. Good old Itzik, he never bothered with easy things or small change.

Then these two jungle-land specimens started in on Simon, how he might be fooling lots of dummies but they weren't stupes, so what was with this religious act? Was he selling phony Bibles door to door? And if he was really bugged out on religion he should sign up with a Jew monastery and keep off the streets where he caused trouble and the bringing back up of old history nobody wanted remembered, like certain papers publishing an old mug shot of him to compare with how he looked now. The old mug shot looked better, they said to insult Simon. Then they started again on Larry about all the money he'd lifted and because Joyce was with him then, she was also a crook along with everything else she'd been. Finally, and before I could get a lot of glow out of what they were doing to Joyce, they started to claw me. Like what made me believe I had a talent? Thinking that proved how bad I need a head transplant. And where the hell was my sense of real to want publicity that in the end could only let people find out what kind of an old tramp a young kid could be, when in their time a girl my age, if she was decent, thought a baby was born from her mother's knee? Wrap it all up, I was nothing but the worst kind of female bum, but what could anyone expect considering the kind of people responsible for putting me here? And the kind of hoogies who'd taken my father's place?

Get this, first they scared me dumb, at least for a while, because from what I'd heard at home and coming up in the car from Sacramento, we were visiting Señor Basqua to be looked over for his keep-on-breathing approval. And if we didn't get it—the consolation prize might be the best cosmetic jobs undertakers could give us. So after we got here and I saw how the place was run like a kingdom with everyone taking orders from one man only, saw how big the place was with cops on the outside protecting it and all sorts of places on the inside to hide things forever like in old mine shafts, those big cellars and elephant-sized barrels, I realized how if we didn't pass the test we could disappear and never be found. The car? Anyone could drive it back to Sacramento where Larry'd rented it from this special man. So he'd say Larry had brought it back. The flight to L.A.? Four people could get on the plane with our tickets, two men and two women. We'd left Beverly Hills in a cab. We'd planned to take one home. And somewhere between L.A. International and our house—we'd disappeared. They might even put someone on the plane who was fat, with a beard and wearing a Jewish beanie. Someone like me, with braces on her teeth. So we were gone. And how would they find us? But who'd really care enough to look hard for us?

Now I must admit that Larry had briefed us—maybe ten times, maybe more—how there was nothing to worry about, but he didn't look or sound confident. And after the way those monsters began to tear us apart at the table, I actually began to wet my pants. Just a little because I'd become so worked up that I screamed and had to call them what'd gotten me beat up by Larry, and that saved me from sitting or standing in a puddle. Still, I was absolutely terrified, more that than anything else, which is why I threw my water glass at them, but it only made Atkinson a little wet, maybe no more than me. Everyone was on their feet and I heard Mr. Basqua tell Mr. Rory to take me for a drive someplace while at the same time, like a king would, he ordered everyone to shut up and sit down. Still, while Mr. Rory actually dragged me away still screaming how I'd like to stomp those two old bastards in the dining room, I began to cry because I was scared of maybe being wiped out to save everyone else. You see—no me, no career, no publicity. Also, it hurts to be looked at as if I was a worm in front of people you're trying to impress or like. And I did like Simon and thought I could also like Mr. Basqua because he spoke so nice and looked noble.

Mr. Rory was nice too. He asked if I had to go and when I said yes he waited outside my room while I got out of my wet pantyhose, cleaned up, washed my face and put on fresh briefs cut like bikinis. I didn't bother with stockings. Then we went out front, got back into the station wagon he'd driven a while ago and started toward the old ghost town which we'd gone through earlier without stopping.

Suddenly I was crying like crazy again, so Rory started to tell me a sort of interesting story about Mr. Basqua, who got started in ranching by making this most famous of all grape bricks. What's for sure, after those tight-ass Tooleyville-types in Congress stopped people from buying their hang-up right out in the open, there were grape bricks around. But they were sort of too big, Rory went on to explain, smelled bad, what they made tasted awful, and what was worst of all, the bricks were made under unsanitary conditions, so that if you didn't die right off you could be sick for the rest of your miserable life. But even before Basqua got to California, he'd already met this mad-scientist-type professor who got this laboratory going on the ranch where they made concentrated grape bricks, most of them no larger than bars of old-fashioned laundry soap, the kind Uncle Simon told me he remembered his mother using when she boiled wash on a gas stove. Made under spotless conditions, bricks and something called wine yeast were sold together for five dollars wholesale. With production and including the cost of the grapes, planting, harvest and all—it worked out to about a four-dollar profit before taxes. And it was all legitimate, because the wrapper on every grape brick warned how it was against federal and state laws to add a certain amount of pure water to make the brick dissolve. That it was against the law to add wine yeast and sugar to the mix. And certainly against the law to build up the stuff —which could ferment up to fifteen percent alcohol—with specified quantities of illegal booster because that could make wine whose alcohol could average up to thirty-five percent per batch. And absolutely against the law to let the batch stand for a certain number of days before it was put into casks. Then any way you looked at it, absolutely forbidden to let the batch stay in casks for a certain time until it was put into bottles and stored at certain temperatures before drinking or selling the stuff, which was also forbidden by law.

Basqua never allowed a grape brick or yeast package to be opened anywhere on his land. Matter of fact, he got some top San Francisco and Seattle distributors to guarantee their taking between three and four million bricks a year, with prices starting at his loading sheds and in their trucks. All legitimate, all within the law, because the wrappers told what the bricks and yeast were really sold for. Like to flavor ice cream, to be used in baking pies, cookies and bread, like for mixing with soda water. Like they could even be used to make paints and dyes, and instructions for these were included with the package.

Even though I laughed some at Rory's telling, I was still sobbing a little, still was scared a lot more, so he kept on driving slow, talking kind to me, until I spoke up.

"Is something bad gonna happen to us or me?" I asked him.

"Of course not," he said.

"Swear it," I said.

"I swear." He raised his hand, kissed his lips and crossed himself, which made me laugh a little. "They were just letting off steam. Nothing more. I'll swear to that."

"My father, I mean my real father, would've killed them." You see, that's how I wanted to think of him.

"If this was another time Larry would too. So would Uncle Simon and your Uncle Fred. That's me," he tapped his chest. "Introducing your Uncle Fred."

"So many relatives," I said. "But not one did anything when they insulted me. Not even my umbilical connection." I tucked one leg under and turned toward him. "I sure was waiting for one of them to call her a big whore. Then I would've shown them how I'd do more for her than she does for me."

"Show them or Don Basqua?" he asked.

He was brains all right, so I kept quiet because that also helped me catch hold of my breath. Those apes. They had to be seen. Still, Mr. Rory had sworn everything was gonna be all right. As for showing them, I had Mr. Basqua but also Uncle Simon first in mind. At least I want to think so. So Mr. Rory kept on driving, kept on dropping his hand on my knee and around it more often, squeezing a little harder every so often. To help out, I'd move away then inch toward him on the seat as if I wasn't aware of what he was doing because everything he said was so comforting I had to hear it real close to him.

"To show all of you," I said as his hand fitted itself real comfortable right behind my knee. "Because none of them seem able to do anything either for themselves or me. If like you say, I'm not gonna get zapped, I've a mind to go it alone."

That was when Rory let go my leg to snap his fingers and say he had a noble idea. See, there was this star—Libby Dorne —who I knew of, so I nodded, and he was an old and intimate friend of hers. Not that he'd been in recent touch, but they were still close friends, so he knew she'd help anyone he sent to her because up to now he'd never sent anyone, which would prove to Miss Dorne how I was someone special.

"Just how close a friend is Miss Dorne?" I asked him.

He puffed his lips before he gave me a Mission-Impossible smile that comes at the finish after everyone's got safe outa the basement. "Legs-around-my-back friends," he laid it right on. "Is there anything closer than that?"

"Not unless you go to live inside her." I patted his hand as it went back to higher above my knee. "Still, why should she want to do anything for me?"

"Three reasons," he said and squeezed three times. "First, because I ask her. Then I'll get Mr. Basqua to speak to Mr. Hammschlager. And Libby'll certainly listen to him. But before they get in touch I'll call and arrange for me to see her personally."

"To fuck her again?" I said that to shake and rev him up good. "But that'd be no time to talk about me."

Rory made I-like-it, I-like-it sounds. "It's exciting to hear you talk that way. Even if it bothers me."

"Suppose I said you were paying Miss Dorne a visit to Rory her again. Or to do some Basquaing? Does that sound better than fuck or fucking her again?" My question startled him enough to snap that roaming hand of his right back to the steering wheel. "You squares," I said in a kind way. "That includes Larry too." To calm him down I brushed at the hair behind his ear, then ran my nails down his graying sideburn. "You're so hung up on words. Is that because you're not so well hung like you used to be?"

By then there was this old mining town, so we got out to look around before he could get car-seat ideas. It was funky junky out there, very quiet, with grass and weeds growing between some of the boards of the old wooden sidewalks, but all-in-all pretty clean. We peeked into some store windows, went into the sheriff's office and I got into one of the cells while Rory made believe he locked me in so I had to listen—which I did—as he went on that everything was all right, no one was getting hurt, how he really wanted to help me and knew enough about what I wanted to do to realize my determination was real. And while he didn't know how good I'd be, he was willing to say I'd do all right, especially if the right doors were opened and important money—the kind Larry talked of—was spent on my package which he was becoming more and more interested in. Still, any help I could get wouldn't hurt, which was why, this very trip, he was going to get in touch with Libby Dorne.

While he yakked on I kept my hands on the bars and made expressions of sadness, hope, slow believing, wonder, excitement, more joy than you can get by shooting up if that's your bag—just like I'd been coached in dramatics by the last teacher who I'd had fired after he said I was plain and simple lousy—before I gave him my caged-cat, under-the-sheets look. But as soon as he put his hands on mine I switched to my round-eyed, young-nun look and said we should go see some of the other sights in this crapped-out dump.

Rory looked put down, which is what I wanted for right then. So without him making passes we saw what was left of five or six saloons, all very crummy and smelling of animals, a place where they once weighed and shipped gold, more empty stores and some shacks where flash girls—that's what

Rory said they were called then—once lived. Everything smelled dry or old, none of it did anything for me, not until we came to the caves near the mine shaft and Rory told me Chinese miners had padded down in them. Try to imagine it, holes from three to maybe ten feet dug straight into the sides of a little hill, caves so low you couldn't stand up if you were more than seven or eight years old. But funny thing, they only smelled dry, not old. I guess animals preferred to do their business in the old houses. In some of the caves there were old busted lanterns, old pots and frying pans. Mr. Basqua had them dug up, Rory said, because someday he planned to fix up the caves. All I could say to that was how in the lousiest, dirtiest commune in the world they had to live better than those dead-and-gone Chinese. No question why that little red-book guy hates the U.S. more than anything.

One of the larger caves was swept clean and had pretty good light in it. There were some stones you could sit on, so we did, and that's when I put it on the line to Rory. No, I wasn't gonna be so stupid to say I expected him to help me out of pure goodness, for nothing, so to prove my gratitude for taking me away from those two awfuls, which probably saved my life, to show him how much faith I had in his good intentions, I wanted to try pleasing him the way he said Miss Dorne had—so did he think we had enough time for a quickie? I meant right now? And while I'd been saying all this, I'd got off my rock, hunched forward and slipped out of my bikini briefs.

"I left my purse in the car." I handed them to him. "So I'd appreciate your putting them in your pocket. Please?"

His hand shook as he looked at the panties, so cute, and he was hoarse as he asked did I mean what he hoped, then said we should go back to the jail where there were some old cots in the cells, some horse blankets piled on an old stand-up desk. But I didn't want to because that's where the car was parked and if someone came looking for us they'd go into the sheriff's office first thing. So I told him to get a blanket and please,

please hurry back before I just burned up with gratitude and passion. Then there'd be nothing left of poor me.

While he was gone I got to thinking that I really needed influence, seeing as I knew without having to be told how I stank in the talent department. That's why my coaches either quit in disgust or were fired. Still, I didn't want to give up. So if I couldn't sing, couldn't dance worth anything, given time and practice I could fuck as good as Libby Dorne. And look where she was.

Thinking this made the fearsome shakes leave, got me to thinking it was almost six months since I'd been under someone, so I started to get excited because this time, for the first time, I was going to do it with someone important, which was all part of my game plan. So while I waited for Rory I decided to take everything off but my hush-puppies before I worked enough on myself to warm up some because it was very late afternoon, so sort of cold to sit there bare-assed. Still, the cold made my nipples hard, which I knew Rory would like, and the exercises I'd been doing had given me body tone. He'd like that too, and I wanted him to like me a lot because Rory was a top man to cozy up with, and if Larry's way didn't help, which it hadn't, Rory's might.

By the time I heard him coming back I felt relieved, warmer and pretty groovy. He crawled into the cave with the blanket which he spread very careful, which I got onto and wrapped around me while he took off some of his clothes. Once he was out of his pants and shorts he told me how he didn't want me to get knocked up. So was I taking pills or something? It broke me up to tell him my diaphragm was at home, and no, I wasn't on pills. So he grinned, all teeth, as he went for his wallet and took out this cundrum which he said was the best quality. Right after that he turned around to dress up and the rest is history played very seriously, even after we were dressed, when I made him kneel on the blanket and hold hands with me.

"Like me?" I asked.

He nodded and nodded. "You're sweet."

"I dig you too," I said.

He kissed the tip of my nose. "And you're not upset? Bad conscience?"

"I loved it." It was my turn to lean forward and give him a little bit of tongue with my kiss. "You actually made me feel like I was wearing a cloud for a hat."

Now he got really concerned. Really began to feel very guilty. "Will you be able to look at me when we get back to the house?"

"With no trouble at all," I said and kissed him once more before I slipped those lousy teeth braces back into place. "You see, I seduced you. Now let's go, my seduced one. Because they're gonna miss us and maybe start looking."

Talk about diplomacy. He made me repeat over and over how I was the seducer, and the more I said it the more he liked, the better he felt. Now he began to talk about calling Libby Dorne right from Mr. Basqua's house. That might mean he'd be going direct to L.A. with us. By now, his saying this convinced me we were getting out of here alive. So believe me, when I hugged him this time, it wasn't faking. Still, when he asked if there might be some way of us getting together in L.A., I pointed out that even if I could get away for a couple of hours, how would it look for a kid to be going to his room? Who knew who might see him, me or us? Even if we could work it out, then it would be him seducing me, and I liked him too much now for that.

"Please, let's think about it?" I said as I reached over to give his fly a special pat. "Because I want to ask you something very personal."

He moved the wheel to take us around a curve in the dirt road that led out of ghost town. "Like what?"

"Like how many times you did it with Miss Libby Dorne?"

"We did it for two days running, so who bothered counting?" he laughed. "That was a long time ago."

"You won't do that to me?" I asked. "I mean make this our one and only? Promise?"

He stepped on the brake, put the shift in neutral to just look at me after he wiped his mouth again—and not to wipe off lipstick, because I hadn't worn any all day.

"I promise, Verney," he said.

"Thank you, Uncle Fred," I said.

Suddenly—get him!—he looked upset. "Don't call me Uncle Fred, please?" he asked before he went on to explain how in the dirty books he'd read when he was in college there was always an Uncle Jack or Uncle George or Uncle Fred who was laying his real nieces and doing some wild things to them. "So you'll call me—Mr. Rory?"

"Mr. Rory," I repeated. "But on your way out here you wanted me to call you Uncle Fred."

"Things're different now," he said and I got it. "Now tell me again," he asked. "Who seduced who?"

"I seduced you." I sort of sang it to give him a sample of my voice. "I seduced Mr. Rory."

He really grinned. "Vixen."

"Should I seduce Mr. Hammschlager?" I asked his advice. "I mean, should I try?"

That bothered him, which is what I wanted to know. "Don't say that, Verney. Don't think it ever."

"I was only fooling." I crossed my heart. "Besides, the only time I saw him—he scared me. Honest, I bet how when nobody's around he flops and crawls around like a monster."

"Keep thinking of him that way," he said and patted my knee again, so I moved closer to him. "If you have to think of seducing anyone, think of me as your next victim."

I touched his fly, then squeezed. He actually crowed and held my hand there and if we hadn't just then come in sight of the main house I'd've taken bets how he would've pulled off the road and made me seduce him again. Just how many did he carry in his wallet? How many did he take on a trip?

After Rory parked I wasn't acting when I asked him please to go in first, to see if it was safe for me. He understood and a couple of minutes later came out with Mr. Basqua and

Mother Joyce, both of who told me that Grobbernasch and Atkinson were long gone back to Sacramento but they'd left apologies behind for saying nasty things to me and nasty things about everyone else in my presence. What interested me lots more was that Joyce looked settled, as if everything'd turned out winners, so I got out of the station wagon, took her hand and let myself be sort of dragged into the house before I busted loose to go to the can. You can bet I wasn't going to wet my briefs with relief.

Because I'd never got beyond soup at lunch, Mr. Basqua made me go to the table where I ate a little of this and some of that, but did put away a beautiful slab of cake à la mode. Meanwhile, he told me how the men who'd left were really good and kind, but Mr. Atkinson's sisters were having trouble with their younger kids, a couple of them who were dropping out and turning on, so he was down on all of us. And A and G were such old friends that if one got upset the other reacted.

Why make a thing of something unimportant? What mattered was that we were going home alive, maybe even better off than when we came up, that Mr. Basqua was on our side, that Rory'd been inside, and the hardnoses had left without doing us harm or damage. Also, I didn't feel sticky or goopy and wasn't worried. After I finished my dessert and milk and before I could brush my teeth, Mr. Basqua took my hand and led me into his library where right away soon the phone rang. He told me to answer it, and there was Mr. Hammschlager saying hello and telling me how sorry he was that business had got in the way of his doing what he wanted most for 1968. Which was to launch my career from countdown to big lift-off to an orbit among the big stars. Would I be willing to see him at our house this coming Wednesday or Thursday afternoon?

Standing in the high-priced spread up to my ass, I didn't know what to say, so he suggested I ask Larry or Mother while he held on. Larry said Thursday would be better, so that's what I told Hammschlager, who I no longer had designs on, not really. Not for the present. Anyway, Rory was more important, I figured, although Hammschlager might be handling p.r. matters for Mr. Basqua. But that couldn't be as important as legal business. Or could it? Really, I wondered how I might go about finding how each of them rated in Mr. Basqua's empire.

"Good." His voice on the phone filled my ear like Mazola. "I spoke to Fred Rory minutes ago," he oozed on. "And I think your meeting Libby Dorne would be splendid. When Mr. Rory and I talk to her, she'll think it's the best idea too."

"Whatever you say," I gushed like he was better than Clorets. "Dear Mr. Hammschlager, whatever you say."

I trilled good-bye, hung up, kissed Joyce, Larry, Uncle Simon and Don Basqua. I was glad Rory wasn't around just then. Next I asked to be excused because it was important to be by myself for a little bit.

I didn't lock the bedroom door. Just the one to the bathroom.

CHAPTER NINE

JOYCE: This particular evening Larry brought his grim expression home about an hour after I got in. But he'd been carrying it around ever since he took Basqua's advice and got himself and Simon out of the market in November. On the following February's worst day the Dow-Jones industrials were off more than a hundred points. That, plus whatever else the don had said to Larry in the couple of long private talks they'd had, made my husband walk around as if like a suppository, a think-tank'd been stuck up his ass. And you should get a load of the reading he was struggling with, per Basqua's advice, all about how much money was made all over the world and in the United States by raping the particular country and people, with the law on the raper's side and ready to put the axe to the people or places that got raped if their cases ever came to court. Since he was following Basqua's advice to the letter, you should see the organizations he was making contributions to. For example where blacks were raising hell to get into good neighborhoods —but not ours—they got contributions from Larry. Likewise the whites who were trying to keep them out got some of Larry's cash. This way all the troublemakers, those who were for pot and against it, those who were for saying prayers in school and against it, those for or against abortion, for or against people on relief—which I'm certainly against—for or against communism or the war in Vietnam or the FBI, they all got something from Larry, just like they did from Basqua and everyone else the don advised. But always—anonymously. And the idea was to make all those people violent and keep them in the news so much that there wasn't room for us. Also, many people might get around to saying how they'd like the good old days back, when crooks worked for a living and weren't interested in headlines or making trouble for good neighborhoods, schools and government.

So before we went over to the guest house where Larry and me were having Friday night supper with Simon, I decided to try relaxing Larry with a story Phil Hammschlager had only just told me. Visualizing the punchline made me laugh before I got to it, but Larry also laughed and said he had to remember to tell it to Mike Loesinger. And he wished he could tell it to Simon, who once'd been a great appreciator of funny stories. Now he'd just stare. But this is what I'd done when Phil told me the story, which got me to wondering why that was my reaction to every one of his funnies.

That afternoon I was sitting in an auxiliary control booth of a TV studio while on the stage below they were taping the sort of kid dance-show Dick Clark'd made so popular but couldn't patent. Verney and her talented back-up group were going to do a number they'd had success with, and the publicity demanded my being around but not making myself prominent, which suited me fine, especially when they took pictures of me and they looked better than I did. Read what I was supposed to have said in *Score*—one of the dumber kid magazines— how Verney's career was my pride and joy, the flowering of dedicated years of planning. But those years had been spent on ambitions for Verney, not me, so no-thank-you, I wasn't interested in the role of stage mother, or in any role, except the one I'd always been in—that of a concerned mom who knew that right now my place was near Veronica for whenever she needed me. So while I sat there in the semi-darkness, watching about fifty assorted school-age kids—maybe some of them dropouts, maybe some of them pregnant or Wasserman plus, maybe some of them come to the studio to put a pipe-bomb in a barrel—shaking on the stage while this group in buckskins and Indian beads screwed their guitars and the drummer actually tongued his sticks, Phil Hammschlager slipped into the seat next to mine and gave my gloves, which I'd put on the dead control panel, a gentle pat.

"You're giving off proud vibrations. Happy ones too," he said.

That called for two smiles. One inside my mouth, the other for him to see. But he still looked dismal. "I hope the same's true for you," I said.

He shook his head the saddest way possible for him, waited until I asked why, then went on to tell me how the past Saturday night he and his wife attended the most important charity ball of the new season in New York, for which guests flew in from Palm Beach, the Bahamas and the big European capitals. And Mary looked absolutely stunning in a silver lamé created for her.

"Until somebody else showed up in the exact same gown?" I asked after he made a stage pause.

That made him pat my hand as well as my gloves, sigh and whisper as if we had a big secret between us, of how perceptive I was. "Yes," he paused to pat again. "And the someone else was Mary's designer. Then, to make the evening a historic disaster, it looked better on him."

Maybe it was Phil, who just wasn't the type to tell a joke or ever say anything funny. Still, every time we met he had one for me, each told straight and very good, but none of them ever made me laugh right then. Later on, some of them convulsed me. Now, thinking about this, I realized how all the jokes involved his wife, which is routine for lots of stand-up comics, especially the kind who look like they just drove into town on loads of onions or pumpkins. Even Phyllis Diller gets the biggest laughs out of Fang. So if Phil, who wasn't a comic, wanted to make weenies about his wife, Mary Scott, why not? Really, he could've told his jokes about any woman, but Mary Scott meant something to people my age. Kids today maybe never heard of her, but about ten–twelve–fifteen years ago she was up there with the big vocalists, the talents whose records sold millions. One big studio tried to use her in pictures but their cameras thought otherwise. Very strange, because she's really wholesome pretty in person, so without being angry she went back to playing the big supper clubs and hotels on the triple-A circuit.

Suddenly, about ten or so years ago, she stopped singing, right after she married Phil Hammschlager because Bruce Dunlop, this Jewish pop singer with the outsize phony stage name and personality, broke their engagement by running away to Europe, where he's been ever since. Mike Loesinger filled us in on the details, how Mary found out where Phil'd made up his mind to marry her before she even knew this very particular kind of fat worm was alive. And how, through a lucky break, Phil—who was a publicity-nothing in New York—came out here with a screenwriter trying to make a come-back with his career and his very first wife. By being soft, weepy, the friend-in-need who'd let you cut him open if it'd make you happy, Phil made everyone feel bigger and more important than him, therefore responsible for him, so in not too long a time he got bigger and bigger in publicity, then public relations, then with Bruce as a dumb-kid client who depended on him for everything, even friendship, until came the day when Phil crossed him up and out of Mary's life.

People in the know also tell how Phil asked Mary to marry him in front of some people he'd screwed into their owing him whatever happiness they'd recaptured or got. During his proposal, which was like his offering Mary the nomination for President from both parties, she put things together until she had the whole picture and frame of how Bruce'd been manipulated out of the scene. No, she didn't try to kill Phil. Instead, she got him off his knees to kiss him, say yes, then go on to say that if he loved her like he swore, then right now, in front of the witnesses to his proposal and her acceptance, because she didn't want to wait until after the ceremony, he would do something very dear to her. What she asked him is so dirty they won't even put it in stag movies made for the worst degenerates. Knowing this always makes me look funny at her whenever we meet, but naturally from behind my dark glasses. But to get back to them, what she asked of Phil sent him flying down the road. Still, a couple of hours later he was back to preach how to save her from this evil, soul-destroying desire, they would be married. Then, working together, made strong by his love, they would tear the devil out of Mary.

Their wedding was small, very quiet. Right soon Phil began to represent institutions and he did well enough to buy a château about a mile above the Bel Air east gate. The place is huge, surrounded by a moat complete with swans, and they say that Mary only allows people inside once a year, when Phil gives his annual dinner-dance business party which takes almost four or five months to plan.

People also say they've never put it together and that one Christmas not so long ago, after Mary opened this big package from Phil and saw the black sable Maximilian coat, she got dressed immediately, went out to the tool house next to their garage, hung up the coat and used four-inch brushes to paint the furs in red, white and blue stripes. Another story about her is that she spends most of her time reading and moving from party-line to party-line phone, each equipped with a headset so she can still hold a book or magazine with both hands. There's supposed to be at least twenty different party-line numbers in the house, and they say for hours on end Mary listens in on conversations. Mike told us she's supposed to be always trying for tie-ins on lines put in for teen-agers, but nobody knows for sure about any of this because all the phones are supposed to be in one special room that has the heaviest shutters on the windows and a door with a steel core and special locks.

Because Mary didn't keep her career or entertain didn't mean she didn't go to important parties and dinners with Phil, where for some wild reason she played the loving, so attentive wife, which made more and more people wonder if it wasn't he who'd made up the wild stories about her. And she looked so good, so pure and all-American wholesome that it was hard to believe about her ruining a sable coat, the phones or what she was supposed to have asked of Phil right after she accepted his proposal. Once in a while Mary would sing for some big charity bash and people who should know say she still has her voice, presence and delivery.

What puzzled the types who enjoy breaking their heads about such things was why Mary stay married to Phil, even if he probably made millions out of playing Humpty Dumpty. With plenty of cash she could call her own, with a real talent even if it sounded old-fashioned by today's standards, what kept her from leaving? Maybe the stories were all wrong. Maybe Phil was a demon lover, a real case of a genuine toad turning into an uninhibited Prince Charming after he shucked his clothes. Still, as I saw it from what was told me, even staying with him under the same piece of sky—let alone a roof—was so unhealthy and sick that by any comparison the worst of what'd happened to me must be rated wholesome. Also, the situation might explain why nothing Phil might say about his wife, even in clever joke situations that probably never happened, could make me laugh when I was with him.

I don't think Phil expected anyone to laugh at his stories, not when he was around, so that afternoon while we sat in the control booth and waited for Verney and her back-up group, the Silent Majority, to do "I'll Tell You Your Fortune, Cookie; You're Gonna Marry Me," we talked about things in general as well as certain specifics to do with my daughter who was really going places. Getting right down to it—it really didn't matter whether we liked Phil or what we thought of him, he'd done nothing where we were concerned to make us dislike him. For example, he was nothing but attentive to me, he'd acted enthusiastic about my house and sent us eight silver-dollar paperweights with solid sterling bases from Tiffany's, two for my desk, two each for Larry and Simon, and two for Verney's, which struck me as one of Phil's better jokes.

And I never forgot how he'd really charmed me months ago, that first time in his office, so why now, even as I wrote him thank-you note after thank-you note for all the special things he did for Verney, the flowers and theater tickets which made Larry take me out, the discriminating little gifts for my collections, why did he make me feel so uncomfortable? Was it because real evil, real bad, should look really evil and bad instead of suffering-saint good? That—Larry said when I made him discuss Phil with me—made sense. Because, you see, we were talking more and more things over with each other, ever since we were meeting each other after hours with nothing between us, and especially since we got back from Basqua's, who'd sent us home with—so he said—four of the original grape bricks encased in plastic. Larry and Verney liked them. Simon, I don't know. I didn't care for mine but the porcelain keepsake boxes that came later in a size just right for the bricks were choice. So Larry's agreeing with my feelings about Phil Hammschlager, and his not caring for him either, made me feel normal, as if I still had some healthy senses left, which, Larry said, was proved even more because I'd told him first, while he was still making up his mind, that no matter my opinion of Phil as a human being, he was a genius.

This is why, when everything is added up, Phil was able to do so much for a kid with absolutely nothing going for her but negatives. Even Phil, after he heard Verney's so-called audition, had to admit that the only talent she had was to be so awful you felt it was right not to feel sorry for her because she wasn't a deserving underdog. However, he went on, in some kind of psychological reverse, her lack of talent was fascinating. So was her determination. Privately, I only told myself, it was insanity. Still, nowadays my feelings about Verney and lots of other things are too mixed up, especially when I get to thinking how through her—of all people—we're getting normal existence because my house is no longer a prison so we can get out of it and even have outside people come inside.

On that day, about a week after we got back from up north, when Phil visited us for two reasons—to see how I'd done my house and to look Verney over—he brought Mary along because she could give us a professional opinion. I got along so well with Mary that I wished she'd say something about having lunch or something sometime soon because it'd been years since I even had a casual acquaintance. Be that as it may, Verney did a couple of songs to piano accompaniments played by Mrs. Droutswood. Then, after she did a little dance, I guess, and before the silence and gloom got so heavy things would buckle under them, Mary told Phil she was having their chauffeur drive her and Verney to Wil Wright's for ice cream. Don't think I didn't want to go along, but I had to stay with the other sufferers—Simon, Larry, Phil, poor Mrs. Droutswood, who thought she saw her work and job go down the drain, and two men whose names I didn't catch from Kerry and Ellison, the p.r. firm Phil'd chosen to represent Verney.

They were sad, disappointed, maybe even disgusted, but I was personally ashamed, furious at Verney because she was a direct reflection on Winnie, God rest his poor soul wherever it might be, and me. Not that either of us were entertainers, please understand I mean in the accepted sense of things, but Winnie could manage a tune even while he jigged, and when I was younger, happier, feeling better and able to sing, nobody told me to quit before all the clocks stopped. And at that time I could dance pretty good. There were times, sometimes weeks on end, when I'd rehearse with the chorus girls at the Riviera because it was good exercise for me. Most times I was able to keep up with them no matter how fast the routine got, so that some of the girls kidded me about joining the line full-time. Which means, by heredity alone, Verney should've been able to do something. But for her the something was proving how she was the all-time *klutz*. For this to see or hear, people don't pay. So before Mary Scott took her away, for the first time, never before that I could remember, I wanted Verney to make good. And I said so after they left. This made Larry take off his glasses to show me how he was glad. And Simon moved to sit right next to me and Mrs. Droutswood squeezed my shoulder as she sat down behind us.

For some of the longest minutes in my life nobody said anything, which made me conclude how everything was finished and now we'd have a worse monster on our hands as she went back into prison with us. But, thank God, how wrong I was. You see, Phil wanted us to feel bottom-of-the-pit hopeless before he moved his chair, then got up slow as if he was weighed down by a cross so heavy it would've flattened our Lord before He could've taken even a single step from the Second Station. This is why, when Phil turned around to show us his palms, I expected to see nail holes and dried blood. Then in a voice of pain, the kind you hear on TV when the broad's having a bad delivery and there isn't a drop of hot water for miles around, Phil told us he was going to take on an additional burden, a project no more difficult than moving the Rockies by blowing against them. In addition to everything else he did to keep the team and clients winners, he was, by himself, going to supervise the preparation, packaging and marketing of Veronica Dobby.

Our expressions, even those of the stone faces from Kerry and Ellison, said it couldn't be done. So as an example to their organization, to us, to anyone present who might have some idea about his not having more talent than luck, he told us how he intended to create something in spare moments that might take them ten years if they worked day and night. And then they'd probably fail. You see, he was going to make

Veronica Dobby—the name she was going to use because it'd been assigned to her by God, not her parents—into one of the country's better-known teen-age singers. And he was going to do it by making Verney into a wind-up toy powered by our resources and positive ambitions for her.

While he talked I was thinking all sorts of things, so I missed some of his monologue and only picked up where he was telling how the word "country" rang bells in his head and the tone of their ringing couldn't be ignored, so he was going to keep on talking until the message from the bells made sense. Suddenly Phil stopped, shivered, then announced in a voice filled with prophecy how the message he'd got was for Verney and her Yankee-Doodle sound to sing teen-age country-freedom music that would appeal to Middle America, whatever Billy Graham and his political friends who'd taken over the country decided it was. First, because what he had in mind for Verney didn't really require a voice because you could just recite the words to the special songs that'd be written for her. Second, the sentiments in her songs would be wholesome, seeing as Middle America was more and more up-tight about the secret messages in the songs performed by hard- and acid-rock groups. Third, what patriotic American'd dare say he didn't like something to be sold as freedom music or Yankee Doodle rock? So it was Phil's idea to have Verney do songs that dear hearts and gentle people in tens of thousands of American old-home towns, where every day was either July 4 or December 25, would like instead of hate.

The faces of the men from Kerry and Ellison were lit up as if they were looking through Heaven's open gates and hearing God's voice loud and clear, so I didn't need Simon's nudge to tell me to smile happy even if he wasn't. So I did, my approval seemed to delight Phil, and he thanked me with a couple of little bows before he gifted us with more of his great ideas.

"I have it!" He clapped both hands over his mouth as if whatever he had was trying to escape before he could show it to us. After Phil panted hard and lowered his hands, we knew it'd stayed captured. "The title for Verney's first LP record, because we're thinking that far ahead. The singles she does we'll use on the LP, plus some new songs, but the general theme and title we work toward is"—he got dramatic again—"*Songs You Can Sing to Your Mother.* Don't worry about the title being too on-the-nose," he replied to Larry's question. "People will thank us for the chance to buy something wholesome for themselves and their kids."

Suddenly he was dressed in his don't-hurt-me appearance as he took a hesitant step toward Larry, put out his right hand and asked if they were on a first-name basis. Larry nodded. How could anyone say no to such a silly question? So he said yes out loud, with us as witnesses who'd heard him.

"Larry, that makes me feel good," he said and proved this by hugging himself like the happiest Charlie Chan around. "Our Veronica deserves the very best," he sort of chanted very dramatically, eyes closed like a Gypsy fortune-teller who actually says cross-my-palm-with-silver. "I see four or five musicians backing up our star. Maybe even more to build the sound. I also see top composers and the best lyricists." Now, eyes open, he turned again to Larry. "Because of our mutual good friend in the wine country, I'm waiving our office fee. Wouldn't you call that good faith?"

Whatever Larry believed, and unless he was out to break Phil's heart, the question called for a yes. Which is what Larry said before Phil boxed Larry in good by asking in front of us —the same witnesses to his generosity—how much he was willing to spend on Verney? And before the old Joyce, the one I knew best and right now was slightly ashamed of could get Larry's attention and signal for him to make some hard cuts in his original figure, Larry said he was willing to shell out even more than he'd first intended, which meant he was ready to lay a hundred and fifty thousand on the line. But he said it in such a way that I knew he wasn't asking now or later for a nickel of mine, which tempted me to say I'd be willing to put up my fair share, but good sense helped me manage not to. Later I got sentimental and took fifty thousand of what Larry'd pledged. Meanwhile, however, no one seemed to've noticed my own little struggle because everyone concentrated on Phil, how he wrestled with Larry's figure before he said something about it being modest, still one he could work inside of. With that—shyly—he offered to shake hands with Larry. When they did, my daughter Verney—a big caliber bust in the talent department—teeth braces and all, was on her way.

Larry phoned all the details to Basqua, who suggested that Verney be incorporated and assigned fifty percent of the corporate stock for her contribution of talent, with Larry and me holding the other fifty. Then, if Verney bombed out we could get some tax relief, because come-what-may, Verney was going to make at least three sides for a company well established in the business. Mike did all the paper work, Fred Rory consulted with him and us by phone, which included his talking to Verney, and soon there was a V-J-L Entertainment Corporation doing business, with Larry and me as president and vice-president. Mike was secretary and treasurer.

During the incorporation we got a happy call from Kerry and Ellison to tune in the four-thirty or five o'clock news on any of our local TV channels and two of the major networks that also started their news at five. At six we could listen to the *Big News* on CBS, because Libby Dorne was being interviewed in depth, which meant a five-minute spot for the major stations, maybe more for the independents. Should Verney listen too, we asked, and were told absolutely. Libby Dorne was the actress Verney told me Fred Rory knew intimately. The way she emphasized intimately bothered me just as much as Fred's always making a point of talking to Verney whenever he called Larry and me.

Anyway, that afternoon at five we gave our attention to NBC on the big set in the morning room and to the local channels on three portables we tuned with their sound turned off.

About twenty minutes into the hour, NBC's chief newscaster for between five and six did an intro for one of the station's on-the-spot local news reporters who'd gone to Libby Dorne's house where she was making some important announcements, like what her next picture was going to be, where it'd be made, who she'd be rubbing up against hardest, what she thought of rumors from Paris and Rome that designers were dropping hemlines way below the knee, world-shaking stuff like that for local yokels everywhere. So there was Libby Dorne all done up for the bedroom in her living room, looking very light-your-fire in her blonde wig and a ski-type harem costume that showed her belly button where—I swear—she actually wore a garnet or golden beryl, which impressed Verney who, as she sat on the floor, back against the foot of the sofa, told us straight out how she'd heard from an authentic source that Miss Dorne was an old-fashioned super-whore from way back, the kind of slinky-kinky who thought it was still fashionable to keep an orchid and a tube of vag-jelly in her refrigerator. Nothing else. Larry shuddered because he realized that Verney must've got most of this from Fred Rory, so for a second I thought there was going to be a blow-off, and it might've happened if we hadn't heard what Libby Dorne said next.

Which started up as a crap build-up how lots of people were interested in eliminating lots of diseases, from bad thoughts to bad kidneys to bad hearts, from leukemia to emphysema to arthritis and anything else you could find in Dr. Fishbein's home medical book. And how all of these were worthy causes. But she and a group of public-minded people suddenly realized how no attention was being given to the nation's teeth, especially those of kids. Personally, Libby said, she thought fluoridation was part of a thought-control plot just like laws that allowed the cutting up of helpless animals for so-called medical studies. What interested Libby in teeth was that they were so necessary to health and beauty, which was why her group was going to do everything it could to provide healthy and cosmetic dental care for children. This would include orthodontia and a program of education to make kids wear their braces.

You should've seen the way I tapped Verney's shoulder, the look I gave her and how her turn away told me to get lost.

Now Libby began to yak how one of her older interests was being on constant look-out for young talents she could help just like she'd been helped as an unknown.

"Commitments keep me from looking as hard as I'd like to," she went on after she adjusted her hips and navel to give cameras a better shot of the jewel, which probably turned on plenty of viewers and filled them full of ideas for self-improvement, "but I always keep my eyes open. So I had the good luck recently to meet an unusual girl just loaded with talent—Veronica Dobby."

Verney screamed as she scrambled to her feet while she pointed at the screen we were watching. "She's a liar! I never met her! I swear I never met her!"

Larry told her to shut up and listen, and we actually got up to stand in front of the tube while Libby went on with nothing but crap how she'd met Veronica at her parents' lovely home and Veronica—or Verney—was cutting flowers in the garden and singing to herself. The girl's voice was clean, sweet, fresh and unspoiled. And she blushed hard after she discovered Libby was listening.

"To encourage a youngster without real talent is cruel," we heard a very serious Libby Dorne while the camera concentrated on the jewel in her navel. "But Veronica has clean talent. So I offered to sponsor her. And she said no."

"Because she doesn't like show business?" a cooperative reporter gave Libby the feed-line she wanted.

The camera moved up to show us Libby shaking her head, as well as one of the men from Kerry–Ellison right next to her. "She does," Libby said so serious. "But she likes her orthodontist more."

That grabbed the reporters, so Libby went on about Verney

wearing braces and how if she ever decided to sing professionally, it would have to be in two, possibly three years, after her braces were finally removed. Right now Verney was wise enough to know an audience, young or old, wouldn't accept a kid with braces on her teeth. This was their loss not Verney's, who in the end would have beautiful teeth, which were lots more important than any popular career could be. Next second Libby clapped her hands, smiled big and told us that in her new picture the script called for her appearing nude front and back, with a passionate skin scene played on one of Hawaii's black sand beaches.

We had it right in the house, the first big proof of Phil's genius and what he had in mind for Verney. She was going to be a unique juve performer—the girl who sang with her braces on—and I didn't doubt at all he'd make a voice for her. Naturally there would have to be publicity stills and what went with them, but I told Larry that nothing was beyond Phil or his coffee go-fors, so we could expect to see Verney looking good, even appealing, maybe pretty in her braces.

Right I was. Later that night Phil phoned, talked first to a hysterical Verney, then to me and Larry, and gave us our instructions. In short, Verney was in his hands. Through Kerry–Ellison we'd be getting orders of our own to follow in dealing with the public, and the first one was to tell Mike Loesinger about writing checks immediately for all bills certified by PAH for payment. We weren't to worry because to date, of the hundred fifty thousand Larry'd agreed to, Kerry–Ellison weren't taking a fee because PAH wasn't and they hoped to work with him on other projects, so only about a hundred and fifty dollars had been spent on hundred-word straight telegrams to the editors of popular magazines for kids as well as six top professional dentist magazines, three of them all about orthodontia.

Every telegram was sent in the name of the president of one of the biggest-selling toothpastes, a company that spent more than seven figures for advertising. Naturally his firm was represented by PAH. And the messages called attention of all editors to the human interest news values they could find in stories and articles about a decent, clean, serious, shy and so-very-talented girl who preferred the advice and discipline of her orthodontist to a career in show business, which only used teen-agers with dental braces for low comedy or as rotten-kid sissies. For sure, everyone knew, no girl could be anything except a drip while she wore braces. No boy could be popular with them on. So the story told by Libby Dorne about Veronica Dobby had to mean something positive for our country, which desperately needed any kind of good news about our kids.

There's no point in dwelling on this except to say Phil got exactly what he wanted from Kerry and Ellison, who were one of the biggest snow manufacturers in a business just filled with it. Anyway, as Mike Loesinger said to us right after Libby Dorne's interview, which he caught as a late-news repeat, if Phil was given the job of selling an alcoholic to the country as a Presidential candidate, the odds were that right after the inauguration the country would be behind him when his attorney-general put the WCTU high on the subversive list of domestic enemies.

So, as in one direction, publicity was making Verney a personality, with her name being mentioned favorably two or three times a week by columnists very important to the dumb public, in another Kerry and Ellison received more and more calls asking for interviews with Verney, with some even offering club dates or guest spots on local TV talk shows. Because Phil and K–E were still selling gas they said no. They meant not yet, not until a kid with no voice was made into a singer, which turned out to be the easiest miracle of them all.

For this operation Phil told us to keep Mrs. Droutswood on as Verney's teacher since she'd be too busy to go to school, and she'd also function as my daughter's chaperone and general nose-wiper. Next from Kerry and Ellison we got a schedule of appointments for Verney that kept us busy for more than a month. First there were photographs, with Verney screaming like she was being killed because she wasn't allowed one picture without her braces. The initial session was short, just rough proofs to take to a certain theatrical stylist and cosmetician who looked at them, whistled hard and told us to bring Verney in for make-over and makeup. She ended up with what we used to call a short bob, but the important thing was he styled it to make her look snub-nosed cute, then he showed me how to help her with comb-outs.

With him along we went back to the photographer where she was made up for lights and freshened up as needed while a hundred shots, maybe more, were made by the photographer who roamed around like a crazy man, even climbing his walls for angles. In the end what really mattered except results? And we had them in pictures of Verney wearing her braces and looking sweet, real Mary-Scott wholesome, so even I was pleased because she looked almost as good now in real life, especially when she wore what became her uniform—a red sailor blouse, white tie, blue pleated skirt sort of short, and white marching-band boots with cute red tassels.

Phil, not Kerry–Ellison, chose about twenty shots for reproduction and two special shots for Verney to autograph and give out, since she was getting plenty of requests for pictures. About seven or eight, maybe ten shots were sent by Phil to his toothpaste client, who began to reproduce them for heavy placement in dentists' offices and for retail displays where they got her points not only as a good American kid but also as a singer—although no one without lying could say he'd heard her sing a note. But enough publicity-hungry psychos that housewives believed in stood up to say they had, so we started to get legitimate feelers from some of the better record outfits.

This, and Verney starting to get substantial checks for the photos that were used for advertising purposes, plus my having to go down with Verney and Mike to stand before a judge who approved a trust and savings program for Verney's income until she was twenty-one, were some of what was happening to me. And how real all this was got driven home when K–E started to coach me for public appearances and give me answers and comments for just about any question a reporter might throw at me, including those that would try to make something of my past. Larry, not so dumb himself, said that K–E must be paid or it would go for taxes, so a fee was arranged and a man on call was assigned to me. Anything Verney could do I could do better, so everyone complimented me for catching on pretty quick and becoming as confident as Verney, who didn't seem to be at all troubled that sometime soon now she would have to sing.

There I was nervous, so were Larry and Simon, but none of the pros were and I found out why after I met the pop composer and lyricist, men with ace reputations, at the sound studio where Verney sang on tapes with her braces off, then on. A couple of days later the composer got the word from the sound engineer that braces didn't make any difference in her voice, which was key of C, with a range of about one and a half octaves, with us getting the best results if the composer wrote music for her between B-natural and A.

This wasn't even a challenge to the composer, who already knew that whatever he more or less created for Verney had to include spirit-of-76 fifes and drums for beat, harmony or background. Everyone agreed the first song had to be pop, something she could fake without trying, so they put together the fortune-cookie song, which I thought was very cute. All the while Verney rehearsed with the composer and lyricist in their studio, they built her confidence with stories of singers they knew with records in the top hundred—some even with sides in the top forty—who didn't even have the voices of ducks.

Came the day when the team was satisfied with the way Verney'd learned and delivered her lyrics, ad-lib lines and little jokes, so Larry and I listened to them give her a no-fooling-around lecture how she was never—repeat, *never*—to sing without her agency's approval no matter how she was coaxed.

This done we left while they put Verney's voice on tape. As they later explained, the sound engineer recorded at flat-out, which is maximum high frequency and the way to put as much sound on tape as it can hold. Then he did the same with the piano alone, which would be the musicians' cue track when they'd come in about a week later to play with headsets on. From his music library of instant inspirations the composer drew on standard marches and tunes as Chinese as chop suey, so he had no trouble working up a bouncy, Oriental and patriotic arrangement for finger cymbals, a vibraphone, autoharp and two clarinets in chin-chin harmony, plus electric guitars tuned to his specifications. And in the background, medium-far away, there were fifes and drums which he personally thought were wild with possibilities for the sound mixer.

I don't know, never cared to find out, how many playback tapes were made and equalized, modulated through dubbing, pasted up and rearranged for more or less trebles, bass and echo-chamber reverberations, how many splices were made where pitch, not synchronization, was changed to give Verney's tinny voice a low, mellow quality that didn't require too much orchestral crowding, but finally we got a call from Kerry and Ellison that the composer was satisfied with what he wanted us to hear. Meantime, he'd also been busy interviewing musicians for the Silent Majority and he'd found a vegetarian guitarist so kosher he wouldn't wear or use anything made of leather, plus he looked just like Abe Lincoln. Not only was he a good musician, he was having his name legally changed to Middle America. He also intended to go around in a stovepipe hat and long coat like Lincoln used to wear. Larry told Mike to put him under contract.

By this time Larry'd heard of a picture called *The Young Americans* which someone in Mike's office had endured on a United flight from Hawaii, and we got to see it in a projection room at Columbia Studios. Afterwards the people from Kerry–Ellison who were with us agreed it was very awful but filled with exactly the types the Silent Majority should imitate in appearance and clothes because they saw Verney and her clean sound appealing to people in their young forties, just old enough to have kids her age who were giving them fits by doing everything possible, it seemed, to ruin themselves along with the country. I understood this, that you can bet, and you can also bet they weren't buying records of the Jefferson Airplane, the Rolling Stones, even the Beatles or any other group who straight out told us to go you-know-what ourselves in every possible way, up to and including ugly pictures on album covers of naked broads and guys, brushes and all, hitting us smack in the face. This is what Verney gave Larry and me as part of her Christmas presents to us and which she thought was so great because someone from Kerry–Ellison's had brought them back from London in his luggage. It also explains why Lawrence Welkers and other straights were doing pretty good in a market just desperate to buy anything they could call decent American and leave around in the open no matter who knocked on their doors. Which brings us right back to my new-image Verney, getting almost a ninety percent favorable response in her unsolicited mail as sales of toothpaste she endorsed went up, while knocks in a bad week from the underground press and the sort of lice columnists who lived by biting people ran no more than fifteen percent.

What surprised, embarrassed, upset, confused yet pleased me were envelopes, more and more of them, addressed to me from people I'd never heard of, with letters that congratulated me for being able in these times to give my dear daughter a decent set of values, so the writers hoped she was grateful for the care, attention and love I'd lavished on her. Some of these letters were addressed to Mr. and Mrs. Dobby, to make me shiver all over, even after Larry laughed them off by saying the writers were probably referring to him because of pictures circulated of the three of us. You could tell that some letters weren't written easily. Others asked if we would please send them an autographed picture of Verney and me suitable for framing. These last upset me as much as anything else they wrote. And what could I say to desperate, out-of-their minds, sick-with-worry folks who asked me for advice on what to do with their kids giving them trouble at home, in school, with the cops, at the doctor and dentist? Or to the doctors and dentists who thanked me for being so concerned for Verney? Lucky we had Mrs. Droutswood because some of those letters got to be too much for me. Once in a while a rotten letter was addressed to me, but not as many as to Verney. These usually came from kids.

It came finally, not long after the first of the year, when a K–E secretary phoned to invite us to Verney and the Silent Majority's dress rehearsal of "Fortune Cookie," so all of us—Simon and Mrs. Droutswood, even Milly and Tom—went to a TV theater on Vine Street rented for the day. Mike and his wife were there, so was Phil with Mary Scott, who I made sit next to me, along with other people from Phil's office as well as Jim Kerry, Norm Ellison and some of their big hands who weren't about to miss something important enough to bring Phil Hammschlager there. Along with other introductions we met an artist-and-repertory man from Home Town Records, a company out of Nashville and big in markets wherever snotty, intellectual smart-asses weren't welcome. He told us what we were going to enjoy was already sold to Home Town, whose contract called for them to buy Verney's next two singles, with options for the next four plus her first LP. No matter how I'd tried to feel noble about it, turning over fifty thousand to the corporation had bothered me, but now I realized there was a good chance my investment wasn't going to be a total loss. In some way I'm ashamed of, this bugged me.

Then, right after the curtain rose, I felt we were going to make money. There they were, six musicians in the center-stage spotlight—pianist, vibraphone, autoharp, a drummer and two guitarists who also could play fifes—nice and healthy-looking clean-cut kids in white buck shoes, gray flannel slacks, white shirts open at the collar and blue pullover sweaters.

Smiling as if they'd always liked people, acting healthy and normal, they followed the pianist's lead as guitarists switched to fifes before they sort of marched to stand next to the drummer. Their marching beat built up as Middle America came on stage, tall, with a beard, looking so much like Lincoln in his get-up that along with Milly and Tom we started to stand as he plugged in his guitar and segued the group into eight bars of fast four-beat tempo of some Chinese-sounding stuff which made us applaud harder than we might've as Verney, playing her finger cymbals, sort of ran on stage in her red-white-and-blue outfit. First Verney blew us a kiss. Then she began to shake, but modestly, like nice kids should do when they groove to nice music. Next she started to sing good into the mike, moving into it for harmony when the arrangement called for that, working the little cymbals to back up Middle America until at the end of the number she was joined in the feature spot by the drummer and fifers who made a catchy little love song with its Chinese-sounding tune sound patriotic and marchy.

By anything you care to name I could swear that Verney was singing. All of us saw her throat muscles working, how her lips shaped the song words so you could understand them, and she seemed so happy and confident, so appealing as the light glistened on her braces, that I began to cry and my shaking off Larry's hand was because he had it all wrong. I was proud and happy, not sad. Verney's voice sounded sweet, she looked fine, and I wished Winnie, even Itzik, were alive to see her, so when the number looked like it was ending I was the first to applaud, to stand, to blow kisses toward the stage, until Verney went off in a snappy four-beat chaser until cut. And I was the first of us to reach Verney and hug her like since I can't remember when. And I was still crying. Later, even when Verney told us with pride on her part how, while her group performed live, she'd been lip-synching into a dead mike, and was overjoyed at it being so hard for us to believe that what we'd heard was tape—I was let down hard. Still, Verney didn't seem to care, nor was she worried about being found out because for personal appearances they'd be traveling with their own sound mixer, which Verney said was standard performance procedure for lots of singers—even those with voices—who preferred to work this way seeing as it eliminated mistakes and goofs. After she rattled off some big names, Jim Kerry helped make me feel worse by mentioning other greats who did this. And he made it sound as if this made them important public benefactors because they were willing to submerge their talents and work plastic so their public could get polished mechanical performances that live could never equal.

Because I kept on sputtering but-but-but, Norm Ellison hurried to assure me more than just a couple of times how no one in the business thought it was wrong or would ever knock anyone else who worked this way. In simplest terms, there was a code between performers which said that as long as the public's satisfied, nothing the entertainer does can be called cheating. What made us wonder—Simon, me and Larry —was how all the mechanics, especially the hollow sound, made Verney's singing mellow, so it didn't matter if her voice wasn't true. While sandwiches, cake and coffee were being served—no hard stuff because it didn't fit the Home Town image—Verney's demo record was played five or six times and even as I tried now to be critical, or be what Mike said was a devil's advocate, at the end of each playing I had to admit the obvious—Verney and her group came across great. And in person, when she grouped with the drummer, fifers and Middle America—a really nice guy in person who saw nothing wrong in making the most of his resemblance, to which I agreed—I actually got chills you could describe as patriotic. Still and all, I couldn't help wishing it was Verney, not machines, who had the talent.

We stepped aside while Home Town's promo people pitched Verney's record to the top-forty radio stations. One man we paid for canvassed college radio stations, which we never knew existed, but he didn't bother with any colleges where SDS and blacks were giving it to the Establishment. Meantime, Jim Kerry took over personal responsibility for plants that mattered about Verney and the Silent Majority in *Cash Box*, *Billboard*, *Record World* and *Variety*, so he was able to get stories printed of how her record would make the top forty in record time for a newcomer. What wasn't true, Jim and others explained, didn't mean we couldn't wish for it to come true, so if suggesting helped the wish along—didn't kids tell Santa Claus what they wanted? Didn't people pray for Him to make their wishes come true?

I was with Verney for her first appearance on a local TV record show where she did so well the producer scheduled her for a second appearance the following week. This started calls coming from San Diego, San Francisco, even Phoenix and Chicago for her to make appearances there. Some of the people around us, even Larry, were caught up in working for the special jackpot that gives you everything including the machine, but I was satisfied to see the company break even. Then, when Jim Kerry called one morning for us to get *Billboard* and see "Fortune Cookie" as 81 on the list, I said we should settle for this and plan to attend church the very next Sunday, at which time we could give thanks and—this I didn't tell him—I would pray for understanding of one particular thing, why Verney didn't mind being an untalented fake. Or does being a fake, or psycho, take some special talent? Because this success proved her view of life, which is—and here I'm quoting her—how it's all a big suck.

"You really believe that?" I asked her as recently as this afternoon while we sat in a star dressing room after she returned from makeup.

To show me that I was no longer dealing with a screaming kid who popped right off if you said or did something against her, Verney fell back in the deep chair, put her boots on the coffee table and stared overhead as if to read from an idiot board. With her that passed for deep thought.

"It's the biggest suck of all," she said at last. "We're all sucking at the foreskin of success. Doing our best to nibble it so good it'll like us best."

"I don't like to hear you talk that way," I snapped because she'd stirred up certain memories I'd rather forget. Be assured, Larry doesn't ask and wouldn't get it if he did. "So let's drop it."

"But, Mother, you brought it up!" She sat up to grin at me with a practiced expression of innocence and goodwill. Unless you know Verney, these—like her lip-synching for which she has a real talent, playing the finger cymbals and laying on four-square sentiments in those phony interviews she did so well—made her look as respectful as one of the original shepherds come to the manger. "Once you've got the hang of it," she went on, "once you're doing it just right, success wants you to keep right on sucking. And it being the biggest john in the reward department, it pays most. Come on, Mother"—she stamped her booted heels into the broadloom so that the sound was of an exclamation mark—"we know what's going on. How it works. How it's paid off so that Larry and you're accepted like people. How no one thinks Simon's a nut, just a lovable kook. So why're you—when I'm not—suddenly so hung up how I make it when we're all of us sucking up such goodies?"

When I got up with a sudden excuse of having to get out of her sight, Verney shoved it deeper down my throat by asking if what she'd just expressed didn't taste good? Because she didn't care, because she enjoyed me having a conscience that suffered as it knew we owed her more almost every day through the interviews she gave—all set up by Kerry–Ellison and planned by Phil—where the people who asked Verney questions were selected on the basis of what they owed K–E.

When questions got around to who I'd been, the same for Simon, Larry, Itzik, even Verney's father or my first husband, Verney would lower her head, chew lips as if she was gonna cry, then raise her chin proud and say how she was never gonna deny us one and all, and how if they got to know us they'd love us too. Proof was our willingness to risk the worst possible publicity to give her a chance to fulfill her ambitions. So she'd like to know how many other parents with skeletons they wanted to keep hidden would do as much for their kids? Sometimes she'd slip in digs how it was the people of respectable society who we'd serviced, then follow up by saying if we hadn't existed, their morality would've created us to supply them with girls, booze, gambling, fenced stuff, money for bad-risk borrowers and protection against goons, which was all we'd ever done. And no one could ever accuse us of robbing anything or peddling drugs, which was more than you could say for certain people who'd had every advantage and now were doing both to finance revolution—why go on? All of it was simple stuff, none of it original or bright, but all of it was being pitched at people who serviced millions of readers who took pride in their not being original or even the littlest bit bright.

Does this explain my unusual low when Phil H. sat next to me this afternoon, and why I left for home without waiting for my Frankenstein daughter, who was to get some more public-relations advice from the boss scientist of the whole laboratory? Larry sensed my disturbance, the way I sank into myself after I told him Phil's joke, so he didn't say anything as we walked to the guest cottage. For this I was grateful.

Immediately as Tom opened the front door of the cottage and Simon gave each of us a *gut Shabbes,* my spirits went up. Larry had his *yarmulkah* on before he kissed the *mezuzah,* and I did too because if it was a lucky thing that protected a house, the one here, and on our house too, seemed to be performing. Milly and Tom seemed to be happier, livelier here than they were with me, which did give me a stitch. But Tom, like always, said how Milly and he were the only *Shabbes goys* Mr. Simon could trust not to make things unkosher, so like always I nodded, gave Tom a big smile and thanks for the little glass of sweet wine he offered.

It was uplifting to stand at the table while Simon in his

shawl and *yarmulkah* said prayers in a language that seemed to be all sounds, not words, with Larry trying to follow but stumbling so much I found it hard not to giggle. The crackling logs in the fireplace, the brass candlesticks on the white tablecloth, Simon's sincerity as he prayed, broke the *challah* and drank the wine, with Milly and Tom standing respectful at the kitchen door—and my suddenly being very surprised to see Tom with a *yarmulkah* and also saying some of the Hebrew —all made me wonder if any of this was realer than Verney? The question almost unhinged me, so that right now I'm not lying when I say faintness was all over me like a shroud and I only began to feel better after my heart seemed to say—this was, this was—say it so hard I had to believe this was one of the few real things which, as it made the rest of living seem not so useless, would also give me peace.

After supper we relaxed in the living room which I liked more with every visit, because everything you looked at, felt, touched and used was real. And I had created the unity. Milly and Tom were doing the dishes and we whispered, laughing because we did, how if Milly and Tom did become Jews it'd better be reform or they wouldn't be able to serve Simon's Friday night suppers or take care of his house on Saturdays. The fire was warm, I began to feel relaxed even though the talk was too much about Verney, with Simon defending the whole operation, which I now, for the first time, insisted was a racket. He did this because he chose to believe Verney had talent and was going along with the *shtik* to make a better show. Also, could I deny that she was surrounded by patriotic people who the country needed as badly as Israel needed her own? One thing I'd learned was not to argue with Simon. Besides it was easier to agree and keep the good mood I was in which might carry itself right into Larry's bedroom. So the evening was going along great. That is, until the door chimes sounded, Tom went to answer and don't bother guessing—it was Verney, still in her stage costume, who made a show-biz entrance to wish everyone *gut Shabbes* before she kissed her Uncle Simon, Larry and me. I swear—she actually gave my cheek a little suck.

Verney said she'd eaten at Cyrano's, wasn't thirsty and didn't want anything, thanks, except to be allowed to sit on the fire bench where she could be warm and comfy as she looked at us—her family, so one for all and all for one. Fortunately for my stomach, Verney wasn't able to give us her whole nauseating act because Larry snapped his fingers for her attention and got ours too.

"I happened to phone Mike late in the afternoon and he said you wanted to see me and your mother tonight," he said. "About what?"

The way he asked and looked, because he'd taken off his dark glasses so she could see that his eyes were no-fooling-around, made Verney nervous. "It'll keep until tomorrow, even the day after," she said.

"But my curiosity can't," Larry told her. "So what's so important you want to discuss?"

For the second time that day I saw Verney go into her thinking bit, with the only difference being how hard her fingers gripped the edge of the fire bench. Finally she began to talk, to say how grateful she was for the hundred and fifty thousand we'd put up to finance the corporation, how happy she was to tell us first what Mike Loesinger'd figured out—that we were paying current expenses and past obligations out of profits accrued beyond her earnings and forced savings. These enabled Mike to make a projection that by the end of the year Larry and me would have most of our investment back.

"That's a projection," Larry said. "We hope it comes true but don't care if it doesn't."

"But I do," Verney said. "So when that happens, and I know it will, you'll"—she hesitated, sort of scared, I felt—"be owning half of me for nothing."

Before I could say something to loosen her teeth right out

of the braces, Larry stopped me by actually putting one of his hands across my mouth. Then he motioned for Verney to go on.

"So I've been thinking," she continued, now looking more confident by the second, "how it'd only be fair if you gave me your fifty shares. Because it's only fair for me to own a hundred percent of me."

"Suppose we don't think so?" Larry prompted her. What surprised me was that there was shock, disappointment on his face. "Then what?"

The act was over, Verney's eyes became mean, which I always believed made them feel most comfortable. "Then I'll have to buy you out. But you'd better not try holding me up."

"And if we don't feel like selling?" Larry's question was a push, a dare. "Suppose we feel like keeping the corporation family? Because if I sold any shares it'd be to an enemy, Verney. And no matter what you say or do, I'm not gonna consider you one of my enemies. You just don't rate that good."

That bugged Verney, but I wanted more. Although I loved what I'd just heard, actually felt as if I should love Larry for saying it, I knew that I would love him enough to do things I'd sworn off if only he'd now let me see how he'd once beaten Verney up. Thinking this, enjoying my anticipation, I also remembered guiltily how, when Larry had first shown up with Simon, the next day I'd lain in bed and visualized Larry's first meeting with my brat, and got enjoyment from figuring the many ways she'd gun him down. Now every cent of my money was on my husband and my heart began to race with pleasure as the old signs of anger began to turn his cheeks and jaws red, then almost black, so I pushed my purse toward him—it was heavy—because there was nothing closer by for him to throw. But he just sat, lips turned down at the corners, breathing so hard air whistled through his nostrils, rubbing his palms together as if to control his itching hands while he waited for Verney to back off, as if he was giving her every possible chance not to get worked over.

"So how about you?" Verney laid it straight on me. "Will you sell me your stock?"

I reached for my bag before shaking my head. "No."

"Because you too are only selling to enemies?"

At that moment I didn't hate her a hundred percent because memory was shaking me up to remember how, after I'd run away from the Riviera because Mitch wouldn't marry me, he'd found me in Greenwich Village drinking with a dyke, really smashed, and I passed out in Itzik's apartment. During which time Mitch agreed to marry me if he got two shares of Riviera stock Larry and Bull-now-Simon were never supposed to know anything about. So I understood, believe me, how it felt to be a commodity. But Verney's case was as different as, say, apples and turnips. She had half the stock. For this she'd put up nothing but learning how to snow the public. If she hated us enough to collapse the corporation, all she had to do was stop faking, which I wouldn't've minded at all, seeing how in addition to Verney being Verney, bad enough in itself, she was now in a position of strength. At least that's what she believed.

"You're a Mitch-bitch," I said after Verney asked if I hadn't heard her question—would I, like Larry, only sell to an enemy? "Which's a type I'd never give anything to—except a good shove over a cliff."

What confused Verney, Larry and Simon understood. And it hurt them. I expected this reaction from Simon, but not Larry, until I realized how it was Larry who'd always taken care of us, in that wild way of his, and how all of us were older, so like it or not, slown up more than just a little. Where a minute ago Larry had looked ready to kill Verney, now he appeared about to cave in. You see, doublecrosses by outsiders and enemies he could understand, but Verney was family, just as Mitch'd been, and to have something like that happen again was asking too much of him.

"You don't understand?" I asked Verney.

She shook her head. "Yes and no. Garbage heads aren't easy to figure."

"I'm ready and anxious to buy Larry's shares," I said. "That'll give me fifty percent of you I can really squeeze. Filthy little bitch"—I was on my feet, ready to swing at her—"is that why Fat Phil was at the studio today? Or Fred Rory's always asking to yak with you? To put you up to this? Believe me, Juan Basqua's going to get an earful."

"They had nothing to do with my decision so you'd better keep him outa this," Verney said as she scrambled to put some pretty good distance plus a sofa between us. "The idea's my own. If I can afford to buy back you've no right to own pieces of me. No damn right!" Suddenly she ripped the braces out of her mouth and threw them across the room. "I hate these fucken things!" she screamed. "Almost as much as I hate the rest of the shit I've been putting out about you!"

"Which is nothing compared to what I could put out about you!" I screamed right back. "And driveway painters come cheap!"

"But I'm doing it!" she kept right on screaming as if I'd said nothing, not caring that Tom and Milly were in the kitchen doorway, very upset and frightened. "Not charging you a cent for giving you a good image! For making it possible for you to get out among human beings! And this's how you pay me back, you fuzzy creeps! By trying to own me! By not letting me buy back what you should be glad to give me for nothing!"

With a sudden screech she went for Larry, who put up his hands like someone waiting to be hit by a wave that would knock him out before it drowned him. She was all over him, scratching at his face, even trying to bite him in the throat, and she might've hurt him if Simon hadn't pushed me aside, because I was swinging my purse at Verney, to grab her—his right hand across the back of her neck—and squeeze so hard she screamed again, but with pain as she let go.

Holding her like a wriggling snake, but not squeezing so hard, Simon marched Verney toward the front door which he gestured for Milly to open before she and Tom were to go back to the kitchen.

"I'm throwing you out," he told Verney, "not only because of what you've thought about and said and done, but because you came here to discuss business on Friday night, which is holy to God and me. So in my house you obey God's laws. And it doesn't matter to either of us if you don't like it. You just obey. On a day of rest there's no business."

His push sent her outside before he shut the door, stood against it and sighed with relief for her having sense enough not to kick against it.

Larry was shook up, and not because of a couple of scratches at the side of his chin that could give him rabies or his ear bleeding a little. First I wiped at the blood with my handkerchief, then began to cry, until Simon said something so crazy it made me laugh so wild it put Larry in the position of changing parts with me, because now I became the patient.

"I hate to say this, Joyce," Simon scolded after he began to look for Verney's braces, "but it's your fault. Your fault," he repeated, "for never giving Verney religious training. That's why we're suddenly dealing with a girl devil."

CHAPTER TEN

SIMON: To Joyce and Larry, Verney's a devil. To me too she is a devil. Even to herself, she's a devil. But to a devil she is a monster. Not only because she doesn't have a conscience, but worse, she's got no understanding of what a conscience is. And this doesn't bother her at all. That's what makes her a monster. An it. Even the people I once worked with had consciences or knew what they were. Most of us, whenever we had to, could choke ours to death. And every time mine came to life again—because a conscience is immortal—I was able to kill it. Until came the day when it got bigger and stronger than me. Then it almost killed me before I saved my life by promising to get well and making up to God for what I done.

Like thunder, while I was out of my head, I realized how conscience was like one of God's very special angels, maybe like the one who almost got beat wrestling by Jacob because he held on so tight, which is exactly what I did while every part of my body, except my mind, wanted to die. Because like it says in Holy Torah, the Old Testament too, which has all of the Torah in it, Jacob saw God face to face. And one day when my fever and head was worst—I did too. Seen Him and got His message. Through exercise I was to make my body whole again, but more important, by repenting, by praying, by being good I was to make my conscience the strongest part of me. Listen and believe—if you don't. After you've had the experience of talking direct to God, or one of His angels, that's when you realize there's no fooling around. When a conscience is called to account by God, even one that's smaller than the teeniest dot and blacker than black, it gets His terrible conclusion. Because size isn't important. Having a conscience is. But if you're a cursed thing without a conscience, then you're damned and you'd be better off not to be born because you're so lost that even angels made up out of one hundred percent pity can't find you. Then, like God's done before in history, He turns His face away and no one on His side ever bothers again to look for you.

That is Verney's terrible curse. So when I threw her out of the guest house, which is my house, it wasn't only because of the way she was talking to Joyce, who after all is her mother, and to Larry who is in such trouble that my head's breaking with thinking of how to help him. It was because she's a very terrible thing. Yes, I understand what I'm saying—a thing, not a person. This, I swear, was a conclusion I wrestled against coming to. Like Jacob wrestled with the man who was at least an angel, I wrestled with my mind not to believe what it told me. And I lost because about a week or so before the night I threw her out for saying and acting so terrible, she'd walked into the grocery with Mr. Middle America. In person and close up he's a sight to see, so not surprising, all the ladies and other customers in our store looked at him, their mouths open. Honest, he looks just like Abraham Lincoln on the five-dollar bill Polchansky took in when he first opened for business, which is now framed under glass and hanging over the cash register.

To stop the commotion I took Verney and Mr. Middle

America into the back room and asked them to what did I owe the honor of a special visit from two such famous people?

That Verney—I've always been more than a little afraid of her since she gave me the Super-Yid poster which made me lose my temper and start a big commotion—she held on to Middle America's hand and said how glad she was to announce she'd become one of us.

"Please explain," I said because I didn't understand.

Verney pushed Mr. Middle America a little toward me. "Him. His real name's Nathan Levy."

Now that surprised me. "Nathan Levy?"

"Doesn't that make him some kind of a special Jew?" Verney asked me. "Kind of like a priest?"

"Very special." I stuck out my hand so we could shake while I wondered that maybe Abraham Lincoln could also've been Jewish, and how this fact was covered up by history? Abraham is a very holy Jewish name. And Lincoln could maybe once've been Levy before this family got lost somewhere in America. Why not? Their name could've been changed by an immigration inspector who wanted everyone to have American names. This would have to be looked into. "Still, I don't understand," I said to Verney, "how this makes you one of us."

Remembering back, I realize how bad, how evil, was her smile. "By injection," she said. "I'm Jewish by injection."

"For chrissakes, Verney, you dragged me over for this?" Abraham Lincoln–Mr. Middle America–Nathan Levy said. "If you want the news to go national that we're putting it all together, why don't you take an ad in the *Free Press?*"

He was boiling and walked right out. Verney's frozen smile began to melt into something that looked like fear and she stumbled over a lot of words how she was going to have him fired and not use any of his songs and she hoped I wasn't mad and she'd really liked Nathan, especially after she found out he was Jewish, which is why she'd done with him what wasn't really considered a sin anymore. Besides, since I read the Bible so much, I should know how many of those original long-beards did it to each other, even with their daughters. But everyone knew that, excepting a few, of which I was one. Jews were very horny, but that's why they were so talented. Which was why she'd first become interested in Nathan Levy, but now he could go to hell and he was going to be fired right away.

"Please, Verney, let him alone," I said. "The group needs him. Enough, I say. Enough. And we're very busy this afternoon."

Can you believe that some customers congratulated me for knowing two such famous people? That some women said Verney was a wonderful girl because she came to visit her Uncle Simon, because that's what she called me as she said good-bye and blew a kiss at me? But how were they to know what they didn't know and couldn't see—how she was a monster? Even I didn't see it then. Not all the way.

So that's how I felt about her before that awful Friday night. Puzzled and upset. Later I realized how she was cursed by being born without a conscience. This is a sad way for one person to feel about another. Then, after I heard her that Friday night and saw how she would've been glad to kill Larry and her mother—I mean actually kill them—I felt sorry for Joyce. But even more sorry for Larry, who at last, I saw, was growing a conscience big enough for more than me in it. And this was how he was being paid back. This and other things that made me ask for answers in my prayers. But God wasn't answering, so I would have to be patient until He decided to. Still I was impatient.

These were the kinds of things I was thinking about all the time, even this morning which I told myself on waking up was to be the morning of the happiest day of my life. Because on this particular Friday night I was presenting a Torah to our congregation. A holy Torah and so beautiful in its blue velvet mantle, all embroidered in gold and silver thread, and wearing over the mantle a silver breastplate, very beautiful, and an even more beautiful silver crown on top. Beautiful as these were, they didn't compare to the Torah itself, which at last arrived at International from Israel.

Larry went with me to pick it up. Also my customs broker, who got into an argument with customs about whether it should come in duty-free. The customs broker said the Torah was a work of art. The inspector said it wasn't because it wasn't old. I said that paying the duty didn't bother me. Then, suddenly, a chief inspector—not Jewish—put a stop to the whole argument by saying the Torah was a work of art, which it is and more.

Imagine, the man who wrote it all out, from memory, mind you, was so holy that he looked like light. I met him and felt honored and blessed. He has the most beautiful penmanship you can imagine. With every letter he says a prayer, so that every letter becomes a beautiful design inspired by God. The skins he printed on were the best parchment without even the smallest blemish and joined so fine you couldn't see a seam unless you used a microscope. The poles for the scrolls and knobs are of olivewood with perfect grains. When I carried the Torah to Larry's car I still don't remember if my feet touched the ground, but if they did it was only my toes.

You should've seen how they were waiting in my *shul*, how some of the men actually cried as they danced with joy around the Torah. Some kissed me, everybody tried to hug me, shake my hand, called me son and brother, even saint, which bothered me as it made me happy. Our rabbi asked to hold off my presenting the Torah for two, three weeks until he could invite some special friends and other people he respected to be with us when I carried the Torah under a *chuppah* held up by people who deserved to be part of so wonderful a *mitzvah*.

Happy I was, especially after our rabbi said Larry could be one of the four men who held the *chuppah*, yet all the time I was sad, disturbed, worried for Larry who, because his conscience had got big enough to hold Joyce and Verney as well as me, was sinking into deeper and deeper trouble.

One example—unannounced, a gorilla in a very shiny sort of green-gray suit comes right to their front door one night and insists to Larry how he's gotta be let in because he's related by family and blood to George Atkinson, the wop bum who sailed into all of us at Juan Basqua's. So he's got a worthwhile piece of a jukebox syndicate in Ohio, Illinois, Michigan, West Virginia and Kentucky, which also means he's got the strongest ins with record stores, radio stations and television people. So what does he want? Only a hunk of Verney, not too big, for pushing every release and personal appearance she'd ever make. Naturally Larry sent him on to Mike Loesinger and Kerry–Ellison for them to brush him off, which made him come right back with a local hulk to warn Larry and me too, seeing as I was there when they showed, how hogging any kind of action had to be resented by certain important people who boiled over very quick.

Without blood we got them out of the house, but not before Verney told them how she would've done business if she owned herself. That put Larry right on the phone to Juan Basqua, who in less than two hours got the musclers picked up. The visitor got put on the first plane going east somewhere and he had to buy a ticket for the local, who was told to do himself good by never coming back.

That's only a small sample of the kind of trouble Larry and Joyce, and through them me, were involved in. And over everything was the bigger trouble of Verney who complained to Hammschlager, Kerry–Ellison, Mary Scott, Mrs. Beverly Droutswood, Libby Dorne that whore, even telephoning Fred Rory and writing letters to Basqua, and calling and writing people in the record company. Also, when she gave interviews she dropped hints about her being unhappy and how when she was a little girl her biggest ambition was to be adopted by people who lived on a farm. Good people who had a pump organ in their farmhouse, went to church every Sunday and would've made her join a 4-H club.

Then really getting nasty, on her own she hired a lawyer

and an accountant, two young wise-cracking sharpshooters with thick sideburns, fairy clothes and three-colored shoes with big buckles. And did they give Mike Loesinger plenty of headaches with demands to see every business paper and bill involving Verney. They were also insisting on the longest explanations of every piece of business that involved Verney, who with her group'd made a couple of more records—"Holy Water" and "Jesus Beat"—which I really hated. But they were climbing the charts down South and getting more and more good mentions all around. Finally, now naturally, Verney seemed to hate me the most because I wouldn't have these records in my house. Also for the other things that'd got her down on me. Because Super-Yid wasn't hanging in my bedroom, but was in the attic somewhere, didn't mean he'd lost his power, so he was always after me to belt her a couple—for her own good, he said. It was a big struggle not to listen to him.

It finally happened. Mike Loesinger insisted that Joyce and Larry come to his office for a meeting, where even before they settled down in their chairs, he gave it to them straight. He was resigning from that part of his work that involved anything to do with Verney. If this meant he'd lose their account, it had to be, because Verney's miserable team were occupying him so much there wasn't time for his other clients and obligations. As well as his wife and children.

"Believe me," Larry told me what Mike said, "you know I've changed my unlisted home number again? Again," he repeated, "and how they get it I don't know." Then he gave Joyce and Larry his new number and told them to please guard it with their lives from Verney because her two miserable bastards never called his home before midnight, which is why his wife's half out of her mind. "So I want them and her off our backs," he finished. "Now tell me I'm wrong."

Nobody could, not really. So after everyone was satisfied that Verney wanting to buy out Joyce and Larry was her idea alone, not suggested by anyone else, it was Larry who told

Basqua and Hammschlager what he thought should be done. Both agreed it was a very good idea to turn over the corporate books on Verney to Fred Rory. His office could handle matters and seeing how he was located in New York the two jerks couldn't call him so easy. When they tried to he was always out and he wouldn't accept their registered mail. Finally when they got so frustrated that with Verney they had a meeting with Larry poolside because he wouldn't let them in the house, he told them straight out to go ahead and sue. So far they hadn't been able to find Verney getting a dime short of her fair share. Besides, because there wasn't anything in the records but an honest shake, an audit—for which Verney'd have to pay—would only prove how square everyone was with her. Another thing, as easy as it'd been to make her, it would be that easy to break her, seeing as she had no one in her corner who couldn't be taken away in less than a day. And yet another thing—any agreements or contracts they might have with Verney, written down or on a handshake, was worth nothing because she was a minor and Mrs. Tunig was her mother and legal guardian.

Afterwards Larry told me how he couldn't stop wishing that it was the old days during the meeting. It bothered me that he felt that way. It bothered me that I felt the same way too.

It was a stand-off, favoring us in points. Still, we had to keep on taking pressure because Verney, the enemy, was living in the house. Also we lost Mrs. Beverly Droutswood, who finally had to resign because she wasn't able to control Verney enough to keep her self-respect and she couldn't stand for what the girl was doing to herself and us. Without Mrs. Droutswood around, Verney was bitchier than ever. Where once she hardly took meals with Larry and Joyce, now she was at the table with them at least twice a day and their only escape was on Friday nights when they ate with me. Verney wasn't allowed inside my house.

Go prove she was responsible for the fire which lucky for us was discovered before it did more than a little damage to a side wall of the guest house. But putting it out involved the fire department and they found firebug evidence. Right then and there Larry got to Kerry and Ellison to keep the fire out of the papers and he ordered Joyce not to file a claim with the insurance company because they'd pay but might cancel her policy. As far as the police was concerned, we sold them maybe thirty percent that the fire could've been started by some of the people I'd had trouble with last year. Still the fire and police investigations brought in building and zoning inspectors who managed to give Joyce a bad time until they were convinced that everything in the building code had been followed to the letter when the guest house was made over for me. So for days on end we had to think more of Verney than anyone else. And I did worry about maybe some night she would burn me alive, a prospect not to be sneezed at, not after you had to take the looks and sneering laughter she gave us.

So this particular Friday morning, which I'd already decided was going to be the happiest day of my life, was already too much occupied by Verney. So the only way to push her and the problems she'd made aside was to concentrate on the day. Right off I washed my hands more than usual in the little bowl on the night table next to my bed and said the right prayer. Then I hurried through my exercises and got into the shower where I scrubbed hard, knowing all the while that later in the afternoon I'd shower again because I wanted to be specially clean for tonight—wondering all the while if for men who were presenting a Torah to their *shul* there wasn't some kind of special bath, say like the bath a religious woman uses in the *mikvah* once in her life, just before she's married.

Putting this in my mind where it wouldn't be forgotten, I dressed, kissed the fringes of my clean *tzitzit* before I slipped it over my head and arranged the fringes over my belt. Then I put on my *tefillin,* taking care to center the little box on my forehead and making a very neat letter *Shin* when I wrapped the strap three times around my left hand. This done I got my *tallis,* kissed its hem and wrapped it around my head by crossing my arms before I put it back over my shoulders. Now I turned toward Jerusalem and the Temple to pray among other things that this day would be a happy one for all good people, for Joyce, especially for Larry and our *shul*. I really felt good as I put everything away.

At the breakfast table I washed my hands again, cut a slice of pumpernickel, sprinkled it with salt, said a prayer and ate. This morning it was very delicious and my morning got better because the doorbell chimed and there was Larry, who after he kissed the *mezuzah,* said he'd invited himself over for breakfast. And if I didn't mind, Joyce also said she wanted to sit at my table. This was unusual because it wasn't more than ten minutes past eight, but Larry said Joyce was up, dressed and hoping she too'd be invited.

My eyes filled with sentiment because, no matter how the morning was already filled with smog, I only saw friendship and affection, and these were lots stronger than thoughts of Verney that'd bothered me so much last night it was hours before I fell asleep. But she wasn't entirely to blame, seeing as I also had thoughts of my family, mostly of my father, who would've been so proud and happy to see me giving a Torah to my *shul*. My father, the most he could afford to give every year was a ton of coal, hard coal, to his *shul,* and when things got bad in the Depression the ton of coal cost him as much as a month's rent for our flat. But every year, even if he had to starve himself and us, the ton of coal was donated. And on cold winter days when the weather was bad I bet it was appreciated almost as much, or by some people even as much, as the biggest gift anyone could give—which is a Torah. So I decided it was time to find out about them, which now put two more things in my mind—to find out if there was a special bath and about my family. That God had forgiven me didn't raise the odds that they had too. Still yes or no, I wanted to know about them, to see them. And God might make me His messenger to Larry's family, to Mitch's, maybe even Frank Goldfarb's and Crazy Sachs's. Who of them was alive? Where did they live? Had time made their wounds more bearable? For sure they didn't live in Brownsville anymore which is all filled up with *reliefnik* niggers and Puerto Ricans. But a detective could find them, especially Mitch's family because his sister married a cop and that would make her easiest to trace. Then through her we could get leads on the others.

Maybe on my family too, what was left of it, because there wasn't any reason for my father and mother not to be alive. Lots of customers that come in every day are over sixty, even over seventy and some over eighty. And I got my strength from my father. This gave me another thing to remember. To speak to our rabbi and ask him to say prayers tonight for my father, mother and family, and the families of the guys who'd once been my friends, as if all of them were alive and well. So I'd have to ask Larry how much I could tell the rabbi about me because it had to involve telling about us if I wanted the rabbi's advice on what to do. By now, with so much on my mind, Verney was pushed way to one side. Still, she was there. So—and this was something else to remember today—should I be forgiving and pray for Verney? For sure no one else was, or would, and maybe on this day God would listen—He always heard—and like He was able to make man out of dust, which is harder to do than anything, scientists will tell you, He might decide to make a conscience for a monster girl born without one.

There they were having breakfast with me, Larry and Joyce, she looking very nice but embarrassed at taking part almost right from the beginning in the biggest day of my life. Tom and Milly were all smiles and looking forward to being at the services tonight—I'd asked the rabbi and he said they could come but Milly would have to sit with the women, which she said didn't bother her at all. So now I asked Joyce if she was coming too because I'd counted on her being there. She thanked me and said yes, of course. Other people were coming. Mike Loesinger and his wife for example. While we were eating, congratulations by telegram were delivered from Fred Rory and Juan Basqua. While we were drinking our coffees other wires came from Phil Hammschlager and Mary Scott, Jim Kerry and Norm Ellison, even from Mrs. Leola Druckman, who is the widow related to Mrs. Polchansky and a nice person but for somebody else.

How to accommodate all the persons who might show at the services was a question. Another thing, that Joyce was coming and her not being Jewish could be accepted. Even Milly and Tom would be all right even if they never went through with changing their religion. There would even be a place for Verney, who I didn't want to think about more than necessary. But I had to, it seemed, particularly since I kept remembering how she once asked, when all of us were getting along pretty good, to watch me pray when I wore my *tefillin,* because she wanted to hear me say a prayer for her and the Silent Majority, and she wanted to see how I worked the magic box on my forehead to make it come true. If too many other *goyim* came tonight and stayed afterwards for *Kiddush,* just what would people think? In every congregation there's jealous *k'nockers,* so we've got our share and one in particular who thinks of himself as very very funny was sure to say again, as if nobody'd heard him the last time, that maybe the congregation should put up bleachers and a big searchlight outside so the occasion could be like a Hollywood premiere. Which gave me some other things to think about, like how nice it would've been if Verney would've been there with her mother. And that first and last I didn't want to lose sight of how holy was this occasion. That was absolutely first. My joy was vanity, so I said a quick prayer to myself for forgiveness.

We finished breakfast almost ten and I telephoned Polchansky to say good morning. Because I wasn't coming in all day I asked if a man from the union had showed. After he said yes and not to worry, we talked about the cakes and wine for the *Kiddush,* how many *challahs* we should have, who was going to help out in the kitchen with coffee and tea, what time the kosher restaurant would deliver whatever else was needed.

Everything was under control, Polchansky said over and over again. Then just before I hung up he cleared his throat and asked if I'd got some telegrams.

"Yes," I said. "And a very nice one came from Mrs. Druckman."

"Leola?" he said like it was a big surprise. "That's nice." Another clear of his throat. "She's coming with us tonight and she'd like to help serve."

"Fine," I said. "That's nice. Be sure to thank her."

On a day like this, what else could I say?

Because Verney was in the house still asleep it wasn't safe to leave it alone, so Milly couldn't go along with Tom as he drove Joyce, Larry and me to Mount Carmel Memorial Park where Itzik rested. Tom drove carefully and with his uniform wore a black homburg, just like Itzik's, a gift from him. Larry wore a dark suit, I did too, and Joyce wore a navy blue suit and hat. Once we got on the freeway the drive was about twenty minutes. Since none of us said very much, it was a relief to see the cemetery. Joyce had the section and plot on a card, so with the map Tom got from the cemetery office we found Itzik's grave in no time.

With all our plans and resolutions to come here, this was still our first visit—Larry's and mine—so we hung back and let Joyce go ahead of us along the narrow path until we came to a plot with marble posts and iron chains turning green hanging from the posts. The plot was large enough for maybe five or six graves, but Itzik's was the only one. Inside the chains, one of which could be taken down for people to go through, were two marble benches each large enough for three people. They were on either side of the grave, on well-kept grass because Joyce'd paid for perpetual care. There also were nice little bunches of flowers and ferns in borders on either side of the grave and all around the border of the plot.

The monument was just like Itzik, a square chunk of granite with a polished face and the Ten Commandments carved on it. Also his name and dates—Jizchock Yanowitz, 1898–1968—

and underneath a real sentiment—"Eternal God, remember the soul of my revered husband, Jizchock, who has gone unto eternity."

Larry took off his dark glasses and along with me looked at Joyce with really different eyes that became wetter and wetter. Itzik'd been married once before he married Joyce. And like everyone else in our past, what had happened to Itzik's first wife and his children, where and what they were, God knew. So all this had to be Joyce's doing, which is why Larry and me —we looked for a long time, it seemed, at Joyce. She was blinking hard until without saying anything Larry kissed her, then I did, and what difference does it make who broke down first? We all did and by that Tom's included.

We sat on the benches, Larry and Joyce on one, Tom and me on the other, with me thinking how Itzik in his way was responsible for my almost dying, my wrestling with the angel of death, my seeing God, my now living good, my giving tonight a Torah to my *shul*. Surely it didn't take an intellectual giant to figure out how Itzik'd been God's instrument. When I stood to put on my *tallis* and say *Kel Moley Rachamim,* which is a beautiful prayer for the dead but not a *Kaddish,* they stood too and I was surprised after we said Amen when Larry showed me how they'd been following along in little books with an English translation of this and other prayers which he'd got from some Jewish mortuary.

The smog didn't seem to be so thick, the sun was cutting through from somewhere, and not too far from us other people were leaving a new grave some laborers were beginning to fill in. This brought me—if no one else—back to a realization that for Itzik his troubles in this world were long over. How things were in another world I couldn't say. But we were still alive, very much, and so were some aggravating problems of living.

Finally it was time to go and as Larry and Joyce went ahead of us, because like I already said, the paths were narrow, Joyce took Larry's arm and to my shock I suddenly realized how both of them were walking middle aged. I mean Joyce's toes were turned out, her steps were short and she put her feet down flat. And Larry walked with his back bent a little, his head moving up and down, each foot coming down deliberately, almost like each step was stamping on something. To make sure, I stopped, motioned for Tom, who was older than any of us, to pass by so I could see how he walked. Exactly the same way as them, as if the experience of everything in his life that'd been sad or hard or heartbreaking rested on his shoulders and back. Yes, that's the way Larry and Joyce were walking. Like they were back numbers. Like they no longer counted for as much with now-people and now-things, which even with his big make-believe could also be said for Basqua, who was living in this country like an old phony *conquistador* on a ranch guarded by grapes and guards against an outside that really didn't care a hell of a lot, I'm sure, whether he lived or died and exactly how and why and when. And those two apes who came to visit—Atkinson and Grobbernasch—and for that matter Fred Rory too, time and things seem to've also passed them by. All back numbers. Since we returned I've heard and read some things about how God is dead. That's really a nerve. But I don't believe this at all. Maybe, like us, He's also a back number. If that's the case, what's good enough for Him is good enough for me. For that I'll settle.

Still, if I was a back number, which I would've wanted to be if Larry—let God alone—was one, why was I—not him—walking so erect? So there were other things for my mind to hold. Like when would Larry and Joyce and me too, I guess, have rest? Know peace? Not worry about being so much on our guards? Be able to take a vacation? Relax?

Walking to the big car I remembered that even before this morning's telegrams there'd been a letter from the rabbi of the Center in Mexico, congratulations and blessing me for what I was doing for my *shul*. Also asking did I ever again intend to visit Mexico City? And *amigo de mi alma*, Señor Tunig, how was he? Did either of us miss Mexico City?

Right then I missed it with a wrench, especially the nice,

big, friendly Chanukah celebration and decorations they'd always had at the Center. I even missed the Christmas decorations all over the city which weren't really religious at all except around churches, so that the Zócalo would have beautiful electric signs over all the streets leading into it, with right in the middle a beautiful red island of poin-something-or-other-they-have-them-here-too flowers.

But most of all I missed going at night on the Center's bus filled with kids to Alameda Park to see the balloons. Tens of thousands of them were sold there, so that the whole long side of the park along Juarez was a solid cloud of flying colors made up of balloon clowns and turtles and Donald Ducks, Mickey Mouses and fat chickens with little balloon chicks on their backs. Also funny centipedes and Bugs Bunnies and big moon faces with *Feliz Navidad* coming out of their mouths. Everything you can name that's good and happy-looking was there in balloons, with thousands and thousands of people walking along under the trees sparkling with colored lights and every so often beautiful rockets sailing into the skies to rain more colors down on us. It was fun to see balloons sailing out of the windows of moving cars, different to see the Indian women selling all kinds of foods, even chestnuts. I watched out who our kids bought food from, and kept them away from *chicharrón,* which is fried pig skin and just about as disgusting *trayf* as you can get. Still I'd buy a couple of fried bananas from a clean peddler whose wagon looked like the kind that used to sell sweet potatoes on corners along Pitkin Avenue, except that his was more fancy because it was fixed up to look like the little locomotive that took kids around the zoo in Chapultepec Park.

Then there were the Santa Clauses with the cutest little sleds and our last Christmas there I must've squeezed myself into at least fifteen sleds so my picture could be taken for every kid on the bus. I liked them and they liked me. Even the bigger kids, boys and girls starting to think of getting married, who hung out in the Zona Rosa, in the Arcade and the Kinaret, told me to bring them some pictures. Which I did. The only thing I didn't exactly like was how on Christmas Day the Santas disappeared and their places in the park were taken by lots of Three Wise Men teams dressed up sort of sultanish, with one of them always making his face black like a *schvartzer*. But they used the same Santa Claus sleds.

Some things to think about on this day. That's what I told myself as Tom drove us back to the house where we had lunch before I rested, read my *Siddur*, did ten laps of the pool, starting sidestroke and finishing breast. Then I lifted some weights because I finally got around to admitting how I hadn't slept sound the night before, so I would've given anything for a tired-out afternoon nap. This wasn't to be, so I just stayed in bed until about three-thirty when I showered good again, let Larry comb my hair and beard, and because it was still daylight allowed Tom to drive me to my rabbi's house for supper. Larry promised they'd all be at the *shul* early.

"What time's the man coming?" I asked. "Seven?"

"Before that," Larry said.

"The same man?"

Larry nodded. "He knows the house and what we want."

"And what to expect," I said with a big shaking of my head.

Larry agreed, but not happy. "He'd know how to handle it. But let's hope it doesn't come up."

Please let me explain. You see, Tom and Milly were also going along with Larry and Joyce. So it wasn't safe to leave the house alone, especially when Verney might be in it. Or if she was gone when we left, she had keys to the front and back doors. Not to the guest house because the locks'd been changed and no key was made for her. Not often were all of us gone at the same time, but today, coming back from the cemetery, we found Milly a nervous wreck because of what Verney'd been doing and saying to her all the time she was alone. And miserable sly monster that she is, Verney drove away minutes before we got home. Sometimes I think she's got radar. Milly was really crying, carrying on how Verney'd gone around lighting whole books of matches and holding them close to the drapes and curtains, kind of holding them under the piano, places like that, all the while saying so innocent-like how she was just looking for an earring she'd dropped somewhere, so why shouldn't she be allowed to find it? Milly got a big flashlight, but Verney just laughed and said books of matches all lit gave more light.

Then she went to the butler's pantry where she fooled around with Joyce's Royal Crown Derby Hat dinner plates, making as if she was having trouble holding them and almost giving Milly heart failure whenever she made like dropping one. Next she began to almost have accidents with vases and china figures. Finally she tried to break into the bookcase in the center hall to get at Joyce's collection of miniature things. Sure there were day-workers in the house, so Milly wasn't really alone. But like everyone else nowadays they weren't going to get involved, so Verney was having things her way until Milly became hysterical. That sort of scared Verney off and out of the house.

Now, like a couple of times since the fire, a private agency detective was going to baby-sit the house while we were gone. We'd had this man, Barney Moodus, before and had confidence in him. In the old days he might've worked directly for Larry, who liked his style and the way he went through the house like a bank watchman to check windows, the garden and cellar. Also he never touched a drop and always cleaned up the kitchen after he ate only what was set aside for him. He'd even wash the percolator. Still, it's a hell of a way to live, another something else to think about in my already overcrowded head.

As I carried the Torah from the sanctuary all around the *shul* in procession, I tried to walk humble. Funny, now that I wanted my back to be bent, my steps small and shuffly, it wasn't to be, not yet. No, like a young man with the most beautiful bride in the world on his arm, I walked with wet, proud eyes and felt love for everyone in the little *shul,* that and more for Joyce, who was smiling at me with wonder, and for my friend Larry as he carried the right front pole of the *chuppah* and turned many many times to look at me like I remember my father had at my *bar mitzvah* after I read the Haftorah so good.

In another Torah already owned by the *shul* we were up to the Third Book of Moses, or Leviticus, in what you call the nineteenth chapter. For a long time this's been my favorite because it tells Israel how God is their Lord and peace offerings made to Him must be of your own free will. With a silver pointer I touched each letter of every word and read very well, no mistakes or mispronouncings, filling in all the unwritten letters, and I stopped after I read how God gave instructions on how much harvest should be given to the poor. But our rabbi told me to go on reading, so I went through about verse eighteen which says, among other things, how you should not bear grudges against the children of your people! So right then and there I begged Verney, who of course wasn't here, for forgiveness. And that's all I wanted to read because I didn't want to forget this, the last, which seemed to me a message verse.

Afterwards at the *Kiddush* Mrs. Druckman was nice, not making a pest of herself. And for the few minutes we talked this time I changed my impression of her because she is intelligent and looks and is dressed like a lady, quite attractive, except she trembles every now and then as if she's struggling not to go to pieces. When she asked my forgiveness for what she'd done in all the excitement at Joyce's house I told her to forget it and accepted an invitation to go with her to an Israel exhibit of ancient things from around the time of the Second Temple, including some Dead Sea scrolls, at UCLA. I also promised to tell her about my trip, what I'd seen in Eretz Israel.

All in all, it was a very nice evening, a good *Kiddush*, my rabbi so proud, even the *k'nockers* keeping their mouths shut. Larry getting along fine, the same with Joyce who was able to find people to talk to who weren't even remotely interested in Verney or old history, Polchansky almost tearing my arm off because I'd been so nice to his wife's cousin and for that keeping his wife from bothering me, at which she is an expert.

So about ten o'clock it was time to go home and Milly and Tom drove away with Joyce because Larry said he was going to keep me company. I don't ride on *Shabbes* and for a long time he's been against my walking through dark streets alone. Carrying our velvet *zeckels* with our *Siddurs* and *tallises* in them, happy with Larry because he still wore his *yarmulkah*, we walked the about four miles to Lexington Road. This took more than an hour because while we took our time I told Larry most of what'd accumulated in my mind since getting up this morning and how in spite of everything this had to be the happiest day of my life. In some way at least I hoped it'd made him happpy too. I also spilled out how I felt about searching up our families.

"I've wanted to talk to you about that more'n once," he admitted after coughing so hard I had to slap his back. "But I didn't know how."

"Then you also think of them? Of our old friends' people?" I asked.

"Since we've had this come up with Verney, more and more," he said. "But suppose you—we—find them? Then what?"

I gripped his arm. "Let's leave that to God. If He wants us to find them, won't He also tell us what to do?"

"I guess so," Larry said after he thought this over. "But you won't start looking without me? Like take off for New York on your own?"

"No," I said. "To both—no. I give my word."

There should've only been one car parked out front, the one belonging to Barney Moodus, the private detective. Instead, there were four. Also, the only house on the block with more than the ordinary amount of lights on was Joyce's, so Larry handed me his *zeckel* before he started running up the path with me right behind. He opened the door in a rush and we went through together before he shouted for Joyce, Milly, Tom—somebody. It was Tom who came out of the living room and he could only motion for us to follow because he was too upset to talk.

Standing with Milly, hanging on to her, was Joyce, with both still wearing their hats and gloves. On one of the two matching sofas before the fireplace, with a coffee table between them, were three young weirdos, thin as snakes, just as dangerous and lots dirtier-looking. They were sitting on a blanket that I later found out Joyce told Milly to bring. Two of them were smoking pot while the third one rested his dirty head against the sofa and was breathing real slow, with a dumb smile all over his face. We found out he'd just minutes before sucked a sugar cube. Meanwhile, Barney Moodus sat on the opposite sofa and covered them with his gun. That wasn't all. Around Barney, who looked very mussed up and in pain, as if a piano'd been dropped on him to give him more than a busted lip, swellings on his cheeks and other lumps, stood three professional hard types no more'n a coupla years younger'n us, I'd say. We found out their names were Lou, Sid and Jerry. Their last names don't matter because they keep changing. While one of them kept his gun on Barney, the other two covered us. And last but not least— on a blanket in the middle of the room away from everybody was an acetylene torch, a five-gallon can that Barney said was almost filled with gasoline and a carton with cardboard dividers in it. In the box were four fire bombs made out of wine bottles. And on the piano was a tire iron, a Boy Scout axe, a couple of hunting knives in sheaths and two sets of brass knucks.

"Shake them down, Lou." Sid meant us. Right off we knew he gave the orders. "But don't hurt them."

Jerry took our *zeckels* and Lou went over us real quick after we raised our hands without being told, for which we got a thank-you look. Satisfied that we were clean he let us put our hands down and move next to Joyce, Milly and Tom. Meanwhile Jerry opened the *zeckels,* poked around, then handed them back.

"Ask him," Sid said as he pointed his gun at Barney. "Ask him if he isn't lucky we're here." Sid now looked from me to Larry as if checking out for himself what he might've heard about us. "The only reason we're covering your man is because he's gotta watch those animals. That's his responsibility, not ours. So go ahead, ask him," he said direct to Larry.

When Barney started to say something the two guys who could move began to laugh and make farting sounds, so Jerry laid his gun across their heads. Just hard enough to shut them up. But that didn't stop him from giving them bonus clouts so they'd remember how to behave. Then he took away their roaches, for which Joyce really thanked him.

Now Barney started again—plenty embarrassed, believe me—to tell how he was sitting in the center hall when he heard a car pull up. Right after the chimes sounded he opened the door on the chain and found himself looking smack into the business end of Sid's gun. Also one of Sid's heavy work-shoes was inside the door. Next thing Sid's got a cuff on Barney's wrist, all the while warning him not to do anything to get himself shot. There was just no way out of Barney's opening the door and giving up. But they were surprised to find cuffs as well as a billy on him, so he had to explain how he was a private investigator.

A bodyguard they understood, a detective took explaining, but Barney wouldn't say anything so they just settled down to wait for us when they heard two more cars park out front.

Jerry covered Barney while he peeked through a dining room window and saw four people coming to the door, one of them a girl. When the chimes sounded, Sid warned Barney to open the door as if nothing was wrong. Standing close behind him in the shadows, if an accident developed he'd be the first to get hurt.

Yet nobody was really prepared for what happened when Barney opened the door. For a second a flashlight blinded him before he heard Verney—he was pretty sure it was Verney although he couldn't really see because of the light—say it wasn't Tom but to get him anyway. The next second he got the flashlight across the face and a tire iron got laid on the front of him as he fell backward. The second after that he got jumped on by these three and all together they were doing a pretty good job of kicking him apart, which might've happened if Sid and his boys hadn't stepped in. Lou said he chased the girl but she got away in the dark. All the same he pulled the distributor caps off all the cars out front except theirs.

Here comes the switch. Barney now asks the guys who're holding him to help hold the three creeps until we got home, especially after Lou found the torch and other stuff, all of which he brought in the house, in one of the cars. So while Barney covered the three narcs, who also wouldn't say anything, with just one shell in his gun—Sid and his boys covered Barney.

Imagine how it scared Joyce to be let in by Jerry and ordered along with Milly and Tom to march into the living room. But not so scared she couldn't tell Milly to get blankets for the sofa and to put them under the gasoline can and other stuff on her Oriental rug. Right away there was no doubt in my mind, or Larry's, why Verney'd brought those creeps. Because the Mustang out front was hers.

What to do about her was a serious problem, but right now Sid said he wanted to talk to Larry and I could come along. Since there was no arguing with the way Sid spoke, we went into Larry's office. There Sid closed the door and put his gun on Larry's desk.

"We're messengers, nothing else right now," he explained. "So after you listen, if you tell us to get out, that's what we do."

"I think the guns're supposed to tell us more'n you just said?" Larry asked.

"If I was in your shoes that's what I'd think," Sid agreed.

"You must carry some mighty heavy messages if it takes three for delivery," I had to say because I'd suddenly become afraid. Not of him, but of who sent him.

Sid looked sort of pained. "My message is mostly for him," he said to me but pointed at Larry. Now he was being very patient and obviously not looking for trouble with us. "Meanwhile, personally, I'd like to know what's going on around here? First a private dick's guarding your house. Next kids come here to beat his brains out and burn this beautiful place down." He thought about this for a couple of seconds. "Verney isn't your real daughter, Mr. Tunig?"

"My stepdaughter," Larry said.

"So maybe you tried to rape her?" he asked. "They say it happens to all of us. Reach a certain age and you start wanting kids."

Larry laughed, me too, so Sid followed. It helped take the edge off things.

"Burn this beautiful house down," Sid repeated. "Or maybe they'd got hold of her somehow? Were making her get them inside so they could clean you out? You've got plenty of high-priced stuff around."

"That could be," Larry said. To back him up, I nodded. "But they're not your bother," Larry went on. "Still you've our thanks for helping Barney hold them."

"But why a private detective?" Sid was still curious. "What's he doing here?"

"To keep people from breaking in, which he didn't do with you." Larry was patient. "Sure you probably saved Barney's life. Maybe of other people too, if anybody else'd been here. And maybe they were gonna burn everything. Still, it didn't happen because you were here."

"Lucky for you," Sid said. "For now."

"Lucky for us," Larry admitted. "Still, you wouldn't wanna go without delivering your message?"

"Not if I wanna be around tomorrow," Sid said. "You're

all right," he went on. "Yeah, the things I heard about you seem to be correct." He sighed deep and whistled. "I'll just have to tell what happened and let them get the why from you. So here goes. You didn't treat George Atkinson's relative friendly. But no matter. Marty Grobbernasch—you know him?"

"I met him some time ago. He's something I'd like to forget," Larry said.

"Not so funny." Sid shook his head. "So be glad I don't repeat it. And just remember I didn't if someday I need a favor from you."

"I'll remember," Larry said.

"Anyway, he says you've been sitting on your ass long enough. So he wants you to go to work." He pointed at Larry. "He says that—not me."

It wasn't my intention to say anything, so Larry didn't have to motion for me to keep still.

"Sid," Larry finally spoke, "I did hear you right? Grobbernasch wants me to go to work? For him?"

"You and him." Sid pointed. "That's if you want him along. But don't ask me what or where. That's not for messengers."

"So where is he?" Larry asked.

"Getting the sun outside Phoenix," Sid said. "Not far outside."

"But I got the impression he'd retired," Larry said. "I distinctly got that impression at Juan Basqua's."

"Sure," Sid said. "Grobbernasch said you might mention that. So he told me exactly what to say—no more, no less—if you did."

"So?"

"So"—Sid began to recite—"he said to tell you that Basqua, what he says, his service and advice, the whole *schmeer* he's involved in, all of it's full of shit."

It'd been a long day, with lots to fill up my mind. But why, God, should this be the last thing in it?

CHAPTER ELEVEN

VERNEY: When you're laying bare-ass naked in front of a fireplace that hasn't got a fire in it so you're pretty cold and your hands are tied behind your back, your feet also, while some old busthead named Quincy Smith is walking around you with all sorts of ropes in his hands and saying—no, he doesn't think he's tied you up to suit your personality a hundred percent—the best thing to do is not think of what's going on because it's liable to make you zonkers. So I put my mind elsewhere, like remembering over and over how Libby Dorne said there was nothing to be scared of, seeing as this lump never did anything else after he tied you up. Unless he made the knots too tight nothing happened except your circulation might get cut off for a little while. Or you could catch cold from laying on the floor in a draft. Or he might get a phone call that had to be put through by his service because it was the very big business kind. Then you could lay there for even an hour. So if the knots were too tight, or your arms or legs started to go asleep, you had to scream real loud to get him to say hold the line and make you more comfortable. But like Libby said, you didn't have to worry about him doing something dirty on you or tearing up your ass with a broomstick.

Sometimes, after you got untied, Quincy'd ask you to wash his hair. That showed he was very pleased with you. Never no more than that, Libby Dorne swore. And if Quincy did ask for the hair-washing bit you went along because he really had lotsa bread, enough to finance big company mergers, stuff like that, which made his backing pictures the small stuff he used mostly for getting people to tie up. That's why anytime at all he could get you shoved before a camera for at least a coupla lines and good close-ups. Libby told me she really liked Quincy, who was the dearest man, even worried about his getting busted, so she'd let him tie her up a coupla times and once'd even liked it. This got her so scared she went to a shrink for advice. What he told her, she wouldn't tell when I asked. Closemouthed, open-snatched bitch, she sure wanted to know everything but everything about me and us. Believe me, what mad stories I made up about them.

So here I am all tied up by this screwloose, who's got the most ordinary-looking straight clothes on—which proves how he's really flipped because for this kind of sex kick he should've been dressed up like a Mr. Witch, Barnabas Collins or maybe even an executioner, and he's not—is sitting on a camel saddle decorated with lots of silver, all the while breathing hard so his dentures're whistling like crazy, which proves he's getting real happy charges, and every so often worrying out loud how my very complex elfin personality is giving him grave problems.

If my personality is giving him problems, it's giving me fits. For right now, here's where it's at. First, we oughta start with my flipping out real bad because Joyce and Larry wouldn't give me back to myself, which right then and there proved how I was a valuable property. Second, what really bitched things was them not believing the idea was mine and mine alone.

Why couldn't they give me credit for being able to have some good ideas by myself?

Third, and here's where I started to go outa mental sync, I've always known about my bad temper, which in screaming, cursing, hitting, kicking and once in a while biting can be pretty scary, even to me because sometimes my mind goes so horror-flick that I feel able to kill off whole countries of people. And want to. Joyce digs my problem, so you'd think a normal mother'd do her best to keep me from feeling and acting this way. Instead, the way she's got things—I mean her and Larry—they give me no choice. I either play with the dirty end of the stick or suck it. And I'd made up my mind that if any sucking hadda be done on the stick it was gonna be done by other people, not Verney. Also part of the third, Simon—who's just as weird about religion as the worst Jesus-freak on the Strip—had no right getting sore when I visited his kike store to kid him about how I'd become Jewish. He doesn't get sore when Milly and Tom talk about becoming yids, which's easy to understand seeing as Jews are just niggers turned inside out. Don't think I wouldn't like to tell him that! But when I said I'd become one, that got him outraged, as if being a Jew was too good for anyone like me. So it's this, I know, and not getting into the sack with Nathan Levy—which was a mistake —that made him boot me outa the guest cottage with a shitty excuse of not allowing business to be talked around him on Friday night.

This brings me to fourth. When I set fire to the guest house —just to put them on notice how they'd better treat me right— I figured on the fire being discovered before it did real damage, so it wasn't my fault they saw it so late it needed the fire department. Naturally I denied it. But the way they looked and spoke when they wouldn't believe me was more insulting than the business called for.

Fifth, after Simon insulted me so bad by throwing me outa the guest cottage, they had no right to turn everyone against me. For instance, wouldn't you think that Fred Rory, after what I did for him, would be on my side? I learned different when he told me to perform and let people who know more manage me. Bastard. I got the same from Hammschlager—not exactly from him because he got back to me through a third- or maybe fourth-string secretary. It was even a bigger mistake trying to see Mary Scott because all she did was lecture me through an upstairs window of her house on going home and no more hinting in interviews about being on the outs with us. Ditto for Jim Kerry and Norm Ellison. Even the kids in my group were against me and that includes your Nathan Levy. One of the worst was Mike Loesinger, who had no right to tell me how he'd handle me if he was Larry. I was really humiliated when I couldn't get through to Basqua. That unhinged me so bad I flew up to Sacramento, where like a no- brain I went to the u-drive guy Larry'd used and gave him as reference.

More and more people who're against you act like pigs. This explains why some guy ten feet tall in his uniform hustled me onto the next plane for L.A., where Larry's waiting for me behind his shades. He doesn't say a word, even after we're back in the house, only shoves me upstairs into my room.

That's frustration enough to make anybody go ape. Because they should've understood, without my having to tell them, how my not seeming to care being programmed to look like a performer did bother me some right from the beginning. Look, the composers had talent. The group had it. Middle America, that yid, had more'n he needed. Only I was just about all plastic. They knew it, I knew it, Kerry and Ellison knew it among others. Everyone who was part of the business, even those dumb record people, were on to me. Sure, I told myself in the beginning, you're doing this for your career. Then I'd ask myself—what career? Take the machines away and what was left that a Disneyland dummy, like they got in the General Electric exhibit out there, couldn't do just as good?

Which is why I at least wanted the satisfaction of owning me. That made sense. If my career had turned out to be a nothing, who would've wanted any part of it? Instead I was doing all right. There were pictures of me in drugstores, dentists' offices, even in Record City where kids from all over come for their sides. And the fan mail kept coming. So only because I was a plastic fake that showed a profit, they hung on to me. That's not fair. And I figured this all out by myself.

Besides, Larry and Joyce and Simon too—when I called him uncle and sort of meant it—owed me something. Seeing how in every interview I said they were the greatest people. How what they'd once been wasn't now. So didn't people think it was great and noble of them to give me my chance, knowing how right from the beginning they'd be exposed to old stuff dug up about them? Old stuff that I must admit was true. But the way I said it only helped them. Even Basqua, who won't talk to me now, said so when he was.

So here we are—me putting out and them collecting all the benefits from good notices. The group and me doing gigs, even working on some new material, all of us giving more interviews, doing more appearances at the openings of shopping centers, showing up in youth centers in Watts, Pacoima, Venice, pretty crummy scenes but where you take your social conscience for the best publicity. Nobody cares that Joyce and Company don't have social consciences, which keep them from seeing how important it is for me to own myself. And that dumb legal-accounting twosome I've got are gonna be axed for getting everyone down on us. Besides they're responsible for all the business stuff being moved east to Fred Rory's—who doesn't seem to remember anything at all about the good relationship we established in the cave. You can believe it, there is a generation gap all right. And they're the ones who made it. So it follows, like it says in logic, that to make the world a better place they should be wiped out.

This sort of thinking dropped me so low I became just prey for those three hustlers I met all because one of the kids in the Silent Majority is real gone gay. Too bad for him because fruits can't bring themselves to make it with groupies. So when after one particular rehearsal I met Acey, Decy and Voltage—I swear that's the names they go by if they're still around, which I wouldn't bet on—without preliminaries they put the bite on me for bread.

"Why don't you types try working?" I said as a turn-down.

"How we work!" Decy said while he wriggled his ass. "Even for you if you come around with some kinda extension."

Not funny unless you're peculiar. Still it just about killed Acey and Voltage. Take my word, they were the dirtiest heads I'd met in a long time. Still certain kinds of boy'hos talk that way to turn on their johns.

"Cut it," I said. "I'm talking about real work."

Since then I've thought lots about saying this to them. Was it the way I said, not what I said, that made them look different at me? What else? So they must've seen more than I said because Voltage signals the other clowns to cool it until we get into their heap parked about a block from the rehearsal hall.

"Now our hair's down," Acey said. "Which makes us available for about anything homo saps can do."

"Anything?" I repeated after laughing because Acey sure hoped I would. Even though I sat by myself in the back seat of their heap while they crowded up front, I couldn't help smelling them. Once I didn't smell much better. Really moldy as they were, I was sitting up to my ankles in garbage. But all the smells only helped to sort of sharp me up, like say, sniffing ammonia. "Give me an example of what you mean by anything."

"Right on," Voltage said. "Like we'll even eat the body to get rid of the evidence." That's just an average example of how gruesome disgusting they were. "But that doesn't come cheap."

"Suppose I was kinky enough to want that?" I asked. "How much in advance?" Not that I didn't realize how this was becoming mighty dangerous rapping, but there's nothing wrong in knowing things. Besides, I was getting a big charge out of discussing getting rid of certain people. Without dreams what would people do to keep their minds in line? "I mean on the whole contract?"

"Depends," Decy said. "But we gotta know right now, Verney, you're serious? I mean serious enough not to lend us five, maybe ten, and forget how we're sitting here?"

I was nose to nose with a decision. There was no fooling around anymore. Either I did them in or gave up. "I'm buying work," I said, feeling more and more electric. "So it's my turn to ask how serious you guys are."

"Serious enough to tell you it costs to keep us serious," Decy said.

"How much?" I wanted to know. "How much to do the worst thing you can think of to people?"

"What we think is worst or what squares think is worst?" Voltage asked right back without even a second between my question and his.

"What squares think," I said straight out.

So Voltage looked from Acey to Decy. And they shrugged back for him to name a figure.

"It still depends," he hedged. "I gotta know more."

"Well" I said after thinking they hadda have something to go on—"suppose there were five squares I wanted outa my life? In let's say a way that looked like they got trapped in a fire? A fire that left no clues?"

"I like fires," Decy said. "They give me the most beautiful hard-ons."

"It's nice to like your work," I said and felt so great I hadda laugh. Why? Because this definitely was the kind of talk to stone you good. Tell me, what bigger decision can anyone make than murder? You see, before they died they'd know what kind of decisions I was capable of, seeing as these three would say to them, loud and clear—With Verney's compliments. "So, for the sake of conversation, a firm figure. How much?"

Can you believe they only asked for five hundred, with half down and half after the house was ashes? It was a fire-sale price but I didn't have five bills so we bargained and finally they got jewed down to three-fifty. That was more like what I had on me, so I gave them a hundred on account. Once this was settled they became all business and told me it would sure help out if I got them into the house, then sort of disappeared unless I'd get some sort of psycho belt from watching them work. Believe me, the way I felt right then it was something I would've liked to see. But if they could actually go ahead and kill five people for less than four hundred bucks and burn the house down as part of the deal, types like that might suddenly decide to put me in the oven with the others. Then there'd be no witnesses. Which got me to thinking how things could go wrong, then I'd be picked up also, so I said no. I'd get them in the house and meet them later. Now I want you to believe I had some second thoughts about this, some doubts, but I was feeling so mad, so keyed up, that when my hired heads showed me how they had an acetylene torch and some fire bombs in their pad, plus the makings for more, plus some tire irons for making ten skulls outa five, I got committed right down the line.

Then, man, stupid me went and did it. Because only after the door was answered did I remember what I shouldn't've forgot—how this was the famous Friday night when Simon was giving something special to that bunch of yids he belongs to, and everybody was going except me, because it wouldn't've done them any good to fix their hearts and invite me, seeing as they would've been turned down cold. But they didn't invite me, weren't decent enough to do something for my pride by giving me the chance to say no, thanks. Instead they gave me another frustration to burn on so hot it made me forget the most important thing I should've remembered and which might've kept me outa this trouble—that nobody was gonna be home.

Still, somebody answered the door and Decy got him with his

tire iron while Acey and Voltage busted right in. But before they could kill him, whoever he was, suddenly—da-daah!—troops come charging. And they've got guns. Lucky for me, I got away. Luckier for me, I guess, I had almost three hundred on me so I was able to hide out in a motel where the manager was hired not to ask questions. Besides, I laid him every night he let me stay, which was most of a week, because the rooms were hot pillow, so each was supposed to be rented four, five even six times a night.

There was nothing in the papers or on radio. Not a line or a single word. Finally I took a chance and phoned Bobby Longacre, he's the gay kid, and he told me Joyce'd left a message for me to come home anytime I felt like because the welcome mat was still out and my Mustang was in the garage. Then Bobby asked if I maybe knew what'd happened to his three friends who'd walked off with me, he was told, while he was freshening up before they all went to a party in Laurel Canyon. We'd just walked out for coffee and Danish, I said. Then I left because they said how they were going back for him. That's about all I could tell him.

After I hung up and got back to my motel room the shakes and twitches really made me suffer. What'd happened to them? Where were they? Nobody except maybe Bobby Longacre missed them. And if I'd've dared ask, which would've been real dumb, most everyone might quit figuring how these three freaks had got weary of the local action and just split. It was enough to drive you crazy.

Finally I had to talk to someone, and of all the people around, Libby Dorne seemed to be the only one who wasn't hostile to me. So I phoned her, sobbing real good into her ear while I told her how I was afraid to go home because everyone there was down on me and she hadda know by now that not so long ago my people were real hard types and still had all sorts of contacts to hurt people serious if they got crossed. It helped when Libby said she'd heard something about our fighting over percentages, before she told me to come over to her place and stay a while until everybody cooled off.

At Libby's I don't know how many more papers I looked at, how much more all-news radio I listened to, but there was nothing about Acey, Decy and Voltage. Nothing about their car, which was right behind mine, or what was in it. Nothing about the man they'd beat up. Not knowing who he was also sent me up the wall. And only Bobby Longacre still telling me —because Libby made me go back to rehearsals and dates— that he couldn't understand where his friends'd gone to. Then one fine day who showed up at Libby Dorne's if not good old faithful Tom with my car keys and the Mustang. His face on purpose was like stone, not to give me any clues about just where I was with certain difficult people on Lexington Road. Still, that he brought the car over had to mean they wouldn't object to my coming back. Now I knew for sure Bobby Longacre'd got Joyce's message right. But that's the way it usually is when an army wins big. They don't object to the loser coming around with his ass dragging.

Which's why I stayed on at Libby's, until at last she started to ask right out when I was going home. Subtle stuff like that. Then, I guess to get me off her back, she told me about Quincy Smith, his hang-up and what he could do for someone he liked. Also, that she didn't honestly think the group or me would ever hack it as big as I hoped in music, which was why an ambitious kid like me oughta think seriously of movies or a TV series. And the man to help me in that department, so I wouldn't have to call on people I was still on the outs with, could be Quincy, a little strange, but then who wasn't?

Quincy sounded all right on the phone, told me how glad he was that I'd called him like Libby said I would, then invited me to his Brentwood house—he had that and others—for some dinner before we drove out to his Malibu place. But you can't see the beach or waves or moonlight on the water when you're all tied up on the floor. So the sound I heard was not—say waves—but only how Quincy's heavy breathing made his false teeth whistle, which Libby told me only happened when he got very high on a subject. Still, he didn't look happy, not the way he was shaking his skinny head, even though I was doing exactly what Libby told me, which was to say nothing unless he spoke to me or there was the kind of emergency I've already mentioned. So there I was, thinking to keep from thinking about what was going on right here, all the while trying not to look anything but enthusiastic about what was happening to me.

Quincy felt the rope and knots around my wrist. "Sometimes it isn't easy to figure out what's wrong," he said. "But now I know."

"Anything I can do to help?" I looked very glad for him.

"Just be docile, please?" he said after he made like patting my *tush*, but didn't. "If I untie you now—you won't get dressed?"

I shook my head. "Until you say different, I'm your slave."

That really spun his wheels. So he took off the ropes and helped me kind of limp to a leather chair so cold it made me yip, which got him to apologize for not offering me a blanket. But when he'd shown this consideration to other subjects they'd wrapped themselves up to destroy the entire mood and thrust of his work. Believe me, I promised to just sit on the blanket, no more, so Quincy's teeth really whistled happy-o as he trotted off for a blanket. He fitted it real nice across the seat and back of the sofa to make me feel lots better even though my hands were so cold I didn't dare touch any part of me to make that part warmer.

Finally Quincy comes back again, this time dragging a very big cardboard carton across the polished red tile floor. His smile was so big when he got near me that reflex made me smile back. He appreciated me more, I could see.

"I've dear and devoted friends all over the country," he began. "Whenever they tear down old movie palaces like the Roxy—you ever hear of the Roxy?" he asked me.

I shook my head. "I'm sorry—no."

"A most beautiful theater. Even more beautiful than the Paramount," he told me. "That's also in New York although there was a Paramount Theater in Brooklyn. Did you know that?"

"I do now," I said. "And I'm glad."

"That pleases me," he said. "To talk to someone young who's interested in theatrical history. Movie history. Allied fields. Which is why I'll take you to see some of the old palaces that're still standing. We'll go soon."

I looked wistful. "You mean that, Mr. Smith?"

"Quincy," he corrected me. "Uncle Quincy. Say it."

"Uncle Quincy," I said. "Uncle Quincy. It sounds nice."

"It is nice," he said. "Anyway"—he looked so dumb serious again—"when they tear down those lovely old palaces, there are people who buy the appointments. Rugs, draperies, marble bathroom fixtures, beautiful chandeliers."

"My mother'd be interested in that," I told him. "Seeing as she's gone on antiques and buys them all the time."

"How tasteful," he smiled. Now he looked at me, rubbed his hands with pleasure and touched the box like he loved it. "What I collect are the plush-velvet ropes. The ones that were used to keep people in the lobby lines while they waited for seats. Look."

I did and saw him lift a piece at least three inches thick, I'd say, out of the box. It was the color of—say, a dark red plum—very *schlongy*-looking with a brass ring on one end and a brass hook on the other. The rope was maybe twenty feet long, he told me. And the ring was for another rope with a hook to be fitted in it.

"Your personality—so wanton yet so elfin—gave me trouble because I couldn't believe what my senses told me about you," he said.

He sounded glad so I thanked him by looking shy and sort of covering my beaver with both hands. "Which is?" I asked.

"That you're a princess. So you shouldn't be bound with ordinary rope like a commoner."

I held out my right hand like a princess does, I guess, when she's got all her clothes on. Quincy kneeled and kissed it. Honest, he did sound like a whistling teapot. Then he helped me stand and after I raised my hands like he asked, he sort of fitted the plush rope right up into my armpits, cinched the hook into the rope and began to wrap me up good. I'm glad to say the rope was nice and warm. After he used up the length he kept on hooking ropes together and finally helped me lay down again while he wrapped me right to the ankles. Next he wrapped a rope around one arm, starting at the shoulder, went down to my wrist, made a kind of knot before he left about a foot of slack and started up my other arm. All the while Quincy was humming to himself like some people do when they're eating good things, but a couple of times he did stop to ask if I was comfortable. I was, lots more. Wrapped up in those warm ropes I felt snuggy, more and more security blanket. Also, the floor didn't seem so hard against my elfin ass and other parts of me. Actually, I began to feel a little sleepy. At last he was done, so he stood up to take a couple of steps back. I had to force my eyes open.

"Beautiful!" he exclaimed. "You are a princess! Do you feel like a princess?"

"Uh-huh," I nodded, so drowsy now. "More'n more like one."

Suddenly he's frowning, very heavy, which jarred me awake so I could see how he's begun to dig into the box until finally he's got another piece of plush rope, a short hunk. Next thing I know he's got it around my mouth and is tying a knot in back. All I could make was sounds.

"It's your braces," he explained. "A princess shouldn't have to wear braces. Now you're so beautiful," he crooned while he brushed my hair until I felt the scared look go out of my eyes so they could become sleepy again. "A beautiful, helpless princess," he was really tripping now, "who isn't afraid of a harmless old beast. You're not afraid of me, little helpless princess?" he said.

Sleepy again, feeling like I was beginning to float, I still forced my head to shake while I made sounds I hoped he'd understand meant not at all.

"When I release you"—he was whistling right in my ear, which woke me up again—"when I remove your bonds, will you wash my hair? Please?"

Believe me, I nodded so hard my head bumped against the floor.

Anybody who tells you it's easy to have a career doesn't know what a kid might be called on to do for it. But with Quincy Smith in my corner—with me playing Princess Elfin Beauty to his kinky hang-up—who needed Joyce or Larry or Phil Hammschlager? Now I was never gonna lay that fat oyster. Who needed Jim Kerry, Norm Ellison, Fred Rory or old Basqua? And for that matter, even Middle America and the Silent Majority? Why should I waste another second thinking about Acey, Decy or Voltage? I felt so good, so warm, so snug in a rug, so inside of something like maybe I was once inside of Joyce.

I gurgled and slept. Slept and gurgled.

The only thing I missed was not being able to suck one of my thumbs. The—left one.

CHAPTER TWELVE

LARRY: Why, once you get saddled with obligations or responsibility for people, does it keep you from really getting ahead? I mean if my business was people—the way Basqua's is—time would be something I could charge for. Also, the headaches and plannings would be part of the operation. So thinking back, which I was doing more and more, and liking it less and less, whatever Fred Rory said to me in Mexico City shouldn't've turned my blood yellow, because nothing that might've happened, or even the worst I could've imagined, would've been as bad for us. By that I mean me and Simon. Now we had a new life in the States, not bad at all, except that I also got loaded down with a big house full of responsibilities. Not that I'm kicking, except there seemed to be no difference in the time I had to spend on big or little problems. Actually, the way things were working out, the little problems took more time because they gave me more aggravation.

Take going to the movies that Friday night not so long ago, seeing as Simon was having supper with some family or other from his *shul*. Ever since his donation of the Torah he'd become such a big *macher* around Fairfax Avenue that lots of people were asking him—Simon!—for advice. Funny thing, after Simon told me some of the things told him, what people asked and the answers he gave, he made very good sense. Sometimes when I showed surprise he asked why, since the problems were as old as the first two people, and the answers to these situations, in every possible form they could take, had all been written down first in the Torah, later in the Talmud. So all a man had to do was listen carefully, with an open heart, then remember at least one of the places where the problem was discussed and answered. Better believe it, more than once I was tempted to ask Simon two things. First, where the Torah dealt with Verneys and Quincy Smiths and Marty Grobbernasches? And second, what did Simon actually think we ought to do about the bad scene we'd got trapped in, a situation fouling up what would otherwise be a reasonable life for me and Joyce?

Because my first reaction to the three heads being guarded by Barney Moodus—with help—was to bury them alive somewhere in the garden. Which was more than they deserved. And my reaction to Sid, the hood who gave me Marty Grobbernasch's message, was to make him do the digging, then let him have it with the shovel so he'd fall right on top of the three creeps Verney'd contracted to do us in. Because seconds after Sid told me what Grobbernasch said about Juan Basqua, I honestly expected lightning would strike him dead. When nothing happened, I realized that like us, Basqua was human, and in the past must've come up against other cases like Marty G. In case he hadn't, dealing with this was as much, even more, his problem than mine, seeing as he was getting paid good money, in a size that mattered, out of Joyce's estate to keep her premises free and clear of pests, even those who'd never got beyond being little kids who got rid of problems by kicking them—they thought—into pieces. What they and I—when I was that way—didn't realize was how the pieces never disappeared. No, they just sank down roots to make them, finally, as big as the original problem, except now there were more of them surrounding you.

So I listened that night to Sid, asked him to repeat exactly, no decorations, what Grobbernasch had given him as a message to me, then asked how I could arrange a face-to-face with his boss for details of what he had in mind for me and Simon.

I'm convinced Sid and his boys never expected they'd become involved with helping a private dick save us and our joint. So my telling Sid how I expected him and his friends to take the three firebugs along, and to call Grobbernasch for what to do with them, affected him like a solid kick in the head. Which is exactly what I wanted. Right away Sid said they were my problem, but I said otherwise. Why? Hadn't they kept Barney Moodus from calling the cops?

"Don't sound like a dumb-dumb when you're not," Sid told me. "How could we let Moodus do that and at the same time keep him from turning us in?"

"You could've first cut out his tongue," was my answer.

"But we just came here to show how we could get into the house and deliver Marty's message in person," Sid argued.

I kept on shaking my head. "You could've put it in the mailbox. But now that you're inside, and not welcome, suppose I won't take your message?" I asked, feeling a little better because he was getting rattled. "Then what?"

"I guess we'd have to work you over," Sid said as if the words were being pulled out of him. "But Marty swore you'd listen."

"And I am," I said, "with thanks for bringing the message and helping Barney out. Now I want them bums taken out by you."

"Suppose we do?" Sid was sore. "Suppose we just kick their ass down the street?"

"Not good enough because they could turn around and do what they first intended," I came right back. "You think Marty G.'d be happy with you? Let alone certain other influential parties who'd be sure to say you weren't responsible types. No"—I put my hand over the phone—"you can't use any line in this house. And listen good," I went on, "if I do business with Grobbernasch——"

"You'd better," Sid interrupted me.

"Then at the very least I'll be standing on your head," I said. "Now get them out of this house and out of my life for good."

Bluff went out of him like he was punctured. "At least let me use the phone," he begged.

"No," I repeated because he had to feel all the pressure I could give. "There's plenty of phones on the outside."

So they disappeared, their car and all, with the only nuisance this fairy kid Bobby Longacre, who called a couple of times to ask if Verney hadn't told us anything about his friends. Naturally Barney Moodus said nothing and was grateful when we paid his salary until he got better, plus a thousand for the wear and tear on his head and ribs which he explained away to people who asked as what could happen to a man when he works in a house crammed full of antiques and he accidently trips. He almost kills himself trying not to break anything.

And I had Marty Grobbernasch's number to call in Tucson, where he was supposed to be retired except for an interest in some Nevada town named Monaco. There he had a piece of a hundred-dollar-a-day health farm. He also owned a small copper mine in Arizona that he let other people operate on a fifty-fifty split. Seeing as the mine did about five thousand a month net and geologists said the miners hadn't hit any of the big veins yet, plus he kept getting big-profit offers from big-board companies, it was a nice piece of property which should've kept him busy and happy. Obviously it didn't.

This I found out after Basqua told me to visit Marty G. and find out, if possible, why his nose'd started smelling around and what he had in mind, seeing as he'd chosen Arizona to retire because of his sinus condition. So a couple of days later, after Joyce was calmed down enough to stay without me, plus we got Barney Moodus to convalesce in the house, which he appreciated since the invitation made it very clear how we weren't putting him down for being taken off his guard, I left for Tucson with my head full of advice from everyone close to me as well as Basqua himself, who I'd met someplace outside of Sacramento. Even if he didn't look aggravated, I felt Basqua was. Not because he was afraid of Marty G. or anyone like him, but after a man puts up what he thinks is a perfect house, he hates to find out that one of the supporting beams might be full of dry rot or termites. So he asked me to do a couple of things, among them to listen, ask certain questions, but more than anything else not to be afraid of telling Marty he couldn't get an outright commitment from me. I wasn't to scare, Juan said, because Marty probably wouldn't do anything more than threaten in a first talk. And if he tried to hit me I was to take what he dished out. Once I got away and home I was to get ready for a long trip with Joyce and Simon, seeing as Marty might have to be neutralized, and during the time he was news it'd be best if I wasn't around for questions. Too bad, Juan sort of kidded me, that he hadn't been able to examine Verney's lice in person before they got DDT'd. Which made me ask a very stupid question—did he really think they were gone for good? Juan nodded, then gave me some more advice. Namely, if Marty G. mentioned them as being the principal parts of some kind of favor I now owed him, it wouldn't be dumb for me to say I didn't know what he meant, or what he was talking about. Let him go prove the favor. I hadn't done anything against the law.

I didn't understand anyone living in a trailer, even if it was located in a good part of Tucson, just the other side of a private golf course which gave privileges to people in Parque los Campos Verde because it was so exclusive the operators insisted on trailers being at least fifty-footers and not more than five years old when they're moved onto a site. Then each has to have built a *ramada* and carport. Of course if you buy a site where these already are, you're at least four–five thousand ahead even on the price you have to pay the park, seeing as when a trailer moves the owner gets nothing for his improvements. These, plus the trailer, could mean an investment of at least forty to fifty thousand, even more, and for that kind of cash in Tucson, a little more in Scottsdale, a man could have a pretty nice house plus privacy.

But a man like Marty G. needed lots of people around him, lots of action, things going on all the time, so Basqua suggested the trailer park and fixed it, since the park considers itself exclusive, for Marty and his wife to move in. At first Marty liked the cover and having all sorts of activities like leather-working or hand-painting on canvas, even sculpture or making bowls plus other things out of clay. Marty's wife enjoyed her jewelry-making classes. Then there were other things to do, like lectures and movies supposed to interest senior citizens, along with standard games like shuffleboard, croquet, horseshoes and darts, and of course golf. People got around the park and went shopping in electric golf carts decorated in bright colors, with fancy canvas tops against the sun, so I had to admit it looked sort of nice. On the bumpers of almost every cart were stickers that said, "Next Time You're Robbed—Will You Call a Cop or a Hippie?" "Legalize Law and Order," "It Isn't Un-American to Be a WASP," "Good Neighbors Are Your Color"—stuff like that, which is why most people I noticed in the park looked like they'd be against me. Also, there was always a bridge tournament going on and Marty let me know soon enough how he always did good because he could've been a big circuit player if he'd put his mind to it. Plus he more than made weekly expenses twice, three times a week playing checkers, dominos, backgammon and Monopoly. So the trailer park suited him fine until his wife died. Then, in due time, he started to get restless, so his sailing into me because of his never liking Itzik was only one way of showing how he hated what really amounted to doing nothing. Still, he had some gripes about Itzik, but I don't think they had anything to do with how Fat Dovel or Joe Foggia got put away.

At the sort of Mexican-style ranch house that was the administration building, a clerk told me Mr. Grobbernasch was expecting me at poolside, so an attendant ran me over in his golf cart almost up to one of the tables that got the afternoon sun. I recognized Marty behind his sunglasses and slowed my walk because one of the four other people with him was the hood named Jerry. Him I hadn't expected to see, until I asked myself—why not?

"Loser!" was the way Marty greeted me, which brought to mind what Crazy Sachs used to say—is he still alive?—how certain people were like the clap, so even if you're in the best of health and can't avoid them, they should only be taken in small doses. "You know Jerry."

I lifted my glasses as if to get a good look at him, then made myself appear puzzled. "I don't think so," I said. That bothered them, which's exactly what I wanted. "But I'm glad to meet you anyway," I said as we shook hands.

It was obvious Marty hadn't expected me to come on this way, but he covered fast and introduced me to this *goyisch* couple in matching Hawaiian prints to show they'd been to the islands. Then there was this friendly woman, a warm person, middle fifties I'd say, with blue-white hair done attractive, in ass-tight stretch slacks and a sweater to show she still had a useful body. The way Mrs. Irene Gauss, who let me know right off she didn't live in the park, looked at Marty gave me the notion she was a widow, or divorced, who'd had enough of getting it irregular. But I liked her for trying to make me feel comfortable by blunting Marty's psychological edge. She and Marty insisted I order something and I asked for the sandwich she recommended—Italian sausage with pimientos on a French roll, no mayonnaise, and black coffee. The couple in the Hawaiian-print *dreck* just had coffee while they did a lot of talking about what a nice place the islands were except for it having Oriental senators. That made them feel funny. Finally, and I was glad, Marty asked if I was ready to go and got up before I could say either yes or no.

I said good-bye politely to the *goyim*, whose names I didn't bother to remember, and Jerry drove the golf cart to Marty's trailer which had a nice flowerbed around it and was named Mon Repos, for whatever that's worth.

Mrs. Gauss offered to stick around but Marty said that would be cutting into the time he'd set aside to talk to me. So she was to please shove off. Jerry would drive her.

After the housekeeper, who looked enough like a big squaw to be in the movies, let us into the trailer, Marty asked how I liked the furnishings, sort of ranch style, then went on to say how high his three boys were on the way I lived.

"That's funny," I said. "Seeing as I never had any of your friends at the house. But I guess they could've heard about it. Lots of people have."

He stared at me. "Who told you to say that?" He started to get sore. "Bucconeri-Basqua? Has that wop grandee filled you up with other things to say that'll burn me up?"

"He sends best wishes and regards," I answered.

"Let'm send cash instead," Marty said. "He's got enough of mine. Say," he brightened up, "what do you think of Irene Gauss? Not bad for an old fart like me? She wants us to make it legal. In my place, what would you do?"

"I'll pass on all your problems," I said. "That's if you don't mind."

"That gym she goes to," Marty went on as if he hadn't heard me, "I bet they give lessons there on how to." Marty opened his belt to sort of give his belly a chance to breathe. "I'll also bet I can still knock the shit outa someone like you," he said. "And don't think for even a second I'm not aching to find out how right I am."

"You can stop aching because you could," I said, remembering what Basqua'd told me about going along with everything Marty G. said.

"I'm still tempted," he said. "But a commotion could get me thrown outa the park, which's a disgrace I couldn't take."

I laughed, which he liked, especially after I agreed how nobody could live down so dumb a disgrace.

"And Señor Basqua doesn't want to deal with people like that." Marty was sarcastic. "Funny how people think Spanish spics have class and wops and Mexicans don't."

"I'm still passing," was all I said.

That made Marty sigh like I was hopeless before he yelled toward his kitchen for Thundertits—I swear, that's what he called her and what she answered to—to hurry up with the drinks and peanuts, so in a couple of seconds his Indian lady wheeled in a cart with cold beer cans, soft drinks, mixings and a couple of bottles of hard, plus bowls of all sorts of nuts. After I took a Seven-Up, Marty started to suck hard on a beer can, all the while looking at me over the rim and now saying nothing. At least not for a while. Whatever he wanted to say, he would, because this was one man nobody could embarrass or shut up. Ever so often he rubbed his chin with the cold can as he tried to see through my dark glasses.

"Take them off," Marty said at last. "It's bad manners to wear shades in someone's house. Especially when I've taken off mine."

"I need them," I said.

"You'll need a tin cup and pencils if you get me sore," Marty said. "And what's with that camera around your neck?"

"There's no film in it," I said as I opened it to show him. "It's just a prop," I explained.

Marty looked the camera over. "It could be a recorder." He was suspicious. "I got a good mind to step on it."

"Then you'll owe me fifty bucks," I said.

When he raised the camera to a line with my head, I got ready to duck in a hurry. But Marty just handed it back while he grinned. "I've got other ways to roust you," he said.

"Such as?" I asked because it was obvious he wanted me to.

"Like having the Revenue people and your friendly local pigs do some more talking to you. Don't say it," he warned me. "Not unless you want to dig this can along with some others outa your head. Sure I did it. Other people including your friend Basqua know I did it. But he's the only one who said he didn't approve. And I think he's lying."

"I'll still think it wasn't unanimous," was the best I could say off the top of my head. Then I thought of something else. "The cops weren't bad, so thanks to you we got them outa the way. But Revenue was a pain in the ass."

"They would've been more than that if the money you copped wasn't covered long ago. You don't fool me," Marty said after he tore the lid off another beer can. "The bank deposit that showed up had nothing to do with you."

I wanted to laugh, but made myself sound sore. "So you knew all along about my honesty and still you put the government on me?" I asked.

"You're cute," Marty said. "Very cute. For someone who's so cute I guess saving your wife, her house, you and that nut friend of yours doesn't mean a thing."

"If you should ever do that," I said, "you'll see how much it means."

That made Marty stand up. Instead of belting me, he adjusted his crotch. For a pretty big man and sort of fat he still managed to look strong and sporty in his brown western pants, tan shirt with big flaps on the pockets and yellow embroidery around them. He also wore tooled boots and a belt that matched, with a big buckle I suspect was gold, and a yellow neckerchief run through a gold slide. Thundertits came in for the empty cans and as she walked away Marty gave her a good slap across the ass which didn't faze her none.

"So that's how you're gonna play it," Marty said after he sat down again. "It never happened. None of it. Like I just said—you're very cute. You'd even be cute dead. But I'll let that good idea sit for a while because I wanna find out if you're the kind of operator who could be taught to steal more with a fountain pen than he ever could with a gun. But first

I've gotta know if you're interested in cooperating? Or do I first have to twist off one of your arms?"

What he'd said about fingering us to the cops and Revenue bothered me, especially as I believed him now that Basqua'd known all along, before and after I'd met him, who was trying to shaft us. Of course it could be that Basqua and the others hadn't said anything because they wanted to see how I'd do, after so long a layoff, when I came face to face again with the law. Like what sort of pressure I could stand and what I'd do if and when it got heavier and hotter.

"I can't give you a yes," I said after Marty yelled at me to open my mouth. "Not if you want the truth."

"Even if it only steals through legitimate channels?" Marty asked.

"Even if it's strictly legit and doesn't steal anything," I said. "I wasn't brought back for that."

"Why?" he shouted. "Because you think you're too good for me, you Brownsville bastard? Tell me why!"

"Because, Marty," I said, very peaceful, "why me?" That didn't make him explode, so I thought another question would still be safe. "In plain talk, what've you got in mind for me?"

"So you can tell the wop?" he asked me on his way to the can. "I'm not worried."

"That," I admitted, "but also to find out how you rate me. What you've got in mind should clue me in."

Before he yanked down his zipper, because he was on the way to the can, Marty turned to look me over as if for the first time. "First I wanna know how a solid mahogany casket, top, sides and bottom, so your ass won't be dragging in a couple of months, sounds to you as a rating symbol? All right, I'll throw in Skinner's satin with tufts. Believe me, I wouldn't do better for anyone else I know. And that includes Johnny the wop." Only when he got ready to flush was the door slammed in my face.

After Marty came back and started sucking on another can

of beer, I asked if he didn't mean Juan Concepción Basqua, a question that put him in a very good humor, enough to start him off on how when he was a little kid living in Ridgewood, which was a German neighborhood in Brooklyn, the tenements he and other Jews lived in on Stockholm Street between Central and Evergreen was all surrounded by *Turnverein* bastards, shanty Irish micks and wops all along Central Avenue. Every year just before Lent, when all the wops and Irish, some of the Germans too, put ashes on their foreheads to show they were Catholics, mostly the Italian kids used to fill up the feet of black, heavy cotton stockings they got from their mothers with ashes. Next they'd come over in gangs to the sheeny tenements, where once you got socked in the head with a stocking filled with ashes you never forgot it, or what kind of people Christians were.

"I might've been a doctor if it wasn't for those lousy *krisks*," Marty told me. "A dentist or a lawyer because I was a pretty smart kid. You know, I can still multiply the first twelve numbers up to fifty, maybe sixty, in my head. Can still add up, even subtract, multiply or divide a lot of figures you could call off. But those lousy kids made me fight back. And I liked beating them up so much I started to go looking for them instead of going to school. Then after I put together a bunch that also liked beating up *krisks,* I started to get paid by certain kids and their bunches to leave them alone. From then on, after the neighborhood don on Central Avenue said he wanted to see me, I was in business. But you've heard that kind of success story before."

"Sort of," I said. "We used to work over boogies and Puerto Ricans if we found them on our blocks in Brownsville. They really ruined that neighborhood."

"Show me what they don't ruin and I'll show you things worth nothing," he said, really hating. "Still, my mother she should rest in peace, used to say there were three kinds of people. Jews, *goyim* and *Italener.* She said that because *Italener* also talk with their hands a lot you can sort of reason with them in certain things. Besides, all the other *goyim* spit on them." He laughed. "I'll bet that's why Johnny-wop became Johnny-spic." Now he looked a challenge at me. "I'll also bet you don't dare repeat that as if it was how you felt."

He waited for me to answer, motioned for me to, but I didn't, so suddenly he's right on top of me, where I'm sitting, and the bottom of his fist smashed hard right down on my head. It felt like a piano landing on me. Then, since I'm not knocked out, so I'm worse off than being unconscious, he's got me by the throat and starts shaking me while he yells that he's old enough to be my father, which, thank God, he isn't, and he isn't afraid to die but I am.

"Tell the truth," he said after he flung me aside. "Admit it."

I managed to get back into my chair, thinking only of what Basqua'd told me to do, not what I felt like trying to do. "I admit it," I said. "So you don't have to prove it."

"Chicken-shit bastard." He looked unhappy as he broke into a fresh can and kicked the empty at me, but missed. "You're gonna take anything I curse and throw at you, you slippery bastard. Slippery bastard," he repeated, "I can't even get you to tell me what you think of Irene Gauss."

"She's very nice," I managed to say in a voice that sounded strange to me. Because he was smiling, I went on. "For her age I bet she's still got young ideas."

"So I found out," he snickered. "And I'll give odds that even though she never was a pro—Irene's as good, maybe better, than what you're married to."

"Do both of us a favor and lay off," I said, feeling stronger again. "Unless you like talking to yourself best."

"You wouldn't dare," he said.

We stared at each other, saying nothing, and in the silence I realized that Marty G. hadn't told me anything specific, unless you call a little conversation about stealing with a fountain pen specific, so I got the bad feeling a mouse must have when it's being played with before being eaten by a cat. Or closer to home, how when I was a kid and surrounded by some guys from another bunch, instead of getting things over with by beating me up, they'd just fool around, talking and joking about everything but me, even ignoring me for a time, maybe giving me a little kick or a shove, so that all the while I waited to be clobbered I had to fight off begging for mercy, and worse, pissing in my pants. We'd do the same to kids we captured. Sometimes they got so afraid they'd puke or faint. And why not? Maybe somewhere near a cactus his boys might be digging a grave for me. The thought gave me more strength.

"Try me." I stood up. "Unless you get down to telling me what you've got in mind—I'm walking."

I ducked when it looked like Marty was gonna throw another can at me, a full one, which gave him a laugh and the satisfaction he wanted. So I was right. He was playing with me. Now he threw an empty toward the kitchen part of the trailer, a signal for Thundertits to keep on serving. She did and just managed to move her ass before Marty could slap it again. His miss told me he was, for sure, beginning to feel all the beer he'd put away, a thought that made me groan on the inside, because leaving—if I managed that in one piece—without knowing exactly what he had in mind for now and the future only added up to lots more worry.

"How big're you in the market?" he asked me suddenly. "You and your friend?"

"Nothing to talk about," I said, which was the truth because I'd followed Johnny's—I mean Juan's—advice and sold out to the bone. Now the market was getting ready to drop below 800, just like Juan said it would, and only the other day when we talked outside of Sacramento he said not to go back in, since the Dow-Jones would be off maybe another hundred points by the end of the year and would drop down to around 700, or even lower, in 1970. So I was to wait until he told me to go back in. "And from what I hear about the economy and earning reports I'm gonna sell the mutual funds," I said.

"You liar," Marty said, suddenly good-humored, as if he hadn't done anything to me. "I got the same advice you did from Johnny the wop. It's all part of the service. So if I listened, you listened." Again he put aside an empty and got up, which was beginning to bother me since he no longer bothered to shut the toilet door and kept the conversation going even when he flushed. "Now you listen to me," he said as he zipped up. "Listen good."

I did, and this really scared me because I realized he was psycho, and only a bad psycho could ramble on like he did of how he was thinking of putting together an organization to be a producers' association for blue movie houses and his people would run it. He was also going to go into publishing an investors' service for brokerage houses that didn't want stocks, securities and bearer bonds disappearing every day out of their back rooms. Then he was going to branch out by buying into health food stores which were becoming very big business. Also, he was going to set up a shipyard someplace below Mexico where tuna boats could be fitted up with armor plate and guns big enough to give it good to the Ecuadorian and Peruvian navies when they came out to capture the American boats that were inside the two-hundred-mile limit they said was territorial waters.

"I've already had word from those soldiers-of-fortune guys who're fighting in Africa. Some of them were fighting sailors and they like the idea of battling on water. That could be very big business," Marty said. "And that's only the beginning of what I've got in mind for you as one of my first-line trouble-shooters."

He liked what he'd told me so far enough to slap my back, a real *zetz,* which added to his beer breath, and what I'd already taken, was like a one-two. Then he asked what I thought of his ideas so far.

"They've got scope," I said. "So they sound too big for me."

"Not if you think big," Marty advised me. "Funny, but I never met anyone from Brownsville who could."

"Which lets me out, I guess," I said. "Because you hit it right on my head a little while ago. I think small."

"But you can be educated," Marty grinned. "Even if it kills you—you'll learn. Because when I'm the teacher it makes me awful mad when someone I'm teaching doesn't shape up. I got into your house once," he still grinned. "So that bullshit you're handing me about never meeting my boys before is just that. I bet you'd like to know what happened to those three hippies."

"What hippies?" I asked, because I was still following Basqua's advice. Also, I didn't want to know what'd happened, seeing as what I didn't know couldn't hurt me. "You know what's wrong with hippies?" I decided to try a joke on him I'd heard a radio disc jockey use that morning. "Everything they eat turns into hair."

The empty beer can landed in my lap. "You're too young to retire, you damned dope," he said after he pinched his nose to show me what he thought of the joke. "So you oughta be ashamed of yourself for just being willing to sit on your ass to the day you die."

"What's wrong with wanting to stay clean and doing nothing?" I wanted to know. "Everything you've told me so far means mixing it up with the law. So where'd you ever get the idea I'm your man?" I shouted, which brought Thundertits into sight, when all I really wanted was not to hear what my cold feet were telling me about myself. That I was scared of him, the size of some of the operations he had in mind, the amount of money and the people who'd be involved. "Look" —I gave Mrs. Thundertits, she wore a wedding ring, the beer can Marty'd thrown at me—"I don't remember a single thing you've said. I swear. I'll tell Basqua you were bored and just wanted to do some bragging. To tell me about old times, seeing as I also came from Brooklyn."

Marty shook his head, no longer steamed, just sad because he was becoming more and more convinced, he said, that I really was stupid. "He won't believe that. I wouldn't either. Would you?"

"I'm still saying no, Marty," was my answer before I pointed toward a window. "You've got people out there, so to show you how much I mean no, just tell me where to go if I'm gonna get it. Because I don't want you thrown outa this park on my account."

My talking interrupted another proposition he was trying to make, to put a sort of sad and frustrated expression all over his face. "You really mean that," he said. "You really do."

"Try me," I said.

"You're not bluffing," he went on, his frustrated expression changing to disgust. "But if your Itzik, who you still think's so great, could get outa his grave he'd be ashamed to see what you've become. A phony. Maybe you'll die in Beverly Hills, Larry, but in my book and in time in Bucconeri's too, you'll be an entry under Brownsville *schleppers*."

How right he was about my liking to live in Beverly Hills and wanting to die there peacefully when that day came. Liked more and more, on the days without worries, the idea of living very rich, right out in the open, just as good, even lots better than the people around us, able to afford all the help we needed for Joyce's house, and all the while not be surrounded by hoods. Wasn't this what Basqua had in mind for us, maybe other people too? Correct. So why should we fight it, which is what we were doing by not giving in to Verney, by getting satisfaction out of spiting her? Believe me, deciding to give her the whole of what she wanted actually made me feel lighter in the head than the rap Marty had given me. But the feeling of lightness in the head seemed to clear out all the pain, the dizziness, even the feeling that I was getting a headache. So it was time to move on, I felt, to get back to Beverly Hills and make things better by getting rid of our share of Verney's company. I was pretty sure, one hundred percent, Basqua would approve.

"Marty, please," I interrupted him in the middle of one of his harebrains—taking the pension fund of a union whose top leaders he had plenty on, "there's a coupla things I think you oughta know. My getting on a plane this morning's a matter of record. Even the don knows I'm here. Also, I reconfirmed a seven o'clock flight tonight back to L.A. That I called L.A. and gave the name of the clerks I talked to here and in L.A. So I'd better get back, Marty," I laid it on him and liked the way he started to look, as if he was gonna rupture a gut, "nice and healthy. Nice and healthy," I repeated, suddenly feeling sort of sad for him because at some other time it would've been a privilege to work with a man like this. "Nice and healthy," I said for the third time because it was making an impression.

"A *schlepper*," was what he kept repeating. "I wasted all this time on a *schlepper*. A bum who never had a bigger idea than to nick shoeshine kids. Or to make slugs for phone booths and the subway. Where the hell did I ever get the idea you had something? Where?"

It was just about five now and as I watched all the strength and enthusiasm, the jism of living sort of ooze out of Marty G., I also heard a golf cart putt-putt to a stop outside. Right after that, Jerry opened the door for Mrs. Gauss so she could come in first. Jerry carried her packages and she gave me a nice, concerned smile before she looked disgusted at Marty slumped in his chair, still hanging on to a beer can. He said nothing to them, just finished off the can and really stumbled to the bathroom.

"How long's he been doing that?" Mrs. Gauss asked me. "From about the time we left?"

"Just about," I said. "But please don't ask me how many cans he's put away. I gave up counting."

That upset her so much she looked ready to cry. Then she got sore enough to go to the bathroom and kick on the door, which Marty, for the first time, had locked.

"What the hell's the matter with you, Marty?" She pounded on the door while her voice went up like a high-speed elevator. "You promised me you'd stop!"

We heard flushing, then Marty opened the door just as he got all zipped up. "My J-A-P." Marty tried to pinch her cheek but she ducked away. "That's a Jewish-American Princess," he explained to me, and I laughed. "Lemme touch your manicure, Irene." He tried to grab her and almost fell down. "When I get real hot, Larry, and she's the same way, she lets me touch her manicure. Special times she lets me smell her scented soaps."

All of us were laughing now, even Jerry and Mrs. Thundertits, who stood in the doorway to the living room and only shrugged like a statue might when Irene Gauss started to bawl her out, but not angry, for not stalling whenever Marty called for more beer.

"Just look at you," she said to Marty, stretched out flat in his Recline-a-Lounger. "Drinking, going to the bathroom and abusing your kidneys. Why didn't you just pour the beers into the bowl and eliminate the middleman?"

"My Jewish-American Princess," Marty's voice was becoming a thick drool. "Maybe tonight, by candlelight, she'll show me a body stocking she hasn't worn yet."

Mrs. Gauss, not Jerry, drove me back to the airport, all the while telling me what I felt, that Marty Grobbernasch wasn't a bad guy, that he had a sense of humor which kept him human, that he was like some little kid who's too active because something's wrong with certain important glands, so he drives his parents and teachers and even his pediatrician crazy. That Marty felt pushed out, that it was bad for him to live all surrounded by a lot of shuffleboard types I wouldn't sit down with even if they guaranteed never to win even once at anything. So anybody with the least understanding could see how he was like an old lion who still had teeth, claws and all his senses, but was stuck out someplace where nobody was, so he couldn't hunt or be king of the beasts. Which was why Marty was dying, drinking himself into a grave. And knowing this, because he did, he didn't want to.

After loading for my flight was announced, Irene Gauss walked me to the gate, where we stepped aside to talk a little more.

"You're not angry at Marty?" she asked, very anxious. "Please don't be angry at him."

"I'm not," I said. "In fact I like him. But I'm not going in with him. Not even if he kills me."

"He just talks," she pleaded with me. "You saw that."

"Sometimes he slugs," I began, then decided to drop it. "Which is another reason I wish I could think of something to keep him busy full-time. But what? I'm not as smart as Marty. Nowhere's near. So the only way I can help him is by not going near anything he dreams up, even if I'd like to."

She held my right hand in both of hers. "Thanks. This man Basqua—"

"Yes?" I said.

"He won't hurt Marty?" she asked.

"No." I wondered if I'd read Basqua right. "He's just as worried about Marty as you are."

So I got back to L.A. with a lump on the head but a whole skin, feeling sorry for Mrs. Gauss and hoping for her sake that Basqua wouldn't set wheels moving to get rid of Marty G. Still, I didn't think he would unless it could be done without headlines. Either way, yes or no, I didn't ever want to see Marty again. I told Joyce just enough to make her believe, I hoped, that she hadn't any reason to worry. Simon the same. With the don, who I went up to see, I leveled and felt like a rat, which was a new feeling for me, so one I hated and wished I'd never have to experience again. Which is why I panicked bad and begged him not to put the blocks to Marty, just to go on controlling him. I took his nod for a promise.

Meanwhile, I'd told Juan how Joyce was willing for us to get out of Verney's corporation. What I didn't tell him was how she screamed, carried on, that she wasn't about to lose a nickel, not through that lousy sick bitch, and how I'd guaranteed she'd get back her whole investment. When she started to yell about the interest she'd lost, I also told her she'd get that from me too. I think this had the effect of making her ashamed.

By this time we'd admitted to ourselves that Verney was living in Quincy Smith's beach house. This also bothered Joyce, especially after she found out what bent Quincy's mind, which I refused at first to believe because it didn't make sense to me, even after we had a meeting with Verney and the two creeps who were representing her again in Mike Loesinger's office, where she showed up looking clean enough, but very snotty and wearing a funny sort of belt, seeing as it was made from a piece of reddish plush rope, something like the kind on the banister of our—Joyce's—center-hall stairs, with a brass ring and hook to keep it around her. Smirking all the time we talked, Verney kept fingering the belt in a way that struck me as sick. But this we knew about Verney, she was sick, but was she any sicker than Marty G., from who I got a long rambling letter how he had some other ventures in mind where I'd fit in and I was to get it out of my head that he wasn't gonna see me working for him?

Suddenly, right in Mike's office, another complication developed, namely, that no minor could head up a corporation, not in California anyway, and until Verney could get responsible older people to act as officers for her, which none of us was willing to do, there was just no way she could operate. Verney suddenly showed enough brains to rule out her attorney and his accountant associate, which meant they got paid off, as at the same time it struck me funny that Verney was now left with a shell nobody would buy or touch. Another thing to give us a lift and make Verney wild was her not being able to get her hot mitts on the money in her trust account, and I must admit that if it hadn't been for whatever it was Quincy Smith said to her when she came to the office with him, there might've been bad furniture-breaking trouble. But he calmed her down, spoke quietly to us and said he appreciated how it didn't look right for Verney to be living in one of his houses, but she was being taken care of, there was a housekeeper, and she was eating the right food and going to the dentist on schedule. Also, seeing as Verney'd lost interest in her rock group but still wanted a career, he was going to get her some small acting parts, which he hoped would keep her happy. What I wanted, but couldn't say, was that I hoped he'd make us happy by keeping her away from Joyce's house, where she'd done enough damage.

Joyce didn't want Quincy around either, seeing as she was revolted by what she'd heard about him. Agreed, if he did what people said, it was a funny way—certainly not one I'd ever heard of or care about to satisfy your hots. But if that was his kick, it didn't seem he could hurt anyone, not unless he tied knots into people the way Kirk Douglas did when he gave it to Luther Adler in *The Brotherhood,* a picture I'll get around to when I tell about the double feature we went to see that Friday night I mentioned some time ago. But suppose, by accident, Quincy did hurt her? That, I told myself, would make me believe more than I did in Simon's God being on top of things and socking it to the right people, those who deserved punishment.

As we argued back and forth, more than once a day now, about what Joyce kept screaming was a dirty, sick and unhealthy relationship for which Libby Dorne was gonna roast in hell forever, Joyce finally went by herself to a child psychiatrist and asked him if bad heredity might be responsible for Verney, seeing as the grandparents on her mother's side were religious nuts who'd actually approved of how Joyce was kept chained to a bed. But that's all she could remember about her parents, Joyce said, and she knew absolutely nothing about Winnie's, so after the psychiatrist said that he could only try to help if Joyce, Verney and me became his patients, Joyce told him straight out he was a fake because he refused to make anything big out of Verney's not getting *her own mother* a gift on Mother's Day. That beautiful experience cost a hundred and fifty for three one-hour sessions which, after I paid the bill out of my funds, made Joyce yell that she couldn't look people in the eye when we went out to lunch, shopping or other places, and that I was crazier than Verney for trying to point out how from what we read about every day in the papers, and saw or heard on TV and radio, Verney was in pretty good shape. With Quincy she wouldn't become pregnant and have to be aborted. And from the way VD statistics were going straight up among kids, anything a son or daughter might do to keep from getting a dose had to be thanked at least a little, maybe more. Personally, I think what stuck in Joyce's craw most was how Quincy Smith seemed to keep Verney behaving so she looked and sounded normal enough. And if he was able to do this by tying her up, or through the funny belt she wore, then why should we fight them?

To this Joyce always said the same thing. That if Quincy did to Verney what people said, and if she liked it, then both of them were even dirtier, sicker and unhealthier than she'd ever suspected people could be.

"So you'd rather have her the old way," I said one night while we were arguing, my voice low, in her bedroom. "You'd rather have her sucking or shacking around getting——"

"Verney doesn't suck!" She began to shake. "Don't you ever say that about my daughter! And a good thing for you her father isn't alive! Bastard! You dirty bastard!" she raved. "To say that about a kid to her mother's face!"

"My apologies," I said and meant it. "Or maybe you'd rather have her go to Tijuana for abortions? That you told me yourself."

Joyce was shaking so hard I had to help her sit. "Now you can get an abortion right here," she said as she pushed me away.

"That might make it safer," I was proud of my patience and logic, "but does it make it better than what Verney's supposed to be doing now, which for the sake of the argument let's say she's doing? But you don't know for sure. Neither do I or anyone else."

"You're just as sick as them!" Joyce was screaming so loud

that sound bounced off the walls. "Maybe you'd like doing to me what that old pervert does to her? Just try it!" she was choking on her anger. "Just dare try, you dirty Jew creep!"

Must I go on? Meantime, doing what Basqua advised me, which was never to start any of the cars we owned but to have Tom, Milly or somebody drive them around to us, was a good, sensible precaution, but it also made Joyce and me very nervous because we couldn't help but wait to hear a bomb go off after the motor was turned on. Also, we never parked on any street, only in parking lots where I paid extra to have our cars locked up front and specially watched. And we never forgot to have the attendant drive the car to us, which is pretty standard anyway in the way of service. Finally, to give us even bigger safety odds, we had the garage added to our burglar alarm system, and big automatic floodlights that went on as soon as it got dark lit up the garage brighter than day. A good thing Simon said the lights didn't bother him.

Also, on my last visit to Basqua, when I reported to him on Marty G.'s plans, like his telling me before Mrs. Gauss managed to get me away that he was going to start up a new union in advanced defense and space industries, which in time would help him get control of the industries themselves, made Juan wonder if Marty hadn't seen *The Brotherhood,* the picture I've already mentioned, because a lot of the movie's plot and action depended on this sort of situation. So he suggested I go see it when I could, and let him know my reaction.

In time, because I'm not much for going to movies when there's so many on TV, almost all of which I'd never seen, the movie section in the L.A. *Times* advertised a double feature in this neighborhood theater in the valley. It was *The Brotherhood* and Jason Robards in *The St. Valentine's Day Massacre,* which I had some curiosity about because it was from a time when Basqua was battling for his own life. Plus I'd heard of the massacre and at the Riviera some of the guys on the payroll said they were in Chicago at the time and went to see how the garage looked after they wheeled out the stiffs. Joyce said this wasn't her idea of entertainment, but after she heard me call the theater and get picture times and driving directions, she changed her mind.

The movie was alongside a big gas station, with a House of Pies right next to the station. We drove into the station, arranged for parking and watching the car, then got into the movie just when they were showing the titles for the St. Valentine's Day picture. Jason Robard as Capone was a laugh, the way he scowled around with a big dumb stogie stuck in his puss, so I rightly couldn't blame the kids too much for talking back to the screen. Still it was hard to hear and I had to tell some kids in front of us to knock it off. They started to get tough until I grabbed one by the shirt collar and twisted. But I liked the old-fashioned cars while Joyce whispered to me if that was how things were in the twenties, between hoods and their broads, she was glad not to've been part of that action. Also, if Mafia people were no more than slobs in tuxedos, she was glad Itzik'd been forced to retire to the extent he had nothing to do with anyone.

Finally they got to the picture's high spot, where these seven guys get put up against the wall, and I must admit that seeing how Capone's men managed things to make the Moraners think they were being rousted by cops, and then, after the killing, how those guys marched the executioners out as if they were being booked, struck me as very clever planning. Something someone who wasn't on the receiving end of the action could appreciate. The kids all around us certainly did.

The picture ended after this important-sounding voice told us how crime doesn't pay, the lights went up so people could load up on popcorn and snacks, and suddenly the whole theater was filled with a roar you just can't imagine until you realized all the seats were practically filled with kids from high-school age down. Older people, like us, were few and far between. Right off the kid whose collar I twisted turns around to make something of what I'd done, but I've got my glasses off, am standing, waiting for him or his friends to move, which gave them other ideas, like climbing over the seats in front to fall down on some wild-looking girls who just loved this sort of attention.

Never in my life did I see so many ushers at one time, at least one for every couple of aisles, and they're hauling kids out right and left and threatening to bust them with flashlights if they don't stop what they're doing, which includes cutting up the seats. This only scared a few of them because as soon as the ushers moved to stop other kids from taking the house apart, they'd start right up again. Now some of them started to come back with all the food they'd bought and I can't tell you how many drinks were thrown on each other, how many rolls of toilet paper and boxes of popcorn were flung, how many hot dogs, ice creams and I don't know what else was used as ammunition. Fights were breaking out all over, which the ushers usually stopped but not before some of the kids really got bloodied so they had to be helped out, but what they couldn't stop was the girls because, you see, they were worse than the boys as they walked up and down the aisles and climbed over seats to pick up boys, and I swear how kids from ten or eleven seemed to have boobs and know-how, and from twelve or so up they all had big tits under loose shirts and their jeans were so tight you expected their asses to bust right through. They looked mean, low, too experienced, like the sort of hookers in some of the streets behind the Zócalo or behind Garibaldi Square, where all the mariachi players hang out, so it can be a lot of fun. The hookers there are tar-paper shanty types, sloppy, smelly, tough-looking, usually dying sick, so ready to steal anything. A guy had to be very suicidal to use one of them. These kids looked no better and believe it, I saw how some of the boys grabbed girls by their bombs and other places, and the girls didn't really mind. Grown-ups looked at each other, not needing to say anything, and some of them left, which is what Joyce wanted and what I would've liked. Except that the don wanted me to see *The Brotherhood*.

I held Joyce's hand, cold as ice, and told her to relax because the picture had to start soon and it did—some dumb cartoon that did nothing to make the kids around us settle down—but finally *The Brotherhood* began, and still holding and rubbing Joyce's hand, I watched. Sure enough there were these top Mafiosos who met in a house bigger than Joyce's and furnished in the worst wop taste, where they got reports on their operations before they went on to new business, in this case to get into electronics so they could take over the whole industry. For sure Marty'd seen this picture. But only Kirk Douglas, who inherited his father's territory and doesn't want to be bigger than he already is, says he's against going into something that was sure to put the government into a big angry sweat. Naturally it starts bad blood between them. Another complication is Kirk's younger brother, who's in with him but is married to Luther Adler's daughter, one of the top men at this meeting. So he sides with his father-in-law but is grateful because he was the only one, really, who didn't want right away to give Kirk a funeral they'd be proud of.

I don't want to go through the whole story, except that Kirk gets told how Luther Adler fingered a lot of old Mafia guys, including his father, to Lucky Luciano. And they all got rubbed out. So one of the old-timers who's still around, and with who Kirk plays *bocce,* makes Kirk promise to kill Luther. He doesn't like to do this, seeing as they are close related by marriage, but finally Kirk decides the old rat must die and he's gonna do it.

After he busts Luther around a little, he ties him up in such a way that his hands are behind his back, and his feet, also tied, are pulled way up his back. Then Kirk winds part of the same rope around Luther's neck, so when he struggles and tries to lower his feet, he chokes himself to death.

You wouldn't believe how the kids cheered, they liked it so much better than the machine-gunning in Capone, the terrible gagging noises they made, how some stood and made believe they were being choked. And they kept right on cheering when the picture got around to where Kirk's brother guns him down. This the kids didn't like so much because all you heard was the shotgun blast, but didn't see the action.

My problem was with Joyce, who, from the moment where Kirk started to tie up old Luther, began to go to pieces in her seat. First she covered her face with both hands while she pleaded with the picture not to, then she started to moan and twist like she was retching or worse, then she seemed not able to breathe. It was terrible, but finally—thank God—I could tell her the picture was over, so we could leave. But she still didn't want to uncover her eyes.

With the lights on, the kids were going crazy again, like they were on a real fun farm. We started to push our way up the aisle where to my tough luck there were kids, boys and girls, all around and right ahead of us. When one of the girls in front started imitating how Luther'd choked to death, Joyce suddenly screamed and grabbed this girl by the hair to wrestle her to the ground, where I guess she would've really hurt the kid if a couple of ushers and me weren't able to break her grip.

In the manager's office I quieted things down and gave the girl fifty dollars to forget what'd happened. And the manager asked us, please, never to come to his theater again.

CHAPTER THIRTEEN

JOYCE: Whereas Larry was reaming his skull when we got home after the movies, I felt very calm and fulfilled. What I'd learned in that movie house between and after the pictures was good for my mental emotions, seeing as right before I flipped and tried to scalp that horrible juvey because she was making strangling noises, it came to me, suddenly like a revelation—Simon's not the only person who can have them—how more or less every girl and boy in the theater was Verney. So Verney was every girl and boy of today. Also you didn't have to see kids at all to know pretty generally what they're capable of. Which is just another way of saying that kids nowadays aren't told or set apart by their age, their size, whether they've got their second set of teeth, or their class in school. You identify now-kids by their capacity for one hundred percent cruelty. Maybe, because I want to be reasonable and not sound like a nut bigot whose idea of solving his personal problems is by killing everybody else, there could be a few kids up to the age of—say twelve—who can still be worked with. After twelve, better forget it, seeing as experience proves that when you hear of a real evil deed, a make-you-sick-to-the-stomach shocker, you'll win more bets than you'll lose by saying it was done by some kid just beginning to menstruate or grow body hair.

Not that adults don't do mighty rotten awful things. One of them, who I hold responsible for everything that happened under her roof, put me in bed now for almost a month so we couldn't go to Europe, when Verney, still wearing her special belt, really proved she was a psychotic episode by getting herself photographed as she kissed the prick of the Mannekin Pis in Brussels, which isn't the kind of statue I'd let stand in a public place. The incident made me sore enough to send cables, and they cost. One to Quincy Smith, telling him to pull the knots tighter on Verney. The second to Mrs. Beverly Droutswood, asking where she was at a time when she was needed? The third to Verney, saying that she and she alone was her own worst enemy. Even after the wire services sent the picture worldwide, no foreign government deported her, which shows how bad our Marshall Plan failed. Proof? All over Europe men and women use the same public bathrooms. And I've been told by people who don't lie that their nuns and priests don't look clean. Also, some old churches have *pissoirs* attached right to their walls. The last is especially disgusting and sounds like something only the worst atheists would do in this country.

Anyway, to take things in order, when we got home from the movies where I'd roughed up the little monster, Larry dragged me right upstairs to the common sitting room and forced me onto the sofa. Then he just held my left wrist and, with his glasses off, glared, so I recognized the old Larry, which suddenly excited me more than the new model. Finally he sort of flung me aside and telephoned Simon to come right up. When Larry realized that Simon never answered the phone from Friday to Saturday dark, he went for Simon, who came back in pajamas, robe and *yarmulkah* to listen, shake his head and say how, as kids, were we any better to our families? But the difference from then to now, he went on, something he saw by looking and hearing what customers told each other and him, in lots of today's cases parents didn't seem to care or know what to do. And of course there were lots of people just as bad, worse, than their kids. That I wouldn't go for, I told Simon. Nobody was as bad as kids. Simon walked out just before Larry grabbed at his head and said he was going to call a contractor first thing in the morning to have every wall padded. Because if he was living in a lunatic asylum with a couple of advanced cases, with the third one out of the house but still carried on our tax return—or was she this year?—it should look like one.

Privately I laughed at how sore Larry was. Also, at how scared the kid I worked over looked in the manager's office. She would've taken lots less than the fifty Larry offered, but if playing the big shot with kids makes him feel good, all I care to say is that it's his money and it'll never again be any of mine.

Seeing as Larry still wasn't talking next morning, even as he drove me to the beauty salon for my every-Saturday appointment, I told him not to bother picking me up because cabs were available. But he had to talk to me when I got home because he'd just found out that we were having company next day. Right after our Sunday dinner, about six, Simon was inviting that dumb Leola Druckman over, for the very first time, to see the slides he'd taken and bought in Israel. We were also invited and Larry didn't want any objections from me. I didn't make any, even though I've seen them at least ten times and more than once of her was ten times too many.

Larry, mine host, also thought it would be a nice gesture if we served dessert and coffee in my dining room. You should've heard the way he emphasized *my* and seen how I stuck my fingers in the corners of my mouth to pull back hard and make the biggest grin, which made him scowl. I didn't care. I'd just had my hair foil-frosted and it looked great. Then, whistling while I worked at supervising, I knocked myself out to make fruits and cheese, sherbet, petit fours and a marvelous torte delicious parts of a beautiful table setting. That Druckman broad was impressed—you should've seen her hefting the silver, how she was dying to turn over a plate to see the mark—but all the time talking very ladylike, with me getting little if anything of what she said because I was wondering what her figure was like without support. Like a matzoh ball? Was she varicose? I figured we were about the same age, give or take a year or two either way, but better the plus years on her than me. So was she like me getting a little blue map of fine capillaries inside her right leg almost behind her knee, hardly noticeable now but growing in size? If Larry saw it when he got into the saddle with all the lights on, since that was how he liked it best, he didn't say anything. Considerate son of a bitch, looking so preoccupied, so worried and tense at the dining room table, I began to sell myself a bill of goods that he appealed to me more when he'd been a real prick.

As for some women, they're just too obvious, so I got very good charges out of keeping that Druckman woman in the house—I insisted the slides be shown in my library—and just never let Simon take her back to his place without us along, which really irked Larry because he was on to me. Finally she gave up, said it was late and got up to make her sad departure. Be assured I was along as we walked her to her car, where I put my arm through Simon's and blew her a kiss just as, really burning rubber instead of maybe feeling it, she pulled away from the curb.

That night Larry and me had at each other again, with Larry saying it was so damned obvious what I'd done and me retorting that if Simon had become too dumb to keep his guard up, then someone else with his interests at heart was going to keep sweet, always enunciating Mrs. Leola Druckman, with her neat clothes and carrying her head high and nostrils quivering as if she was recording everything within sniffing distance, from sinking her hooks into Simon. Furthermore, if she was hot for pushing then it had to be on somebody else's property because the guest house was on mine. Larry said that seeing and hearing me tonight, he couldn't exactly blame Verney for being what she was, which was reason enough in my book to try braining him with a Derby candlestick. Lucky for him the one I picked up of the china pair was the Venus, not the Mars. They date from about 1760 and are in perfect condition—important things I realized in a flash. By the time I put down the candlestick and got my hands on a silver beadle's staff, lots older and able to make the neatest hole in his head, Larry was on his way upstairs and I couldn't get to him because both doors to his bedroom were locked.

To prove he wasn't going to get away with that, I had six brass plates made up to read—Suite of Jizchock Yanowitz, 1958–1968. I intended to mount them on both sides of the three doors Larry used to the center hall, his bathroom and the common sitting room, until I realized this involved drilling holes in my beautiful doors, so I just put the plates on Larry's dresser, bathroom sink and other places where he had to notice them. He used them as bookmarks.

Like any big argument which runs out of steam, in about ten days we were civil enough to make up in bed, by which time I'd begun to use leg makeup on the little map. It was a nice reconciliation, so the next day, after Larry got home from Mike Loesinger's office, where he'd gone to wind up our end of Verney's corporation and give her back-up group a chance to go out on their own and still call themselves the Silent Majority, I met him, very excited and happy, to tell him that Sally Mercer had phoned to invite us to a dress-up dinner party three weeks from Saturday night, so we didn't have too much time to get ready. Sally's husband, Marvin—I told Larry—had developed and was executive producer of a TV situation comedy that was in its ninth year on a major network. Only the first three years were in syndication, so between that and his outright ownership of forty-two percent of the show and more than fifty percent of subsidiary sales like comic strips, toys and clothes, plus the right of annual audit for which the network had to pay, they were rich enough to have their kids driven to school in a Rolls Royce that'd been made over into a pick-up truck. Once again this proves that them who has gets. The Mercers were millionaires and getting bigger for all time to come. Their house was down the street from ours, a big French Normandy place with too many fireplaces for best overall symmetry and ivy instead of grass lawn, which is one way of economizing if you're willing to settle for second best.

Although I'd begun to meet Sally Mercer in Gucci's and Giorgio's and other nice shops on Rodeo Drive, and we'd exchanged phone numbers at *her* suggestion, I'd never called her and was surprised that with her first call to my house, she was inviting us to a big party of the size she only gave two or three times a year. She admitted it was a late invitation, but to prove it was sincere she brought one over and wouldn't leave until I said yes. She also brought an invitation for Simon, knowing from what she'd heard that he wouldn't come to dinner, but she'd be delighted if he would come afterwards, say about ten-thirty, and he could bring a guest.

"I'll die if he brings that Leola," I told Larry as I showed him our invitation and Simon's. "So why're you hesitating?"

"Isn't she the lady whose maid I had trouble with?" he asked me. "The one who quit the day of the riot and got hired right off by some other woman?"

"Yes," I said. "I hope that miserable coon's stolen that maid-stealing bitch blind." Then I looked around, went to the door of the morning room to see if Milly, Tom or some other *schvartzer* was around, which would've been a catastrophe. "You have to be so careful," I whispered to Larry. "From one second to the next you don't know where they are." I took a deep breath of relief. "I've accepted, Larry. So we're going."

"It's your decision. Your responsibility," he said.

He could be exasperating. "Look," I began, "I asked Sally Mercer straight out, right there"—I pointed toward the center hall—"if she had anything against us for losing her maid. She laughed and said absolutely no." I was still whispering, which was ridiculous, so I stopped. "As a matter of fact the new girl she got to take her place is a hundred percent better and more educated."

"That's good news," he said, but still didn't look happy about the party. "And you say it's formal?"

"You can rent a black tie," I said, then changed my mind. "You'll buy. And I want a new gown. My God, Larry," I shook him, "when was the last time you went to a party with civilized people?"

My question shook him into looking blank. It even sent chills through me. Because, as I looked back, I'd never been to a real party where I was a guest since I was ten or so and stole back the birthday card I brought because it was so pretty. From then on, until I got into the trade, which was after Winnie saw me in Longchamps, where I was a hostess, and made me a better proposition, the kind of parties I went to—as a working guest who got paid just like the bartender but a lot more, a lot more—would've been raided if the cops hadn't got their cut. So if I looked as if I was having fun, why that was part of my act, a very important part. At the Riviera we'd sit around the private table, and if it looked from other tables like we were partying, we weren't. Not with Larry sitting up there bawling the crap out of everyone for what they'd done that day he didn't like. When Itzik and his people showed, we might have something going in the suite, even with music, but it wasn't a party in the sense that the girls who were there didn't have to put out if they didn't want to, and still, to this day, I can't see what's funny in busting down a bedroom door to see people doing it. Or having a lot of couples piled on one bed or actually showing off in front of everyone else.

After our honeymoon in Florida, when Mitch and I got back to the Riviera, Larry gave us a party in the dining room for everyone to see. No sir, he wasn't gonna waste a private room on us or not be able to see what was going on during the supper hour and show. Some people at the table, all bums. Some party. Some Larry. That nobody killed someone else was a miracle. Before I married Winnie in a quiet ceremony, Itzik sent word down there was to be no party. There wasn't. We never had any kind of party for Verney, poor kid. So here I am—admitting to forty and that I was older than Mitch and maybe older than Larry or Simon, but not by much and I do look younger than them—and not having been to a party that would be defined as a party in your Funk and Wagnalls for at least thirty-five years.

I know how anxious I looked, maybe more than after my first contraction with Verney, so finally Larry smiled, not big though, and admitted how he'd been thinking, now and then, of us beginning to entertain. So our going to a party to see what other people in our circumstances did for entertainment when they put on the dog mightn't be such a bad idea. That was good enough for me and I even agreed that he didn't have to wear a frilled shirt with lace and the rest of the gay stuff that people wore on TV shows and even in magazines supposedly for good dressers. He wanted a simple dinner coat, straight pants without flair or faggoty stripes or materials, and shoes that were right but still masculine. For a couple of seconds, as his face got black, then pained, then wild again, he seemed to be wrestling with himself if he should say what'd come to mind, and he finally did, which was that he remembered how, when he was once going somewhere in New York with Mitch, they'd stopped off at a store called Rogers Peet because Mitch'd started to buy his clothes there. Also there was a store that advertised in the local *Times*—Brooks Brothers—and their clothes looked like they were tailored for solid, important people. That's the kind of store Larry wanted to fit his tuxedo.

No trouble, I said, we'd go to Bullock's Wilshire, where I liked to shop most because they always had something beautiful in china, marvelous crystal, table accessories and Boehm birds, which I'm sorry now I never collected. Also their linens, those that can be made to order and that includes lace tablecloths, are something to see. Before Larry could have any second thoughts I phoned BW, asked for the men's department and was assured they had in stock what my husband had in mind. So we went there, after phoning Simon at the grocery and he saved my life by saying to give the lady his thanks but he had a previous appointment.

Larry liked everything shown him and didn't need major alterations. He also promised to go back to the store for my shopping in the French Room, so my good humor was so good I didn't care a hell of a lot when Quincy Smith phoned and asked me to meet him somewhere for a talk, seeing as he'd got Verney a little part in an olive-oil Western, which meant it was being shot in Spain. Then he planned to take her to a film festival someplace in Italy whose name I didn't catch because anything other than Rome, Venice or Capri sounds all the same to me. Thinking of it, I can't remember if they were going to Spain first or the other way around, but who cares. I wouldn't have Quincy in my house so we arranged to meet in a bar. Naturally he was going to have a chaperone along and he wondered, if I agreed, what did I think of Beverly Droutswood if he could get her? Also, he'd like to have Verney's birth certificate which was needed for her passport and he wanted me to see them off at the airport.

"Yes and I'll try to do everything, Mr. Smith," I said, controlling myself because he didn't look like a Dirty Old Man and I could tell that he was asking me only out of politeness, nothing more. But what the hell did I care, really? Her life was her life and wasn't going to ruin mine. "If you want me to, I'll call Mrs. Droutswood and if she says okay, both of you can meet right here."

Beverly took a little persuading because she'd had it up to here with Verney, plus was she to be a real chaperone or just a beard? I told her to do me and Mr. Tunig a favor, please, to go along and do what she could to keep Verney civilized in public and to forget whatever went on between her and Quincy Smith in private. Finally, to show how much I'd appreciate her saying yes, I offered to buy her a set of matched luggage at BW, up to three pieces plus a tote bag. I don't want to think it was the luggage that persuaded her, but who knows about people, really?

Larry insisted we be at the airport to see them off, seeing as the press might be there and it would be better all around if it looked like there was harmony and we cared. I didn't argue and in a way I'm glad we went, mainly as it gave me another chance to buck up Mrs. Droutswood, whose face was one big pucker because of what she'd begun to hear about Mr. Smith, who looked so distinguished, so benign, she said, so much the courtly gentleman, until she remembered that in the time of Charles Dickens and a poet named Tennyson how the nicest-looking Englishmen, ones who, if they were alive now, could get jobs on TV and in class advertisements as bankers and other kinds of great leaders, were the ones with the worst sexual crazies, like whipping or being whipped or dressing themselves up in wolf skins. It just made her shiver, so she was looking forward to the day when she no longer had an erotic thought. Thank God, they were becoming fewer and far between, but most important, never beyond her control. She hoped I believed every word she said.

"Oh I do." I was sincere. "Just keep your eyes on Verney in public. Never let her slip away. And see what you can do about stopping her thumb-sucking because both're raw and ready to get infected. Why the hell she's started that now," I wondered, "is something you can't learn from me."

"I'll do my best," Beverly said without heart. "But whatever that turns out to be, it'll be my best."

"Good," I said, glad that we'd insisted she get paid a year's salary in advance and always have her return ticket. "If he really loses his mind and marries her"—palms together, I looked up at the ceiling—"then you can quit right off."

Lucky me, just then the first call for first class to start boarding came over the p.a., so I kissed Mrs. Droutswood, pushed her toward the door, shook hands with Mr. Smith while I pitied him, then walked toward Verney who'd been standing with Larry. Sure enough, we had to pose for a picture, for which all of us managed smiles.

"You've got to stop sucking your thumbs," I said after we got rid of the photog and Larry went over to Quincy for last-minute talk and handshaking. "They look awful. Besides, the dentist would say it'll throw your teeth more out of line."

"Fuck the dentist. And nobody photographs thumbs," she said.

Don't flare up, I ordered myself, and obeyed. "Promise you'll see a doctor," I asked quietly. "I don't want to ask Quincy to make you. But if I have to———"

Verney sucked on her braces, then nodded. "Okay."

"As soon as you get to London? Promise," I said.

"I promise." She raised her hand and looked around to see if we were being watched. "Seeing as I have a doctor's appointment right after we get settled at the Dorchester. That's where Liz Taylor used to stay. You've never been to Europe," Verney taunted me. "Never been to the best hotels all over. But don't worry, you'll live big through the picture postcards I send."

"I've been to hell and back," I said. "So there's nothing else for me to see. This doctor"—I changed the subject—"why're you going to a doctor?"

My concerned look made Verney laugh. Her laugh made me repeat my question, which was what she wanted—to upset me all she could—before she opened the jacket of her light suit and turned sideways to show me what I hadn't noticed, but then I hadn't seen Verney much in the past two months. Her breasts, they did look a little bigger.

"Silicone injections," she answered my open, astonished mouth. "Quincy's paying for them and the doctor's promised when I'm all finished to shape me a pair just like Marilyn Monroe had. That'll make me a unique Mia Farrow type, seeing as I'll have tits." Suddenly her eyes were mean, so hateful she had to turn away when she began to button her jacket. Somehow she hit her right thumb against a button, which hurt.

"Don't you try stopping me," she said. "I'm gonna have my career, no thanks to you for screwing up my company. And maybe some of my friends." This last was said with each word spaced.

"You could've kept the group going," I played dumb. "Breaking it up was your decision."

"Don't change the subject." She was able to look at me again. "Shit, who cares about them?" Suddenly she sounded cunning. "Better just remember this. I've got old Quincy so hung up he wants to adopt me. Belt and all."

"Good," I said. "The sooner the better."

Another photographer aimed his camera at us, so Verney put an arm around me and leaned forward to kiss my cheek, which she actually nipped with her teeth. "Drop dead," she whispered as I jumped. "That's the least you can do for me. And the most."

At home, after I was able to stop crying, I told Larry some of what Verney'd said, and specifically how she'd insinuated that we'd given it to some of her friends. What could I expect him to say? So why did I blow up when he shook his head and picked up the phone to call TWA and find out if the plane'd landed? Was it because I was sorry it had? But the lives of innocent people had to be thought of.

While planning for the Mercer party occupied me a hundred percent, two things that bothered me most were what sort of gown I should get and what to do about Sally's invitation to join her social service group, which was named EROS, a word—I let her know—that has a lot to do with sex. Sally said how right I was, but the broads in this chic group wanted to be with it while they did social work. So among other good ideas and activities that EROS might have for them, it also stood for the first letters of Eliminate Racist Offensive Symbols.

You see, when I got up enough courage to call Sally and ask what gown length her dinner party was, Sally said any length was all right just as long it wasn't so short pussy showed. She laughed, so I had to, even though I never expected that kind of an answer from someone I didn't know well but respected and was grateful to for inviting us—or sponsoring us, was how Basqua put it when Larry phoned him for advice and was told we should go—into respectable and pretty important society. I thanked Sally, which is the thing to do before you say goodbye to someone who's answered a question, but she asked what I'd heard from Verney, so I made up having got a long happy cable from her, which made Sally say what a wonderful, exciting life kids had nowadays. Then she invited me to join EROS, whose only purpose now—with other activities to come later, but what they were she and other board members hadn't figured out yet—was to go through every street in Beverly Hills, even those south of Santa Monica Boulevard, which makes the addresses less important, block by block, house by house. Then, when a member saw one of those little cast-iron black jockeys at a house, she reported it to EROS. After the research committee found out who lived in the house and the type of people they were, the public relations committee made an appointment to call on the lady to explain why she should get rid of the little jockey boy. Or at least to paint his hands and face flesh-color white. If the lady cooperated and looked socially okay, she was invited to join EROS.

 I thanked Sally, said we'd have to talk about it after the party, then got hold of Larry right away and told him to get rid of our jockey boy which stood to the side of our garage so it couldn't be seen from the street. After I explained why, he said that because other people were stupid it didn't mean we had to imitate them. But, to please me and because it was my statue, and an old one, not a recent casting, he put it somewhere in the attic.

 All indecision about hair styling and makeup, gowns, hose, shoes, gloves, an evening bag and the jewelry I'd wear, also should I wear an evening coat because summer evenings in Beverly Hills are cool, Larry was so patient I worried at times if he wasn't in bad health, maybe with high blood pressure and following his doctor's advice not to get excited. At last, after dozens of changes of mind and finally deciding not to wear any jewelry, I chose a simple blue sheath trimmed at the neck with long silver beads, the kind of thing Jackie Kennedy wears so well and which Larry swore looked great and refined on me. Underneath I was only going to wear a two-piece body stocking.

Then, God bless her for really being a faithful family retainer, like right out of an old MGM movie showing on TV, about a week before the party Milly whispered she had something to show me in private, and in my bedroom handed me an envelope with maybe ten sheets of paper in it that listed the name of everyone who'd accepted a Mercer invitation. A part-time secretary had helped Sally make up the seating list for the caterer, who was setting up a dining and dancing tent in the garden. Besides that, the list told something about the people, who they liked and who they didn't, what they did and why they'd be comfortable with other people at their table. Besides that, Milly and the particular girl who'd given her a Xerox copy of the list had filled in what they knew about the guests.

"We used fan magazines and gossip columns," Milly told me after I hugged her. "Which is why, if I was classifying that list, I'd have headings like drunks, bums, deadbeats, whores, sleeping with each other and to-be-sure-to-count-the-silver."

"Thanks, Milly." I loved her, so glad that I'd made Larry put the jockey away, even though none of my people'd ever said anything. So glad that Milly was concerned for me, then not liking myself for wondering if she ever discussed us, thumbs down, with help from other houses. "Now I can go over the list with Mr. Tunig and know something about people we're meeting for the first time. It'll make talk easier."

"Sure," Milly said. "Talking with trash is always hard."

The invitation said cocktails at seven-thirty, dinner and dancing from nine, so I made myself take a nap that Saturday afternoon, and with Larry alongside of me reading the latest *Forbes* when he should've been going over the list and memorizing people's names and who they were, I fell asleep, without taking anything, from two to almost four-thirty, which was about an hour more than I intended to nap. With my hair in a net I stepped into the tub and Larry did my legs and back and *tush* with scented soap, which made him call me a princess and made me ask if Simon's appointment that night was with the Queen of Israel, Mrs. Leola Druckman? But I didn't ask it nastily, so Larry said Simon's social business was his own, and why kid anyone, I was glad, he knew, that Simon wasn't going to the Mercer party, and he understood why. That made me sit up to look right into Larry's eyes, and they were a little bit ashamed, just like mine were, I guess.

He held a thick terry robe for me, patted my back to help me dry, and I remembered how right after I'd got to New York from Mexico and taken my first bath, Winnie'd also helped me bathe and dry off. That scared me because I just couldn't take another accident, like the kind that'd happened to Winnie, so I grabbed my Larry hard, rammed my tongue into his mouth and moved it all around while I smacked my crotch against him. Finally I whispered hot in his ear that tonight after the party I didn't care how late it was, whether or not he was tired, he was going to get the fucking of his life. Then I freed myself, laughed, and held his face in my hands to kiss him gently before I said I liked him now, the way he was, much better than what he'd once been, and he was never to believe me if I ever said otherwise. Then I asked him to please ring for Milly to help me powder and get into the body stocking, the top half of which had to be slipped carefully over my hairdo even though my hairdresser was coming over to comb me out.

Would you believe that when I went into Larry's room to hear from him how great I looked, he was staring at his camera on the dresser while Tom was still helping him with studs and tie and vest? After Larry saw me in a mirror he turned to say before Tom did how marvelous I looked, which I appreciated without getting soft, because I pointed at the camera and shook my head before saying no.

"And you'll please not wear dark glasses," I went on.

I rested against a slantboard so as not to crease my dress and liked the way Larry looked when he came into my room for inspection. Hand-some. Tom wanted to drive us over to the Mercers, which wasn't even a block away but that would've meant sitting down, something I wasn't going to do for as long as possible, so with Barney Moodus along because he was sitting the house tonight, they walked us up the block, right to the Mercer circular driveway where a uniformed crew in black pants and red military jackets with lots of gold braid were helping other guests from their cars, then parking them.

"You'll call before you leave?" Barney asked us. "Good," he said after we said yes. "Have a good time."

Larry felt good because with Barney there was a gun in the house. When he was gone, there wasn't any. I felt good, even grand as well as confident, because we weren't the first to arrive. I felt even more confident once we entered the house, where a maid took my evening cape and told me that ladies were using Mrs. Mercer's section of her suite for rest and comfort, because I looked better than any of the women I saw around me and the expressions of the men with them said I was right. Plus the way some of the quote-unquote ladies cased Larry told me he was doing all right in the comparison department with the men around us, some of who were wearing—you guessed it—dark glasses. Larry was nice, didn't make a thing of it, said he'd be all right but there was nothing wrong with my hair or anything else that was part of me, but he didn't mind being left alone if I didn't take too long. So with a little wave and my lips forming a kiss, I went upstairs slowly, taking little steps so I wouldn't trip in my sheath, which is a style I'd never worn before. Going slow gave me the chance to take in the light fixtures—undistinguished, no imagination—and the color scheme for the center hall, the landing and upper gallery only made me sneer. The odds and ends of pieces I saw—especially the paintings, very badly framed and every one of them a reproduction, mostly of florals without life or good color values—made me more confident with every step I took on the wall-to-wall carpeting, another proof that the Mercers didn't have style enough to live with rugs on polished wood.

A uniformed maid, about the sixth I'd seen, welcomed me to Sally Mercer's bedroom where I had to step right up to the black velvet and gold headboard of her bed. It was real. Every other piece of furniture was covered with the most awful gold leaf and all the mirrors, even the one over the dresser, were so Venetian you only saw reflections. Angels holding clusters of light were lamps. The fireplace, obviously with its mantel removed, was of yellow marble with gray streaks. Setting off this unbelievable example of inferior desecration were the sort of figures you'd see on old sailing ships. Attached to the wall on either side of the fireplace, they held sconces in the shape of gold and black torches.

Four dressing tables were ranged along one wall and the women sitting before them either looked in their mirrors to size me up or turned around. The dressing room door was open and I might've gone there to join those voices when a woman at one of the tables told me she was about through.

"I'm Beatrice but call me Bea Bofford," she said. "And I like your dress. Especially the way you look in it."

"Thank you," I said and introduced myself, pleased that I remembered her name on the list. The Boffords, Sam and Bea, were at table five. We were at table four. Sam headed the art department for one of the major TV stations and was personally responsible for network spectaculars. To those in the know, Sam was an important man.

"Joyce Tunig?" the woman at the next dressing table said as I told her my name. "You look like someone named Joyce Dobby, whose pictures I've seen."

"The same," I told this woman, Patricia—and please don't

call me Pat—Daggett. Her husband, who didn't mind being called Bill, was business manager of some pretty big stars. "Dobby's my daughter's name. Since I remarried last year, it's Tunig."

"Of course," Patricia said. "Verney Dobby. She's just left for Europe to star in a big picture."

"It's not a big picture and she's only walking past the camera," I said for the record. "And I'd rather she was in summer school than Europe."

"You beautiful innocent!" Patricia's eyebrows waggled when she laughed like a horse. They continued to waggle when she stuck two fingers inside her big mouth, with little cakes of lipstick in each corner, to whistle louder than a traffic cop. The blast brought about five or six women out of the dressing room, plus some maids ready for an emergency. One woman threw the towel she was wiping her hands on into a corner, for a maid to pick up. "This is Verney Dobby's mother," she introduced me. "Verney Dobby," she repeated because some of the women looked puzzled, "the kid who sings with braces on her teeth." Because they still looked blank, she gave them up as know-nothings. "What did you say your name is now?"

"Joyce." I felt very awkward and sorry I hadn't stayed with Larry. "Mrs. Larry Tunig. We live just down the street and I'm glad to meet all of you."

"I know the house. A lucky house for a lucky mother," Patricia said and I realized she meant every word, "because in that jackpot business there's no such thing as a little picture or a little part. And American kids who look cherry ripe do great in the foreign press. Especially with Italians."

"They're shooting in Spain," I said.

"The Italians send people everywhere. So when you next write to Verney, be sure to tell her that when she poses, especially for the Italians, she's to be sure to give them high inside thigh shots"—she lifted her gown to illustrate—"it makes them come and come back again."

At this funny Patricia's eyebrows actually danced, the other women broke up, and like a crack across the head it struck me that none of them saw anything wrong in Verney being in Europe with an old rich pervert. A *poor* pervert would've been something else. So I smiled, thanked them one and all for their friendly good wishes and advice, and said I hoped to see them downstairs so I could introduce them to my husband. Believe me, please, that one nicely turned-out woman with a happy way about her and older than me—Delphine Gavere, husband's name Sherman Gavere, MD, facelifter to the stars—squeezed my arm to make me feel how lucky Verney would be if she got Quincy to marry her because an old psycho like him, with not a living relative or favorite charity to screw things up for an heir who could be called child bride and wife, couldn't last forever. She, personally, after finding out about Quincy from Libby Dorne, a patient of her husband's, for what she wouldn't say because it would violate professional ethics, had researched Quincy, then done her best to bring him to the attention of a dumb niece now freezing her ass off somewhere in Canada with a longhair freak who'd run away from the draft when a bad kidney had to make him 4-F, except that appearing for induction wouldn't've been standing up for his principles. In letter after letter she'd begged her niece to leave her zero in the zero weather he seemed to like and come home to put her neuroses to work, seeing as she liked strange sexual *shtik,* and try to make it with Quincy who she—Delphine—could get to through Libby. But some kids are so anti-Establishment it makes them blind to any appreciation of the good life as we see it, so Delphine was glad someone with sense had tied herself to Quincy who, if he didn't marry Verney, could still be forced to make her rich for life if he didn't want to be hung or lynched with his own ropes.

"He'd never go into court because, thank God, the laws about corrupting minors were passed by constipated bigots. Sherman says all bigots suffer from irregularity." One by one,

Delphine lifted her bombs and moved them around in her gown. "These built-in bras never work for anyone over A. And I just managed to squeeze into a D-cup. I'm running now." She patted my cheek. "Look for me downstairs, please?"

Still standing, I pulled in the side mirrors of the dressing table she'd just left, stuck my head forward to see myself three ways, and decided I needed nothing except to tell Larry how friendly these natives were.

"I never thought that big mouth would leave you alone," I saw Bea Bofford talking to my reflection. "You of all people don't have to ask mirror-mirror," she added.

"Thank you," I beamed. "From one woman to another, that's more than a compliment."

"Does my compliment entitle me to a personal question?" she asked.

I moved a little to one side to see her better in the mirror and nodded. "Ask and find out."

My saying sort-of yes made Bea hesitate in all sorts of hand and facial ways, including touching her throat and shoulder straps with nervous fingers. "I—some of us've got to know about you," she finally spoke, "when we read your daughter's lovely interviews. Those where she defended you so beautifully. They actually made me choke up."

"Phil Hammschlager'd love to know your reaction," I said because I'd tensed and she sounded so sticky.

That puzzled Bea. "I mean—what I mean to say is—your life's been so dangerously glamorous. Glamorous," she repeated because I looked scared of her. "Exciting and defiant. So what I want to know is—what's it like?"

"What's what like?" I asked, so's not to jump to a conclusion.

She hesitated, then sort of squared her face. "To be in a house. That kind of house." She grabbed my shoulders and shook my head for me not to turn around, just to keep on talking to her in the mirror. "Wanting to be in a house is driving me crazy."

It'd all started to bug her hard, she explained, this past

winter after she'd seen this marvelous movie of some Spanish director, very famous at film festivals. The picture starred a French actress, Catherine-something in *Soup*—no, *Belle de Jour*, and showed how this very beautiful, upper-class wife spent a couple of afternoons every week as one of the girls in a Parisian whorehouse. Catherine did this for kicks. Bea envied her, except that the house didn't appear to be at all exclusive, so we wished Catherine'd been in the one shown in *Lady L*, which starred Sophia Loren, who I agreed was too beautiful and gorgeous for just one woman. In *Lady L* the house was in an elegant mansion, all gold, velvet, crystal and plush, with little rooms fixed up like railroad compartments, Arab tents, whatever was your bag, so for a man to get into this establishment he had to be a somebody. Now Bea dreamed of working like this Catherine did, a couple of afternoons a week, in a mansion that might be situated in, say, Hancock Park or Bel Air.

"I don't think of anything else," she whispered, her eyes bright in the middle mirror. "My pants just steam thinking about it. Then I worry that no madam would want me, and being turned down would just kill my ego and the dream. So, meeting you"—her hands moved like they were being shocked—"I just had to ask. Tell me it's exciting!"

Nobody so intense and torn apart could be kidding. But looking in the mirror because right then nothing could've got me to turn around, I shook my head.

"Forget it," I said. "Movies aren't life. Not even when they show people going to work. And it's hard and dangerous and dirty work."

Now she appeared angry. "Why not help me find out for myself?"

"You asked and I told you," I said. "And even if I knew a joint—and on my life, I don't—I wouldn't help you get in it. Bea"—I made myself sound kind even when I felt only fear and anger—"I was lucky. Very lucky," I said before I turned the subject away from me. "What's the matter with your husband?"

"He's a john," she said. "No good, so he actually pays so I'll act like he is. That's what started me thinking about it."

"I'm sorry for both of you," I said.

"Some sorry," she mocked me, then looked helpless. "Are you saying no and that you're sorry because I got out of line?"

"No"—I lifted her hand off my shoulder—"you talked to the right number."

For seconds we stared at each other in the mirror. "What table are you at?" Her smile was forced. "Because I must talk to you some more. I swear our conversation'll never be repeated to anyone."

"Table? I don't know," I lied.

"I don't know either," Bea said. "But we'll talk some more?"

"Absolutely," I lied some more.

She looked so grateful my heart ached for her. "Most any table is all right as long as you're not sitting with Marv Mercer. You've met him yet?"

It was safe to turn around now, so I did. "No."

"You'll have to," she said. "You'll recognize him by his big head. I mean it," she was serious, "his head's bigger than ordinary. Almost macrocephalic." She looked as if she'd just thought of something very ugly. "His press agent says it's packed full of ideas. Other people in the know say it's packed with conceit and larceny." Bea once-overed me again. "You're not angry?"

I didn't mind taking her hand because I was thinking of something else—to remember that word "macrocephalic" and look it up. "Of course not," I said.

Traffic on the stairs was very heavy but halfway down I stopped to look for Larry or Sally Mercer, seeing as I hadn't said hello to her yet. Then I saw a man with a bigger than ordinary head and knew immediately what macrocephalic looked like. After he moved to let a waiter by with a tray of glasses, I saw that he was talking to Larry, who had, in the time I was upstairs, gone home for his dark glasses. I can't tell you how affectionate, tolerant, even maternal his doing that made me feel.

Larry wasn't the only one around Marv, who bowed the big light globe that was his head when we were introduced, as it struck me that to lay such a freak a woman would have to be very Sigmund Freud, so I marveled that Sally Mercer could've had four kids with him. Four kids! How many times did they take? Even the thought that it could've only taken four gave me goose pimples. And I wondered what Sally's kids looked like? Or should I ask—Bea?

I brought my mind back in time to hear Marvin say he wasn't going to introduce me to the people around him because he wanted us to be friends next morning. That got a big laugh which made his chest swell before he went back to what he was discussing before I came along. Namely, he was telling how certain network surveys had concluded that a lot of the sitch shows and comedies like *Beverly Hillbillies, Green Acres* and the rest of that barnyard shit were up in the ratings. That nobody denied. But the over-forty Serutaners who watched the shows didn't even want to buy laxatives to make them feel better. So advertisers and networks were looking for new, now ideas for shows, the kind that would appeal to young marrieds with cash or willing to go into debt for things they could do without. Which was why memos out of New York solicited exciting ideas.

"You got a call, not a memo," some man whose name I didn't catch, but it should've been Egyptian grave robber, said. "On your level you get calls."

At least another two hundred watts went on inside Marvin's head, which was sort of bald, very shiny and veiny under too smooth skin.

"The call came," he agreed. "About a week later I made my move."

"Which was?" another brown nose asked, like he was doing a play.

It was a play all right, the way Marv rubbed his hands together before he told how, with his attorney along, they went to New York all expenses paid including his attorney's daily fee, which cost. After a deal was hammered out, a deal that left some executives dying in their chairs and others afraid they'd pass on before they heard what they'd bought, a deal that guaranteed him a million-five spread over ten years, which he figured was education money for the kids, and absolutely payable, even if the series bombed in the first ten weeks, Marv said he went to the window of the conference room way up in the company tower and looked out over New York. That was for added drama, heightened suspense, before he knocked them out with his series title and theme.

"*The Decadents*," he said slowly. "I sold them *The Decadents*. It'll be in the trades, et cetera, Monday morning. See it," he went on, "the biggest, most beautiful and luxurious private yacht in the world sails into the harbor at Cannes. This yacht's the size of a destroyer, at least. Bigger than anything Onassis could even afford to dream of. And as the yacht's tying up at the private dock the camera cuts away for a tie-in shot of this big helicopter coming in to land on the dock. Then our lead gets out of the helicopter. Big, handsome, an international buccaneer of finance——"

"I'd rather be an international fuccaneer of binance," the grave robber said.

"For that I'm getting you laid Monday," Marvin said to him. "By Tuesday your cock'll've fallen off," he went on, which showed us he didn't care to be interrupted when he was center stage. "Our man's all of forty-five, not more. All personality and balls. And he goes aboard his yacht to an office that's got to be bigger than the Astrodome, which is furnished. Furnished!" Marvin's head sweated with creation. "In a couple of minutes our man disposes of just average problems for him —two governments, a revolution, building a pipeline across the length of Africa and getting the channel tunnel started between England and France. In one second"—Marv snapped his fingers—"he buys all of Nevada from Howard Hughes and California from Ronnie Reagan."

"Forgive me, Marvin dear," a sincere-looking woman I hadn't met yet said. "But yuch on Ronnie."

"No politics, Ann, please," Marv said soothingly. "And especially not Vietnam. Not tonight. That's a dear." He pinched her cheek. That taken care of, Marv took a deep breath to help stoke the fires that lit up his head. "Business disposed of, our lead dismisses everyone and the camera in a medium close traveling shot follows him as he starts to take his clothes off—everything!—until he's bare-ass naked when he reaches a magnificent door at the far end of his office. Now"—Marvin began to sweat with the tension he'd created—"the camera shows his hand slowly turning the knob."

Mouths were open, jaws were dropped, some people wiped at their faces, others licked their lips as Marvin framed what could be the scene inside a camera lens. I looked at Larry. Behind his glasses was a stone face, but his hand around mine was warm.

"It's our man's bedroom," Marvin ended the suspense. "Rich but simple, seeing as the pan shot only shows this big round bed with shining black satin sheets and the right lights concentrated on the bed, in the middle of which is this gorgeous hunk of blonde ass absolutely naked. But she's got blonde hair as long as Godiva's so you can't exactly see her crotch. Still, enough tit is showing to blow sets all over the country."

"I can't help it," some man groaned, "but I just popped. Which is something I haven't done since I was eighty."

"There's more," Marv said after he patted this man's back to prove he could appreciate the right comment at the right time. "Because this gorgeous piece of *shtup*, she's having her toes sucked one by one by"—he lowered his voice—"a beautiful octoroon. Or maybe"—he touched his forehead—"one of them high-caste Hindu cunts. Naturally the toe-sucker's naked. And when the blonde sees our man, she dismisses the broad and stands like a Venus to welcome our lead. And she's got the most gorgeous pair, pure alabaster, hair under her arms and no beaver."

"Like Botticelli's Venus," the woman who was asked not to discuss politics said. "But I don't think she had hair under her arms. I really don't remember."

Marvin smiled and clasped both hands behind his back. "I like her with hair."

"All right," she said. "Then what?"

"That was my presentation," Marv said. "From that point the network develops."

People looked from Marv to each other. Some women looked uncomfortable. Others as if they'd give anything for that particular part.

"Marvin, you mind-fucker, they bought that?" somebody asked, not exactly believing. "For a million-five?"

"I should've asked for more," he said. "Because their reactions were just like yours. Silence. Awe. Until somebody who really counts with the network, and always has, screamed that he was taking solo credit for selling them on bringing me to New York. 'Genius!' this simple shit screamed. 'We've bought genius!'"

"Mr. Mercer," Larry got his attention, and I was glad now that he'd gone for his glasses, "I'm not in the business. But you can't show stuff like that on TV. Not yet."

"Of course," Marv was so tolerant of Larry. "That's one of the problems that'll take some front-office licking."

It's hard, impossible to beat that sort of curtain line, especially when Marv stuck out his tongue and held his hands as if he was cupping the cheeks of some broad's ass. Everyone laughed, cheered, tried to shake hands with our host, who let them touch his flesh, then excused himself because he had to circulate around and make everyone there feel wanted.

"I'll believe anything," Larry said as we worked our way toward the French doors of the living room for some air. "After I saw somebody clinch a cigarette by throwing it into a champagne bucket I made up my mind to believe anything, even after the jerk who did this told me the rottenest dirty story I ever heard."

"Namely?" I asked.

"Forget it, Joyce," he said. "I wish it was past midnight and time to say our polite good-byes. Especially to our host's head."

"It's macrocephalic," I said. "Now the joke. Give."

Larry squirmed. "I don't think it's funny. All right," he turned away from me, "when does a cub scout become a boy scout?"

"Tell me," I said.

He hesitated. I mean he did! "After he's eaten his first brownie. Dirty bastard," Larry looked around, "but what the hell can you expect from a hog farm like this? Look"—he pointed—"just look."

I did and laughed, not at the joke which was very sick, but at myself for having driven Larry and everyone else around us wild with what he was going to wear, what I was going to wear, would our choices complement each other without looking stagey, with what we would say to certain things, what, how we would react to certain situations like if snails were served and which Larry swore he wouldn't eat no matter what, would we dance only with each other or with other guests, which meant my making Larry practice, and how we would explain Verney, what we'd do if a man asked an embarrassing question or said something mean or stupid, or if it was done by a woman. Nobody put us down, nobody cared to, not yet, seeing as most everyone around us was busy selling himself up river and everyone else they knew downstream. In loud tough voices, not caring who heard, they knocked everyone and everything, even Marvin and Sally Mercer for not knowing how to give a party that wasn't a disaster drill, but then someone who wore tennis shoes with his no-button tuxedo coat and flared trousers said the Mercers didn't know a dozen—better make that one—person they could call a real friend, so how in the name of style could they ever have a small civilized evening? Which was why their parties were always too large, too noisy, too much help for too much to eat and drink, so that on the morning after the awful night before remembering the Mercers was the real hangover. Still, the parties proved that Marvin Mercer was a showman with balls of brass because no one else would dare have so many people who hated the air he breathed under his roof at any one time. So, if they were here for his trophy count, let it cost the son of a bitch, even if it meant pouring full bottles into toilets and damaging the furnishings because stealing Marvin's Sulka and Charvet ties had become some sort of a tradition which Marvin now expected of his guests, so that on the Monday immediately following a Mercer party lots of men wore a tie stolen from his dressing room and they put in calls to Marvin to tell him about the classy tie they were wearing. Everyone in the know thought it a class joke and Marvin would've been terribly disappointed to find a single tie left on his rack. They were freaks, and that went for a lot of women too.

Then to prove my point I saw this thing, sort of under middle height, with big violet glasses so large they hid most of his face, who wore a cape of pink feathers almost to the floor. The cape matched his pink Afro, which I found out later was a wig. After he gave the cape to a maid having trouble keeping her face straight, he preened and moved his arms like they were bird's wings to show us slobs his lemon-yellow shirt with its ruff collar and lace front, like the kind nobles wore when they wrote with feathers. Since his dinner coat was sans sleeves, so it looked like a long vest, you just couldn't help noticing his shirt and maroon pants with yellow stripes on the outer seams, and that he was barefooted.

"The party's officially on its way," Delphine Gavere said as she introduced us and our amazement to her husband and his big moustache waxed at the ends, an absolutely emaciated man with the biggest hands I'd ever seen. "If you don't know him, don't bother. That faggot writes for Marvin under the name of Johnny Jump Upp—double 'p'—which if you look it up in the dictionary—single 'p'—is defined as an American violet or a wild pansy."

"He looks simpleminded," I said.

"Don't let his camping around fool you," Delphine told me alone because Larry'd turned away in disgust. "The little bastard is very sharp and a karate expert who loves to cripple people. Whatever else he is"—she shook her head—"thank God he isn't Jewish."

"I wish that still didn't bother you," her husband said. "But how can you be so sure?"

"Because I once gave him twenty dollars to show me his prick," she said. "I just had to know. And knowing was worth the twenty, even the hundred he asked for and didn't get. That eighty bucks went to a charity."

"Delphine, please," her husband was amused, "it's a medical fact that even Christian boys are circumcised."

She poked her husband with an elbow. "This one wasn't. Let's get away from here," she included us by tugging at Larry's sleeve, "and get something to wash the sight of him out of our eyes."

Larry and me, before we started out, decided to say that I'd had some hay fever symptoms and taken an antihistamine, and he had a beginning ulcer, reasons enough for our not drinking anything stronger than wine. But before we had to make any explanations Sally Mercer saw us and charged through to wrap her arms around me like we were the oldest best friends, which may explain why my thoughts were so bitchy at being detached from the Gaveres, who waved so long as they continued toward one of the bars. I didn't like Sally's dress—too nothing, her hair—too streaky, her jewelry—junk or too flashy if it was real, and there was nothing nice I could've thought about her makeup because it was too much. Furthermore, she looked awfully put out, which somehow activated my sympathy, so to cheer her up because she isn't much, with the way her mouth twists at one corner when she talks and too skinny legs for her big butt, I said how wonderful she looked and her party was just as beautiful as her house.

"You know so many people," I said because I couldn't remember Johnny Jump Upp's name on the guest list. "I won't be able to remember even half their names."

Sally's thank-you kiss left my cheek oily. "That son of a bitch, like always, ran in extra guests at the last minute. I'm speaking of Marvin," she explained because I looked blank. "That's one of his special little cutsies, to add people I really despise after he, personally, has called the caterers."

"Like that Johnny Jump Upp?" I asked.

"You're clairvoyant!" Sally thought she rewarded me by slobbering against my cheek for a second time. "But Marv says it's considerate and exquisite to have someone at a party that everyone can feel superior to, can hate and be afraid of at the same time. So he always invites Johnny."

"That sort of refined reasoning is way over my head," Larry said in a voice that told me again how he wanted to go home.

"I know he does it to give me fits," Sally said. "Somehow to get even with me for marrying him. He sees himself in a mirror, so he knows I said yes because how else could someone like me ever get all this? God"—she looked at me, then at Larry—"you're so lucky." When she spoke again her eyes were *che sera sera*. "Have you stolen your tie yet?" she asked Larry. "Please do. Marv made a special point of telling me how he hopes you do."

"Go ahead," I pointed toward the stairs. "And pick a nice one, Larry. A Sulka."

"Take two," Sally said. "One for your friend."

We watched Larry make his way through the crowd and he only turned once toward us, but I waved him to go on.

"Now there's another one of my special hates." Sally nudged me to look in the direction of the Steinway grand in its inlaid walnut case, a handsome instrument but too large for the room. "Sometimes I hate her more than I even hate Johnny. See who I mean?"

"She's wearing the white accordion-pleated mini?" I spoke of a girl with so-so looks but a good body and legs.

"The same. Does she look disgusting to you?" she asked me. "Of course not," she answered. "So would you believe that she blows Marv right in the office? To relax him during creative and production crises? Isn't that disgusting?"

"What she does, where she does it, or why?" Because this had to be heard, I wished Larry hadn't gone for a tie.

"Cocksucking aside, she's an absolutely marvelous executive secretary and budget analyst," Sally went on as if I'd never asked my questions. "Worth every dollar of the twenty thousand Marvin pays her. Which, when you figure that someone with her educated mouth could get fifty a trick from *schmucks* on our income level, isn't too much money. Seeing as she probably blows Marvin twice a week, more if his Nielsen's off, that makes her salary about fifteen or less, wouldn't you say?"

"Both are doing all right," I said, surprised at my self-control as I went on to say that she didn't have to pay for a room, for travel, protection or cut in people she had to depend on. A very big savings was her not having to split with a pimp. I paused because some women approached us, but smiling sweetly I asked them to excuse us girls for another minute seeing as I was giving Sally advice on a personal and intimate problem. That, before they left, put stars of curiosity in their eyes. Then I went on. "From his side, Sally, he doesn't have to make an appointment, travel, hand out tips or run the risk of a raid. Still, taxwise, she'd be better off if he paid her fifteen and gave her the other five under the table. This way your Marvin writes off the whole twenty, so you get part of the tax benefit. Right?" Larry was coming toward us, so I pinched Sally's cheek, but not to hurt her. "Right."

Stupid bitch, I left her like that, even though she apologized so hard her nose began to run.

"Dear Abby, move over," I answered Larry's silent question

—what was eating me? "Twice so far I've been asked what it's all about. You know—the trade. Damn them," I turned away, "I need your handkerchief."

"I can do more than that," Larry said as he gave me one. "I can take you home."

"No," I got stubborn. "The party's not even started yet. We haven't even had dinner."

"I could get the car and take us somewhere people dress up to eat," he suggested. "That could be fun. And you'd be doing me a very big favor."

"No," I insisted. "We're staying. I don't want to argue!"

He folded the handkerchief and returned it to his pocket. "Suit yourself, Joyce."

I managed to inject a little humor into a tense situation by pretending to peer under his dark glasses. "Did you steal one of his ties?"

"No," he said. "I went to the can and just sat."

"Because there were other people in his bedroom?" I asked.

"Joyce"—he was patient—"I didn't go to his bedroom. Since when've I become a sneak thief?"

"But it's a game, nothing else," I explained. "You've been told that."

"Then I don't have to play," he replied. "Joyce"—he used my name again to show how bothered he was by everything, people, the way they looked, behaved and the things they said—"I think they're getting ready to serve dinner."

He was right. At the French doors to the garden porch, staff at two tables told people where to sit. The lines were pretty orderly for people who'd been belting the booze and each other, but no one bothered to lower a voice so we heard all sorts of snatches of interesting conversation, particularly from a group almost right behind us who were so razzmatazz they never stopped snapping their fingers and shuffling in little dance steps, even while one man advised his friend, poor guy, that if he did come to the party with a wife in no condition for later-on hacking, at a circus like this it wouldn't be any trick at all to make it with a chick in a broom closet. Or he could go over to the Strip and get himself a teeny-bopper and feel like a Roman emperor because those kids had no inhibitions at all and they went at positions and you-name-it like they were in creative playschool.

"And think of it this way," he continued to lecture. "With those kids, if society can't get them on their feet and off our backs, then let's get some personal relief by putting them on their backs, which gets them off our feet at least for a little while of pleasure."

This guy's wife, shiny and smooth as plastic, applauded by tapping her thumbnails together. "That's more profound than the bright quip you were throwing around all of last week," she said. "Whenever oral sex came up in conversation"—she told the other woman—"Derek would grin and say—show me a man who doesn't and I'll steal his girl."

They saw us listening, waved friendly and introduced themselves, but we were at the assignment table, so I called out how we hoped to meet them later, then turned toward the table to be told what we already knew. That we were at table four. A circus tent of red and orange stripes enclosed part of the garden and pool area, over which a dance floor and slightly raised bandstand had been set up. Chinese lanterns in artificial trees provided light, and radiant heat from standards made us comfortable. Portable bar carts flanked the bandstand. There were at least twenty-five tables set up on the flagstone and they looked very bright and cheerful with their orange tablecloths and napkins. Floral centerpieces were California poppies and short-stemmed red roses. Captains' chairs with red cushions were very comfortable. Portable kitchens stood outside the tent, behind the bandstand. While a team of maître d's helped people get seated, waiters served the shrimp cocktails. The band, about seven pieces, played music you could digest by and some couples danced toward their tables.

At our table, which like several others was set up for three couples—not five as I'd expected—Larry shook hands with both men, bowed to their wives and introduced me in a quiet, confident way. The couple to our right, Genevieve and Harvey Caxton, were in their late thirties, and after a few general remarks Harvey let me know he was a TV producer and working on a new series he'd developed for the network, whose watchdog over him was Marv Mercer, information which made Genevieve blow a silent one with her lips. The pretty woman to Larry's left was Myrtle Richards, who let us both know before we talked about anything else that Casey, her husband, very handsome, was going to play one of the two leads in the show Harvey Caxton was producing. No, the other lead was out of town and stinking up a pretty good play, so the critics said.

"Our show's sold for next season," Myrtle said, understandably happy. "They've been shooting for a month now even though there's some script problems." Now she lowered her voice. "That's why they've put him under Marv, which he hates."

"I hope the show's a success," Larry said for both of us.

"Thank you, it will be," Myrtle said but looked put out because we hadn't asked the obvious—what the show was about.

Frankly, being hungry, which is unusual for me, I was more interested in the shrimp cocktail, very good, choice, marvelous sauce, and I told Sally so when she appeared at our table to say we looked comfortable before she hoped we'd find each other *vrai sympathique,* the meaning of which I got, and if I hadn't, wouldn't've shown it to her or anyone else.

Nor will I give Sally Mercer the satisfaction of describing anything else on her store-bought menu, first class but no trick, seeing as all anyone has to do is call a good caterer, tell him how many you're entertaining, so that it becomes like a Chinese restaurant, where the more people in the party and the more expensive the dinners you order, the more fancy and elaborate dishes you get. That settled, let's get on to where Marvin Mercer came over, right after our entrees were served, to kid around generally until he stood between Larry and me to confide how the people on either side of us—the Caxtons and Richards—had specifically asked to be at our table.

"You're both authentic," Marvin told us. "Real people who haven't, like the mass of men, led lives of quiet desperation."

That was eloquently put, but before I could upgrade my opinion of Mercer, Harvey Caxton caught my eye to signal hold it. Later he told me what impressed me should, seeing as it was a very famous quotation of the American writer who invented civil disobedience.

I'm rambling and don't want to. So to be orderly again I'll tell how Marvin went on to say he hoped Larry wouldn't mind his saying what everyone or almost everyone aware of events around them knew—how Larry'd once been a public enemy.

"That was long ago." Marv continued to pat Larry's shoulder, which I was sure was stiffening. "Now half the people in America think the other half are, which gives Larry—like it or not—the whole nation for company!" He laughed at how smart he was, so did the other two couples, but not Larry or me. Hands in my lap, I let the food get cold, which ruins it, while Larry's jaws firmed up and his old scar began to show. "Because we're proud of who you are, Larry," Marv said after he signaled for his four-stooge chorus to stop laughing, "one of the purposes of this dinner party is to welcome you to our television team—I hope."

That said to confuse us, before Marv walked away he told Harvey Caxton that explaining things to us was up to him. Sort of nervous, Harvey asked if I'd mind exchanging chairs so he could sit next to Larry and elaborate on what Marvin had started. I moved myself next to Genevieve Caxton, who thanked me more than it was worth for being so cooperative. She wanted to talk but I wanted to listen while her husband told Larry what this was all about, and which's why whatever she had to say got lost on its way to my ears. All put together, the show was about big-league crime and Harvey's concept'd been corroborated in important part by *The Thomas Crown Affair,* which starred Steve McQueen as a brain who planned big capers for his kicks and at the end got away with another robbery that gave him a couple of more million, plus he's laid the girl detective assigned by the insurance company to trap him. Research proved how audiences liked the switch of McQueen making it all the way because it proved that like in real life, big crime paid big. So Harvey Caxton's series was about a top syndicate group opposed by a top group of lawmen. Each side, though they fight to the death like the German and American aviators do in *The Blue Max,* respect each other. Like the McQueen picture, I hadn't seen this one either. To go on, in Harvey's series each side would win and lose some, and if the network brass got with it, the percentages would never be more than fifty-five to forty-five in favor of the good guys.

"Casey here"—Harvey told Larry—"is our college-educated syndicate man. A young captain of an old, very powerful family. We think it's just right for him. Another reason why we intend to make this series—we're calling it *The Arena*—authentic. And that's where you come in, Larry. You don't mind my calling you Larry?"

"After being called a public enemy, why should I object to Larry?" he answered. "Let me get this straight," he went on. "You want me to work on this series? As some sort of expert? For pay?"

"On the syndicate," Casey said after Harvey's nod gave him permission to join the conversation. "With you on the series as a confidential, behind-the-scenes man, because your office won't be at the studio, we'll be able to get authentics and not the kind of shit writers dream up while they're jerking off, the no-talents. Then Harvey and me—I—won't have as much trouble with directors who think they know it all because who else gets the last credit on the title crawl? Man"—he didn't like what he thought—"talk about thieves. Directors are on top of the pile."

"Of crap," Larry said. How he'd done it, I couldn't say, but his complexion was normal again, so I guess his scar had disappeared. "That's a joke."

"Sure," Casey said. "And very inside."

"It's been cleared," Harvey took up the pitch and sell. "Some of the network brass in New York—real stiffs—didn't like the idea. But Marvin sold it to them after they bought *The Decadents*."

"You don't say?" Larry marveled. "That they liked, but putting me on your show they didn't?"

"You're not going to turn us down because they objected at first?" Harvey was anxious. "Who's your agent?"

"I haven't got one," Larry said, and I felt he was playing along to keep from hitting Harvey, Casey or both of them. "But I've got an attorney who can negotiate for me. I don't come short-term. Or cheap."

Harvey hesitated, then made himself appear forceful. "I'm starting right at the top because that's where you are. Where you belong. So there'll be no giving in, thousand by thousand, for me. We've got thirty shows to do for thirty-nine weeks, with nine serving as repeats if we stay a full season. So the first ten are guaranteed. You'll get fifteen thousand for them. Naturally, it's understood, an office and secretary. If we get picked up for the second ten you get another fifteen. For the third ten—pray to God it goes thirty weeks—you'll get twenty thousand. If we're canceled the first year, any time, you get your salary for the segment plus five thousand as severance pay. But if we get picked up for the second year, all of us"—he included Larry—"negotiate better deals."

"That's an offer?" Larry asked. "Or a commitment?"

"There's an office waiting for you Monday morning," Harvey nodded. "All you have to do is say yes. Or you can work at home and have the secretary plus some phone lines.

Believe me"—he leaned toward Larry—"you're absolutely hush-hush. No writers, no directors will know. So how about winging me a yes and make our night?"

"I've gotta think," Larry said. He took off his glasses, not to wipe them but to let me see that if I was surprised, he was too, but he was also bitter. Not angry. Bitter. Because he wasn't being hired for what he knew best and was proud of, how to run a hotel or resort operation, but for something he knew very little about and certainly wouldn't be allowed to do. Not if I knew Señor Basqua right. "Some people I really respect are rolling over in their graves," he told their looks of disappointment. "So after they stop rolling and settle down again, and I've had a chance to think about it, seeing as I've never done business at a party—that's the truth—I'll let you know before Monday." To impress them, Larry looked phony mysterious. "Because I'll have to make some important calls," he added, "to important people."

"Important people." Harvey was really awed. "This show's gonna be a smash."

"I hope so," Larry said. "Now mind if I do some eating?"

Harvey stood to exchange chairs with me. "We'll talk some more later?"

"Sure," Larry said. "Fifteen hundred a week for openers?"

"Believe me," Harvey crossed himself, "that's the top figure."

"Even if I squeeze?" Larry asked.

"Don't," Harvey begged. "Please don't press. We'll show real gratitude if you don't."

If truth is important, I was fascinated and wanted to say something but didn't because Larry shook his head. So I listened to him tell Harvey and Casey that he wanted their phone numbers to let them know yes or no by tomorrow afternoon. Meanwhile, our food was so cold would they mind if he signaled our waiter to serve us again? That pleased everyone, me too, and we were very tolerant when they played kissy with us by pointing out some well-known personalities we hadn't got to meet and told us inside stories about them and other people that, even if they were fiction, took imagination to make up. When Casey asked me to dance, Larry did the right thing by moving Myrtle around the dance floor. Then I paired with Harvey, a really smooth dancer, who told me how much he hoped Larry—who was one-two-gliding on the floor with his wife—would agree to their proposition because with him the series stood a better chance of survival. Plus it seemed to him that Larry was too young a man to retire.

"We'll arrange for both of you to visit the locations where we'll set our stories. Maybe even one or two in the Bahamas or the Virgin Islands. You've been there recently?"

"No," I said.

"I'll bet you haven't been to New Orleans in years." He looked sorry for me. "That's why this'll be so good for you. Getting out, traveling, being directly involved in the creative end of the world's most important form of communication."

Honest, I was sold, and what I wanted from Larry was to move a mountain if he had to so that he could participate. And I feel, really feel, it might've worked out if Sally Mercer'd had spine enough to tell Marvin that no matter what, there were some people she wouldn't have in the house. And first on her person-non-gratis list was Johnny J. Upp. He'd been moving around from table to table, very obnoxious and making people uncomfortable from their expressions, and right after we got back to our table because the band had taken a break, there he was, coming toward us, looking very snotty, which we could see because he wasn't wearing his clownish glasses. But he was smoking a little cloisonné pipe and the odor was sweet and sort of heavy.

"Very exclusive beautiful people," he greeted us by lifting his leg like a dog. "I was stuck at a table very elbow to elbow with an awful assortment of laboratory discards. But you"— he sucked in deep on the pipe, held his breath for a longish time, then let go—"you're so comfortable."

"We'd even be more comfortable if you took off," Larry

said before he told us something we all knew. That Johnny was smoking pot. "If this party got busted it wouldn't be good for us," he said but meant himself and me.

Understanding is one thing, trying to do something about it another, so when Harvey Caxton got up and put a hand on Johnny to steer him away from us, I guess, the next thing we saw was Harvey flat on his back and only Genevieve's scream saved him from much worse because Johnny stood over him, smoking, smiling and ready to deliver some kind of crippler. Then I remembered what Delphine Gavere'd told me—how the little queer was a very dangerous karate expert.

I told that to Larry, who nodded, and said nothing as Johnny helped Harvey get up and waved to everyone as if it was all some kind of joke before he made a big thing of brushing Harvey's coat and pants, which gave him a chance to goose poor Harvey and make him jump. Poor guy, he was shaken and bruised, I know, but he did his best to laugh off what'd happened to him while he asked Johnny to please go away.

"That's not friendly," Johnny pouted, aware as we were that more and more people were watching us and enjoying our unhappiness. "Not friendly at all. But your husband isn't friendly either, Mrs. Mafiosa," he spoke directly to me. "How do you explain that?"

"I don't," was what I said. "But I approve."

Johnny clowned grief, which was his way of baiting us. This we—I—understood. What I didn't, what shocked and hurt most, was how more and more people around us enjoyed the way Johnny was working us over. They laughed, roared, as he acted being broken-hearted and crying, at the way he tore at his pink hair and trembled as if he was being flogged by the cruelest people who were too much for poor little him, which explains why some comics who thought they had senses of humor began to call out that we were going to be reported for cruelty to nice little barefooted guys.

"Let me handle this, please," I said to Larry who was killing himself in his chair. "He won't dare manhandle a woman."

Larry nodded, not happy, and I stood up to put me just about on eye level with the monster. "We're asking you, the nicest way we know how, to please leave us alone," is what I said to him, very civil and polite.

"But I came over, smoking my little peace pipe, to establish friendly relations," he said and began to dance around, all the while pumping his hips like male dogs do after they've mounted. "Relations," he repeated after a long drag on his pipe, which he tapped out and stuck in a pocket, "because thinking about fucking an old pro who's still got her looks stimulated what I never knew I had. Male hormones! Mother! At last"—he shrieked in a way that just doubled up some of the jerks who were watching him—"I've got the hots for you!" He stopped to put a hand inside his shirt to make believe his heart was thumping like crazy. "Think of what you'd be doing for society," he said as he danced closer to me, still moving his hips in and out in a way that made me sick. "Making me into a straight would save the assholes of hundreds of little boys. Their mothers would love you. Their fathers would——"

Larry's chair hit him in the upper chest and as Johnny staggered, surprised, Larry swung my chair overhead with one hand and let fly. It caught Johnny hard enough to knock him flat and as people screamed, Larry kept moving forward, deliberately, almost casually, not excited or wasting a movement, with another chair in his hand. When he swung this chair, which he didn't let go, it knocked Johnny's arms down. When Johnny tried to roll clear and get up Larry clubbed again with the chair. Johnny was stunned, but like he was working a poisonous snake, Larry turned him over with the chair, then brought it down to trap him under the four legs. Coming to, Johnny began to wriggle, so Larry stepped down hard on one of Johnny's bare feet to make him scream before he got kicked in the side of the head to really put him away.

I started forward, other people did, but after Larry handed me his glasses his look sent me back and stopped other people because his eyes were the kind you see inside the black mask of an executioner who uses an axe on you after he's torn out your fingernails.

"I need napkins," Larry told me. "Clean or used. At least a couple of dozen. Hurry up."

Larry took the napkins I'd collected, and scared as I was, it was a delight to see the way he made a knot in one and stuffed the knot into Johnny's mouth before he tied the ends tight and hard. Then, with two napkins tied together, he tied Johnny's hands behind his back. Before Johnny came to, his ankles were tied so he was helpless when Larry lifted him into a chair. Now he tied Johnny's upper arms to the chair back. After he slapped Johnny across the mouth very hard, Larry untied his wrists and tied each of them to the chair arms. Next Johnny's ankles got tied to the spreader between the two front legs of the chair. Not once had Larry hurried, so after he checked every knot and was satisfied it would hold, he took an open bottle of champagne out of a bucket and poured the ice water and cubes over Johnny's head. He shuddered but was still groggy, so Larry gave it to him with the contents of a second bucket. When Johnny's eyes opened and he was able to think, he struggled, tried to speak, strained against the napkins and knots, even made some sort of cry when Larry grabbed his hair, which came off. That started some people laughing again, especially after Larry threw the wig away and poured some water over his hands before he gave Johnny another rap across the head you couldn't help feel. Then like an artist might, he stepped back to evaluate Johnny and think some before he saw Marvin coming toward him, very slow and uncertain.

"Hold it right there," Larry ordered Marvin, who did as he was told. "You invited us because you wanted to get—I mean hear—some authentic inside stories on syndicate procedures. Or are you saying I misunderstood you?"

Marvin hesitated, maybe because right then his attention was on Johnny, how, while he was struggling to get free, he began to froth against the gag. "Untie him and I'll throw the little bastard out," he bargained with Larry. "You're fired, Johnny!" he began to shout. "Send your agent around for your check and things because I don't ever want to see you again!" Marvin's righteous effort winded him, but at last he had enough breath to talk to Larry. "Now you can untie him."

"Not yet," Larry disagreed. "Since you wanted to know how they operate on top or close to it, I'll tell and show you what happens now and then, once in a while at their dinners and parties. Not as big as this one, Marvin, but it's still a party."

Marvin just stood, not moving, as Larry dragged Johnny in his chair to about the middle of the dance floor before he invited everyone to come in to the edges so they could hear him without straining. When most everyone was around the dance floor, with some people standing with the musicians at the edge of the bandstand, Larry told them how it was stupid to believe that every breach of syndicate discipline or doing something wrong, like holding out collections or saying something bad against religion, was punished by death. Sometimes the wheels who were judging the man just decided to fix him a special way that never failed to teach a lesson. That was done by inviting him along with his wife or best girl to a dinner party, where right when the man was enjoying himself most, he was knocked out and tied to a chair just like Johnny was.

"That's after all his clothes are taken off," Larry explained, "which is all right if the guy's human. Then it isn't disgusting. But this"—he gave it to Johnny in the face with an elbow—"would look too much like a puked-up worm."

Why, why did I have the feeling that Larry was waiting now for someone to plead for Johnny, someone who wasn't connected with him in a business way, someone who had nothing to do with him, didn't like him, but still felt sorry for him? But no one did and as Larry stepped toward the chair, where from his movements and expression it looked like he might untie Johnny and just maybe throw him out, people looked disappointed, with some of them even making protesting sounds. No doubt about it, they wanted Larry to go on, just as I did because of what that slug'd said to me for everyone to hear—not that he wanted to fuck me, which at my age was a compliment, but that I was an old pro. For that I could thank Sally Mercer and probably the head that was her husband.

The crowd, and that includes me, wanted Larry to go on with the educational entertainment, so he thought for a second before he clapped his hands. "All right, what happens next to the man tied up just like this? But with his clothes off? Somebody ask me."

"With pleasure." It was Delphine Gavere, loving every bit of this. "What happens next, I hope, I hope, I hope?"

"Good," Larry said. "So let's not disappoint the lady. Now I need some volunteers to start things off. "You"—he pointed to Harvey Caxton and Casey Richards. "You," he motioned for Marv Mercer to join them on the dance floor. "You three," he chose some other men who looked like they wanted to be part of what was going to happen. "All of you out here."

They looked self-conscious, laughed, waved to friends as Larry told them to stand in a circle around Johnny, just about two feet from him. From where I stood with Genevieve and Myrtle, and with Delphine who'd left her husband somewhere, I began to get some idea of what Larry had in mind. So did other people. And that's why some of them, then more, began to laugh and call out for things to get started.

"Gentlemen," Larry said to the men around Johnny, "start pissing on the rat. That's right," he told them, "unzip and get started. People're waiting."

They hesitated, Harvey looked as if he was going to step away but Marv Mercer's look held him, and when Marv's head began to grin like a happy pumpkin as he unzipped his fly, Harvey and Casey hurried not to be left behind, which got the other men going. All their pricks were out, the drummer sounded a roll on his drum, and just as he hit a cymbal they all took aim at Johnny—who again looked like a choking animal being driven crazy—and let go to wet him down from head to foot. I can't now or ever describe how everyone loved it. Marv pissed at one of Johnny's ears, Harvey aimed at his eyes, Casey asked the men to hold while he pulled back the ruff collar of Johnny's shirt and let him have it right down the back, which got a big round of applause from people who appreciated originality and style. After this group emptied their bladders, when Larry waved for other men to step forward he had to motion some back because he wanted no more than six at a time. Then, after Marv called to Sally for some of their steady help to bring mops and buckets so their guests wouldn't have to stand in someone else's piss while they did it on Johnny, Larry let as many as ten at a time piss on someone who for all intents and purposes would've been better off murdered.

Suddenly Dephine ran onto the floor, where right after she lifted her dress and leg to share in the fun, her husband rushed out to drag her away while she screamed how he never let her have any fun that counted and she'd never forgive him for denying her something she'd never again get the chance to do.

"At least let me spit in his face," she pleaded with Sherman. "Please!"

Because he hesitated, Delphine broke away, got through the crowd that parted like the Red Sea, I guess, and didn't seem to mind the wet she had to step in as she let go with what Itzik would've called a big *chyackeh* right in Johnny's face. And she looked actually radiant as people screamed because of what a beautiful thing she'd done.

It went on for maybe another five minutes before we left, with an inspired Marvin, who, after he got his regular help to bring him some clothesline to retie Johnny, had them bring bottles of catsup and barbecue sauce, jams, jellies and pancake syrup, which he poured and smeared on Johnny for other men who waited in line to piss off him. And to prove that this was a family affair, Sally came charging out with some other women, including Marv's secretary, all of them carrying specimen bottles half or more full which they poured on Johnny's head. By now it looked as if Johnny'd fainted, or was dead, but no one cared.

Suddenly it happened. Someone pissing on Johnny began to throw up, which slowed things down, and as I began to gag in sympathy, which I always do when it happens where I can see, hear or smell it, Larry was at my side, looking as scared as the doctor who'd created Boris Karloff, and people didn't seem to notice as he walked me toward the front door, where I told him I wanted my evening cape, but he said forget it, we could afford another. So with his dinner jacket across my shoulders we started across Lexington toward our house, not saying a single word to each other and not because we wanted to hear the racket going on under the tent in the Mercers' garden, which, thank God, got fainter and fainter with every step we took away from that house. I'd roast in hell before joining EROS.

I began to cry, very hysterical, but only when we were safe in my house and upstairs, only after Larry told Barney Moodus to stay the night and sleep with his gun handy.

"A real party," I wailed while I actually tore the gown off me because it had to be burned. And that went for Larry's clothes too. "I still haven't been to a real party since I was a kid."

CHAPTER FOURTEEN

SIMON: It doesn't take even half a brain to understand why, for the public, the murders of Sharon Tate and her friends, and right after that this Italian grocer and his wife being slaughtered just about the same way, were lots more interesting and exciting than any suicide could be, unless the person who did away with himself was so important that his dying changed history. For that, Johnny Jump Upp couldn't qualify. He was dead, and as someone who felt himself to be a human being, I was a little sorry for him, or whatever it was, but certainly nowheres near as sorry as I was for the poor people who were murdered so terribly. Because a suicide wants to die but people who're being murdered don't, especially not in the horrible way these were, which was even worse than some of the killings in Brownsville, say like the Shapiro brothers, with the third of them, the kid who tried to make it in song sheets, ending up butchered and buried alive in Canarsie. Or the Ambergs—I'm sure there was more than one of them—being hacked to pieces in a garage. Though I hate being made to remember this, I won't deny it happened, or that if God hadn't taken over my life I could've been one of those being put into a lye vat. Or I could've been doing the putting.

What troubles me most about this particular suicide, which might blow her house down, is how Joyce refuses to believe it happened. Even after she heard about it over radio, saw things about it on television, read about it in the papers, even after we had cops over and everything, Joyce just said to them and later on to us that it never happened and was all some part of a very sloppy publicity stunt because people don't go around finishing themselves off like that. There she made sense. People didn't. But what about not-people? Because there were the Tate murders and those of the grocer and his wife, which affected me in a personal way. Could people—I mean human people—have done those? Absolutely not. So they also had to have been done by not-people.

Let's go on, please. That Saturday night, not too long after twelve, when Barney Moodus came to get me after he saw my lights go on, Larry was still putting Joyce to bed. She was under the covers, flat on her back and crying without much sound, which made Larry ask me to look and tell him if *I* thought she was going to be all right. His asking showed me how bad he thought things were or could get. And after Larry told me how Joyce'd been so disappointed in people at the party, I was more than glad I hadn't accepted Mrs. Sally Mercer's invitation. Still, being with a lot of snotty people who thought they were so great that they didn't need manners didn't sound as bad as what I'd gone through with Leola— who I'm not gonna see for a while—at her house, seeing as how she started to carry on like I alone was doing something terrible by using her phone to call a cab to take me home and away from the argument between us. How I was tearing up her self-respect by refusing to stay over. How I was humiliating her by turning down a reasonable suggestion to go to a motel which would've been a neutral place with a neutral room to be used by us, who she called consenting adults. These are things I don't understand. And right now I've no time for such education. What Leola—right away crying and carrying on—didn't see was that I liked her, was beginning to think of maybe marrying her, which meant working up to proposing. But I wanted everything to be done right, respectable, like the way it had been for her before she got married, so that when she had come to her husband as a virgin without a blemish, she would come to me—a widow without a stain. And for such a wedding, as I saw it, I could have all the reasons anyone would want to look for my family and invite them to California, all expenses paid. Also Larry's family and with the same arrangements. So who knows, maybe after I help Larry get Joyce on her feet and strong enough in the head to admit how there had been a suicide, I can take up again with Leola, explain my feelings to her, propose to prove I was sincere, and then make plans for a wedding attended by family and going somewhere for a trip, maybe even to Israel which my Leola says she'd love to see. God help us all, if by that time Larry can get along without me so close, I could move into Leola's house, which is very nice no matter what Joyce might say about it. In Leola's house I wouldn't be afraid of spilling something on the floor or of making, though not on purpose, a little scratch on the furniture. But all of this must be put aside until things get better under the roof where Larry stays. Then, if God's willing, I might be able to make plans involving the roof I think I want over me.

What can you say that's good about someone who climbs over the back wall of the garden around the fairly new art museum in that old mansion big as a palace this family used to live in when they owned an awful lot of what is now North Hollywood and Studio City? A couple of years ago the museum was willed to Beverly Hills and in no time at all through other gifts the museum was in business with such a fine collection of paintings that other museums, lots older, were already asking for loan of them. In a loan for loan, some paintings for some sculpture, this New York museum sent out a collection of sculpture so big it took freight cars and auto-carrying trailers to deliver. It was very modern, I heard, mostly of steel, shining or painted, in all sorts of shapes that people who know about such things write are beautiful.

Anyway, so here's this big outdoor and indoor exhibition of modern sculpture, with some pieces in the courtyard up to maybe twenty feet long and maybe as high. And come the Sunday morning right after Mr. and Mrs. Marvin Mercer's party, when the gardeners and janitors got to work a couple of hours before the museum opened for the day, there's a little skinny man without a single piece of clothing on him hanging from the end of a tall piece of sculpture made to look like some kind of grass-edger with a square wheel and a very long, bright steel shaft. It was Johnny Jump Upp, all naked, with his feather cape dropped near the square wheel. Then he must've crawled way out on the shaft to which he tied one end of the rope, with the other end very tight around his neck before he dropped off. Dying that way is terrible—like one of my customers said, a *miesse meshina*—but what was worse for the living was how bad Johnny smelled and the piece of cardboard dangling from the end of his dingle which told how he thanked Marvin Mercer, his shit of a wife Sally and their crappy guests for making up his mind to do this now instead of later. He also wanted to be cremated and flushed down the toilet in the master bathroom of the Mercers' house. Some people said this was a switch on an old joke about the last wishes of a dying actor who says that ten percent of his ashes should be blown in his agent's face, but if Johnny meant it as a joke, or to prove how temporarily insane he was, or still sane but so mean he had to kill himself in a way that closed the museum for more than a week to ruin the exhibit which was shut down during that time, he sure succeeded. Besides he gave Beverly Hills another black eye because everyone considered where the Tate murders had happened to be in Beverly Hills, seeing as her house was an easy walk from Harold Lloyd's estate, which really is in Beverly Hills.

Bright and early, because I also stayed over in one of the guest rooms where I was very restless because my head was filled with Larry's problems and mine, I heard the phone ring and it was Mr. Marvin Mercer insisting on coming right over with his wife, who he described as a case of walking shock. Right in Larry's office Mr. Mercer began to carry on how it was Larry's fault that Johnny'd killed himself, bad news he'd got from a friendly reporter who knew Johnny was one of his top writers. And right after that call came another from the cops, who told Mr. Marvin Mercer how they wanted to see him and would he please, to save time, maybe have his attorney present when they discussed a very strange suicide note and what it meant? The note, which Mr. Mercer got the cop who called him to read over the phone, was a disgrace and what was worse it implicated Mr. Mercer as well as Mrs. Mercer, who was so upset she might have to go to the hospital. This too was all Larry's fault.

Lucky I was there, lucky I hadn't gone to the guest house for even a little while to say my morning prayers because this poor Mr. Mercer's head might've got cracked like an egg. But I was able to grab Larry in time, force him into a chair and order—believe me—order him to tell me what this was all about. Then I got the whole story, the part that mattered, from before the time when Johnny began to bother Larry's table until he told—no, insulted—Joyce with how she was an old-timer who he, a dirty fairy not ashamed of his condition, was going to—fornicate.

"You're very lucky I wasn't at your party," I told this Mr. Mercer. "He would've been torn to pieces."

Mr. Mercer and his wife didn't see it that way, but before they could tell me, Larry did, so I found out how he'd handled the *faygelah* karate expert. Very good, I nodded, because when someone works with a wild animal or a snake, a chair or long stick sort of evens things more or less. If I'd been there, and Larry would've wanted to handle this thing alone, name your bet and odds and have them covered, I wouldn't've worried for a single second. But take my word for it, that's where it would've ended. Not with Larry shooting off his mouth about things he shouldn't of, no matter how sore he was by this time about being invited to this party because one, some stupes wanted him to work on their TV show as an expert on the mob, and two, Joyce being insulted with lousy questions about a long time ago, when all I care to remember is how she helped Larry get me into Mexico and put it out to strangers so things could be done right for me. No, people that Larry told of, the kind that hang you on a meat hook, are ones I'm glad to say I never got to know close. But were these fancy-shmanzies any better? Still, if I'd been there Leola wouldn't've been able to get so sore at me and no matter how sore Larry was, he'd never been allowed by me to start people off in that game.

"Who did the pissing?" I asked right out. "My friend here or you? And who got stuff from your kitchen to put on him? Your help or ours? Don't interrupt," I told this big head and his *ongeblozzene yenta* of a wife who began to look like she'd been caught stealing used clothespins but still wanted to make it seem like everyone else was responsible for her being such a cheap *Telebende*. "You invited him and Mrs. Tunig, who's now sick in bed, to your house not as guests but to hurt them like they were no better than sideshow freaks or carnival coons who used to get baseballs thrown at their heads. You're lucky I didn't accept your invitation." I kept on talking to keep them busy blocking my words and hard-look charges. "Very lucky because if whatever you had in mind for me'd happened—— Lucky," I said to knock in very deep the word and what was behind it. "Very, very lucky."

Without any ceremony I ended the talk between us right there and threw them out. Their trouble wasn't ours and if they sent cops over then I, personally, no matter how Larry felt about talking to the law, was going to blow the whistle on why Larry and Joyce'd been invited and how bad they'd been insulted. But what could people expect, I'd ask the police and reporters, of certain people capable of making up and selling something like *The Decadents* or of having degenerates working for them like this Johnny, who'd thought it very smart to advertise his freakiness, while they thought it was very inside for someone with his kind of sickness to sit down with them?

Enter the cops, almost right after I got through phoning some people like Mike Loesinger, Mr. Fred Rory and Señor Juan C. Basqua, all of them surprised to hear I was calling for Larry and Joyce—she in bed and he in no shape, although he wasn't exactly come unglued, I swore, to do any talking right now. Then, while I was fired up, I telephoned Leola and gave her some orders too. She was to quiet down and not get upset by things she might hear or read. No, I was all right and if she really cared about me then please, she was to stay home and not come visiting to our house or even the grocery. If she did what I asked, I'd call her every night.

Certain people, with plenty on their consciences telling whoppers that anyone with the least sense would've realized was a put-on, wasn't anything Larry had anything to do with, is what I told the cops. But last and certainly not least, I also pointed out, this Johnny was dangerous. He'd already hurt one guest. And the host, Mr. Mercer, hadn't done anything. As for what he'd said to Mrs. Tunig—well even cops who were trained to take guff hadn't always been able nowadays to hold themselves back when kids and revolutionaries called them pigs, worse names or asked who their wives were screwing while they were on duty. Or were the papers and television telling me lies? When the cops tried to make Larry do his own talking, Mr. Loesinger said he didn't have to. Because he hadn't done anything a man with blood in his veins wouldn't've done if his wife was insulted. So when, Mr. Loesinger asked, were the cops going to grill the people across the street? And if there wasn't going to be a cover-up, what charges might be brought against them?

The conclusion was obvious. There were too many people at the party who counted with the statehouse and even better clout to make charges stick for something the DA might call a shame against common decency. Also, how can you arrest—maybe a hundred people—when all of them've got cash for expensive talent to keep them free while they fight the case for years, especially, as Mr. Loesinger pointed out to us privately, if they stuck together and insisted they were all equally responsible so they wanted to be tried at the same time by one judge and jury? Another thing, practical and important, in any case that's prosecuted to make points with Mr. John Q. Public, is that the person or thing hurt has to be popular. For sure, Johnny wasn't. As for hanging himself, for which he was personally responsible, as his note proved, in the place he chose, reminded me of how people in New York used to feel about suicides. Generally, when someone took his own life, you felt sorry for the poor slob. Except if the guy didn't jump from a building like he threatened, which made you waste a lot of time for nothing, or if he did jump suddenly because then he could hurt people on the sidewalk or make them sick by splattering all over as he busted up. And not if the *schnook* jumped from one of the bridges between New York and a borough because then he tied up traffic and most people in the jam never got to see him. And least of all if the inconsiderate bum threw himself on a hot summer day in front of a subway train during the after-work rush, which could keep people from getting home for hours while they died in the heat. So the way Johnny committed suicide, naked, and the place he chose, so the museum and exhibit had to be closed down, didn't sit well with the locals and even less with Mr. Silent Majority after he found out how he'd been a big writer on a show the whole family could watch together and make believe it was themselves they were seeing on the tube.

Sure there was an inquest and the jury agreed that Johnny'd killed himself because he must've been of unsound mind. Sure some fan magazines tried to connect Johnny with the Sharon Tate murders, even if they had to print November and December issues, for sale from Labor Day to Yom Kippur late in

September—with their as usual made-up stories about movie people like Mr. Richard Burton, Elizabeth Taylor who's really Mrs. Burton, some others I didn't know so well, along with some about Mrs. Jackie Onassis and her husband that didn't make sense either, and how President Nixon was gonna have old-fashioned Thanksgiving and Christmas celebrations at the White House with Billy Graham as master of ceremonies—all this was filler for the story they were really interested in for right now, whose scary titles asked in big letters if Johnny was a devil worshipper who'd betrayed certain secret ceremonies which had the effect of getting him killed by the same devil priests, or their gods, to make him another name on a long list of unsolved murders in the files of Hollywood cops? It was weird, especially after some, then more of these magazines ran stories of how the bash given by Mr. and Mrs. Mercer was a put-on, nothing more than a run-through for a big, sort of Grand Hotel party that was going to be the subject of maybe a couple of episodes in Mr. Mercer's very important new project for television, *The Decadents,* and how when Johnny, wanting to give up writing for acting, found out he wasn't going to get one of the important parts in the series, he decided to kill himself and at the same time get even with everyone, especially his old boss, who was gonna fire him from writing his family show because he'd become emotionally screwed up and not a nice character.

Go tell with people like that—the Mercers and their real friends—maybe the party had been staged, is what I tried my best to convince Joyce. To back up my supposing arguments, some of the more reliable trades carried more or less the same story of how one theme in *The Decadents* involved the Mr. Tycoon putting together for profit and personal fun a TV show of organized good guys against organization bad guys fighting each other all over the world, with both sides winning and losing some, so for being right on the nose about this, which might lead to the spin-off of another series, Mr. Mercer was negotiating for someone to be his technical advisor who knew all about such things, seeing as he was in real life a very important Cosa Nostra figure so up-front in behind-the-scenes politics that involved even war and peace that he couldn't've spared the time to spit on Mr. J. Edgar Hoover. This, along with what'd happened down the street, struck me as purest bullshit without any filler. Which was why, seeing, as Joyce agreed with me one hundred percent about this, she wouldn't believe Johnny's suicide had ever happened. Bullshit, none of it really had, she now started to say. Maybe that was why she asked Who? when a certain Mrs. Delphine Gavere came to see Joyce with flowers and a letter to prove how much she wanted to be friends. Very foolishly and sort of dangerous, I thought, especially after Larry told me how Joyce'd told him of this particular party and how she'd like to know her better, for her to now say she'd never met Mrs. Gavere, which was reason enough not to see her. It figured, because Joyce'd already said she'd never met Mrs. Sally Mercer or ever been to a party at her house. Just why was everyone trying to confuse her?

Even if only Barney Moodus was around, Joyce wouldn't set foot outside her room until he and the day-help'd gone home. So once again she started to become a night person, even staying in bed around the clock, with Larry not having to tell me how dangerous this was for her. So the house began to be run like a hospital with one patient, very carefully, all of us not doing anything to disturb Joyce's mind, which was why a particular cable from Verney—who must've thought she was being funny as she told us how she didn't care a button that the shot of her kissing the *schmekel* of a naked little boy statue in Belgium'd caused dentists all over our country to throw her picture out of their offices—somehow got seen by Joyce. Nor was the one that came a day or so later, also from Verney, which said how in her opinion kissing a tool was nowhere near as bad as the kind a dentist usually put in your mouth. But what could we expect from a kid, very sick in her own way, who'd spend so much money to send us still another cable to tell us how in Holland lesbians were called Dutch dykes? All of this was news we could've lived without.

For the time being we let Joyce operate in her delusion, which gave me time to think privately, only to myself, of where were things going to end for us? You see, Larry was beginning to look worn out and sound sort of desperate because right off Fred Rory'd flown out, fit to be tied as he told Larry—in a way he wouldn't ever've dared before—how stupid he was for letting some little lump put us in this sort of rotten fix that'd got so much attention called to us. Right from the house Fred phoned Juan Basqua, who Larry'd tried to reach until he was almost climbing the walls because he couldn't get El Señor to take his call, and Fred told Juan—who wouldn't speak directly to Larry but gave orders how, until he said otherwise, Larry was to lose his number—that for the present Larry was, please for all our sakes and he meant our sakes, to stay home and just jog around the garden if he needed exercise.

After Rory—who was a very strong temptation to me to commit a big sin—left, I made calls to Leola and my partner to say they'd be hearing from me when I phoned them, which was how it had to be right now. Later I made Larry sit with me in the garden for some sun and talking.

"Larry," I began, trying to believe what I was gonna say, "it'll blow over."

No surprise to me, that only made him shake his head harder. "My temper," he said. "When in times past, without thinking, I blew up and started breaking up people and things, they'd turn out all right where I was concerned." He pulled up a sort of green and pretty little plant, which he said killed dichondra. "But Freddy Davis and this Johnny," he went on, "with them it was different. I could've let Freddy go or paid someone else to chop him, and not have something that's hung over my head for twenty years."

"My head too," I said. "But I don't remember saying no at the time."

"I wish you had," he sighed through very bitter lips. "But then I might've busted you one."

"Like you did times before," I said and rubbed my jaws through the beard to show him how well I remembered and that whatever I might've felt then, I wasn't sore now.

"When I make plans of personal satisfaction, with nothing really to do with business, to cash someone in, that's when I buy trouble in job lots," he went on. "That's when I dig a grave for myself, which sometime before I want to, I'm gonna fall in. I should've done what you would've."

I shook my head no. "Sometimes I don't."

"I shouldn't've done anything but leave those creepy Mercers. Him with his head and her with her specimen bottles," he said, furious with himself and disgusted with them. "Gone right on home when I saw who they were. Did we respect them when they were our customers in Vegas?" he asked, really getting sore with himself. "Be accepted by them?" I guess he was thinking right then of Señor Basqua and how we were supposed to be a social project. "What the hell for? So we could steal ties together?" He stopped to shake his head again, like none of what he'd thought and done was to be believed. "But Joyce wouldn't hear of it. Why"—he asked me as if I had the answer or could get it—"why should what she calls a real party've meant so much to her?"

"Because Joyce's who she is, just like you're you and I am—or became—me," was the best I could say. "Come to *shul* with me for Yom Kippur," I said. "Say you're sorry about Johnny where God can hear you. It can't hurt." I waited for him to say something, but he only shook his head, so I had to go on. "All right." I was serious. "What do you think might happen?"

"How smart is it to wait around and find out?" he asked.

Good-bye, my dear Leola Druckman, I thought to myself. "We've got real passports, I think?" was my answer. "And the other kind where you said I'd have to shave?"

Larry held up two fingers. "It took some fixing to show you in the fake one without hair all over yourself. But it'll pass. But suppose we do have to shave you?"

"It's done with some kind of face powder, a special kind

that eats away hair," I told him. "And you shave with a little stick like the kind a doctor puts down your throat when he tells you to say aah. But God forgive me," I looked up, "with us it'll be a very big hurry, yes? So you'll have to cut my beard and all with a scissors and razor. Then I won't be doing it by myself, please?" I grabbed his arm and heard him say yes, sure, of course, I shouldn't worry. "So come to *shul* with me for Yom Kippur?" I went on. "Please, Larry, please?"

"I'll see," was the best I could get out of him before he mentioned our traveler's checks and some cash hidden away at the bottom of one of the upper drawers in his highboy, and how he checked them every day. "I'll really try."

I nodded as if seeing and really trying satisfied me. Would I, somehow, be able to write to Leola? Would I want to? "So all told, Larry my banker, how much is there between us?" I asked because he was waiting.

"More than"—he looked around, but we were all alone—"a million. It's a responsibility," he agreed with my whistle. Suddenly he slapped my knee. "But maybe we won't have to pull out," he said. "Maybe the worst that'll happen after everything cools off is that we get fired by Basqua, which won't be bad at all, if they tell us to go back to Mexico? From there I could divorce Joyce." For a little bit, after he stopped talking, he looked unhappy, guilty like he was thinking the way a rat might. Then he slapped my knee again. "You'd like Mexico again?"

"I like Fairfax a lot," I leveled the truth at him. "Still, it won't be going to a strange place." Would Leola mind living in Mexico? "But if you're asking," I said after telling myself how I didn't think she would, "I'd rather go to Israel. You want the truth," I sort of snapped at him. "So you're getting it."

What I'd just said shook him, so when he went on that we were just speculating—no harm in that, was there?—I thought things over and decided to tell him something I really hadn't wanted to worry him with. Like how a couple of days before,

Mike Loesinger's wife showed up in the grocery and asked me, please, to step outside.

"She's out of her mind in her way as bad as Joyce's in hers," I said to Larry. "She wants so bad for Mike to give us up good and final that she swears to leave him and take the children if he doesn't."

It was nothing new, I'd seen it before, the way Larry's face got so red it looked black. But not for the longest while now. Still he didn't do more than walk to the pool, grab the skimmer off the rack and run it over the surface to catch a few floating things.

"So what'd you tell her?" he finally asked.

"That as far as I was concerned, Mike didn't have to handle us," I said.

"Did she tell you what Mike said?" He hit the net part of the skimmer so hard on the decking that an edge bent. "Did she?"

"Not at first," I admitted. "But I asked the same thing you did just now, right after I told her not to be scared because everything was gonna be all right." My nose was full, so I sniffed hard. This was no time to catch a summer cold. "Then she said Mike was scared too," I went on. "How he'd begun to sleep bad and didn't want her to leave him. But what could he do if we said no?"

"Which's what I'm saying," Larry said. "A big, fat no."

"No you don't," I said. "If you want out and I want out, why can't he?"

"Because I don't like the idea of rats dressed to look like people leaving us," he answered, very stubborn. "So he stays."

"It's wrong," I insisted. "If you don't let him go——"

"What?" his voice jumped me with both feet. "You'll stay behind or something like that?"

"Never," I said. "But like I said, if we go—and you say we are—why keep him and ruin his life? His family's?"

Larry looked as if he was gonna hit me with the skimmer before he slammed it down and pointed toward the guest house. "Call him," Larry said. "Go ahead and call him! Call the dirty bastard to close us out and send a full bill! A final bill! Let him steal something too!" he began to scream so hard it brought Tom to the back door and I had to motion hard to make him go back inside. "Call him before somebody gets hurt!"

He was shaking with anger but didn't want me to touch him or do anything except to get my big ass to the phone. So after he promised to sit down, not move or do anything because I actually believed he was going to get heart failure or break a blood vessel and bleed to death from the nose and mouth, I plugged my phone into one of the jacks in the garden and called Mr. Mike Loesinger's office. He was out so I called his home, spoke to his wife and told her how sorry we were to lose Mike as a lawyer, accountant and friend, but her peace of mind and his was more important to us than anything else and our giving him up should prove how much we thought of him and all the services he'd done for us. So, before she could begin crying so hard she wouldn't've been able to understand anything, I asked her to please have Mike call me on my number. He was to talk to me, no one else. Did she understand? By this time she was crying very hard, but I'm sure she said yes, yes, yes.

It took time, plenty of it, for Larry to quiet down inside, so I said nothing while we sat on a stone bench together. He was breathing very hard, I was sniffing just as hard but didn't want to leave him for aspirin. And the garden was so beautiful, so still except for birds and breeze, so peaceful that I wondered if this wasn't a dream. Maybe we were sitting in a modern Garden of Eden? You see, it all fitted. The garden was beautiful. Joyce could be some sort of Eve becoming dissatisfied with a healthy mind and peace, and the devil and hell could be trying to break in and get to us through her.

It fitted so much it scared me. Because we all know, even those who don't believe, how the devil fixed up like a snake got into the garden and how from then on everything's gone downhill. The good days in the garden here, after we got adjusted, were over. Which was why I couldn't tell Larry right now what was bound to be even worse for him than losing Mike, who Larry really liked, trusted and believed in. Couldn't for the present tell Larry how a new snake named Bobby Longacre had stopped me on Fairfax as I walked past a free clinic he was going into that's been set up there to help hippie kids with all sorts of terrible problems.

The kid, this snake, looked awful, no longer clean-cut American like he used to be when he was part of Verney's group, and his eyes told me that he'd become a head very into something bad. He was looking to talk to me, he said, was actually going to come up to see me after he got himself some treatment, because he wanted to discuss with me some of the things he'd heard about the Mercer party and how this Johnny—the word said—got worked over there in some crazy way which led up to his suicide. There was something wrong with us and our house, Bobby said, seeing as people connected with us didn't last long on earth.

"I'll lay it on you straight," this Bobby bum said. "First, maybe you got some loose change?"

I gave him everything in my pocket plus a dollar and told him to come up to the grocery, on the next block, where I'd give him a bag full of food, which he looked like he could use.

"I'll be there," he said, all the while looking at the money in his hand as if he hadn't seen so much cash in the longest while. "Where exactly was I?"

"Going from first to second," I said.

He tried to snap his fingers but couldn't. "Right," he said after giving up. "Second, I've gotta find out exactly what happened to three freaky friends of mine that just disappeared right after they were seen hassling with Verney. Acey, Decey and Voltage, if you don't know their names," he went on as I could feel my heart and stomach dropping like I was in an elevator on the hundredth floor and the cable'd just been cut. "So when's Verney coming back from Europe?"

"Soon, I guess," is what I guessed. Then we'd have to deal with another snake.

"It better be soon," he warned me. "Because otherwise the pigs might get a call. You're Establishment." He poked some dirty fingers at me, which I pushed aside. "So I don't mind calling Establishment. Not in this case."

"Don't do anything foolish," I said. "Where can I find you if I want to get in touch?"

That made him back away. "No you don't." He looked scared. "I'll find you."

People on the street were giving us the eye. Some I knew well, some not so, but all were curious. One lady, a customer going to our grocery for the couple of things she bought every day instead of all at once because it gave her, she said, a chance to get out of her four walls, even tried to stop and talk, so I moved Bobby away and she went on, looking insulted.

"Any way you want it," I told Bobby. "Come to the grocery for food."

Then I left him, thinking how this past year I hadn't been so bad at all in my heart or mind or doings. Hadn't sinned big, unless maybe you count my upsetting Leola or keeping quiet at times when I should've spoken, or spoken when I should've kept quiet and done what Leola wanted us to do. So why, I was going to ask God on Yom Kippur, why was this happening to me through us?

Right then, as I'd made up my mind to have a serious discussion with God, a messenger—Super-Yid—popped into my mind to really make me sweat as he kidded me for making a mistake about him not representing God. He certainly did and maybe he was and maybe he wasn't the messenger who put into Larry's mind what he'd made happen to Johnny Jump Upp at the party. Now that I was scared of this Bobby Longacre, I'd better listen to him without asking questions if I didn't want to get God good and sore at me again.

More scared by the second, I turned right around that morning and went back to my *shul* for super-praying. And I prayed wild, rocking and hitting my chest, believing but pleading for Super-Yid to go away, but he wouldn't. Because he liked my company, he said, and hadn't been around to see me for a very long time, for which he was very sorry as he wished me a Happy New Year.

CHAPTER FIFTEEN

VERNEY: Suddenly my feelings went way down. Why? Because we were flying west. Besides, no matter how comfortable you are, what fun you're having, anything more than five or six hours of nonstop flight is for the birds. So about an hour and a half out of Los Angeles I went to one of the johns to wash and dress for my triumphant return as a star in foreign-made films to the land of up-tight straights and hysterics by Joyce, Incorporated. It was sort of crowded and cold for stripping down to the buff, but I managed all right. Then will you believe it for happening right then, just as I was soaping my ass I heard this real hard pounding on the door, so I yelled to Beverly to give me more time. Because the pounding continued I had to stick my dress in front of me before I opened the door a little. And there's this woman looking straight at me. She was past thirty, very tony she'd tell you, the kind who has a shiny health-farm complexion, a comb-out every day and does the world a favor by living in it. And they hate us most because they've started over the hill so we're their biggest rivals.

"What's the matter?" I asked her, getting sort of scared because, man, we were way off the ground. "There's trouble?"

"You've been in there an awfully long time," she snarled every word. "That's the trouble, miss."

"Oh," I got the score. "And that's troubling you, missus? Just why, may this poor little peasant ask?"

"Because you're giving my kidneys trouble," she said to put me down.

"So go to another can," I came right back.

"They're all full. And like I've said, miss," she gave me—common clay—the benefit of a lecture by Mrs. Supershit, former crap artist supreme for the Junior League of Azusa, "you've been in there an awfully long time. Just exactly what are you doing?" she asked very suspicious because of me holding instead of wearing my dress.

"Getting ready to tell you what nobody's ever had the sense to." I set her up for a real fatal slash. "So here goes—fuck off!"

With that I slammed the door. When she kept on pounding I rang the bell for service, which brought one of the hostesses. In no uncertain terms I told her to take the dumb but dangerous creep away. To which reasonable request the hostess whispered that the woman'd told her of the dirty insult I'd said.

"Dirty insult!" I put on the look I used in my second Western, when I told the cowpoke what he could do with his idea to explore the barn and learn what a hayloft's for. "When I told her I'd be through in a couple of minutes, no more than five," I started in, "she told me to get the fuck out of here before she came in and stuffed me down the toilet! And flushed it! That's what you said, you evil witch!" I yelled over the hostess's shoulder at this dopey snatch who was having trouble keeping her eyes open, seeing how weary it was for her to look at the lower class. "Now you've upset my stomach and made me sick!" I wailed as if I was doing a take. "You dirty filthy mouth, after we land I'm gonna have you arrested!"

The bummer didn't know what to say because I'd shoved her right to the wall with my sincere sounding accusations and act. The hostess, closer to me in age, looked upset because of the way I'd been insulted and abused, so I firmed up my advantage by begging her to please take the dirty-mouthed woman away and maybe have her locked up because anyone with eyes could see she was dangerous. Then to please page Mrs. Beverly Droutswood, my chaperone and traveling companion, to come and get me because I didn't dare leave the bathroom alone, seeing how afraid I was of the nut behind her, who she was keeping from hitting or scratching me to death.

Feeling beautiful, I shut the door again, sat down, really enjoyed my leak, and continued fixing myself up. Then I heard another knocking, firm but polite, which I recognized, so I opened the door and there was dear dear Mrs. Beverly Droutswood, very concerned and puzzled but holding the Pucci slack suit of the most beautiful silver-blue jersey knit which I'd chosen to wear for my press and public. After Beverly got into the can with me, I told her what that awful woman'd said, so I wanted her sincere advice. Should I have her arrested?

"It would be your word against hers. Hers against yours," Beverly said. "When we start for our seats and if we pass her, just point her out. I'll give her my toughest military look. How about that?"

"Okay," I said, looking at myself in the mirror, especially the side views. "How do I stack up?"

"Very nice," she said with no heart in it. "Because I can't help feeling you want to become more than just a little overbuilt." She sighed because my ultimate ambition was too much for her to dig. "I'll wait outside if you have to go."

"I went," I said. I stuffed my old things into the carry-all of my new matching luggage and let her carry it. "So I'm ready."

Sure enough, going to our seats and appreciating the looks

my Pucci was getting because of me in it, I saw this particular mother, really acting shocked as she told—I guess—her husband, a fucker who looked like he'd never been allowed to start up a farting acquaintance with his wife, what she swore on her Social Register soul had really happened. She noticed me, looked scared, so Beverly, my warlord, made me move along while she got ready for battle if she had to.

It was very tempting to look back but I didn't as I—an American Dream come true—went straight on forward to the little lounge where I'd been making time with some smooth guys, international types who looked as if they'd had successful plastic surgery to make them all cock. That sort of operation made them especially able to appreciate me as a 30 so firm I hardly needed a bra, formerly a little more than 26, and still growing because I wanted them to be so gorgeous that *Playboy,* who'd beg me to be a playmate, would have to use two issues to show all of me. Guillermo, the one I dug most, said I had to visit his beautiful house in PV, even higher up Gringo Gulch than the Burton place. He also owned, he swore, a private beach in a little cove a couple of kilometers past Misma-something where they'd shot that *Night of the Wigwama* picture, in which, without trying, I could've played Sue Lyons's part a lot better. With Guillermo's speedboat to take us there and musicians to play while his houseboys prepared drinks and stuff, we could swim in the moonlight. No suits of course. It sounded very *me gusta* but impossible to make, I said to myself privately while I blew kisses at him and the other studs before I moved along the aisle without twitching my *tush,* since that would've made them whistle or howl. Getting into my window seat I thanked Beverly after she told me how the woman and her husband wanted to forget the whole thing.

Why not, seeing as I could afford to, because in the entire history of the world, maybe no more than a couple of kids at most ever had such a good time as me, which began from the moment more than a couple of months ago when the wheels slammed into the belly of the plane, so I was sure we were up, up and away, really flying one-stop to London. That's where Quincy had his most important European office. Naturally, like I'd told Joyce and Larry, at the Dorchester I'd be sharing a suite with Beverly. Quincy had his own suite on a lower floor, but both of us knew that all he had to do was phone me for room service and it'd be delivered shazam.

Beverly'd done a tour of duty in England and knew all about London. So to start our trip on notes of keep-the-peace—which Quincy insisted on—even though it drizzled off and on, I let her take me to the Tower, interesting all right, but not so much as it was when you could see heads lopped off. Still it was fun being photographed with one of those guards dressed up so neat and getting to see the crown jewels which really knocked me over, Downing Street—a real dump where the prime minister lives, and the changing of the guards, a very impressive ceremony. Then Beverly wanted to take me to the British Museum or to see the American Embassy, plus a couple of art galleries, all of which was vetoed by me in a polite way because I voted for Soho and Piccadilly Circus—really a circle—where right off I connected with hippies from all over the world who make the center of the circle their American Express. Some of them recognized my name and said they were glad I'd given up my straight group and rejoined their generation. First they filled me in on what the local scene and other places was like, and said I just hadda get to Amsterdam where the city'd set up two clubs in old mansions where kids could smoke really good hash under controlled conditions, whatever that means. Then they touched me for a couple of pounds. We had lunch at the Caprice, very many swanee types, before we —because I made Beverly do it or I was going alone—headed for Kings Road, then on to Carnaby Street for some outasight rags and a maxi psychedelic-designed raincoat at Apple before we got one of those old-fashioned cabs to take us to Chelsea where I went wild on every floor of the Drugstore, had the greatest sundae and wished I could've worked there for a little bit because the waitresses looked so great and with it. Then I remembered how they were waitresses and I was on my way to Spain to make my film debut.

That night, after we—get it—dined at the hotel, which Beverly loved and I hated because it was a stiff, we went with Quincy in the limousine he'd hired, complete with chauffeur and guide both dressed to match the big old Rolls, as it took us all around London. Seeing the city at night was somehow supposed to improve my outlook. Next morning I was pretty rested, even after Quincy told Beverly he wanted to see me for a little while. That meant we had a session, during which he told me again how much it pleasured him to've found someone who really liked being tied up as much as he did the tying, but I had to stop sucking my thumbs. Also, he wished I'd give up on the injections. That I wouldn't do, so we made a bargain. He could tell Mrs. D. to stop my thumb-sucking, I'd try on my own not to do it, and he wouldn't say anything anymore about the injections, for which he was paying. Also, he'd let his sideburns grow longer and start wearing fatter ties with bright colors in them. It was really nice to lay there all in plush, yet talking friendly and concerned for each other, so nice that he fell asleep in a deep chair and I slept on the carpet, a little pillow under my head, very comfortable inside my ropes that made me feel so good.

The sun coming through woke him about five and he let me sleep a little longer because I looked so young and at peace. We had a good laugh and made up to meet at the hotel about four because he faced another long day with his business affairs. I went back to our suite, opened the door very quiet and sacked out on the sofa facing the TV, so when Beverly shook me about eight, I said how I'd come in around eleven and wanted to see what English TV was like but fell asleep before I could turn on the set. The nine-hour time difference sure had screwed me up.

"I read until midnight," Beverly said in her stop-the-bullshit voice. "I heard clocks chime."

"Quincy told me to tell you that anytime you see me sucking my thumbs you're to make me stop," I said.

That made her sigh. "There's some other things I'd like to stop," she said, looking at the floor as if she wished she could see through it. "Mr. Smith does seem like such a nice man."

"Which is your way of saying I'm not?" I asked.

"You're nice, Verney," she said. "If only—"

"Only what?" Believe me, I was polite.

"Only"—every feature of her face looked confused—"only —"

"Quincy thinks you're very poised and well informed," I said, like a diplomat would. "And he's leaving it up to you what we're to do today. Which goes for me too. Only he thinks we oughta lunch at the Empress. He says it's the tops."

That made her smile because she enjoyed a good meal. "I'll make a reservation," she said.

"Then he wants us to go someplace called Burley-something," I said, then surrendered because I couldn't remember the name.

"Burlington Arcade?" she said and looked pleased when I told her how right she was. "To do exactly what?"

"He gave me a list of stores and what you're to get for who if you don't mind. And to what account to charge it," I went on after she said how delighted she'd be. "Christ"—I began to dig through my purse—"I hope I haven't lost the fucken lists. Lists," I repeated, "because he made one for me."

Beverly looked at me again, the look she gave me whenever I threw her with something I said or did, the look which said that in her whole life she'd never met anyone like me. "I'd like to fill your mouth so full of soap you couldn't speak or get your thumbs in it," she said after she put away that look. "Thank you," she said as I found the lists and gave her one. "Then what?"

I looked at my list and told her how Quincy'd written down that she might take me to a place called Fortnum and Mason for tea, because it was a grocery where everyone dressed like a butler. Then we were to get back to the hotel about four or so for rest before we dressed for dinner at a very expensive restaurant, the Café Royal, where we'd eat and go on to see something called *Canterbury Tales,* which Quincy said was very good, then back to the Royal for dessert. Looking up from my reading, of which I was proud, there was Beverly frowning, so I had to ask what the f———— hell was the matter now? And I swear she said it, how some of those stories weren't for girls in their teens. Now I was interested.

"You don't say?" I said. "If I don't understand something you'll explain it in simple language, please?" I tried kidding her because the thing or person I needed least on this trip was a drag. But Beverly didn't react except to tell me to go on with whatever else was on my list. "Then we're going to a gambling club where it's fixed for me to get in, no questions asked. That's as long as I don't stand at the tables too long or try to play. Still, Quincy says you should help me look older."

"I can accept, even like most of the evening except going to the club. Is that all?" Beverly asked as she looked at her list and nodded over things on it.

"Not quite," I teased her. "After we get back here, Quincy and me are gonna have a private talk about my movie work. And"—where did the urge come from to really stick it to her?—"if you don't like any of these, wait until you hear what's on for tomorrow."

She didn't look sore, angry or scared, just cool, which revolted me. "Namely?" she asked.

"Taking me to the doctor," I said. "Where I'm supposed to rest for at least an hour after the injections."

That scored because she thought for some long ponderosa seconds, until she said she wasn't my parents and we had a couple of full days ahead of us, so for today, could I be ready, dressed for breakfast by nine-thirty? And not in my most spectacular clothes?

"Sure," I said. "For you—anything."

And right then, suddenly switched off mean and on to good, I meant it, the anything. And I think Beverly got the vibes changing in me, which could be why she grabbed and hugged me, and I thought she was going to wet down a little because, you see, I don't think she's any older than Joyce, at least not by much if she is, and I got the feeling that salary had nothing to do with it, she was concerned for me and got frustrated how all of us, especially me, were locked into each other in sad, not satisfying and dangerous relationships. But the old military stanced her up in time, so all she did was sort of hug me again, give me a shake like I was someone who had to be protected against everyone, even herself, before she snapped off a command for me to get dressed and wear comfortable shoes for walking. She also reminded me that I would be flying back to London once a week for attention, that's how she put it, so on the same day we'd go to the American dentist recommended by mine at home. Not for work, she hurried to say, because even thinking about dentists and my teeth was making me wilder by the minute, but just to check how my braces fit. That I didn't have to wear them so much was something, but really not enough.

"I'm going along with you on things I'd rather not," she said as I began to complain how this was a vacation, yes or no? "Now you go along with me," she went on. "Besides, I'm supposed to deliver your charts and medical history."

I was anxious to get out of London where most everything's too old and what's so great anyway about a wax museum? But no, we weren't going right to Spain, the picture I was in wouldn't be started at least for two more weeks, which Quincy'd known all along, but I hadn't. To me this was sort of sneaky. Anyway, he wanted to see a film festival in Brussels, then take care of business in Amsterdam and Paris, places from which, he kidded me, he got some of the bread to keep us happy. Because he knew I wouldn't like Switzerland he was going there alone after the picture started, when he'd leave me in Beverly's charge, who I wasn't to push around, he told me.

The idea of a film festival was plenty all right because from what I'd heard, festivals are where lots of actors and actresses can't be told apart from other crazies, with all sorts of great parties and way-out things happening. Like, for instance, in San Francisco, where people having their own festival were raided by underground movie types who started to throw pies and tomato paste and other goopy stuff so that it looked like old-time comedy and was lots of fun even after the pigs came with wagons, because they also skidded around all over the street when they tried to arrest people and didn't know who was who, seeing as both sides decided to give it to our common enemy.

So how was I to know that straight types had film festivals too, and the one Quincy wanted to see in Brussels was all about industrial films? Imagine, the movies showed different new ways of doing things in factories, even with machines you punched in to do jobs that got rid of assembly-line, blue-collar types who're becoming our country's straightest joes. But if that was the attraction of this festival, what was I supposed to do for fun? Nothing except be dragged here, there and everywhere by Beverly, including the Battle of Waterloo where it was fought on some big old fields that you just looked at if you didn't want the trip out there to be a total waste. Then I was dragged to see other sights and sights and sights, which in the end got me in a kind of trouble after I let that fink photographer who was free-lancing around Europe talk me into posing for a shot he said would get me lots of publicity and help my career with kids, who were now the new movie audience. Imagine it. There was Beverly up in that museum looking at costumes sent from all over the world for the little statue to wear on special days. And here was I letting this free-lancer—who I should've known was evil once I found out he was from Canada someplace—promote me on doing what he suggested. But to tell the truth he didn't have to sell awfully hard because his idea struck me as a real original and kinky wild.

All set, we moved off that big square which is all surrounded for the most part by buildings hundreds of years old and just like the kind they have standing on some of the backlots of big studios who haven't got around to selling off their real estate, except that these buildings are for real because those smells can't be faked. And here's this statue, the cutest naked kid with curly hair, the right hand on his hip while his left hand holds his little prick, so cute, which he's using to pee. Honest, don't people kiss the bare asses of their little babies? Did Joyce—or my father—ever kiss mine? Don't all those books on how to do it tell you to kiss and eat each other for what they call firing up for mutual stimulation and exquisite sensations that skin you alive? So why all the noise because after I looked at the statue of that little boy supposed to be a prince, liked the stream of water coming through his weenie, I climbed up to give it a kiss? People all around who were watching—most of them laughed or applauded, honest they did. And a couple of other kids did the same thing but their pictures weren't taken by an evil. Lucky I had sense enough not to tell this free-lancer who I was traveling with or anything else except my name and how I was an actress on my way to make another movie, which in publicity is standard, because you always say more than the facts. Also, if I would've known how much he sold the picture for I could've got Quincy to buy it.

Anyway, a couple of days later, right after we checked in the best hotel in Amsterdam, which isn't the one I wanted because it's too far out from the action streets right behind the American, an older hotel that would've suited me fine, Beverly comes snorting into our suite. Man, I never saw her so angry ever before. For a couple of seconds, while she stood there with this newspaper, I thought she was gonna try knocking me around. So I got ready for her with a lamp I pulled out of a socket. Because she was still trying to control herself and not do anything physical, I had time to take off the shade and make it a handier weapon. At last, I guess, able to control herself, Beverly tossed the paper at me, told me to turn to page three and sat down as far across the room as she could.

The rag was English and the picture wasn't a good reproduction, so that if my name hadn't been spelled very correctly, you couldn't've told who it was who was kissing the little dingus of the statue they call the Mannekin Pis, which proves how if you can call a statue something-pis, it doesn't make what he's doing bad at all. And bad or not, pity the poor bastards who can't. That's trouble.

By the next day lots of other papers, including American, had the picture, still not very good, which proves what a lousy fotog that Canadian was. Because Quincy only shook his head and said how important it was for me to learn who to trust, and since one picture never made enough words for a book, we were to forget about it, so I didn't really feel bad or care too much until that cable came from Larry and Joyce in reply to my cable in which I tried to laugh off the picture. Their first cable asked why about the picture, their second was full of opinions I won't bother repeating, which made me send them other cables to show that if they took the incident seriously, I didn't. You'd think that after a couple of days Beverly would get over her mad, but forget it, she wouldn't talk to me at all, even when she was alone with me, when she said only what was necessary. It was uncomfortable. Worse, it kept me from asking her if we could go to those hash mansions the kids in London told me about. Also, I couldn't get rid of her the one night I had to walk behind the American Hotel where the narrow streets were full of discos and scads of kids from every country you can ever name are having themselves an international ball to which every other right kid's invited.

But the one night Quincy was free and not too tired because everything'd broken his way, he said, he took me out by himself, which gave Beverly the chance to go to a concert she had the sense not to try selling to me, so just with Quincy we went to this old restaurant in this older old building that's not able to stand up anymore if it wasn't held together by giant clamps going every which way, side to side, top to bottom. Inside it was wild with things from hundreds of years and outside, well, if it'd been in Venice—I mean our Venice in California—it would've been bought up for an awful lot of money by some biggy who wanted the kinkiest pad. Anyway, the meal was great, beefsteak all covered with cherries floating in wine sauce, great rolls and butter, ice cream that was the most, and what made it all especially good was Quincy not making me wear my braces, so I didn't have to worry about carrying them or putting them in my mouth after eating, a living pain which always involved first brushing my teeth.

About ten, I'd say, we left the restaurant and had to walk a couple of blocks to a main street because this restaurant isn't very far from the American, just at the edge of a canal, but on an old street without traffic. Believe it, I wished Quincy would become generous and say how he was going back to the hotel and as long as I came back before daylight, to have fun. But he didn't. Instead the old fox gets us a cab and tells the driver to take us to some damned square and drop us in front of this hotel with a sort of Polish name.

Once we got there in no more than a couple of minutes the cabby gave Quincy a sort of funny look and asked in pretty good English if he didn't want to be driven? But Quincy said no, in pretty good Dutch, I think, and waved for the driver to take off.

Still trying, I asked Quincy maybe there was a movie he wanted to see, but he just took my hand and walked me into this narrow street past the hotel with the funny name, a street which looked very old, was very narrow and looked sort of tough, although other people who were walking along, some toward us and some away, didn't. There were lots of cheap bars with signs that made me feel they were for sailors and people like that, but there were little nightclubs too, and finally, I swear, we got to another old canal where I just blew my mind because even if I'd been a head on the very hard, absolutely uncut, I couldn't've imagined what was all around me.

Along this canal, even the little narrow narrow streets just off, are lots of houses with small rooms right at the street level. All the rooms have big windows. Right next to the windows were doors with dull red lights over them. But get the windows, filled with girls sitting in them, most dressed in mod-mini and boots, while others wore leather, animal trainer and harem costumes. One girl even wore a mermaid costume with just gauze over her boobs, a very nice pair to me, who looked them over with the eyes of an expert. And the girls, through the windows, are kidding around with people, men and women, young and old, who are looking in on them. Some of the girls are eating, drinking coffee or pop or beer. Some are playing cards, even writing letters. But if they spot what they think's a live one looking in the window then they become all smiles and movements and signs as they invite the johns in pants or skirts to come inside and enjoy the flesh. And the impression I got was of being in a sort of amusement park where everyone is having the best time, since the place isn't cluttered up with little kids yelling for no reason at all or pushing to go everywhere at the same time, meanwhile getting themselves and you all dirty and sticky.

I couldn't say anything but wow as I ran from window to window to look at the girls, lots of them no more than fifteen just like me, and when I finally caught my breath and looked up at Quincy, he was standing with hands behind his back, smiling at my excitement.

"No wonder you didn't make Beverly come along," I said after he got my biggest hug. "She'd've run for the cops."

"There's a police station around here somewhere," Quincy told me as he moved us aside to let by a bunch of people he said were Germans. "Want to see it and make a complaint?"

"Why?" I asked. "What for?" I made him get close to the building while a taxi filled with tourists made it slow alongside the canal, with everyone moving aside very good-natured. Behind us was this window and I looked in at the two girls, waved to them and made the signs of peace and right on, which they understood was me rooting for them. They smiled back. Then noticing Quincy with me, they looked at each other, said something in a hurry, then signaled for us to come in. "Can we?" I begged him. "Please say yes."

So he laughed okay and went to the front door which was open and before we could get accustomed to the dark in the hall, or have to take too much of the old smell, the door to the front room opened and in we went. You know, the ceilings of old rooms are low because when these houses were built, maybe more than a hundred years ago, people were lots smaller, which was why the top of Quincy's head almost touched the ceiling and he had to duck to get by this old-fashioned lamp all beaded with some of the bead strings hanging loose in just about the middle of the room. The curtain across the front window was already drawn, so people couldn't look in, and the front room was furnished in poor so-so furniture and a very bad tapestry of Jack Kennedy hanging on the wall under which was a table with a Holy Family group on it. I thought this was a very nice touch of respect for a man who I've been told had a heart and swung and wasn't a tight-ass like Nixon who once actually tried to make a thing of Kennedy saying damn in an interview or something. Mike Loesinger, who's a liberal, told me this. And I'd have to remember to tell Mike how in Amsterdam there's an actual square named damn.

The girls were around my age, blondish, pretty and cute. Maybe the one who spoke pretty good English was a little older. The other just spoke English words, mostly dirty, and I had no trouble making myself understood when they suggested how maybe me and Quincy were looking for a couple of girls to ball with. If we got together on price they'd close up shop for the night, like other places had where they'd put out all the lights, and they'd guarantee us a better time than in any book we'd ever read or maybe any stag movie Quincy'd ever seen. Don't think I wasn't tempted to do something that would make me a woman of the world, but I had sense enough to keep my yap shut while Quincy, in that polite way of his which proves he's real class, told the girls we'd come in to get acquainted and they weren't to look disappointed because he was going to give them enough to shut down for the night after we'd leave, which was in about half an hour, maybe more, depending on how long I wanted to stick around and talk. And to prove he was more than bullshit, he gave each of the girls fifty guilder, which is more than double what they get for an in-and-out trick. For a night they try to get a hundred guilder or a hundred and fifty if they're one of the special dress-ups who're selling something they say can't be got anyplace this side of Tibet. Believe me too about the next—I was tempted to tell them about Joyce, but Quincy wouldn't've liked that either.

Cash relaxed the girls, so they showed us their permits and health certificates, then told us how they were doing this to get dowries for when they got married. Next the younger chick, who said her name was Betje and only spoke, like I said, mostly dirty-word English, got a great idea in Dutch which her friend Marlene passed on to us. How would I like to sit in the window with them to see how I'd do? That presented a problem because what would happen if I sold enough for a guy to come in?

"I'll say they are sad mistaken if they come inside," Marlene told us. "That it is month time for you."

I liked it enough to look at Quincy.

"Why not?" he said. "Meanwhile, I'll stand outside, right near the window, and listen to what's said."

"And you'll tell me every word?" I wanted his promise.

"Every word if I understand it," he said.

It was an absolute gas. Quincy went outside while me and the girls sat at the table in the window. Betje dealt hands of cards to make like we were playing, but it was very difficult to make believe I was interested in my hand, my heart was pounding so hard. Soon we heard this little rap on the window and there were these guys, nothing special-looking which was a disappointment, looking in on us and making zigzig signals. I smiled along with the girls, winking and making signals like them, until one of the guys, not the best or the worst of the four, sort of decided to speak to me, which got me itchy excited you know where. I think they would've come in but they were four guys and we were only three girls.

Other people looked in. Two guys who looked drunk and sort of stupid—Marlene just drew the curtain on them. Others talked at us through the window until finally one guy came by who knew Marlene and wanted to come in, so I was introduced as an English friend not doing it, just traveling, and when he started toward a back room with Marlene, I felt it was time to go, even though Marlene and this friendly Hans asked if I wanted to watch, but I said no. I signaled Quincy, who came in and gave another hundred guilders to Betje, who promised to give half to Marlene. Then we left. Now I wanted to see the police station, so we got a cab some other tourists—stupid-looking Americans with dumb wives who giggled how they just couldn't believe it—were getting out of. When we drove past the station, with little VW police cars parked outside, I got a kick out of being in such a civilized city.

And how did still sore-at-me Beverly spend her time for fun and profit after she got through with her longhair concert, during which time—we said—we drove around the city to see how government buildings were lit up? Why, she'd found a pharmacy near the concert hall and got some dragon-vomit stuff to put on my thumbs. She said it'd help my withdrawal from this juvenile habit. I think she was trying to make me upchuck for days to come.

Anyway, I felt so good that I gave Quincy's hair a good wash like he hadn't had in a long, long time, which also got rid of the stuff on my thumbs, then asked him if maybe he wouldn't like to try getting into me? Or me doing it other ways to him? But he only smiled in that wise way of his and suggested I lay down alongside of him on the bed while we talked, during which he told me that if I learned good manners, and how to control myself when crazy notions or ideas got into my head, we could have a marvelous future together, even doing some of those notions or ideas, but only after things were fixed so we couldn't get discovered—or if discovered, hurt—in any way whatsoever. Besides, I had to understand how he was so much lots older than me, and if we could work something out, with his depending on me even when I was someplace else, the rest of my life would be taken care of in a way that most people weren't even able to dream of. It all sounded like a proposal, so I asked him straight out if it was, and he said he didn't have to give a damn about public opinion, especially since a big-shot governor of one of our important states, just as old or even a year or two older than he, had just married one of his secretaries and she was already knocked up. Naturally Quincy didn't say knocked up. The word he used was French, which got me to thinking that I was so grateful to him it was exactly what I'd've liked to do to him right now, for hours. But I knew it would be bad manners to interrupt his lecture to me. He certainly knows a lot, maybe even has as much brains as money, which should make him one of the very wisest men in the world, if not the wisest, because that's how —after he gently stopped my thumb from slipping into my mouth—he scolded me, indirectly, for kissing Mannekin's cute little prick. Which got me to thinking down another dangerous road, I realized. How I'd never seen Quincy undressed naked, an idea that I made, without good manners, get right out of my head. Still, that it got in there put me in a very cold sweat.

Next day at the airport, we separated, Quincy going to Paris while me and Beverly went back to London for dates with injections and teeth. This time we had reservations at a hotel just as nice as the Dorchester, but smaller. Sure enough, the rain we had on landing in London lasted all night and into the next day, so going to the American dentist, who must've been crazy to move here, then to the injection specialist took all morning before we had lunch at the Cheshire Cheese, which did nothing for me at all, maybe because I was beginning to feel blah and to look the way I felt.

Good-bye, Paris. We never got there because I'd caught the worst cold, so bad my tits ached. The hotel doctor said for me to stay in bed for as close to a week as I could stand, which is what I did, watching black and white, and color TV when it was on. With BBC so bloody determined to stuff brains into people through their eyes and ears, the best things were old American reruns on the commercial channels.

Yet it was sort of nice to stay in the sack, listen to the radio, try to read scandal newspapers and watch TV, have meals sent in and maybe just as I was falling asleep, try to listen to the rain, a very restful sound, especially when you're not in it. Sometimes when Beverly wasn't in the room and the rain made that nice sound, I played with myself, thinking all the while of Betje and Marlene, two of the nicest kids I'd ever met. Also, Quincy called from Paris at least twice a day and told me among other things how the weather there wasn't good either, and like me he was looking forward to Spain because it was warm there, the way a summer should be. For example, Quincy made me laugh when he said how a couple of years ago he'd spent a glorious summer in England one day in July. I sent that as me saying it in a cable to Larry and Joyce. I also sent them other jokes. I also made a compromise with Beverly. Once we left London I wouldn't go back for injections or to that dentist. But I'd wear the braces most of the time except naturally when I was working or at night. She agreed because I guess she was getting a little tired of fighting me.

At last we took off from London on Iberia and were in

Madrid about two hours later, almost at three, where there was Quincy, who'd flown in from Paris less than an hour before us. We had two hours until plane time, then it takes an hour to get to Almeria, so we didn't bother leaving the airport because it was sort of hot and I still felt shaky now and then. Only Beverly was sorry we couldn't spend even a day in Madrid, but when Quincy said she could stay and come up later in the week, she said no. The restaurant was cool, pretty nice, and Quincy had presents of perfume for me and Beverly, who he promised a full week in Paris if she wanted to take it at the end of our trip. Or when we went to Rome, she could go to Madrid, Paris or both before she joined us in Rome for going home. Beverly said she'd see, but she also said I'd been well behaved, not too much of a pest as an invalid, taken all my medicines and made really good progress with my thumbs, which she wanted me to show Quincy, so he could see how good they were healing. That seemed to please him as much as a great tie-up.

Even at night, Almeria is hot, but by day during the summer it can get past a hundred and fifteen. Later, when I got around the landscape outside of town, in more and more ways it reminded me of Southern California because the ocean and hills, canyons and mountains and desert are all pressed together. It even looks like parts of Africa, they told me. But there isn't smog anywhere near this place, and a couple of American cameramen, old-timers who can't work in Hollywood anymore because they won't shoot psychedelic, swore this was how all of California was maybe fifty–sixty years ago, when it first got discovered for movies. The town isn't much, actually a nothing, but there are an awful lot of Gypsies all over the place, thousands of them, and they don't bother much now with the things they used to do, like fortune-telling, because now they work in movies as Mexicans, Indians and cowboys, all kinds of ancient-history soldiers from Europe, Asia and Africa, even Mars, or even as monsters when they're needed in crowds. People who aren't Gypsies but live there also work for the movies, which they dig a lot because they like to dress up, and an American buck and box lunch for twelve hours of work in the sun is very good pay for them.

The Eñon is a first-class hotel which Quincy didn't like because it was built low down instead of way up on the hill, so the views we had were awful. From our suites all we could see was a lousy pier with all sorts of junky ships, cargo and lots of noise. In another suite Quincy had them show us, we faced a dried-up riverbed where some enterprising type had put in a school to teach you how to drive a truck. From other windows of other suites we could be inspired by railroad tracks and freight cars. This wasn't any sort of selection, so Quincy used the phone because he also knows Spanish, lots better than Larry or Simon, to call this place Aquadulce, which is about ten kilometers out and absolutely super, to see if they could accommodate us. No, because they were all filled up.

I motioned Quincy aside. "How long're we gonna be here?"

"Two weeks for you—no more," he said. "Meanwhile, I'll be going in and out of Madrid. And one day to Barcelona."

"The air-conditioning feels great," I said. "I like the first suite and don't care what it looks out at. Likewise the people we saw in the lobby looked okay. So let's stay, please?" I lifted my arms and waved the cool air toward my throat. "I just don't have the energy to move. At least not today or maybe even for the next couple of days."

That's how we left it. Quincy called the Aquadulce again, told them to let him know immediately if a reservation was canceled and we went back to our suite that looked down at the dock while Quincy said he'd stick with his view of the driving school which had to close down at night.

By the time Beverly'd unpacked, I'd showered and got into my tan Levi's and boating shirt, because that's how people dressed here at night, that is everyone except Beverly, who stuck to dresses because she has a big ass even though the rest of her is kept nice and tight through exercise. But even in a dress she couldn't help but look like anything less than chief hellcat for a roller-derby team always booked in as villains.

Anyway, we met in the lobby, me in my boating shirt and Levi's, Beverly in what was for her as always a sensible linen dress and Quincy in a cotton suit with white shoes, white shirt, sort of louder tie and, I'm glad to report, sideburns growing longer. We went into the bar on the second floor, not a bad room at all if you don't mind imitation red leather, and after we got seated Quincy told the waiter to get the two men he pointed out on the other side of the room.

"They're the whole ball of wax." Quincy told us more about them, because he'd already started to on the plane down here. "Producers and directors. Even actors in crowd scenes. Writers and cutters. Two of the most amusing but versatile small-time thieves I've ever met," he went on. "So Crapshoot Productions—yes"—he answered Beverly's look of don't put me on—"that's the name of the company, describes them all the way. I'll talk," he said when we heard and saw both men coming toward us like we were what they lived for. "You just listen and be entertained."

Right off I liked Lew Hooper and Q. E. Dee, who always told his new friends to call him Cyooey, which he spelled for you and said not to ask what the Q and E stood for because he was liable to tell you Quiff Everlasting. Right after they insisted on giving Quincy a big *abrazo*—because when you're in Spain, you do like—they wanted to know what he'd done businesswise in London, Paris et cetera, because that'd tell them how much of a tap to put on the profits he just made over one weekend. Two percent or three? Maybe four? Asking for so little, instead of say, ten or twenty percent, clued me in hard to some idea of the *dinero* Quincy had. Maybe carloads of it, because when someone tells you he's loaded, he usually has less than his bragging, but when other people say the man's rolling in bread, it pays to listen.

Lew and Cyooey, I'd say they were about forty, very suntanned and happy on the outside, moving like promoters going somewhere, with both of them hiding behind the sort of beards and sideburns that tie in moustaches, just like—Quincy said—some people named Hapsburg wore when they were important grand dukes and kings, which made Cyooey ask fast if there was anything in those Hapsburgs they could make, while they were here and shooting, for a worldwide market of popcorn chompers? Both these characters had round faces, round mouths and round eyes they kept wide open. This gave them honest looks, which was just about all the honesty they needed or wanted because their *shtik* was to yak a lot, start right off with lots of facts and figures on long sheets of paper or writing them on napkins and tablecloths, while they'd say over and over how figures couldn't lie, as if that proved how people didn't. They were so good at this routine that if someone wasn't careful they got things their way, which always meant cash out of your pockets and the doorknob of their hotel suite—you'd get stuck for this too—right up your ass. Facts, figures, lots of friendliness, kissing your you-name-it and promises—just what're they worth when you're dealing with any sort of sharpies?

But Quincy knew all about them. Besides, he'd told us on the flight down from Madrid, they amused him. So a tight-pockets could make money worth the time and effort through them, but only if they weren't allowed to get within touching distance of the green stuff, not until they'd delivered at the price first promised by them. If not, they had to be crippled by penalties so that Mr. Tight-Pockets walked away with what the contract said he'd get. In their operations, which Quincy let us know he bankrolled now and then for profits and laughs, he'd always supplied the comptroller. Now from reports he'd got in Paris, the one picture Crapshoot'd been set up to make was turning into seven. And for not much more than forty or fifty percent more in salaries, film stock, processing and editing, which, if true, meant they couldn't help but come out very good and this would also show them how to do this again and again so it would pay to set up their own distributing organization.

Naturally because Quincy said this tab was on him, they ordered champagne, and between toasts used the tablecloth to show how they were going to make the same picture, with just about the same cast of principals, seven different ways. Four of the ways were as Westerns set in North, Central and South America. In the first one, to be released mostly in states where they don't give a damn about *la raza* or live Indians, the Americans knock the shit out of the Mexicans and their savage Indian allies. In the second, to be sold mostly in Mexico and Central America, plus certain theaters that Mexicans go to in the U.S., the Mexicans knock it out of the Americans and their redskins. In the third way it's Mexican rancheros working over their colonial oppressors and their Indians. In the fourth picture they'd have gauchos bolaing it to American bushwackers who've lost the Civil War and want to set up a new Confederate States, complete with slaves, in Argentina. Naturally these dirty bastards would be using bad Indians. The fifth picture proved out as my favorite because those costumes were the best. In it Spaniards from the time of El Cid, and riding dressed-up horses, kick the *cagajon* out of what'll look like thousands and thousands of lousy Moors on their horses. In the sixth make these same Moors become the heroes, so they kick the *canina* out of the dirty Arab slave-trading dogs. In the seventh, which I wouldn't work in because of Simon and Larry too, I guess, it was modern Arabs living in a little village someplace who're being persecuted by Israelis until a young Arab teaches them how to be guerrillas. Then they'd win the big battle with horses against tanks. It was the seventh which was going to make them the biggest bundle, Lew said and Cyooey agreed. But they understood why I couldn't be in that picture. Lots of regrets but no sweat, they'd slot in some other kid.

"Besides," I said, "I was only gonna be in one picture, I thought. So now I'm in six. And we're staying here two weeks?" Six pictures in two weeks. How could I believe it wasn't a put-on?

Cyooey looked at Lew, then gave me his confidence. "I'd say three. No more than four. But what do you care, sweetheart?" he said when I began to hit myself in the head. "Look at all the extra loot you'll be picking up. All the extra publicity. Think of it, you lucky, lucky kid. You'll make six pictures in no more than four weeks because we can't afford more than four. And six pictures add up to an awful lot of active credits. An awful lot of footage your agent can show around. Color stock. By the way," he paused, "who's your agent?"

"Quincy Smith," Quincy said.

"That was a question, not an argument," Cyooey said. "Of course she gets more money."

Why should there be a beef when about every *peseta* in their company came from Quincy? But the problem was two weeks becoming three, maybe even four, because in art, you know, unplanned things can happen. What Quincy had to consider was how a man in his position, who planned his business moves months in advance, could spend two more weeks down here? He hadn't figured on being in Europe to the end of October or maybe even November, if we still went to Rome like first planned. And by then the film festival he wanted to attend would be over. But there's the difference between parents and people. Larry and Joyce wouldn't give me their fifty percent of my company, when it wouldn't've made them lose a cent— not when I got around to asking for it. But Quincy, who made money in fistfuls, was actually thinking of letting an awful lot of it slip through his fingers just to get me a list of credits. Larry and Joyce—I bet they were sorry now, but not as much as me, seeing as how their turndown got me involved with three electric-named heads, who, I had the feeling, if they were ever found, would be in a sad condition that called for an investigation with only one possible ending—unhappy. Thinking this, while Lew and Cyooey were doing their best to make Quincy see things their way—how seven pictures instead of one, for no more than fifty percent more than he'd invested, ought to do all of them a lot of good—made me remember one particular day of the week before, while I was sick in London. Quincy'd called, he said, to tell me first, before I got it from an unfriendly or exaggerating source, how Larry and Joyce'd gone to a party at some neighbors where a fairy writer, very mean and poisonous, who, when he was born should've had his head squashed instead of his ass slapped, had insulted Joyce in the worst ways possible, for which Larry'd worked him over good. Then certain things had happened at the party which might've made this writer commit suicide.

Even though I don't like Joyce, really hate her more now, I tell myself, and I'm not exactly sold on Larry because I can still remember and feel how he beat me up, I was relieved for them because a suicide only involves the person who does it and nobody else. That's what Quincy told me and he should know.

"Verney's dreaming," I heard Quincy say, smiling just as big as the owners of Crapshoot, once he got my attention. "On a separate frame to run at least ten seconds, you're getting 'and-introducing' billing on all six pictures," he said. "And your part is going to be built up. So you'll stay the three–four weeks and get paid for four weeks even if you work less."

"And you?" I asked him.

"I'll have to do some reshuffling," he said. "Don't worry, please. But we haven't asked Mrs. Droutswood if she'll stay on. Will you?"

"Sure she will." Lew was about to put an arm around her, then saw how it would be the wrong thing to do. "And have I got an idea! How would you like to be in the pictures? Why not?" he went on because she was so surprised. "Without lines if you don't want any. But we'll guarantee you shots that won't be dropped in cutting. Come on," he sold by looking at us for help, "let's all of us make movie history." Before Beverly could say yes or no, though I could see she was tempted, Lew turned to Cyooey. "She goes on the payroll as of tomorrow. Right?"

"As of right now," Cyooey said like he sometimes had to wonder about Lew's judgment in not signing up talent as soon as they found it. "And I know just the part for her! The woman with the gun who tries to run off the raiders and gets killed!"

Grateful as anything, Lew shook hands with Cyooey. "We needed someone who looked rugged. A woman to sort of match the mountains around here. Mrs. Droutswood"—he got hold of her hand—"you're perfect!"

Later I found out there never was such a part. But when they wanted something they didn't mind manufacturing as they went along, like big Swedish and Italian directors, who Americans are imitating all the time, do. Suddenly we're both in show-biz and Quincy's laughing because both guys've proved how they're everything he's said about them. Who— even God for instance—doesn't like to be shown even more right than he says he is?

It was all settled for us to stay three weeks, absolutely no more than four. Meanwhile, between scenes she worked in, Beverly would help me learn lines in Spanish as well as English or at least to read them pretty good off the idiot board. With my bigger salary Quincy also got me pieces of these seven pictures, even in the last one which I wouldn't do. Believe it, Lew and Cyooey battled this right down to the signing, but Quincy let them squeal, which he said was all right, seeing as he wasn't cutting their throats so they'd never heal up.

"You made me proud handling them like a very, very rich

man Indian chief," is what I told Quincy later that night, while I stripped down in his suite. "The money's yours, right? So why shouldn't you get back as much as possible?"

"I've never argued with that point of view," Quincy said while he watched me with interest.

Undressed now, clothes folded neat like Quincy taught me, I turned slowly to show him the front of me, then blew a couple of hairs from my beaver at him, which made him do what he calls chuckling. Next I gave him a side view to show how neat they were growing, and finally turned around to show him my ass, small and lean with the cheeks drawn in tight, the way he liked to see it. That done, my eyes asked him where he wanted me to lay down, and he pointed to the exact spot before the window.

"I'm wondering," I said while kneeling to the carpet. "Wondering if Beverly's working in pictures, why shouldn't she be taken off your salary? Maybe even pay you—or me—what an agent gets? I mean, why should she be paid twice? That isn't right."

"You have to learn when it pays to be generous. Or to look generous," Quincy said while he patted my head, so I kissed his hands and licked between his fingers with my tongue doing little bird kisses. "And I'm sure you will."

"From you, the only teacher I've ever loved and will always be able to love?" I asked while I looked toward his fly. Now, like before, there was no bump or lump.

Quincy switched off the lights. Moonlight filled the window and fell all over me like it was a spot. "Yes," he was breathing very heavy for him. "Oh yes."

"I want you to start teaching me about money," I said before I stretched out on my back, spread-eagled the way he liked so he could position me in any particular way he wanted this time. "How do I look in the Spanish moonlight?"

"Beautiful," he said. He sat on the carpet near me, just looking while he touched my hair. "A beautiful Medici."

If the air-conditioning hadn't been going full blast to make me chilly I'd've asked what a Medici was, but I was also beginning to feel very raunchy and heating up fast. Raunchy because I'd missed what Quincy did to me and couldn't think of it all day up to now because a lot had happened to me that required all my attention and thinking. Six pictures. Pieces of seven. "And-introducing" billing. More salary. Three weeks, maybe four, even more, away from Beverly Hills and people there I could do without. Maybe that week in Rome after this. My inside thighs were becoming squoochy because so much good had come my way and was going to keep right on coming. And something else. Tonight, for the first time, I knew I'd come when Quincy tied the last knot, so very adult and sincere I called him Quincy darling and whispered for him to hurry, darling, to hurry because little baby couldn't hardly wait anymore.

There were up to twelve hours of daylight but hard or big action scenes had to be shot early in the morning, before heat fried the desert so you could hardly stand or breathe. Right off I met the people we'd be working with in front of and behind the camera, and everyone, you can bet your sweet ass, treated me and Beverly de luxe for standing in so big with Crapshoot and its chief bankroller. First we got taken around to Costume for what we'd wear, which for the first four pictures was pretty much the same, but in as bright colors as they had so it would look good in the color they were shooting. Still the fitters got instructions from me and Lew, who like Cyooey was all business once work started, that my pants were to be very tight, low hip-huggers to show my belly button and lots of skin. Since I wouldn't be working with a bra, Cyooey wanted to know if I'd mind doing some scenes, like where I'm getting raped, without my shirt on, maybe even nude but only my ass showing to the camera? These would be put into the negatives of prints that would be made up for countries where you could show such stuff. Naturally I said yes. Naturally Beverly said no. So it was left up to Quincy and he surprised me by backing Beverly. The only thing he'd go for is the raper tearing off my shirt and the camera getting a quick shot of my boobs, which I wished now were lots bigger.

That settled, we went on to my outfit for the fifth picture, where I'm an Argentina señorita, so they fixed me up with a fandango skirt, still cut very low to show the button, and one of those scoop-neck, off-the-shoulder blouses, to wear with nothing underneath. The sixth outfit, where I'm a young Moorish beauty, but still raped—which made me say to Lew and Cyooey, when Beverly wasn't around to be sore or shocked, how in real life, by the sixth time around, there'd be no snatch left—my outfit was pretty kootchy, the one I liked most. Except later the breastplates really heated up in the sun. Besides giving me a pair of roasted knockers, my nipples became so sensitive they had to be kept in lotion.

Shooting six days a week meant working Saturdays, but this had to be done if the first eight days of shooting hoped to do seven battles with hundreds and hundreds of soldiers and riders, including the one in the last picture, where the Israelis fight in tanks but lose to the fierce horsemen of the desert. Everyone around who knew the Middle East said the Arabs would go to see this picture over and over and over again.

Every day we drove out to that part of the desert assigned by the town and government to Crapshoot, where crews, extras and principals got ready for the battles in which I had a very good part. It's like this—after Beverly gets killed dead for gunning down some of the dirty bastards who want to rape me, I can't no longer resist this featured stud—a sort of Marlon Brando type people can root for even if he's a baddie —who, after he cops my cherry, turns me over to his troops for their amusement. That's supposed to break my spirit, and it looks like it does, seeing how I start throwing myself around like a weirdo. But it's only an act, seeing as even the worst bad guys think it's very rotten to *shtup* a crazy kid. So I'm left alone but not allowed to escape until finally, in the big showdown battle, when the bad side seems to be winning, I sneak away, get lots of powder, dynamite or grenades—this depending on what time it is in history—and use it on them to blow up the bad guys' ammo, guns, cannon, lots of their horses and, if I would've worked in the seventh picture, the Jewish tanks. Naturally I am mortally wounded but not in a messy way, and after the good guys win the victory and come over to pick up their dead and wounded, somebody important recognizes me, who they thought had disappeared forever.

Naturally they're glad to see me even though I'm wounded so bad I'm dying, so they look sad, which makes my big scene come naturally, because I say something like how I didn't mind dying since they'd won and freed our people forever. Also, if they would've rescued me all healthy, I would've had to live among them as someone who was horribly dishonored, so they'd always have to pity me. But this way, when my dying helped them even a little in winning, they wouldn't remember me as dishonored, someone who had to be pitied, but as a heroine who gave her life for a just cause. For the plain old shit that's such a big part of history, these were beautiful sentiments in what I considered a beautiful scene. Later on, when we were shooting it in different costumes, and getting better with each take, Beverly started out watching me with grim expressions, then she'd get wet eyes, and finally when I'm wearing my kootch outfit, she actually cried.

My action took less than two days, which didn't give me any time to learn lines, so they told me to use the boards and not worry about Spanish or Arabic but to just say the lines in English since they'd dub dialogue and loop it in when they were cutting. What Cyooey, who was directing me, wanted was sincerity all the way. Because some of what I was supposed to say and do on the battlefield seemed awfully simpleminded, my hardest job at first was not cracking up with laughter. That only happened twice. After I pulled myself together for the second time, Cyooey grabbed one of my nipples through the shirt and twisted so hard I actually wanted to faint. Beverly moved in to give him a karate chop, but before she could take us both out of the pictures, Lew blocked her off with a rifle that had a long, sharp bayonet on it.

"Laughs are for after we break for the day, Mrs. Droutswood," Lew said while I was fighting back tears and telling Beverly to lay off. "Right now we're working with Mr. Smith's money and our time. And the only way all of us come out is to use time like it's worth more than money. You"—he pointed at me with the rifle—"tears'll make you look better in the next take. That's if you're settled down and don't blow it. So what do you say?"

"I'm ready, you bastards," I let them both know. "But don't think for a second how I'm forgetting this."

From then on I worked harder than ever before in my life, worked so hard there wasn't time for thumb sucking, so I began to feel older again when I was with other people. Everyone worked hard, especially the American and English actors because production was so way down back home and working hard here might get them with another company coming into Almeria who didn't want to pay for transportation or people who had to get accustomed to how things were done down here. In real life an actor without loot plays a deadbeat bum or whore, so here at least they not only cleared some cash but got some of their expenses, and most important, were making movies and keeping their images on movie screens. And who knew, what'd happened to Clint Eastwood could happen to them, which was a hope that made them work harder, I bet, than anything else.

Still, there were the wildest side effects. Like suddenly forgetting what picture you were making, whether you were now playing good guys or bad, which is the way life really is—all screwed up so nothing makes sense the very next day. For me, in the first picture, I'm a Kansas sunflower—an orphan—who's gone with her widowed aunt—that's Beverly—and other settlers to Texas. There, after we homestead our little home on the range, I'm raped by greasers and whatever dog-eating

Indians they've got with them. So I had to play how I hated Mexicans and their Indians. But in the second picture I'm Chiquita—same sort of family history—and it's a bunch of lousy blue-eyed gringos who take away my honor. Then, like my part change called for, I'm the orphan of a nice guy who left me a hacienda, and the time comes when I scream— "¡Madre! ¡Madre Dios! ¡Me están violando!"—because of what Spanish oppressors are doing to me. Now, as the orphan of a gaucho, it's done to me again by Kentucky-fried-chicken-and-yam types, and next to finally, when I'm the orphan of a royal house, it's done to me by Moors, which is another way for saying coons. Finally, I'm a coon being raped by other coons, only they're not coons you can respect because they're Arab gooks, who everybody knows would rather fuck camels than women.

So it was not only confusing to me but to all the other players, some of them with lots of experience, sometimes even to Lew and Cyooey, the cameraman and script girl, as to who we were yesterday, what we'd be today, were they good guys or bad guys, although for me and Beverly it was easier because we played the same part. Still, to be part of the American team, which was good one set of takes, then to have the Americans bad the next, made nothing seem real as we changed heads and sides, working mostly all the while under a sky that seemed to boil in the afternoons, so at any second we expected to be covered with hot blue glass melted down by the sun which seemed always to be fighting against the night, seeing as how it didn't want to set. And always there was the pressure of costume changes, doing the same set up against people whose natures became different, depending on the picture, having Lew and Cyooey always timing us with stopwatches because everything cost and the people in NATO, who'd been stealing film stock and other stuff for them, had got themselves caught and it took time to establish dependable sources you could work with in Germany and Vietnam to get us what we needed at a price the company could live with. Meantime they were paying big-studio prices, which was just killing the budget, so the only way to save the pictures was to stay with the scenes, know our lines or be able to read them like an intelligent person, and after the master shot was established, to work fast through the medium close-ups and close-ups, one head and two, shooting from over shoulders and straight on, and always always always trying to remember in what picture we were so that we played good against the same character sometimes, and bad against him after he or you'd changed into whatever costume this particular picture called for. Yet day by day I got better and better, because—as one person who was jealous of me said when she didn't realize I was around—it was obvious I had no depth, no real feelings, no ethical values, couldn't tell crap from gold, so I was able to act convincingly no matter what I was told to do. So what? Why's that bad?

By six, dead as we were, those dirty bastards usually managed to have principals around until seven. Then it'd be back to the hotel for maybe falling into the pool with our clothes on, then sitting poolside with drinks and trying to put away as many as possible before our producers showed and raised hell about what would happen to anyone hungover next morning. Most of us ate like we were, then changed for doing something to forget the day just passed and not think about the one coming up. Some of us swam at night, others talked shop about ourselves and other pictures shooting around us or coming in. Those who'd got connected for putting it all together would take off to get started, those who were breaking up looked for new connections and some of us might go down to around the docks to see how the friendly natives relaxed. Then we'd usually end up at Extraño's, the saddest place with even sadder-looking old whores in body stockings that looked like they were made from old fishnets, so you didn't know for who to feel sorrier—them or the poor guys who had to make it with such holes.

Yet we—me and Beverly—we had it better than all the other

people around us, because those who came down to work in our epics were for the most part trying to get connected with other companies, which meant an awful lot of hustling in every way you want to use that word. Sometimes I felt sorry for the girls, seeing as I was one, and to help them out if they had nice things with very good or better labels that were brand-new or not worn more than once and if they looked good on me, I'd buy, but I never paid much. If they had gold jewelry I'd buy that too but for never more than what it weighed, which I learned how to do because Quincy got me some scales and they had weights that worked in my favor. The Pucci I wore when I got off the plane cost me ten bucks and it was never worn. For the Valentino that was worn once I gave the poor broad five. But what the hell could they do? They were actresses who had to end up on garbage heaps from which they could never be recycled.

Meanwhile, Quincy flew up to Madrid. When he next showed, it was in a leased Lear jet, very rich interior. So on Sundays he'd fly me and Beverly to Madrid—once we even made it to Malaga—so that day was for us like getting out of prison. Most of the time Quincy'd leave by Tuesday for most of the week, so there were guys all around who tried to move in, not an easy thing to do because Beverly was an all-time *duenna*, so I couldn't even make it with the one guy I wanted, a hippie kid who showed up with real American peanut butter and different kinds of jelly in his knapsack, for which I was suddenly dying.

By this time I was smart enough to realize, and appreciate what I'd realized, that where a career was concerned, no one could deliver it like Quincy. Another thing which kept me pure after the peanut-butter kid left town was a feeling that if I ever had to have it the real way and told this to Quincy, he wouldn't mind at all. He'd just get me someone who'd satisfy without giving either of us any sort of trouble.

By the middle of the third week Beverly was climbing the walls, with me right behind her because both of us wanted out of there so bad, but we were trapped for a full fourth week. Then business made Quincy go back to the States before us, but like always, nobody was more generous and he insisted that I be nice to Beverly who he said he'd had some nice talks with while I lazied around in the pool at night, so we were to go to Rome for a week because there were reservations for us at the Excelsior, which movie stars liked best. Also it was close to the Via Veneto, and all Beverly had to do was call the hotel and give them twenty-four hours' notice. Then we'd have a good suite, limousine and chauffeur, the works.

We refused to consider staying for the seventh picture, even after Lew swore how they'd enlarge both our parts, so we spent the fourth week doing retakes and going to sleep early, Beverly with a snore ball tied round her neck and me with my plush belt under the pillow.

Rome was okay and I liked best seeing all the whores, from cheap to big-time, working everything and every place from the Borghese Gardens to the Via Veneto, along which the cops would make sweeps at least once a night. But in the end it was good to reconfirm our flight reservations, do some last-minute shopping because Quincy on his call to us from Chicago said we could and should. And we weren't to try smuggling anything. Just pay the duties, he said. So without caring about it, I bought presents for Joyce, Larry, Simon, even Milly and Tom. And I bought something expensive, a beautiful velvet smoking jacket almost the same color as my favorite rope, for Quincy.

In our first-class seats in a first-class plane where I connected right off with some first-class guys, I realized how I'd been gone for most of the summer, part of the fall and had, among lots of other goodies, which included a bundle in unused traveler's checks, the swellest suntan.

So all in all everything'd been just about perfect except for one thing for which Joyce's to blame. That was my finding out how when they saw the rushes how Lew Hooper and Cyooey didn't think my tits were big enough in that bare close-up they took of me after my blouse got torn off before I was raped. So they used someone else's pair—I know whose, the bitch—because she's built like an abnormal cow. When I found out and began to scream Cyooey said they were doing it for the pictures and why should I care since audiences would think the big pair on the screen were mine, which couldn't hurt my career. That cooled me down some, especially when I figured that by the time all my pictures got released, I'd be lots bigger than right now. Putting it all together, I had to admit my trip'd been a groove. And that was in spite of Joyce not helping me physically through heredity.

Which should explain why I didn't look forward to going back, because in my experience that meant exchanging a groove for a rut. Which is the real reason, I guess, for my taking that woman apart on the plane when Quincy would've liked me better if I'd apologized for monopolizing one of the cans. Going back. Notice how I didn't say going home? In my mind there was a difference as big as the one between having money and shagging your ass for mighty little bread. Between having a career, which is, after all, work and having it made so you can be entertained, even lapped, by people who have careers.

The difference—Quincy recognized it in my voice when we talked across the ocean and he didn't get the right reaction after he told me that a couple of good reporters who owed him favors would be waiting for me at L.A. after I cleared customs. That's why, I know, Quincy went on to ask how I felt about things in Joyce's house? Where did I really want to unpack? Because the beach house was all set up and waiting for me, with a cook, maid and handyman-gardener from one of his other places to say hello and what's-your-pleasure until he got there.

"From the very first I've loved that house," I thanked him over the phone. "Still, don't you think I oughta make a try at, say, going home? At least, say, try sticking my head through the door?"

"You should." His pause told me he had something else to say, so I just kept quiet. "That particular party, the one your mother and stepfather——"

"Hold it right there." This time I had to interrupt. "Her husband. Let's keep him as her husband."

"As you wish, Veronica." He understood. "Well, it's all blown over. They're in the clear."

"Good," I said. "You'll tell me exactly what happened?"

"As much as I know. You've been a very good girl, Veronica," he complimented me like he was glad to be able to. "You'll send them a cable after you've confirmed your flight. And one to me so I can have the reporters there. Go home, princess," he advised me. "Try it. You'll phone me shortly thereafter?"

"Whatever you say, Quincy darling," I said.

"Suppose I said go direct to the beach house?" he asked.

"Beach house. Dog house. You name it and I'll call it home," I said. "Just as long as the refrigerator's filled up with every kind of peanut butter and all sorts of jellies."

That made him chuckle and with last-minute final instructions that our bill was all paid for at the Excelsior, not to be stingy with anyone, not to forget the concierge, not to smuggle anything and to give his best wishes to Beverly—which I did through signals because she was sitting in the living room with me—Quincy hung up. And Beverly had the good sense, I must admit, not to talk to me for a little while and never even once to mention my unpacking problem.

I promised to keep in touch with the studs, especially Guillermo, whose PV address I'd already torn up. Then, whatever bitchy mood I was in on the plane got worse in customs where this dumb Establishment bureaucrat in her lousy uniform wasn't satisfied with my declaration, which Beverly had filled out to the last pair of pantyhose I'd bought, so that we could pay the duties without arguing about a single thing. No—the bitch in uniform insisted how I—not Beverly—had to be searched right down to the skin. There was no way out of it and in a dressing room when I spread the cheeks of my ass and the woman doing the searching said she hadn't asked me to do that, I asked why not and said how I had a good mind to report her to the inspector in charge of assholes for not doing her job right. Half an hour later they admitted I was clean and let me pay the duties, which I think were awfully high, especially if they go for the salaries of people like that. We were the last people out of that lousy room.

Then, as the reporters spotted me, I saw old reliable Larry in his dark glasses and camera, sort of dangerous handsome, so it might've seemed to the reporters how he was a pretty big director come to get me, his star, and take her away before she could answer a single question. Which is exactly what he did.

All the way out, with a couple of porters following us, I kept my mouth shut to control my temper and let Beverly do our talking. At the curb Larry put her in a cab after she kissed my cheek and I sort of kissed hers. The long walk from customs seemed to have got his wind, but he got around at last to saying how I looked fine, just fine.

"Now I'll get us into a cab," he said. "Because you must be tired."

"Where's Tom?" I asked. "Why isn't he here with the car?"

"He had other things to do," Larry said.

That didn't satisfy me at all because in any family a daughter coming home from her first, very long and triumphant trip to Europe, the whole family including the chauffeur, if they had one, would've been at the airport with at least a ton of flowers. But my family wasn't *any* family, something I'd known for the longest time, which, right that minute, bothered me more than the customs examination.

Only after we got off the freeway at Sunset Boulevard, which is just a couple of miles from Joyce's, did Larry get around to asking anything about my trip, did I like working in pictures, what foreign countries and cities in Europe looked like? All of it was the simple time-passing questions people ask and get answered to keep sounds between them. He remarked again that I looked healthy and Beverly didn't look worn out, proof he was glad to have that I hadn't given her a bad time. Only when the cab got to Lexington did he ask me how Quincy was, but before I could say more than splendid, the cab started a left turn into our driveway and I knew I was home all right when Larry told the driver to park at the curb.

The cabdriver stopped right in the middle of the street. "But that means a long walk with luggage," he argued.

"Just do as you're told," Larry said, sort of tired. "You'll get a big enough tip for carrying them to the front door."

"Thanks," the driver said as he got his cab around and parked right where the sidewalk met the path. "But what's a driveway for anyway?"

From the sidewalk I looked at Joyce's house. Somehow the lawns didn't look as nice as usual, which made me wonder what'd happened to the good and careful gardening? Then, before I could think more about something I couldn't care less about, our front door was opened by Milly, who just stood as I waved hello and ran up the path alone while Larry checked to see that six pieces of luggage and my carry-all were taken out of the trunk.

"Milly! Tom!" I sort of sang their names as they stood at the door, very dressed up. "So good to see you!" I looked around for a welcome-home sign, for flowers, for Joyce or Simon. Nothing was there, but I covered fast. "Is it really months since I last saw you?"

"It's nice to see you home, Verney," Tom said. "You look very well. Very suntanned. Very elegant and grown-up."

"I had the most marvelous time," I thanked him. "And wait until you see me in the movies! But to see me in all of them you'd just about have to go halfway around the world."

"Will you be doing that?" Milly asked me. She showed the cabdriver where to put the three bags he'd brought to the door. "Your room's ready if you want to go upstairs."

"Not yet." It was late afternoon, so why weren't all the hall lights on? Was it my imagination that the house didn't smell crisp? "My legs are still rubbery from all that flying. So I'll sit down for a minute." I flopped on the oak thing at the foot of the staircase that Joyce'd always thought was so great. It was dusty. "How've the two of you been?"

"Not so well," Tom said. "I mean Milly isn't feeling like she should." He looked terribly upset, really about to break down or something just as bad, so he hurried toward Larry and the driver who'd just brought up the rest of my luggage. When the cabby smiled because of the way Larry'd taken care of him and got ready to leave, Tom told him to wait. "Have you got a fare?" he asked.

"No," the driver said. "Who wants to go somewhere?"

"We do," Tom said. "My wife and me. In just about a minute." He looked at Larry, hesitated, then decided to ask. "Could the cab go up the driveway to the garage, Mr. Tunig? There's a lot of luggage."

Larry took off his glasses. Christ, now he really looked worn out. "If I said no, Tom, would you stay?"

"I'm sorry, Mr. Tunig," Tom answered him. "We just have to go. It's best all around. We agreed so last night. This morning too."

"There's no way to change your mind?" Larry asked, now actually pleading. "There's no possible way?"

"No," Tom said. "Please, Mr. Tunig, I don't want to cry in front of you."

It looked like Larry tried to fight, at least wanted to scream or something, but he just gave up. "Go up the driveway to the garage," he said to the driver as he took money out of his wallet. "You'll carry their luggage down from the apartment over the garage. And remember, their ride and tip's been taken care of."

I really believe Milly and Tom wanted to kiss me, but they

were so unstrung they couldn't do more than shake hands with both of us before they hurried toward the back door through the kitchen.

It took me seconds, no more, to collect myself and ask Larry exactly what the hell was going on around here.

"Where's Simon?" was my next question.

"He went to work because I made him," Larry said.

"Work's more important than saying hello to me," I said. "And I suppose Joyce's also got a job?"

Larry shook his head. "She's upstairs."

"The house and grounds—they don't look or smell right," I said. "So for the second time, if you didn't hear me the first —what's going on around here?"

Larry sat on a step and gouged at his eyes with both thumbs, which he only stopped as we heard the cab going up the driveway.

"Joyce—your mother, she's become impossible," he began. "That's why Milly and Tom finally had to leave. I can't blame them."

"The lawns look neglected," I said. "The gardener quit too?"

"The gardener. The pool man. Day-help. The grocer and pharmacy. Even the laundry and dry cleaner've given us up," Larry said. "The mailman doesn't want to come to our door. He says he'd rather take his chances with a mean Doberman pinscher."

"Nuts I know she is. Half out of her gourd she's always been," I said. "So what else's the matter with her?"

"When you look in her eyes you don't see a vacancy sign," he said. "Just a wild storm that looks like it's never gonna let up."

That bothered me, but it also made me laugh, which I thought would make Larry sore, but if it did he seemed too tired, actually worn out, to care. "So she's become crazier than normal about her precious, beautiful house?" I remarked. "Is that it?"

"Those're symptoms," he nodded. "What's causing the symptoms we don't know because she won't let anyone treat her." Now he just stared off into nowhere. "Right now I'd be happy if she'd even see a fortune-teller. Yes," he said when I asked if Joyce knew I was arriving, coming home today. "But she said she wasn't up to seeing you. At least not today."

"Let her go to hell!" I yelled, crying when I didn't want to. "Who wants to see her?"

"Milly and Tom leaving—that upset her. But she made their lives miserable," he went on. "It started a couple of weeks after you left. Joyce started to go after everyone. Even them. Everyone includes Simon too," he let me know. "It's been awful."

"She started after the party?" I asked him.

"So you know about that?" he replied. "Yes, soon after."

"Then, Larry, I'd better not stay?" I asked and knew that whatever he said, there was only one thing I was going to do.

"In your place, I wouldn't," he was honest. "But keep in touch, please?"

Suddenly feeling very tired blood, and very tired brains, the best I could do was curse because the cab was backing out of the driveway. My presents for Milly and Tom were in my luggage, along with those for Joyce, Larry and Simon. All that money wasted.

"Really," I said after I dried my eyes, "they shouldn't've taken my cab. Not if they had any idea I mightn't stay."

"Shut up." Larry got off the step to go to one of the phones. "Please, if you have any pity."

CHAPTER SIXTEEN

LARRY: In desperate situations, even where everything solid is falling down on itself, it's pathetically funny what your mind thinks of. For example, how when things were pretty good between Joyce and me, so that we were beginning to feel better and better and better about each other, one nice afternoon we lunched at the Beverly Hills Hotel where one of the places you can eat is in a sort of garden patio. We especially liked that, seeing as we could walk from Lexington in just about ten minutes, which gave us a little exercise and a chance for Joyce to look at houses and grounds along the way—we always tried to walk down a different block or so—and tell me why hers was lots nicer. Or better. Anyway, that particular afternoon my mind was now thinking of, we had a nice umbrella table next to another one where six people, substantial types, in-looking, were seated sort of crowded.

Since the three couples at that table talked a lot and didn't bother to lower their voices, we got interesting earfuls about people all over and even in Europe, until we sort of figured out that two of the couples were visiting these parts for the first time in a long time, and the third was hosting them for mutual friends living in Hawaii, where these two couples had just come from. Finally one of the visiting firemen got around to saying that their mutual friends in Hawaii had said they were to be sure to ask a specific question of their host—what kind of business was he in? And this guy leaned back to grin at his wife, a really nice head. When she smiled very big and broad, which told him to go on and not mind how she'd heard his business explained before, he said very slow, but distinctly, how he was the most prominent building finisher in the United States.

"What's that?" The guy who'd first asked what he did looked puzzled. "Something to do with flagpoles or aircraft warning towers?"

"Way off," their host said. "Very cold." Really enjoying this, he pushed his chair back far enough so that everyone at his table—and I think he was aware of Joyce and me listening—could see him better. "I'll have to go into details," he began, "because building finishing is extremely technical."

Now he went on to explain how his company only contracted to finish finely detailed commercial or office buildings six stories or more, which with land cost at least ten million. And the buildings—if they weren't government—had to be in the best business or residential districts, either established or developing. Commercial buildings included hospitals and exclusive apartment houses, even hotels. His listeners got the picture. We did too.

Well, just about when the building was ready for occupancy or business, this man and his company stepped in to render their service, which was to assure the public—not the owners, he emphasized—that the building was finished. And most important, was safe in every way. So he and his architects and engineers went over the blueprints, every specification and step of construction like they were detectives and scientists in a crime lab. Using professional terms that impressed us, he explained how every window, wall, ceiling, floor, cable, line, heat and air-conditioning ducts, you-name-its big and small, were checked out. And if building inspectors had faulted something during their earlier once-overs of construction, then this man's company checked the correction doubly hard. Finally, when they'd approved the whole building, the last step was his engineers checking out the elevators, which most people usually were most nervous about. And if these reacted a hundred percent safe to their tests and instruments, then he personally went in to certify the building.

"And how do you do that?" one of the visting women asked, seeing as their host had paused as if this was the question he wanted to hear.

"By getting into each and every one of the elevators," he began. "Without a ladder or anything else, I climb right to the ceiling. How I do that is a professional business secret. And then, with a small screwdriver and making no attempt to be neat, I scratch FUCK YOU in big capital letters right across the ceiling. That's all the proof people who're going to use the building and elevators need to know that everything's A-okay. Then I have my men go through the toilets and write things in the booths like—if you want a good lay, to get blown or to try it with a dog, or to measure the size of yours against theirs—to call certain numbers."

Believe me, once they got the significance of his joke, the people all around him laughed hard, even his wife, who was enjoying herself through seeing how the other people appreciated the put-on. Even we thought it funny in a very sour way. Matter of fact I phoned Mike Loesinger and he couldn't stop laughing.

"But the numbers?" the same guy, who'd first asked what their host did, asked again. "What numbers do your people write on the walls?"

"The zoo," their host said. "John Birch headquarters. The DAR and Sons of the Golden West. Colonel Sanders. Health clubs and beauty salons. Some of my people just draw pictures of parts of people. Or of people doing it. One of my men invented the bit of drawing a television set on the booth door and lettering above it—Smile. You're on Candid Camera."

"Your business must be very successful," the woman who hadn't spoken said after she stopped laughing. "Is there an opening for a lady? I letter very well. Can even make up rather good dirty limericks."

That was it. Something good, even beautiful, gets finished and somebody comes right along and writes "Fuck you," "Kiss my ass" or maybe "Shit shit shit" right across some part everyone has to see. I guess what this joker described that sunny afternoon was the feeling of security most people have in damage, like for instance in their cars. Not being able to drive them without being nervous, without worrying, until someone puts a dent in a door or grille while they're parked in a supermarket lot. Or until some crazy's run a bunch of keys right through the paint from rear fender to front. Or your aerial or windshield wipers been busted off. Or a couple of hubcaps've been stolen. After this happens you get that what-the-hell-everybody's-a-bastard feeling. That makes you relax and stop worrying, which is all to the good.

But I didn't like the feeling with me, all the time now, that someone or something had clawed "Fuck you" across Joyce's heart and mind and still pretty face. Which is why I was able to pity her and take the kind of guff she was putting on me. Not that you could see most of the scratches or the words, but they were there, inside of her, which is worse because then the person so damaged never stops feeling them. Awake or sleeping, they're always visible. Take a dozen sleeping pills, swallow a quart of booze, shoot yourself full of dope, the gouges and words stay in your heart and brain, so even if you're out cold they show on your face and right through your eyes.

That man was joking about being a building finisher. But one way or another, everyone—living or dead—is a people finisher. Lucky Simon. Poor Joyce. Simon became sick because of what he thought he'd done to finish off people and things. Joyce was becoming sick because of what she thinks people and things are doing to finish her off. And as far as I could see, especially since she refused any treatment that could help her, except sleeping pills, which she got through her gyn. man, Joyce was through. Not a little, halfway or just about through. But through. Worse off than Simon once'd been, since at that time he finally went far enough out of his head so he could no longer fight off help. Then he was able to get it—since we had the big money that kind of help costs. Joyce was way beyond me but not far enough gone, so the only help I could give was through making her comfortable and taking her anger until the time came when she became like Simon was. Then, maybe, she too could be helped.

Meanwhile, waiting for Joyce to change from a raving witch into a helpless bundle that breathed was giving me a long run of blue fits. When I asked Simon for advice, which was the help I wanted from him, he said that once Joyce was in a sanatorium, he'd pray very hard each day and every day for her. Mrs. Droutswood phoned a couple of times to say she was available if I needed help and discretion, which was nice of her but I was too ashamed to tell her or let her see what was happening to Joyce. Mike Loesinger didn't refuse my calls, actually got back to me if he was out, but he also suggested psychiatrists and sanatoriums, but not particular ones, which gave me the feeling he wasn't ever again going to do anything specific for us. Whenever Johnny Bucconeri—because like Marty Grobbernasch, I found it harder and harder to think of that meatball as Juan Concepción Basqua—took maybe one call of mine out of ten, he'd sound very fed up with what he called my lack of judgment, which was responsible, he said, for my wife going to pieces. And Fred Rory, that son of a bitch, kept passing me back—whenever he took one of my calls, which wasn't often—to Bucconeri, until one day I screamed over the phone how if I had him here in front of me this second I'd hang a hit on him, cut his heart out and stuff it down his throat. It wasn't any real satisfaction to hang up on him before he could do it to me. And don't think I didn't think of calling Marty G. in Tucson, or going to see him, but thoughts of how he'd chew on my pride squashed that temptation. And then, I told myself what my mind not my emotions had to hear—that he was nuts too.

Which, after I discounted his hang-up and who he practiced it with, was something I couldn't say about Quincy Smith. He called the day he got home from Europe, and right after he saw Verney, to ask what was wrong with Joyce? And was there something he could do?

"Sure," I said without having to think. "You can help lots by taking the lady off my hands. How about a mother-and-daughter package?" I went on, tempted to ask if maybe the two of them laying on the floor in straitjackets wouldn't give him a high he'd never had before. "At your place or this, because I'd pay plenty for being allowed to cop out the back door. Maybe that'll end my losing streak."

Quincy came over a couple of days later. He fixed light Scotches for both of us and waited patiently, a real gentleman, until I was able to start talking about only the highlights of what was going on in this beautiful house, seeing how anyone with eyes and a nose could tell it was slipping downhill in a big hurry.

Right from the very moment I was told about it, I had reservations about that lousy party invitation. Still, although to me it seemed more silly than crazy, I thought Joyce got the disappointment out of her system by tearing up her expensive gown and making me do the same to the clothes I'd worn. After I got Joyce into a nightgown and put her to bed with some sleeping pills, Simon came in because I'd sent for him and he saw how Joyce was carrying on. Laughing, laughing and crying, laughing and crying and cursing, until suddenly Joyce sat up and in a groggy voice started to tell Simon how awful, what hypocrites everyone at the Mercer party was. Then while she was trying to prove their miserableness by comparing them with the hoods, slobs and muscleheads we'd known and done business with, she began to pass out, and did.

Simon didn't like at all what I told him and he went to sleep in one of the guest rooms, sort of angry I felt. I got into bed, wanted to sleep more than anything else, did and didn't, so I heard the phone ringing about seven, and managed to answer it just about the time Simon got to my door. It was Marvin Mercer screaming that he had to come over that very minute, and they—Marvin and his hysterical wife—were at the front door by the time I got into a robe and Simon was in his shirt and pants. In the library we got the bad news of Johnny's suicide and lucky for Mercer that Simon was there. Because some of the things he said to me couldn't be let pass. But Simon stopped me, then threw them out. I was shaking too hard to tell Simon not to phone, so he used it to call Mike, Johnny and Rory, and I must say his being there saved me because I couldn't've spoken so calmly on the phone, at least not to Johnny, who at that time was still Juan to me. Then Simon helped me get back to bed, made me take a sleeping pill so that finally, thank God, I bombed out.

Believe it, I could've slept right through to next morning if Joyce hadn't awakened me about five in the afternoon, but not by shaking me or making noise. Instead, through my sleep, which I hated to give up, I realized that extra weight was on my bed. When I managed to get my eyes open, there was Joyce, in a pair of white silk—not see-through—boyish pajamas, sitting cross-legged to one side of me and watching me—like a kid watches a fly whose wings he's torn off—while she balanced a large dinner plate on her lap and ate a toasted water bagel filled with cream cheese and jelly. She was bathed, combed, smelled fresh and sweet. Calm, beautiful, youngish and innocent-looking, while she took small, dainty bites and nibbles of the bagel, after which she wiped her lips carefully with a banquet-sized linen napkin, her eyes were always on me. Still groggy from the pill, it took me a little time to realize where naked me was, what had happened just hours before up the street and somewhere around a museum, and that Joyce, looking like some kind of college kid, the sort you see in old-fashioned movies only showing nowadays on television, so beautiful and innocent yet sexy in her boyish pajamas, never stopped eating the bagel as she stared at me all uncovered, still sleepy and laying there with half a hard-on.

"If you sit up and don't get crumbs, cheese or jelly all over the bed, I'll give you a bite," she said.

"Of what?" I asked, really embarrassed about my bone since all I wanted right then was to keep on looking at her with happy wonder that someone, in a matter of hours, could change so much for the better.

"Of the bagel," she answered, her expression straight. "It's delicious."

It was. Then, after I got dressed, I told Joyce about the really bad news the Mercers had brought over. Where I expected more hysterics, there was calm because Joyce told me that although she never liked jokes that didn't have an ending, if Sally Mercer thought it was funny to have an actor dress up and behave crazy, while she went around introducing him as one of her husband's writers, why, then, there was just no accounting for taste. Other people besides her must've recognized how bad a joke it was, so if Sally was trying to come out on top by now saying that the actor had killed himself, then all she wanted to say was how sorry she was for not listening to me.

"You're a pretty good judge of character, Larry," Joyce said while she folded and refolded the used napkin. "In the future I'll also take your advice about situations because you're a pretty good judge of them too."

A couple of hours later Joyce said she felt tired again, which I could understand, so she went back to bed, where she stayed most of the time for the next two–three weeks during the day, and only coming down at night when Barney Moodus and everyone else around her house, with the exception of Milly and Tom, were gone—complaining all the while that somehow, no matter how hard she tried, she couldn't get over feeling upset because more and more people were helping Sally Mercer along with her suicide joke. Were these people, like Delphine Gavere, who tried to get in to see her, really of the opinion that they were good actors and actresses? Things like that, which, with the unwelcome publicity it'd got us, were becoming too much for her to take standing up.

Tired myself, I went along with Joyce only moving around at night, while Simon went along with my worsening temper and talk about our pulling out of here. Finally, after a couple of really tense days and nights when Joyce didn't get out of bed except to use her bathroom and ate practically nothing off the serving tray which she made me—no one else—bring to her bed, I asked if she ever again expected to get dressed and come downstairs? She asked why I wanted to know.

"Because this isn't good or healthy for you," I said. "Do we need any other reasons?"

"Are there others?" she asked me a second question.

I moved my arm to indicate her suite. "Sure. You don't let Milly or Tom bring your trays. Then you say you don't want the girls coming in here to clean up while you're in bed or up here. But you don't get dressed anymore or come downstairs. So how can they clean up?"

"I still let them change the sheets every day," she said.

"That's when you lock yourself in the bathroom." I had the distinct feeling of getting nowhere with her. "What's with this hermitess bit, anyway?" I wanted to know. "You had a bad time at a party. I'll buy ——"

"What party, Larry?" This question jolted me.

"The Mercer party," I said, slow and distinct.

Joyce shook her head. "We're not going, that's final. And I'm not letting you go alone. That's also final."

"I see," I said, smart enough to drop this until I could speak to Simon about it. "This staying in bed," I started on that again. "It's upsetting everyone in your house."

"You've learned," she replied in the nastiest voice since

when, "that it's my house. And it was going along pretty good before you came through the front door."

"Say the word and I'll be on my way out before you can say another," I said.

Joyce started to pound the pillows behind her in a way that told me she was working herself into the screaming meemies. "No you don't." She punched the pillow once for each word. "Then things were different, very quiet around here. Since you've moved in what've I had except a skinful of scandal? Of keeping you away from bad company like the Mercers? So never again"—she was screaming—"do I want to hear another word about the party they invited you to! We're not going! And that's final!"

"Whatever you say, Joyce," I said.

Now she was breathing heavy. "You want to pull out— fine," her voice was a little calmer. "But first you clean up the mess you've made around here. Which goes for Simon and that Jew slut who's moved in with him."

"Leave him out of this, please," I said. "He only lives here because I make him. And Mrs. Druckman isn't living with him. She doesn't even come over."

"Did you ever hear of one Jew not covering for another Jew?" she asked after laughing at me.

I actually moved to a chair to sit on my hands. "Don't say things like that, Joyce," I began. "If Simon heard you talk this way—I don't know what it'd do to him."

"He did plenty to me and my house and my street," she came right back. "Filling up my street with Mexicans and niggers and all sorts of garbage. And lots of Jews too." She leaned back against the pillows, then locked hands behind her head. "You might's well know now as later what I've made up my mind to do. Go ahead, ask me what?"

"What?" I repeated.

"I'm thinking of having Itzik dug up and baptized a Catholic, which is what he wanted——"

"You're crazy and you're lying!" I yelled.

"—and then I'll have him reburied in a Catholic cemetery," she finished. "That way he'll never have anything to do with either of you in the next world."

I pressed down on my hands until they ached enough to tell me that I wouldn't touch Joyce. "If you do that I'll have to go into court against you," I said. "So I think it'll be better if we move out." Where, where was the woman who'd done the college-girl, bagel-eating bit I kept remembering with such—longing? "Better all around," I added.

"That suits me," she agreed. "But what I said about you—because I'm willing to leave Simon out of this—goes. So first you'll clean up! Put things back the way they were. Then you can take off without even saying good-bye."

I looked at her and she nodded, raised her hand like she was swearing on the stand, then crossed her heart. "If that's the way you want it," I said and wondered—did she really mean it? Would her meaning it let us go? "So tell me exactly what I have to do."

"You won't do it, Larry," she said.

"Joyce"—now I raised my hand as she had—"try me."

"And find myself bitched, buggered and bewildered?" she laughed at me. "Not a chance."

"Try me," I repeated. "Take a chance on giving me one."

"All right," she pointed at me, "I can't make you stop people on the outside trying to have fun with me while they talk about me——"

I interrupted her again. "Nobody's doing anything."

"But in the house I don't want people joking or talking about me!" She punched again at the pillows. "So make them stop!"

"Them"—I asked—"includes me and Simon?"

"The hell with you two!" she was screaming again, hard enough now to bust a gut. "Make them stop! The help, you stupid strong-arm jerk! They're talking and whispering about me when they pass that door. I hear them laughing as they pass by. They think the joke was funny. That's why I don't go downstairs anymore. And get rid of Barney Moodus too because he's no better than they are!"

How do you argue with meanness, with whackiness? Lucky us, we'd had the same day-help coming in for a pretty long time now and every one of them worked well with Milly and Tom. Besides, they did their jobs as if they were interested in earning their money. We could leave cash and other things around, and when the help got through they'd still be there, except that now the cash would be in a neat pile or stacked alongside the other things. We were polite and pleasant to the help, they were the same to us, with an occasional *kibbitz* now and then, but no familiarity, so that in many ways the house and its operation gave me the same satisfaction—in a smaller way of course—I'd gotten from the Riviera when it ran like silk. The help—I knew—weren't talking, whispering or laughing at Joyce. Barney Moodus was a good man. But if she believed they were, who could convince her otherwise? It would be like arguing with someone who believes the world's flat, in astrology, or that thirteen really is an unlucky number.

"So what must I do before shoving it and off?" I asked, which was a stupid question even before it left my mouth. "You want me to fire Barney Moodus. So he's fired. What else?"

"Give him company," Joyce said. "Everyone goes except Milly and Tom."

"They'll be laid off tomorrow," I said. "Do I give them a week's pay? Maybe two, since they've been with us sort of long?" I asked and bit down on my tongue not to say—plus they were being fired for no good reason at all. "It'll be out of my pocket."

"Why should I say no if you want to be stupid with your money?" was her beautiful answer. "Firing includes the gardener and pool man too." Suddenly kneeling, she pointed toward the windows. "Don't tell me I haven't seen them looking up here and laughing!"

I didn't tell her anything. What would've been the use, seeing as she was becoming a victim of things that people shouldn't allow in their minds for even a little while? So I paid off the help with excuses lots worse than none would've been. Milly and Tom got in touch with help agencies for new day-workers while I went through the newspapers and Yellow Pages for a new pool man and gardener. We got nowhere. Because as soon as Joyce realized there was someone new in or around the house, she had them brought up to her sitting room for a grilling session. Hiding behind a large pair of shades, in one of her expensive dressing gowns, looking neat but sort of pale because she wasn't getting any exercise or air, Joyce would order me to draw the blinds and drapes, and not to put on a single light. Then, like some sort of Mrs. Munster, she'd have the person brought in and begin to ask questions. First, names and addresses if they had references. Then she'd want to know if they'd ever worked for really rich people who'd given big parties like the kind reported in the society pages. If they said yes she next asked if they'd ever helped at the parties? Then she wanted to know exactly why they were coming to work for her? Was it because they'd been fired from their old jobs for bad-mouthing to reporters and gossip columnists? Most of the scared women would walk out right there and then, others didn't know what to say and would look at me for some kind of clues or help, but in the end it always wound up the same way. Paying them for the day and telling them to go with my apologies.

Getting a new gardener and pool man proved impossible, even after I started to walk up and down the streets around us, with Simon helping me, and tried to hire gardeners and pool men to work at our address. They never lasted past their interviews with Joyce, so I settled for a floating vacuum cleaner for the pool and an electric mower and hedge trimmer for the lawns. Besides never learning how to operate any of these very well, swimming pools, grass, plants, shrubs and flowers have schedules of care. And what in the world did I know about chlorine, pest sprays, soil feeders, fertilizers and weedilizers, and something called Bandini Plush? Simon tried to help me as much as he could, but like me, knew nothing about pools or gardens or flowers, and one Sunday afternoon, after he managed to get the lawnmower started and running a little bit before Joyce opened a window to scream at us that she couldn't stand the racket, he remembered a joke that some stand-up comic told at the Riviera so many years ago—how he was visiting someone very rich who had the most beautiful garden and when he asked the name of a certain flower, his host said how should he know? He wasn't in the millinery business. Maybe I would've laughed more if there hadn't been some kind of greenish-black algae that felt like slime growing in the corners of the pool, along the steps and behind the pool ladder. It was even growing in the pool light receptacles. Also, that morning, for the first time, Tom approached me to say that he was afraid of Milly having a nervous breakdown, so would I mind if they gave us notice? That really put me in a panic and I begged, like I've never remembered begging before, for them to stay and not leave us—particularly Joyce—when we depended on them more and more every day.

"Let's all of us have a talk with Mrs. Tunig," I pleaded. "She won't want you to go. We'll increase your salaries. Go ahead," I said to him, "just name it."

"It's not money," Tom said. "I want you to believe it's not."

"But the new people you're going to," I went on, "they must be paying you more. So I'll match it plus."

There weren't any new people. They were just leaving, for exactly where they didn't know, although Tom said that maybe he and Milly would take a trip around the world, stopping off in black countries in Africa and also Israel to see if they mightn't move from the United States, which was going to hell through a war in Asia that nobody understood anymore. Still and all, I was able to persuade them to at least talk over how they felt with Joyce—they owed her that much—

and her hearing right from their lips how awful they felt about no longer being able to be of real service, so they were giving notice.

Did I really think this would snap Joyce into reality? If I did, it shows what a jerk I'd become, because the meeting turned into the worst kind of disaster. Joyce took over from the second they stepped into her bedroom, with accusations of how she held them responsible for letting us go to the Mercers' party—all the proof she needed that blacks, no matter how good you were to them, were disloyal and could never like whites, so if that was the way they felt way down deep, then she wasn't going to have any part of them around and as far as she was now concerned, they could get out of her house after they shut the bedroom door behind them. Later, in the kitchen, Milly cried like a baby and Tom sat shaking as if he had a high fever. There was no doubt in their minds of Joyce being sick, but if they stayed they would go to pieces too. Still they agreed to helping me the best they could until we got word that Verney was coming home. Once she set foot in the house, they'd go.

Meanwhile, meals just about stopped because no one dared shop after Joyce got it fixed in her mind that all of us were working as a team to rob her blind, so she insisted on going over every bill, then carried on it was too much, padded, double and way more than it should be. The next step in her mind was logical—she insisted that every piece of mail be delivered to her unopened and she took out the envelopes with her name on them, saying all the while that she knew we'd hidden the really important letters addressed to her, so it was a job getting the others out of her hands. Joyce wouldn't open her letters so it became impossible for me to balance the household accounts and her checking balance.

My best meals became the breakfasts Simon made, the rest of the time I ate sent-in pizzas, fried chicken and any other garbage advertised on TV and radio, which I watched and listened to at the same time to keep my head filled with pictures and words that had nothing to do with my situation. Don't think, meanwhile, that Simon didn't try talking to her, that I didn't try along with him, but neither of us got through and I couldn't bring myself around to checking out how to have her committed before she became Queen of Outer Space or Marie Antoinette, a possibility that scared me diarrhetic, seeing as it was sure to make certain people, recently become less friendly, decide that I'd failed to do something very simple—like take care of Joyce who deserved every consideration because she'd been a good wife to Itzik Yanowitz and fixed up such a beautiful house for his last years on earth. So in a very real way I was glad that Joyce was back on sleeping pills, which gave me the chance to take some for myself, otherwise dreaming all night kept me from getting a wink of sleep. But my taking pills bothered Simon, who was now spending more and more nights on a folding cot in my bedroom. Still, I was awake lots more hours than Joyce, and while she slept I had a little peace and kept myself busy trying to dust the house and do other things that didn't tire me out.

Finally, there was Verney's cable, which Milly brought me. Since there was no keeping what it said a secret, they got ready to leave.

"And I wished I was going with them," I told Quincy. "That way I'd be letting Simon get out from under and start living. Like people do who get married," I explained when Quincy's eyes asked if I'd mind giving him some details.

"I see," Quincy shook his head. "Things have deteriorated."

"I think of them falling apart as if they'd never been held together by anything more than spit," I said.

Quincy's fingertips touched the dust on an end table. "I could send some of my people over to help you."

"Joyce would spot them, so they'd have to get out," my voice thanked him as I explained why not.

"Do you think a pet might help her?" he suggested. "Most

women like little French poodles. Or how about a Yorkshire terrier? They're cute dogs and very feisty for their size. I'd enjoy sending her a good puppy."

I had to keep on shaking my head, which somehow gave me some sort of emotional rest. "I don't know, Quincy," I told him. "If she doesn't go for the puppy—then what? I'd hate to get rid of a cute doggie. And can you imagine how she'd carry on while it got housebroken? Or wouldn't stop crying or barking? But keep thinking," I said. "You might get a usable idea yet."

Lucky for us, Joyce was asleep when he came over, so when Quincy asked if he could see the house, because this was his first visit, we walked quietly through the downstairs and tiptoed around the second story, but only looked out at the back garden. He was impressed, very much, especially by the dining room and the china and silver in the butler's pantry. And the living room with Joyce's collections also made him shake his head approvingly. After I asked how Verney was getting along, he smiled wisely and said fine. What she intended to do now, they hadn't decided, but in a couple of weeks he was swinging back to Europe for a busy ten days and Verney was going along. Lucky kid is what I said. I wondered if she knew how much.

My routine continued, no help and learning the very hard way what lots of other homeowners—which I wasn't—had got to know. How it's become a hell of a state of affairs when you spend fifty thousand dollars and more for a house, so you can have the privilege of being your own janitor. Thanksgiving dinner was what Simon brought me from Leola's. Soon after that, the second week in December, TV, radio and all the papers told how the L.A. cops had caught up with this Manson character and some of the broads in his bunch for their murdering Sharon Tate and those other people, with all the write-ups bearing out one hundred percent what Johnny Bucconeri'd told me when things were going up-grade for us—that nowadays people committed murders which made no sense at all. Really hating that wop now, I wished there was some way to make him tell me exactly what to do before I—in some of the dreams I had on nights when Simon wanted me to try making it without a pill—finished him off.

Because, by this time, I'd become so worn out by the way Joyce and me were living in a big house filled with silence and burying itself under dust that I thanked God for Simon, who put a clerk full-time in the grocery and came right back after he went to *shul* mornings. Since he now had to make better time getting around, he'd brushed up on his driving and got a license. After *shul* he spent most of the time with me, except that some Friday nights he slept somewhere around his *shul* and didn't get back here until sometime Saturday afternoons. Figuring that he was sleeping at Leola's, but not knowing for sure or wanting to look as if I was interfering in even the smallest way, I didn't ask. Otherwise, he was with me, or not too far away, seeing as he'd go no farther some afternoons than the little park across the street from the Beverly Hills Hotel, where Leola would drive to meet him. At no time, Simon told me, did he tell her more than the minimum, which was, that Joyce was sick, refused the sort of help someone in her condition needed, and Leola would just have to be satisfied with things as they were until Joyce either got better or so out of it that something could be done without her realization, which would be doing plenty for someone who knew what was going on—me. There were times when Simon returned looking so sad that I wanted to throw him out with orders never to come back, which would've been my way of doing something solid for him, and maybe Leola.

Come Chanukah, while I had nothing for Simon, he'd bought me a beautiful cashmere pullover at Saks, with a diamond-pane front and solid-colored back and sleeves. He also had a gift for Joyce which she took and wouldn't open. So where there were bright lights and decorations on the houses and lawns and trees all around us, with people visiting back and forth, having fun, I watched television with the sound tuned out and the radio volume turned low. Which was why,

I'd say, when the phone rang about noon on December 31, cold but sunny for the last day of 1969, and it was Verney telling me how she wanted to come over to visit and talk at least to me, I said welcome home again from Europe, called her international jet-setter and invited her to lunch, for which I was willing to have Simon go out for anything she'd care to have.

"Thanks, Larry," she said. "But I can't make it until about four-thirty or five. I'll see you later."

Simon helped me dust and I was so glad to see someone, anyone, even Verney, that I didn't mention her going up the driveway and parking just outside the garage. Since the back door was closer, Verney came in that way, her arms filled with presents for all of us from Quincy and her, which made me glad that Simon had used his head and some of the time before Verney came to get gifts for her and Quincy from all of us. These he'd had wrapped in Christmas and Chanukah paper, depending on whether they were supposed to come from Joyce or us.

The kid looked well, even wore her braces, but made a point of showing us—by unfastening a belt of plush material, lifting her sweater and opening her bra—how thanks to science her tits were still getting bigger, before she suggested going to my office for talk since the rest of the house was a depressing drag.

"Next thing you know it'll be filled with bats and other yuchy things that squeak," she said. "Which brings Joyce to mind. How is she?"

"Your mother's not so well." I let pass what Verney'd just said. "Right after you called, I looked in on her."

Verney flicked her eyes at the ceiling. "And?"

"She was sleeping. Still is." I hesitated for only a second. "If you want me to try waking her——"

"Let it be," Verney said. "Seeing as I'm really here to talk to you about two people. Bobby Longacre and her."

"Too bad I can't see the connection." Tiredness, I think, made me sound casual. "Should Simon go for a walk?"

She shook her head at him. "He can stay."

"Thanks," Simon said, also in control of himself. "But if at any time—just say it."

"I will," Verney told us. Now she thought a bit as she pulled on the tops of her boots, sort of gulped like she was having trouble starting the motors of her thoughts and voice, but finally both were under control and meshing. "First, Larry, let's talk about Bobby Longacre. One of the kids who was in my group," she added to give me more of a lead.

"I remember him," I said after a nod. "Nice-looking. What's with him?"

"The other day he was waiting for me outside of Quincy's house. The one in Malibu." She didn't look or sound happy while she told me this. "Christ, he looked awful. A living reason why fags shouldn't take up on a junkie's life."

"Every so often I saw him on Fairfax," Simon said, which was surprising news to me. "When I was working. He looked terrible."

"Which was no reason for giving him my address and number, Simon." She started to get sore. "No reason at all."

That startled Simon but didn't throw him. All he did was look a little unhappy that Verney should accuse him of something like that. "I swear by whatever good things I prayed for this morning, which the New Year should bring to all of us, especially to your mother, that I never gave him anything except a little food and some money," he said. "He's a pathetic case. But why should he bother you? Except maybe to get a little money? So give it to him."

"He says I've got something to do with the way three of his friends suddenly disappeared!" Verney said, losing some of her snotty cool. "And I don't know what he's talking about!"

"Then why worry?" Simon said after he'd motioned for me to let him carry this. "On Fairfax he told me some sort of story about some of his friends. It didn't make sense, even the part where he mentioned you. How I could help him, he really didn't say."

Verney looked from Simon to me. Our faces were controlled, we didn't look anything but curious, but patient, which had the effect of messing her up further. What could she do? Admit that the three creeps Bobby Longacre was looking for'd been hired by her to do us in before they burned this house down on us? She really was a little murderer. Definitely, this was one thing she'd never want Quincy Smith to know the least thing about.

"So, you two smart skulls, what'm I supposed to do about him?" Verney said at last.

"Forget it," Simon said, which is exactly what I would've. "What're you supposed to be? Some sort of information agency for a poor hooked *faygelah,* who, I'm afraid, is going to be found dead under garbage?"

That made Verney point at Simon as if he'd said something to give us away. "Meaning exactly what?" she asked.

"That if an overdose doesn't kill him, some pervert will," Simon explained.

It was time for me to interrupt. "Verney," I began, "if he bothers you by hanging around Malibu, any place at all, put the cops on him. Believe it or not—even coming from me— it's good advice. Now"—I waved my right hand for her to keep quiet a little longer—"let's talk about your mother." I made quote-unquote signs. "If she is your mother."

"Good," she said, "but I want to go back to Bobby Longacre again before I cut out. Anyway, about her—Joyce—my dear mother." Saying "mother" made her look like she'd just found half a worm in a peach she'd been eating and enjoying. "Why doesn't she have a will? With me as her one and only heir?"

Both questions shook me up, but not that she could see. "The answer to both is—I don't know," I said.

"Not good enough. No way," she came right back at me.

"Because if she doesn't have a will, she should, especially now, the way she is. And when one gets written, everything should go to me."

"That's not for me to say," I said. "Your mother's money and other things, what she does with them is her business."

"I'm not buying that either, seeing's how if she was to die right now, this minute, you'd inherit fifty percent of everything because she hasn't got a will. A will," Verney repeated. Her laying it on me this way made her look like what she basically was—rotten. "Do you know how much money she's got?" she asked me. "Even some rough idea?"

I shook my head. Simon watched me, not Verney. "I'd say something," was all I admitted. "A place like this doesn't operate on markers."

"Millions," Verney said as she leaned toward me. "At least ten. Maybe more."

Even if I'd been made of stone, I would've reacted. So the kid had just looked rotten. Why not?—I sort of forgave her. For even a million, even lots lots less, most people would do the rottenest thing you could mention while you were delirious. "Ten million? That's what you said?" I asked. "That's a very solid figure. And how did you get this information?"

"By stopping off in New York on our last trip back from Europe," she began, "and by going up to Fred Rory's office." Boy, her smile was cruel. "I laid it on the line just like the time when he laid me. So either he told Quincy and me what we wanted to know or I phoned his wife. It was that simple."

"Some things come natural to some people," I said. "So go on."

"So Quincy went over Joyce's tax return and explained it all," she said. "He did this because he's concerned for me. Do you know she's got just over four million dollars—repeat, four million," she said slow and heavy, "invested in tax-free three-percent municipals that pay her about a hundred and fifty thousand a year?"

"There's something wrong with your arithmetic," I said

while my pulses were trying to thump, it seemed, ten million times in less than a minute. This—not what we had—was what Simon would call *schvere gelt*—heavy money. "If what you say is true, which I still doubt, it would only be a hundred and twenty thousand."

Instead of answering right off, Verney dug into her big leather purse with fringes hanging down to come up with a sheet of paper that she unfolded. "I'm talking about yield," she said after reading, for which she could thank me. "That means if you buy the bonds under face, you get more interest on your money. Joyce's getting the income from five million in double- and triple-A municipals. But they only cost Itzik about four. Then she's got money in banks. In the best stocks and"—she read some more—"convertible debentures." She looked at me as if to say how about that—words of more than three syllables. "Quincy says it's a very solid, professionally put-together portfolio. And everything, even her municipal bonds, could be turned into ready cash in say just about four days."

"I wouldn't recommend her taking a loss right now," I said. "Quincy wouldn't either." The judge-like-looking son of a bitch. He'd come over to find out and case the joint. And he'd got a good long look at Joyce's return, which was something I'd never seen because this past April, when Joyce had to sign them for federal and state, a man'd flown out from Fred Rory's office and Joyce'd met him at the airport, in a VIP lounge, where she'd had things explained to her before she signed the returns and drawn checks for payments due. Then the messenger'd flown right back. "So I think you oughta wait for a market turn-around."

"I'm in no hurry," Verney said. "But the way Joyce is going —Quincy only told me what you told him———"

"The fucken old bastard," I had to say this or go crazy. "Here I'm spilling my guts and he's taking an inventory. Presents"—I pointed toward the library, where we'd left them— "I wish mine was the kind he'd better not open until a bomb squad's worked on it. How much, if you don't mind my asking, did he say Joyce's house and everything in it's worth?"

"On today's market, because it's free and clear, and Joyce could carry all the paper, an easy half million. And"—she looked again at her notes—"if we put Parke-Bernet, they're the top art and antique auctioneers, in charge, Quincy says they could certainly get her another half million, at least."

"Then nobody but those people should handle it," I said.

"If the stuff goes up," Verney said, not at all bothered by my sarcasm, "Quincy says he'd like to buy the Orientals before they go to auction. He's willing to pay top of the market for them and some other pieces. So don't let him jew us down."

"I'll keep that in mind, you shitty little *goy*," I promised, one hand on my heart, the other stretched out toward Simon, for him to sit still, which he did.

Verney was so satisfied with herself, she didn't even bother to get sore. "So that's how it figures out to at least ten million, depending, like you say, where the market is. But Quincy also says that from these circumstances, and the way Rory clammed up, there could be money in Swiss accounts. We'll have to work together to get that out of Joyce. Or maybe that Basqua character."

We sat in silence, the office filling up with shadows since I'd gone and cut off all the lights except from one lamp because I couldn't stand seeing more of Verney than I had to. Verney was impressed for one reason. Simon and me for another. We'd always figured Itzik to be a big man. But never this substantial.

"The will Itzik wrote said Joyce was to inherit everything. Then that she was to make her own will and choose her own heirs. So we've got to get to work on her because Rory said how they could never get her to sit down and do it." All this Verney told us while we just sat. "Quincy said for me to be generous," she went on, looking directly at me. "So don't worry how you'll be taken care of."

"That's good to know," I admitted. "Now tell me how to thank you besides kissing your mean little ass?"

Then I heard movement. And there was Joyce, barefooted and in a quilted dressing gown. Looking terrible, she hung to the door frame for support. She cursed me when I moved to help her and told me not to stand between her and Verney, at who she wanted a good look.

"Who let you in my house?" she put it to Verney. "And how come you're not holding up your camera with someone like her around?" she said to me.

Verney put away her paper and touched her belt. "I phoned Larry to ask if I could come over," Verney said. "I came here to bring presents from Quincy and me. And to wish you a Happy New Year."

"Take your presents and wishes to someone who wants to die of cancer," Joyce said. "What's this about me making a will and what I put in it?"

That question rattled Verney because it told us that although none of us'd heard Joyce because she was barefooted, she must've got an earful before she made sound enough for me to hear her. Verney looked at us for help, advice, some sort of support because of what she'd just promised—to be generous—but Simon said nothing and I shook my head. This was between her and Joyce, and she could forget about being generous. Simon and me—we had enough to live on.

"That's it exactly," Verney finally said. "What you put in your will, which you should make immediately. Who's to get the estate, be the executor. Stuff like that."

"It's all gonna go to snakes," Joyce said.

Verney looked from her mother to us, as if sometime soon we might be called as witnesses. Then she said, "Snakes?"

"Poisonous snakes," Joyce nodded. "And only the kind that rattle, seeing as they're honest enough to tell you what and where they are."

And then, in a voice that never got loud or emotional, with

her eyes always on Verney, who moved to sit next to me for
protection, I guess, Joyce began how all along her luck had always been so bad it kept her from praying in a church because if she'd ever decided to go to one some Sunday, on that
particular day it would not only collapse on her, but also kill
lots of innocent people. With no luck at all, she'd known all
along that only her money interested us and we were waiting
for her to die so she could be robbed stiff before her body
became that way, just like the pathetic old broad in *Zorba the
Greek*. And if we wanted to know, Itzik had left every dime
of every dollar he had for her to do with exactly as she pleased.
And if she couldn't take them along in her coffin, then next
week, after she'd made herself get well which she could do
any time she put her mind to it, she was going to have a will
drawn and leave everything to a home for poisonous snakes,
the rattling kind, she repeated, and Verney wasn't going to
get a plugged nickel of anything and neither was I or anyone
else because none of us deserved a cent and that included Tom
and Milly who'd left her in the lurch, surrounded by leeches
and wolves and perverts and phony fairy singers who did nothing but prove over and over again what she'd known all along
ever since she was a little kid who'd never really had anything
she didn't have to be first abused to get—that people were rotten. And she'd made a tough living giving them the things they
wanted and which all the while they'd considered rotten, so
how come they were now showing wide open the kind of
rotten work she'd done? Showing it in pictures and books and
magazines, in plays and movies for anybody who wanted to
see cocks and cunts and fucking and sucking and anything
else the animal mind in humans could think up, showing it
done larger than life and in the brightest colors? Which was
the way Verney and Quincy lived—in the brightest colors—
seeing as Verney's gone again to Europe to stay in the best
hotels, while she, God pity her—her mother, had got herself
locked in with a couple of stumblebums, one of who she had

to marry in a proxy ceremony that was a disgrace from beginning to end. And nobody cared—not even Mrs. Droutswood—how Verney was living and doing things that once upon a better time would've gotten her put away for life—with the same at least going for the dirty old man she was living with. But as soon as she'd gone to a party she thought would be civilized it'd turned out to be a conspiracy dreamed up to make her feel more ashamed than if worms were crawling all over her. So why should she leave anything to anyone? Could any of us tell her why? Without lying right up from our toes?

"Because you've blown your mind!" Verney screamed at her. "That's why, lunatic!"

"I know it better than you," Joyce said. "That you're alive today proves for how long I've been very sick."

Then she dragged herself out of my office and we didn't say a word until from the distance we heard her upstairs door slam.

We were all breathing hard, me as if heavy rocks'd been piled all over my stomach and chest. And I don't know how long we would've sat there, saying nothing, if Verney hadn't looked at her wristwatch, fished another slip of paper out of her purse and asked to use the phone on my desk. She asked whoever answered for Bobby Longacre, got him, then they argued until she said all right, she'd go to his place to have it out once and for all, which was a good way to finish up the old year. She repeated his address, wrote it down, then repeated it again.

"I'll be there when I finish up on other things," she told him. "It'll be before ten. I promise. Before ten!" she yelled into the phone. "Seeing as I've also got a party to go to!"

Then she hung up and stared at the address. "Shit," she bitched. "Why did I promise to see him? But he's got to be told off. How the hell do I get to Van Nuys?"

"By going over the hill," I said. "Up Benedict to Mulholland. At Mulholland——"

She sort of smirked. "Which I've had some small acquaintance with. Then what?"

"You turn left on Mulholland until you get to the traffic light. Then you turn right and go down more than a mile until you come to Ventura. Then it's left to Van Nuys." I looked at her. "Man," I was glad to say, "he's really got you scared."

"Maybe some," she admitted. "But not enough so I won't use that kid to tell something against you that's gotta be said."

"Namely?" I asked because that's what she wanted.

"Namely," she repeated to make fun of me, which was not sitting well with Simon, "that unless you do something about her—my mother—making a will right now that leaves me everything—"

"If that's what your mother wants—why not?" I interrupted.

"Correction," Verney said. "What I want. You're not so smart, Larry, we can't tell you how, if Joyce died this very minute, you'd inherit fifty percent of everything. Everything," she repeated while she swept both her arms to sort of take in the house and all. "And if she dies five years from now, when I'm past twenty-one, and there isn't a will—there'd be a good chance of you getting every last cent. Which is not gonna be, Larry. You can bet it's not."

"What makes you think I could get her to write a will favoring you?" I asked and meant the question. A kid like that didn't deserve a dime, let alone ten million. "Seeing as she feels like she does about all of us?"

Verney pointed at me. "How she feels about you is your problem. My problem isn't how she feels about me. But how I'll stand in the will she's gotta make."

"I wouldn't worry about that," I said. "I wouldn't touch a red cent of what's Joyce's." I couldn't stop the thought—wasn't it, after all, Itzik's? "So when she feels better I'll see if I can get her to oblige you."

That made her laugh at me, at all of us. "In your time you

were a pretty powerful influence," she said. "Now maybe you're not so powerful. But you're lots cuter. So she could decide to leave you five million."

"I swear I don't want even a dollar," I said and realized how very dumb it sounded.

Now Verney really laughed. "We'll have to have that added to the world's most famous last lines. Like—I just put your check in the mail," she began. "Or some of my best friends are niggers. Or Jews." Little bitch, she slung that in to throw us, but it fazed me more than Simon, who just looked at her in wonder. "Or I won't stick it all the way in unless you say so. Or"—she pointed at me hard—"I swear I won't come in your mouth. Not in my mouth or pocket you don't," she let me know. "So we're right back to something I might have to tell Bobby Longacre. Which is a something you certainly don't want told."

I said it again. "Namely?"

"Namely that since Joyce doesn't look like she's in any condition to make a will, you're gonna help us get Joyce committed and declared outa her skull. Say by this coming Monday. That's so I can move fast to ask the right court to appoint a"—she got out the first sheet again—"a conservator."

"And suppose I drag my feet?" I asked and wondered how I could. Joyce needed the conserving from Verney.

This last thing I'd asked made her shake her head like I was stupid and she was surprised at finding this out. "Then I'm gonna blow the whistle so hard it'll stop your breathing. By that"—she looked from me to Simon to the ceiling so that I figured she included poor Joyce—"I mean for all of you."

"For exactly what?" I also looked at Simon. That he didn't look confused or upset was some sort of relief. "I'd say we've been good citizens."

That, for reasons I knew and understood, and which Verney was guessing at, just broke her up. "I'd like to ask those three friends of Bobby's who disappeared if they feel that way about you," she said between laughs and looks of sort of admiring my cool. Then she was serious and mean again. "So what I'm gonna say to Bobby really depends on you."

"Depends on Larry doing what you want?" Simon broke in and I let him get a say because he'd been quiet and patient for a long time. "Helping you put your mother away? For you, Miss Veronica Dobby, never."

"I hope that's not the way you feel, Larry," she said after she'd looked at Simon like she'd like to destroy him for contradicting her. "In case you do," she went on, warning, "here's what's gonna happen in a coupla days. Before Monday. Take bets on it."

"We're taking," I said as if we weren't worried. "And listening."

Like she already owned the place, Verney sat first in my chair, then on my desk, chewing her lips a little as if to sort out her evils until they were in the order best suited to bomb and destroy us. That done, she started to tell us what she had in mind. It was plenty. First she was gonna take Bobby Longacre, Quincy and a lawyer Quincy had in mind—a Pro America who hated organized crime even more than he hated commies—right to the Beverly Hills bigs. Next she was gonna tell them how awfully scared of us she'd been for a long time, ever since we'd moved into her mother's house. But now she felt grown up enough, with real sincere friends who were interested in her welfare, to tell the cops something they should've known a long time before. How, after a fight—she meant an argument—with me and Joyce about the corporation we'd formed to exploit her, which gave us fifty percent of her group, Simon'd gone ahead and thrown her out of the guest cottage where we were having supper with him and where she'd never been welcome. That made her look around for a place to stay. Feeling low and needing laughs, she decided to accept the invitation of three funny, winging freaks with electric names, who'd called her Snow White, to flop in their pad. With them along to help her carry out clothes and stuff, she'd gone back to Joyce's house, rung the bell, which got the front door opened and the next thing she knew—her friends were having the living shit kicked outa them, which made her so scared for her life that she took off and hid out for some days and nights here and there until she thought of going to see Libby Dorne, an actress who'd said nice things about her on television. Her—Verney only told that she'd been booted out by her mother. But she was alive. While her three friends'd disappeared. Now another friend of theirs, Bobby Longacre, who'd been in her group and introduced her to the funny freaks, had put pressure on her to tell what she knew. So still very scared of us, who we were and our connections, she was telling.

"Then it'll be up to the fuzz to see what kind of story you tell after they've heard mine. Personally," Verney said after a couple of you-can't-change-certain-things shrugs, "I think they're dead. All three of them. But that's the sort of thing that keeps cops in business."

"Suppose they buy your stupid story, which never happened?" I asked. "What'll it do to us?"

"That depends on their finding the bodies. And what was done to them," she said. "If my story proves out—with no reason except that cops can be pretty dumb unless they're helped by rats"—she tapped her chest and nodded that she didn't mind my accusing, shoe-fits look—"then you'll all be fighting murder charges."

"All of us? Don't you mean me?" I asked more questions because they were the only stall I could think of while she had me on the ropes of this rock-bottom situation. Personally, and I swear to this by everything Simon believes in and which for both our sakes I hope comes true, that what we'd learned about the money didn't make me the least bit greedy. As for Simon, I knew it meant nothing to him. But Joyce—why should this kid, of all the undeserving people I'd ever known, rob her of Itzik's cash? "Or do you really mean Simon and me?"

"Simon and you," she laid it on me. "And Joyce."

I was still struggling for the time required to think of holes in the story she was going to tell. Even if she was lying in her throat, was that an excuse to make three corpses?

"You don't mean that, Verney," I said nice as possible. "You really don't."

"Try me," she said. From the way she'd taken over my desk I didn't need eyes to see how Verney was sure she had a lock on us, so she was enjoying every second of this, of paying me back for the beating I'd once given her, for Simon throwing her out the night she'd just mentioned, for Joyce despising her. She had us on our backs, making us suck blackmail, which tasted worse than it smelled. "Either Joyce makes a will"—she interrupted my thoughts—"the way I want it, so that I'd be willing to wait, or she's gotta approve a conservator and say right out how everything goes to me. The conservator'd be Quincy," she told me what I'd already guessed. "He'd protect me and really put her money to work."

"For a kid, you sure know how to hurt a guy," I said. "Still, the cops won't buy your story," I insisted. "It'd be your word against ours. It's just too insane."

"Since when, nowadays, are people sane?" she laughed at me again. "So it'd be my word that counted. Because why would a kid want to turn in her own mother? Unless she'd been part of something so awful no honest kid could live knowing what she'd done? Why would she?"

I really didn't have the answers so couldn't stop Simon from getting out of his chair and walking back and forth, up and down around my office, with both hands clasped behind his back. Meanwhile, Verney was actually sprawled across the top of my desk, with one leg way in the air to admire the fit of a boot and to give me a look of way up her pantyhose. It wasn't often, I guessed she felt, when someone'd got the best of us. But she had, was enjoying it, and didn't mind seeing us squirm because it would make our final, unconditional surrender—to her—all the sweeter. It was then that I remembered the particular lunch I've already mentioned, and it was then that I thought of Verney as a big finisher. First of this house—Joyce's pride. Then worse, of her mother, by really scratching "Fuck you" across the loyalty people connected so close—by a cord that'd once been tied from Joyce right to Verney's belly button—were supposed to feel for each other.

"If the kid was a social disease, say like a Nazi, she certainly would," Simon said suddenly.

Verney rested on an elbow in what looked like a Cleopatra pose. "Come again? A Nazi?" She was puzzled. "Who's a Nazi? They were Germans, I know. Though some of our power-to-the-people niggers think your kind are operating as Nazis in Israel."

"Don't mention that holy country," Simon warned her. "Your mouth and mind aren't fit."

"So why'm I a Nazi?" she asked, sitting up.

Even after Simon leaned his knuckles into the other end of my desk, Verney didn't look scared. "Because," he began, "only a Nazi would turn in a parent. Even one who's sick and suffering. Even if, like you say, your mother knows about murder, you know she couldn't've done it."

"That doesn't make her less guilty," Verney said. "But her being nuts—that could save her life. I guess the same goes for you, Uncle Simon," she was nasty. Then she turned to me. "I guess you'd be the only one who'd sniff gas." She let that sink in before turning to Simon again. "So why don't you forget about Nazis and start telling Larry to play ball?"

"Then you don't care?" Simon asked, looking very shocked. "I mean about being a Nazi?"

Verney shook her head. "No, Uncle Simon," she told him. "Not if it gets me what I want. Say like putting you down and giving me ten million."

It happened faster, it seemed, than a mickey finn taking apart someone with a weak stomach. The way a rhino can move like an express train was the way Simon went around the desk to catch Verney, smother her first and only scream so it sounded like the end of a gurgle, swing her up and off her feet with a reverse figure-four chokehold he'd put on her before he pressed in hard and twisted in opposite directions to break her neck before you can repeat what I've just said. Meanwhile, before Verney died, I'd grabbed her wrists to stop her from scratching Simon's skin or some of his clothes. After I let go, and her arms dropped, he still kept the hold as he lifted her away from the desk. Finally he walked slow and very careful not to knock against anything before he put her down in a corner where the shadows were thickest. After that he got me to a chair and made me sit down while he looked me over and all around the room for buttons or threads, stuff like that. He didn't touch Verney's purse, only looked at it after he thanked me for holding her wrists.

"You're all right?" he asked me. "I'm going to worry if you're not all right."

"All right? Not worry?" I repeated. "When you've just killed her! And I helped out!"

"Which I'd do to any Nazi I'll ever get my hands on. Keep sitting, Larry, please. I want to think about this just a little bit. You know," he said after a while, "I wish we could get in touch with Marty G. Find out how his boys got rid of three stiffs. Which takes some doing," he added after I didn't answer.

So I sat, elbows digging into my knees while my hands covered my face so I couldn't see any part of my office. Simon—I could still hear the little snap as her neck broke. Simon—I heard him still walking up and back, until he finally sighed and said since we'd always depended on each other, we'd do just that again. So the very next thing we had to find out was —what was with Joyce? If she was asleep, it would help things. How, I couldn't see. But because Simon seemed to have—no, had—taken over, we went upstairs, where very quietly I opened the door to Joyce's bedroom, also all full of shadows, but we could see Joyce laying on her back, sort of half under the covers. She was breathing heavy enough for us to hear but after we tiptoed closer I couldn't stop a groan of pain, of real agony because of the empty bottles of sleeping pills turned over on the night table, and under one of the bottles an envelope on which Joyce had written To Whom It May Concern. Then I groaned again because in my mind I'd just seen Joyce sitting on my bed—before the work the finishers'd done got to her—looking so fresh and alive in those white silk boyish pajamas.

"She's gonna die if we don't do something," I croaked at Simon. "And"—I pointed toward the floor and right through it—"what the hell can we do?"

"I could stick Verney in a closet until later," Simon said. "No good," he changed his mind. "No good at all. Don't look at her, Larry. Please."

But I couldn't turn away as, very carefully, he took a handkerchief from a pocket, moved aside the bottle over the envelope, picked up the envelope and used the other end of the handkerchief to get out and open the notepaper, which was folded in half, before he moved toward the open door where there was more light to read by.

"I'm reading," he began. " 'I don't want to live in the same world with Verney and people just like her.' " Simon shook his head. "I don't think she included us, I hope." He looked at the note again. "She signed it Mrs. Juday Joyce Domziak Adams Wolf Dobby Yanowitz Tunig."

"Are we gonna call a doctor, a hospital?" I asked Simon as he put the note back the way we'd found it. "They could save her life."

He turned to me. "For what? Tell me?"

"But we can't let her die!" I insisted, even though I thought in a flash what might happen if Joyce recovered. Not her facing a murder rap for those three boys, but her digging up Itzik's body to make it Catholic, which would be finishing him off. "Before I'm asking you, Simon, I've already asked myself. How can you be so calm?"

"And why not?" was his answer. "I'm calmer by the minute because Joyce doing what she did is gonna help us with downstairs. Trust me, please, Larry. Just trust me."

I let him take me to the library, where he sat me down again. After he put a finger across his mouth for me to be still, and I nodded, Simon dialed Leola Druckman and told her how terribly upset I was about Joyce—no, that wasn't going to keep him from coming to her party tonight—but this afternoon, to make things worse than they already were, Joyce's daughter'd shown up with presents, which didn't stop her from becoming awful to her mother about a will that would make Verney inherit everything, right now, even while Joyce was on this earth. So bad words'd been said back and forth between Verney and her poor mother. Now Joyce and Larry were very depressed, with Joyce gone back to bed which wasn't good for her, so please, could he invite us along to the party? It could only do us and him good. Naturally, Leola said yes, so Simon said we'd be at her house about ten, or not much later, he promised.

"That's it," Simon said after he hung up. "Now we move fast and leave it to God whether Joyce lives or dies. Because after we get rid of Verney and everything else works out, when you go upstairs to see if Joyce is already dressed or needs help—say with a zipper—however she is, alive or dead, we call the police because they'd get here soonest with an ambulance. If she lives—you'll be able to put her in a sanatorium. Then, maybe she'll get well again. It's going to be all right, Larry." He shook me gently. "Now lend me a pair of dry dishwashing gloves because I want to put Verney, her purse and our presents in her car."

While he did that I vomited in the toilet which I kept flushing to get rid of the smell. Soon enough Simon was back to say that it'd been no trouble getting Verney and everything else into the front seat of her Mustang. He was also glad to report that she'd left her keys in the ignition.

"She was going to the Valley," he said. "Right. Up Benedict and over Mulholland?" He looked at his wristwatch and talked the way generals do in movies before they move up their troops for the biggest crunch of the war. "It's after seven. So by this time and especially tonight there's little traffic up there. We'll make more sure by pulling toward the curb along Benedict so there'll be none behind us as we go on up. You in your car while I'm driving Verney's."

"I'll drive Verney's," I corrected him.

"Right about where down below they found the clothing of those Tate murderers, there's no houses close by," he repeated what we both knew, because we'd gone up there to see. "So that's where Verney's gonna lose control of her car. You'll be coming up right behind to pick me up. After which we come home and do what people do who're getting ready to go to a New Year's Eve party."

Hope was like a damp match in my gut that was catching fire and beginning to burn very strong.

"I'll be driving Verney's car," I repeated in a voice I once again was able to recognize. "You're too heavy to get out quick. I'm driving," I said again. "Otherwise I don't go. Another thing, we take the phones off so there'll be busy signals."

That's how it was. I wore gloves. Verney, her purse and our presents were on the seat next to me as I backed her car down far enough for Simon to open the garage door with the remote control and follow me into the street. For a rich city like Beverly Hills, the streets aren't really lit up at all, something I was very glad of now as we turned right from Lexington into Benedict, where Simon stayed about fifty feet behind me. All the way up toward the hill I only spotted two cars coming down the canyon toward us. At the hairpin turn, where you start climbing, Simon dropped back a little more while I stayed at about thirty until I came to the place where a sign says fifteen an hour is safe speed. Then it was only a couple of hundred feet more to the place where there's a drop-off from the road of hundreds of feet into rock and brush. Right there's a dirt shoulder of maybe six or eight inches at the edge of the road, so I got the front wheels and the right rear over the shoulder before I put the gear lever in Park and pulled Verney toward me and into the driver's seat as I eased my way out. From where I stood I could've seen car lights from a long way off in either direction, but there weren't any. Now the next thing was the hardest, because I had to move fast and pray that no car lights would show up right then, or if Verney's car exploded it would burn up but not start too big a brush fire.

I aimed the front wheels at the edge, then reached in fast, over Verney's lap, to pull the lever into Drive and slam the door. The shoulder held the car until I got to the rear bumper to lift and push until the wheel went up and over. By the time the Mustang picked up speed to go over the edge, not making too much of a racket it seemed to me, I was across the road and in beside Simon, who put his beams up to normal and had our car going good until, in less than a minute, we were at Mulholland, where as I got the all-news station that broadcast instant accidents as soon as they were found out, he turned right, went along and down into Coldwater and around to the house. When we reached our block, which was deserted, he cut the headlights and pulled into the garage, where after he shut the door with the control, I turned the radio back to XTRA Music, which comes up from Tijuana and broadcasts nice arrangements and information about Mexico. But no news. Door to door, it hadn't taken forty minutes.

We started to dress right after we put the phones back. Showering and shaving, I fought myself all the while not to look toward Joyce's room until a little after eight-thirty, when Simon fixed my tie and arranged the points of my handkerchief in the pocket of my oxford gray suit. Simon, as always, looked like Simon, even to his *tzitzit* hanging down from under his vest. Satisfied with the way I'd shaped up, he put my hand on his chin to make me look into his eyes and see how calm and clear they were. It also gave him a chance to check mine. Still and all, I had to hug him to give myself strength before I knocked on the door of Joyce's bedroom, called her name, then opened the door.

She was so still she looked dead. Now we both handled the

note and I really fell apart, so Simon had to help me downstairs to the library where in about another hour he'd call the operator to get the police and make it snappy. After that, he told me again, he'd do the talking—tell the police about the argument, even where Verney said she was going, but everything reluctantly.

"Naturally we'll tell about this Bobby Longacre kid bothering her—even me," he said as he made me take a little Scotch. "At the right time you'll help me tell how Quincy Smith stopped off in New York with Verney to look at Joyce's tax return—which takes a helluva nerve—find out she had no will and how he helped Verney out with notes on what to say while she twisted arms. So Quincy'll clam up if he knows anything because that's the only way to water down the publicity he's gonna get and doesn't want. No, it won't sound good." He nodded and looked satisfied, then made a long face, the kind someone long married puts on, I guess, when he has to tell his wife some bad news that can't be helped yet he'll be blamed for. "After I call the cops it'll be time to call Leola," he explained his expression, "and tell her why she won't see any of us tonight. She'll want to come over but I'll insist no."

"Don't let her talk you into yes," I said.

"Depend on it," he said. "Later, if there is a funeral for Joyce, after which you'd sit *shiva,* can she be the sort of hostess?"

"Sure," I said and looked around, "if we're still at this address. Poor Joyce. Poor, poor Joyce."

"Poor Joyce," Simon agreed. "She never had any strength of character. Remember how she couldn't stand living with Mitch at the Riviera and not be married to him? At the Riviera," he repeated. "As if anyone who came there had an opinion about anyone else that mattered. But even then, you must remember how Joyce carried on about people laughing at her. And talking. You remember, Larry?"

"I remember too much I'd rather forget," I said.

"In time you'll forget what shouldn't be remembered," he said. "So will I."

"Here's something you didn't remember," I said. "To find out about our families like you wanted to."

Again Simon whistled under his breath before he pointed from him to me. "You stayed tonight when lots of other people would've powdered. So who needs more family than what's between us? Besides"—he paused—"for a long time now, which is why I never followed through, I've had the feeling that if they were interested in knowing if we were alive, and where, they would've somehow gotten in touch. Especially after the big fuss I made soon after we got back here," he explained. "It put us in the news."

"Where we're gonna be again very soon, right after you start using the phone," I said as panic hit me so bad I almost dropped my drink. "But this time even worse. Because I don't think we're gonna make it. There's just too many things that gotta hang together."

"Of course we will," Simon said as he wagged a finger at me. "Absolutely." Now he looked at his watch. "Soon now, I'm calling the cops."

I managed another small sip. "Simon," I began, "let's face it. How can you be so sure?"

For a while he stood with his head raised toward the ceiling, as if he himself had asked the same question and was now waiting for an answer. Finally he looked satisfied and nodded. Then he got around to giving me his answer by stepping right up close, putting my drink aside and forcing me to stand up before he put my hand under his chin to make me look into his eyes which were just like they always were, clear and calm, trusting and as filled with believing as they'd been when we stood at the Devil's Knee in that park in Uruapan.

"Because"—he said sincerely—"because God is on our side."